HOME AT LAST

Ginny followed him through his apartment to the kitchen, past the long shelves of books, the leather chairs and sofas, the rack of pipes that held the pungent odor of his tobacco. She opened the refrigerator: nearly empty.

"I always eat out," he said.

"Maybe I could . . . whip up an omelette?"

Strains of Debussy drifted through the apartment, dreamy and romantic. She felt the heat of his body as he moved closer to her, reached for her, pulled her into his arms.

"I can't believe you're here," he whispered, caressing her in a languid, sensuous motion. "I've dreamed of this so often." His kiss was deep, hot, demanding. It left her whole body pulsing with need. "Tell me," he said huskily, pulling her closer. "Tell me you love me."

"I love you," she whispered, her breath mingling with his. "Oh, yes, my love, I love you."

D1115392

DISCOVER DEANA JAMES!

CAPTIVE ANGEL   (2524, $4.50/$5.50)
Abandoned, penniless, and suddenly responsible for the biggest tobacco plantation in Colleton County, distraught Caroline Gillard had no time to dissolve into tears. By day the willowy redhead labored to exhaustion beside her slaves . . . but each night left her restless with longing for her wayward husband. She'd make the sea captain regret his betrayal until he begged her to take him back!

MASQUE OF SAPPHIRE   (2885, $4.50/$5.50)
Judith Talbot-Harrow left England with a heavy heart. She was going to America to join a father she despised and a sister she distrusted. She was certainly in no mood to put up with the insulting actions of the arrogant Yankee privateer who boarded her ship, ransacked her things, then "apologized" with an indecent, brazen kiss! She vowed that someday he'd pay dearly for the liberties he had taken and the desires he had awakened.

SPEAK ONLY LOVE   (3439, $4.95/$5.95)
Long ago, the shock of her mother's death had robbed Vivian Marleigh of the power of speech. Now she was being forced to marry a bitter man with brandy on his breath. But she could not say what was in her heart. It was up to the viscount to spark the fires that would melt her icy reserve.

WILD TEXAS HEART   (3205, $4.95/$5.95)
Fan Breckenridge was terrified when the stranger found her near-naked and shivering beneath the Texas stars. Unable to remember who she was or what had happened, all she had in the world was the deed to a patch of land that might yield oil . . . and the fierce loving of this wildcatter who called himself Irons.

Available wherever paperbacks are sold, or order direct from the Publisher. Send cover price plus 50¢ per copy for mailing and handling to Zebra Books, Dept. 3789, 475 Park Avenue South, New York, N.Y. 10016. Residents of New York and Tennessee must include sales tax. DO NOT SEND CASH. For a free Zebra/ Pinnacle catalog please write to the above address.

MRS.
PERFECT

PEGGY ROBERTS

ZEBRA BOOKS
KENSINGTON PUBLISHING CORP.

ZEBRA BOOKS

are published by

Kensington Publishing Corp.
475 Park Avenue South
New York, NY 10016

First printing: May, 1992

Printed in the United States of America

One

The sweating, that damnable sweating had started again! She felt the prickly tightening along her scalp and thought briefly of her careful hairdo. A flush of heat crept up from her neck, over her cheekbones and brow to meet with the moist burning sensation at her hairline. I don't need this, not now, Ginny Logan thought, flipping another card in her presentation. Things weren't going well. Turning to face the men seated at the gleaming mahogany table, she smiled brightly, hoping it didn't look forced.

"Our thought is to show the excitement that Ozzie's Secret Sauce can add to the average ho-hum meal. We'll begin with a family around the dinner table. Everything will be black and white. Everyone will look bored. The mother will appear to be worried until her face lights up as if she's had an idea. She goes to the kitchen, which is also all black and white. We'll pan to the bottle of Ozzie's Secret Sauce sitting on the counter. It will, of course, be in bright living color. The mother picks it up and hurries back to the dining room, where it's passed around. As each family member puts some sauce on his or her dinner, the food and that person are shown in color. Finally they'll be wearing dazzling smiles. The voice-over will say, 'Put a little color in your life with Ozzie's Secret Sauce.' " She swung around and smiled brightly at the circle of skeptical faces. She felt like a mother trying to convince a roomful of little boys that spoonfuls of this medicine were just what they needed. Well, she'd done it before.

The room was ominously silent. Burgess Osgood, known to his friends and a few privileged plebes as Burr, made no comment. His face was poker straight as he stared directly at her. Ginny had seen him use this tactic before, scowling and fixing his own sales people with a stony glare that often left them quaking in their shoes. He was a large man with an entirely bald head and such pale brows and lashes that his round face appeared hairless as well. His eyes were small and of a dark indiscriminate color, and his lips were thin. He had a habit of tightening them, which made them appear even thinner. His presence was imposing if not downright intimidating, and Ginny had had trouble with this account right from the beginning.

"I'm giving him to you because you're experienced in handling difficult people," Alex Russell

6

had said. He was her boss and the sole surviving partner in the Russell and Taylor Advertising Agency. "Don't be fooled by Ozzie's Secret Sauce. This is an important account. Burr is a conglomerate. He controls an endless number of items our firm could represent. Give us your most dazzling work."

So, Ginny stood before them all, Alex, Burgess Osgood and his assistants, not exactly dazzling and most definitely sweating. She could feel the beads on her forehead. They almost had a cooling effect in the air-conditioned office.

She had a hunch Burr Osgood wasn't looking so much for dazzle in their advertising campaign as in their female staff. She'd caught his assessing stare at her assistant, Nola Sherman, and it had made her feel handicapped. Not that she'd ever used her sexuality to win a client over, but she'd been aware when one found her attractive and had known that was a plus when it came to getting her job done. She pushed the thought aside, tried to ignore the shifting, itching moisture on her brow, and stepped closer to the board's table, resting her hands on its smooth, cool surface and leaning forward slightly to show confidence and enthusiasm.

"We can, of course, carry this same theme over into magazine advertising, superimposing a brightly colored bottle of Ozzie's Secret Sauce over a hazy black and white of our family at the dinner table—or at a picnic or backyard barbecue or church potluck."

She knew exactly when his hard, bright gaze fixed on the beads of sweat on her brow. "If you want to bring in the teen segment of the market, we can use the same layout using teens in the background at a drive-in, school cafeteria, a picnic on the beach." Her voice dwindled in spite of herself. Her eyelashes flickered once, in annoyance and panic. A bead of sweat had gathered enough moisture to slowly roll down her brow and into the hollows beside her nose, then down to her chin. Burgess Osgood watched its progress in wordless fascination.

Never let them see you sweat. Ginny swore silently, thinking of a deodorant ad that had run a few years back. She resisted the insane urge to giggle and ignored the itchy sheen of sweat that was ruining her careful makeup job as well as her campaign. Her discomfort only seemed to increase the heat rushing to her face. The silence stretched out, and Alex Russell cleared his throat.

Taking a tissue from the pocket of her silk crepe de chine jacket, Ginny straightened and moved back to the easel that held her presentation cards. Briefly, she dabbed at her chin before turning to face her audience, her wide mouth curved in a smile. Damn it, she had created some damned good advertising campaigns. She hadn't gotten to her present position in the agency by sweating in front of customers or appearing unsure of herself. She'd taken this account as a favor to Alex. He'd asked her to do her best, and she believed she had. There was only so much you could do with catsup, no matter how secret its ingredients.

"We believe depicting a middle-class family environment will present your product to the widest market," she said firmly and clamped her lips together. She would say no more. The presentation had either done the job or it hadn't. If she went on, she would appear to be pleading or padding up a less than solid approach. Turning her back on Burr Osgood's obsidian gaze, she dabbed at her brow under the guise of straightening her poster cards.

"I had in mind something a little classier, a little more youth oriented," he said now. Ginny carefully replaced the boards on the easel, counting to ten to calm herself and halt the flow of perspiration on her brow and upper lip. She was surprised to see that her hands were trembling. She clenched them together and prepared to answer Osgood's complaint, but Alex was ahead of her.

"Our research shows the family is going to be big in the nineties. As Mrs. Logan pointed out, we can bring in the younger consumer as part of the campaign, just to start them now on your sauce. By the time they're married and have kids of their own, Ozzie's Secret Sauce will be a natural part of their lives. But we need to concentrate

9

on mothers who want to give their families something a little different."

"All right," Osgood agreed reluctantly. "I'm sure you know your business." He glanced at Ginny. "How long did you say you've been at this?"

"Fifteen years," Alex answered for her. "She's the best we've got. She knows her stuff."

Osgood's quick glance slid over Ginny's trim figure, from the Ferragamo alligator pumps to the Louis Vuitton scarf knotted loosely around her shoulders. Deliberately she kept her face blank as she returned his stare. His thin lips tightened, and he was the first to look away.

"We can flood the media with ads, send out free samples through the mail, donate some sauce to school cafeterias and soup kitchens."

"I wanted something with a little more pizzazz. After all, I gave this sauce my name. It's my secret. I made it in my own kitchen."

"We could have the mother say, 'I've got a secret!' then go to the kitchen for the sauce," Alex said hopefully. He could see the account slipping through their fingers. Osgood's expression remained closed.

"How about if we use a jingle that makes a play on your name?" Ginny said, suddenly understanding Burr Osgood's ego a little better. He glanced at her, a shimmer of interest in his dark, flat gaze. "We could do something like Ozzie's Secret Sauce makes all your food taste good, Ozzie good." He sat as if considering it. She could tell Alex was holding his breath. Hell, Osgood could tell Alex was holding his breath. He held off a while longer, keeping them waiting, enjoying his moment of power over them.

"I like that," he said finally. "Ozzie good!" He nodded his head. "It's catchy, don't you think?"

"I'll get our music department onto it right away," Ginny said.

"Didn't I tell you she was the best?" Alex declared expansively. He shot Ginny a grateful glance.

I'm going to hit him up for a raise, Ginny decided. Then she shivered slightly. The sweats were gone now, replaced by a slight chill. She pushed at her dark hair and felt the dampness. Damn!

"Do you have time for lunch? I've made reservations at the Black Swan," Alex was saying. "Ginny, you're joining us, aren't you?"

"I'm afraid I have another appointment," she said, coming around the table to shake hands with Burgess Osgood. His hand was large and fleshy like the rest of him, and the hair that refused to grow on his head had taken root on the backs of his thick fingers and heavy wrists. He held her hand overly long.

"Perhaps your assistant, Miss Sherman, could join us?" he suggested in a soft tone that held steel behind it.

"Of course, I'm sure Nola would be delighted," Ginny said lightly. "I'll send her down

11

to your office, Alex."

After spouting a few stock phrases and some reassurances that the Ozzie account would be given top priority, Ginny slipped away, glad to leave the manipulative, overbearing man. She was sorry to have thrown Nola to the wolf, literally, but she knew her assistant would survive. Nola was attractive and smart, and she had a way with handling difficult people. No doubt she'd have Burgess Osgood laughing at some risqué joke and be calling him Burr before the waiter had taken their order.

"How'd it go?" Nola asked, poking her head around the door as Ginny stored the promo boards on a side table and settled herself at her littered desk.

"Harder than I expected," she sighed and gratefully took the cup of coffee Nola handed her. Bemused, she studied her assistant. Thirty-five, dark-haired and petite, Nola Sherman had stated frankly at her interview three years before that she was lazy and hated physical exercise, and she hadn't been kidding. But Ginny had never known anyone to possess such a quick lively mind. Nola's mental gymnastics more than made up for her physical inactivity. She had an uncanny ability to zero in on another person's strengths and weaknesses, and her humor and warm approach often drew people out, leading them into revealing more of themselves than they might have. But Nola was ambitious—and determined. Ginny recognized in the younger woman aspects of herself fifteen years before.

"I take it Osgood wasn't pleased with your presentation?" Nola said sympathetically.

"He likes being a hard sell," Ginny said, and told her about the song idea. "Now we'll have to come up with some catchy little jingle that exudes some taste, no pun intended."

Nola grinned dutifully. "I'll give it some thought myself if you don't mind."

"Think away," Ginny said, pushing aside the empty coffee cup and shuffling the papers on her desk. "By the way, Mr. Osgood has personally requested you join him for lunch. Are you up to it?"

"Me?" Nola's dark eyes widened. "Will that be a problem for you?"

"Why would it?" Ginny asked, absently studying another account.

"Just since he asked for me and all." Nola flashed a brilliant smile. "You're a pretty terrific lady, you know, and not a bad boss either." Ginny made a face and turned to the mound of papers. Nola headed toward the door, then paused.

"I almost forgot to tell you, Scott called. Wants you to call him back."

"Thanks," Ginny said, reaching for the phone. She paused as the door opened again and Alex poked his head in. His thin tanned face lit with a grin as he met her gaze, and his fingers closed in a circle of approval. Ginny placed the handset back in its cradle and turned to greet him.

"What a gal," he said strolling into her office. "I knew my trust in you was well placed. Never doubted you a minute."

"Come on, Alex, you have to admit, for just a minute there, you thought we were going to lose him."

"Maybe I did sweat just a bit," he said, easing one slender hip onto the edge of her desk. His dark eyes fixed on her face. "For a minute there he even had you sweating. Everything okay with you?"

Ginny flushed and looked away. "We just landed a big account. Why wouldn't it be?"

"I just wondered." He fell silent, but she could feel his measuring gaze on her. She picked up a pencil and checked off the corner of one page without knowing what was on it. She'd go over it later when he left the office.

"You don't reveal too much at one time, do you?" he asked softly.

Ginny raised her head. Her gray eyes warmed as she looked at him. "A woman likes to maintain her mystique," she said. His brown eyes darkened, intensified until she glanced away again. Sighing he got to his feet.

"Sure you won't join us? It's a pretty fancy restaurant. You did the hard work. You should come take the kudos."

"You know how I feel about lunching a client," she answered absently. "Besides, I have to start thinking Ozzie good!"

"That could wait." His tone was slightly reproving. "All work and no play—"

"I don't consider lunch with Burr Osgood play."

Alex sighed and stood up, straightening his suit jacket. He was pencil slim, so there was always a rumpled elegance to him.

Ginny glanced at him. "Straighten your tie," she said automatically, and turning back to her work, she didn't see the look of surprise and then exasperation he bestowed on her bent head.

"I'll be back around two. Talk to you then."

"Right!" Long after the door closed behind him, she sat staring at the wooden panel. Lately, she'd had the strangest feeling that Alex was on the verge of saying something to her, of reaching out to her in a way that had nothing to do with business. She shrugged and reached for the phone again. Insane! Alex's life was filled with beautiful young women. He was a handsome man and the years had only made him more sought after.

Besides, she wasn't interested in a man like Alex, not after David. She glanced at the framed picture that had sat on one corner of her desk the whole ten years she'd been with the agency. A slender fair-haired man, not so handsome as Alex, not so flashy, but still attractive, stood with his arm around a man who was a younger version of himself. The two were laughing as if they'd just shared a joke. They'd been golfing and come home full of camaraderie. She could remember the day as if it were yesterday. She'd sensed the warmth between father and son and had proudly rushed to get the camera to capture it. Two weeks later David had died of a massive heart attack.

But she still had Scott and his three daughters. If life takes away the people we love best, it tries to compensate by giving us someone else in return, and though she wished every minute of every day that David was still with her, she'd mended and gone on because she had Scott and her granddaughters. Her finger jabbed eagerly at the buttons on the phone, and she felt a little catch when she heard Scott's voice, strong and sure, on the other end of the line.

"Nola said you called," she said into the receiver.

"I did. How did your presentation go?" He was smiling. She could always tell because his voice changed.

"Ozzie good!" she said and laughed a little, suddenly pleased with life. She'd survived the worst thing that could happen to a woman, and she was reaching for the sunlight again.

"How good is that?" he asked, playing along with her.

"Good enough to land the account."

"Congratulations!" She could hear the change in his voice as his thoughts turned to something else. "I'm flying out of town tonight, Mom. I have a meeting first thing in the morning with American Steele in Pittsburgh. Mrs. Lansky's going to stay over and watch the girls for me, but I thought if you'd go by and have supper with them one night, they might not miss me so much. Do you have plans?" His asking was a mere formality. He knew her social life had pretty much ended with David's death. Still, she appreciated the fact that he didn't take her for granted.

"Actually, I do have plans for this evening, but I'll get together with them tomorrow night."

"Just don't take them shopping for any more toys or clothes. They have enough as it is," Scott admonished.

"What else have I got to spend my money on?"

"You spoil them, Mom."

"It doesn't hurt them," she answered. There was silence across the line as they both sat thinking of the mother who was no longer there to spoil the girls.

"Do you ever hear from her?" She'd wanted to ask the question a thousand times before, but never had, not wanting to cause him pain. She wished she hadn't now.

"Just from the divorce lawyer. She's somewhere in California." He took a deep breath. "Look, Mom—"

"I'll spend tomorrow evening with the girls," she said when he didn't continue.

"Thanks," he said softly, and she knew it was more for not probing a raw wound. "My flight doesn't get in until after midnight tomorrow."

"Maybe I'll just take the girls home with me for the night. We haven't done that for a while. Have a safe trip."

"Bye, Mom." His voice was warm, filled with love and care. For an aching moment he sounded so like his father she wanted to weep, but she bade him goodbye and hung up the phone.

Immediately she plunged into her paper work. She'd learned long ago not to let sentimentality build up. Keep your mind busy and don't think too much or the tears come.

"I'm back," Nola stuck her head around the door. Her dark eyes shone with some special mixture of humor and triumph. Obviously, she hadn't been intimidated by Burr Osgood.

"How'd it go?"

"Boring!" Nola answered. "Man talk! Not one word about the latest fashion or Liz's most recent wedding."

Ginny chuckled. Nola always gave her a lift.

"By the way, don't forget about tonight."

"I haven't! Where are we going for supper?"

"Paddy's Pub, okay? Some of the girls are joining us and afterward we thought we'd take in the new male stripper revue."

"Oh, I don't think so, Nola. That sort of thing's not for me. I don't get anything out of seeing young men shake their naked backsides." Ginny pushed back from her desk and rose in a smooth liquid movement that won a touch of ad-

18

miration from Nola. She hoped she could move that way when she was Ginny's age.

"The girls are counting on your coming along. They want to make this a special night for you," Nola wheedled.

Ginny had crossed to the file cabinet. Now she whirled to look at her assistant over the rim of her glasses. "You didn't tell them about my birthday? You did, you rat."

"Just that you had one, not about the big five-oh part."

"Don't!" Ginny bent over her desk again. It should have been a signal to Nola to leave, but the younger woman stood studying her boss.

"Are you ashamed of your age?"

"Mmm, no I'm not. But let's face it, this is a youth-oriented culture."

"Then come tonight and prove the girls wrong."

Nola's words were strangely needling. Ginny paused, trying to sort out her ambivalent feelings about this birthday, and finally shrugged her shoulders.

"All right, but if you spring a cake and happy birthday songs on me in the restaurant, I swear you'll all be looking for jobs in the morning." She was talking to empty air, for Nola had already slipped out of the office. Ginny chuckled. Maybe it would be fun to get out with the girls. She glanced at David's picture. "A male strip show, imagine!" she muttered.

"Things have sure changed."

The rest of the afternoon was relatively quiet, so she was able to work uninterrupted. She was surprised when Nola poked her head around the door.

"It's six o'clock," she declared reprovingly. "Time for even you to quit and come play a little."

"Is it that late already?" Ginny shuffled the few remaining papers together. "Did Alex come back to the office after lunch?"

"He's been shut away all afternoon. Do you want me to ring him for you?"

"No, I'll just check out with him and join you in a minute." Ginny rose and gathered up her handbag and tweed coat. Outside her window it had snowed, and cars and buildings were covered with a soft mantle of white. She made her way to Alex's office and tapped lightly.

"You're working late?" she said. "No pretty young thing to squire about town?"

"Not tonight." Alex glanced up and grimaced, pushing his glasses up on his tanned forehead to rub at his bleary eyes. His dark hair was rumpled and lay across his brow. The grooves in his cheeks seemed deeper. A five o'clock shadow was darkening his chin.

He's getting older, too, Ginny thought with a start.

"Want to go out for a bite of supper together?" he surprised her by asking.

"Thanks, but I've already had an offer. The girls are dragging me around for my birthday tonight."

"I'm sorry, Ginny. I forgot."

"Frankly, I wish I could forget," she grinned good-naturedly, "but Nola told everyone and now they're taking me to a show of some sort."

"You'll enjoy it."

"I'm not so sure about that. I'm not into exotic young things." She paused, realizing she might have insulted him when she hadn't meant to.

Alex grinned. "Actually, they hold less appeal for me every year. Amazing, isn't it?"

"I suspect it's different for you men than it is for us. Once we've nursed a babe at our breasts, we feel an eternal mothering bond."

Alex looked annoyed at her words. "Pity," he said cryptically. "You might be missing out on some really special relationships."

"Maybe so." Ginny got to her feet, willing to change the subject. "Did things go well at lunch? No new surprises or demands from goody Oz?"

Alex grinned as she'd intended. "A few things were discussed but nothing important enough for you to worry about now. Nola came up with a couple of suggestions on the 'Ozzie good' jingle."

"Umm, she works fast. She just mentioned to me at lunch that she wanted to try her hand at it."

"You don't mind?" Ginny was puzzled by the question and sensed he was closely watching her reaction.

21

"Of course not. Why would I?"

"That's what I told Nola. She seemed worried that you'd feel threatened."

A prickle of surprise swept over Ginny. "What did you tell her?"

"That you weren't that kind of woman, what else?" He shrugged. "She seemed relieved."

"How strange. I reassured her before she left for the luncheon. Besides, she's worked for me long enough to know I'd never object to anyone trying something new."

"Yeah, well, you know how Nola is. Despite any misunderstanding she's always a team player."

The obvious admiration in his voice was unsettling. Evidently Nola had worked her magic on him as well as Osgood during the luncheon. Getting to her feet, Ginny pulled on her gloves.

"Sounds as if everything went well then," she said. "I'll go off to supper with a clear conscience."

"Ginny . . ." Alex's voice was troubled. His dark eyes regarded her, some emotion she couldn't name in them. She waited for him to continue while the pause stretched between them. Finally, it was Alex who looked away.

"Tell me about Nola," he said, and his request further surprised Ginny.

"She's really not your type, Alex," she snapped and bit her lips, wishing she could call back the words. His expression grew dark, and his cheeks flushed beneath his tan. "I'm sorry. I shouldn't have said that."

"No, you shouldn't have," he said with deceptive mildness.

"Look, I'm tired. It's been a long day."

"You're right. Perhaps we should talk tomorrow instead." His posture was unusually stiff. His dark eyes avoided hers. His lips were clamped together in a thin line. She'd hurt him with her thoughtless remark. Intuitively, she crossed the room and placed a gloved hand on his arm in a silent plea for forgiveness.

"I'm truly sorry for my remark," she said softly. He met her gaze then, his liquid dark eyes pinning her. He saw concern and regret on her face. Ginny would never knowingly be unkind to anyone and to deliberately give offense was beyond her. The thought only made him feel sadder.

"You'll never get over thinking me a lecher, will you?" he asked, laying a slender brown hand over hers.

"Never that," she replied. "I only meant by my remark that Nola isn't like the girls you usually date. She's not a . . . a bimbo. She has a good brain, and she knows how to use it."

Surprisingly, he laughed. His hand squeezed hers, then he released it and moved back behind his desk. When he faced her again, the old carefree humor was back in his eyes. "Bimbo?" he repeated. "Do you think I date only bimbos?" He shook his head. "Ginny, Ginny! One of these days you're going to change your opinion of me, and what a day of revelations that will be."

"I hope not," she answered, glad to see his good humor had returned. "I kind of like you the way you are."

"You do?" He looked bemused, then nodded toward the door. "The girls are waiting. Go have supper, and someday soon we'll take up this conversation again."

The words were a promise that both troubled and reassured her. "Good night, Alex," she said and made her escape.

Two

Nola and the other girls were waiting, coated and booted, gloves and bags in hand. Their voices and quick, ready laughter showed they were anticipating the evening. Ginny stood watching them, seeing how they gravitated around Nola, laughing longer at her quips, looking to her to lead the way to something brighter and more exciting than anything they might come up with. There was no doubt Nola had a way with people, and Alex would have to be dead to be immune to it. Still there had been undertones of things unsaid in Alex's office, and Ginny felt a tremor of disquiet. She didn't want to acknowledge it, so she shrugged it aside and moved toward the girls.

Nola glanced up and saw her. "Everything all right?" she asked, her gray eyes studying Ginny a little too intently. "You were in there so long we thought something was wrong."

"Not at all," Ginny answered. "Alex and I were just talking."

"Uh-huh!" Mary Preston teased, and the other girls grinned.

Ginny smiled back at them but didn't deny their words. Everything was said in fun anyway. She sensed she was being enfolded in their light-hearted camaraderie. It felt good. She'd missed these girls' nights on the town. During her marriage to David, she'd seldom gone out without him. She hadn't needed get togethers with women, not when she had David and Scott. Maybe she did need them now! They all piled into the elevator, everyone talking at once.

"You look great, Ginny. It's hard to believe you're really fifty," Fran Whittaker said, squeezing in beside her.

"What makes you think I am?" asked Ginny. Darn that Nola.

"Well, it's your birthday," Fran stammered. "I mean, that's what we're celebrating, isn't it?" Her voice dwindled as she realized she'd offended her boss.

I should let her off the hook, Ginny thought.

"Whatever age you are, you don't look it," Fran babbled.

"Thank you. I don't think I look thirty-nine either," Ginny said. Fran smiled but she contrived to move away as soon as she could.

Way to go, Gin. How to win friends and influence people. Instead of smarting over Nola's ways, I should be taking lessons from her.

They all decided to forget about cholesterol and calories. Sizzling hot steaks and sour cream abounded at their table. Talk flowed, light-hearted and fast changing. Glasses of wine were consumed. Cheeks grew pinker, eyes brighter. Everyone was feeling tipsy and daring.

From the warm semidark interior of Paddy's Pub, they went back into the cold snowy night, piled into a taxi, and headed downtown to a gaudy-looking nightclub. The wine they'd drunk had added a shriller note to their laughter, and their jokes had become a little more ribald. Get into the spirit of things, Ginny chided herself, but she'd long since grown impatient with the evening and with the company in which she found herself. These women were younger than she was, their responses held an edge of youthful recklessness she'd long since left behind. Ginny no longer wished to let her hair down as Nola had several times suggested. She was feeling every one of her fifty years—and they didn't feel good. She was outdated, a dinosaur left behind with only extinction to contemplate.

"You're becoming morbid," Nola said and dragged her from the taxi.

The nightclub was packed with women seated at small tables. Dominating the cavernous, low-ceilinged room was a large stage with runways, all empty and dark now.

"Good. The show hasn't started yet," Nola said, and led the way through the throng. Miraculously, she found an empty table up front near the corner of the stage. Ginny contrived to squeeze into the seat farthest from the stage, but found there was a runway at her back. The waiter was young, very good-looking, and, Ginny guessed, still in college. He was nude from the waist up except for a bowtie and white collar. A mat of dark hair swirled down the front of his muscled chest. Ginny's companions giggled, but she wanted to tell this young man to cover up and to take his vitamins before he caught a cold.

His dark eyes were bold and intimate as he took each woman's order. Obviously, he was aiming for a big tip. Ginny didn't meet his suggestive gaze. The last time a man had looked at her like that, they'd made love far into the night. She was angered by the young waiter's nonchalant promise of intimacy, believing such looks should be reserved for people who care about each other.

"What'll you have, Ginny?" Nola asked.

Ginny glanced around the table. Everyone's eyes had turned to her, while she was still grappling with her feelings about being here. "I . . . I don't know," she hesitated. "A glass of white wine, I suppose."

"Aww," Nola reprimanded. The other girls joined in the chorus. "Why don't you really

28

live?" Nola suggested. Her bright gaze swept around the table and came to rest on the waiter's lean bare midsection. "I know. She'll have a fuzzy navel." She wiggled her eyebrows, and the other girls laughed. Even the waiter grinned, although he must have been used to hundreds of such remarks by now. He disappeared toward the bar.

"Ummm, I could spend a few hours alone with him," said Mary. Ginny knew she was married and had a six-month-old baby; she would never think of being unfaithful to her husband. What made women assume this attitude when they went out like this? There were as macho as men.

"Wait until you see the lead dancer," Nola warned. "He tops them all." Ginny found the conversation inanely juvenile, but the girls were trying so hard to help her have a good time. The young waiter returned with the drinks, and Nola passed the peach-colored one to Ginny, then waited for her to taste it.

Ginny sighed and nodded in feigned approval. The noxiously sweet drink was every bit as bad as she'd feared, but she didn't want to hurt Nola's feelings. Talk swirled around her as she sat watching the others. Nola glanced at her often as if to reassure herself that Ginny was having a good time. Obligingly, Ginny smiled and sipped her drink. After a time a relaxing glow enfolded her and she decided the drink was stronger than she'd suspected. When her glass was empty, a full one replaced it. Laughter came easier now, even if the remarks were silly and sexist. The fact that they were without any substance had no bearing on their responses. They hadn't come to this place to be intellectual. They'd come to ogle young men's biceps and pectorals and whatever they called backsides and thighs these days.

"Ladies and gentlemen . . ." The emcee, dressed in tight leather pants and a stud-encrusted leather jacket, laughed. "Ladies and ladies," he amended, "welcome to the Chez Rue Review. Our show is about to begin!"

Bright lights flared to life, illuminating the stage in a silver-blue glow. Music, deafening and frenzied, flooded the room. Ginny flinched from it and placed her hands over her ears. Four young men danced onto the stage, their lithe hips writhing to the wild beat. The women behind Ginny screamed, and Nola leaped to her feet and raised her arms, calling out some ribald remark that was lost in the din. The dancers played to the women, inciting them to further demonstrations of approval.

"What do you think so far?" Nola asked after the first number ended. Her hair floated around her head in a wild tangle, her eyes glittered with laughter.

"Now I know what the Roman arenas must have been like," Ginny answered dryly.

"Don't be stodgy," Nola reprimanded. "Forget about who you are and have some fun. That's what this is all about." Without consulting the others, she motioned to the waiter and ordered another round of drinks.

Cut by Nola's words and by fear that she might appear condescending to the other girls, Ginny made more of an effort. When her drink came, she downed it, then clapped and cheered with the rest of the women as the revue continued. She could feel her inhibitions slipping away. She was actually having fun. She told herself she would regret her new attitude in the morning, but for now it was enough to feel daring and young again—and carefree. What had Nola called her? Stodgy. Old people were stodgy. She wasn't old, and she wasn't stodgy.

When Nola rose and danced in the aisle, Ginny egged her on, snapping her fingers and wriggling her shoulders to the music. She was enjoying this new freedom of her body. Vaguely, she was aware of cameras going off around the room. She saw their popping brightness, but it blended with the strobe lights into the kaleidoscope of dancing colors. Ginny stood up and gyrated her hips the way the dancers were doing. She heard the girls laughing behind her. They hadn't expected her to let her hair down like this. She smiled and kept moving because the music and the moving lights demanded it.

The dancers moved forward, wriggling their

nearly nude bodies. Some leaped off the stage and danced with the women in the audience. This occasioned more laughter. Everyone was having a good time.

One of the dancers, a tall blond man who reminded her of David when he was in college, came to dance with her. Ginny laughed and then put a hand over her mouth in dismay before quickly sitting down, but the dancer took a stance directly in front of her. He wore only a G-string. His fair, hairless body was very muscular, his middle lean and flat. Sweat gleamed on his skin as he twisted his hips in a primal, sensual movement that spoke of raw lust and hot desires about to be met. Ginny felt her breasts grow hot, and a strange pulsing ache arose between her legs. The dancer's eyes were blue, and they held her gaze. His glance was hot, sharp edged. That relentless rhythmic movement of his hips continued as he motioned her to her feet. Slowly, Ginny stood up and began to move. Their bodies twisted and jerked in an erotic dance, without touching. Suddenly, she wanted to touch him, to feel David whole and alive again.

"Put some money in his jock," someone at the table shouted, and suddenly she felt cheap. He was playing her for a bigger tip, using sex to up his earnings. Blindly she reached into her bag, grabbed a bill, and stiffly held it out to him. The young dancer sensed her change of mood. Languidly he smiled and, taking her hand, guided it to the thin strap near his groin. Ginny could feel the heat of his body. His eyes still held hers, but his expression, too, had changed. It had become arrogant, triumphant, as if he'd won some battle between them. Hastily, she shoved the bill into the strap, aware that his pubic hairs grazed her fingers. She tried to jerk away, but he still held her hand.

"Let me go," she said firmly, and with a crooked grin that said he'd learned all he needed to know about her hidden needs, he moved on to someone else. Abruptly, Ginny sat down. She felt used and foolish and angry, all at the same time. The music ended and the dancers leaped back on stage, their bare legs and buttocks gleaming in the strobe lights. With a final thrust of their pelvises, they ran backstage. Ginny gathered up her coat.

"Where are you going?" Nola asked.

"I have a headache." Ginny realized it was true. "No need to leave because I am, I'll get a taxi."

"We'll come with you," Nola said. "You've had a lot to drink."

"I'm all right." Ginny took a step and knew immediately she wasn't. The room was spinning. She staggered a little farther and had to grab a chair back to keep from falling. A man in a dark business suit came forward. He took hold of her arm.

"Are you okay, lady?"

"I'm fine," Ginny said, putting a hand to her fuzzy head. She couldn't seem to focus, and suddenly she felt like grinning at all the witty things that flitted through her head. "I'm right—right as rain." She smiled up at him. "The rain in Shpain shtays mainly in the plainly." She enunciated her words with precision then peered up at him for approval.

"She's with us," Nola said, taking her elbow. "We'll take care of her."

"You'd better get her home," the man stated flatly as Ginny peered at him.

"Hey, are you the manager here? Great show!"

"Come on, Ginny. Let's get you home." Nola guided her to the door.

Women at other tables were staring at her. Sobriety, stark and blessedly brief, claimed her. "Nola, get me out of here," Ginny pleaded in a slurred voice. Dark shadows were pressing at her consciousness. She couldn't humiliate herself further by fainting.

"We'd better get her home," Mary said. Taking hold of one of Ginny's arms, she looped it around her neck.

"Poor thing," Nola muttered, taking Ginny's other arm.

The cold air was a welcome sting against her face. Ginny gasped in the sharp coldness and tried to stand upright, but she felt fuzzy. Now she understood the name of the innocuous little drinks she'd been downing.

"Shorry to spoil your fun," she said, gripping the rough texture of the building with her fingertips.

"That's all right, honey. It's your birthday. It's not every day a woman turns fifty."

"Damn you, Nola," she hiccuped. "You promised not to tell."

"It slipped out." Nola shrugged. "I can't cover for you all the time."

What is she talking about? Ginny wondered dimly. But there was no time to ask. Her wobbling head was about to fall off her shoulders, and a cab had slid to a stop in front of them. Sinking onto the upholstered seat, Ginny moaned, her head rolling from side to side.

"She ain't going to throw up in my cab, is she?" the driver demanded.

"I promise she won't," Nola answered, ignoring Ginny's head bobbing an affirmative. "Here. Put your head over this," Nola whispered in her ear. The cab moved up the silent, snow-covered street and headed west into the suburbs. Ginny sat with her head over her handbag, praying the night would soon be over and she could quietly die and end the enormous pain that had engulfed her.

Nearly a half-hour later, the taxi pulled up in front of Ginny's apartment building. Nola got out and helped Ginny to the street.

"I'll make sure she gets in okay," Nola said. "Wait for me!"

Ginny wanted to say she didn't need the help, but she did. She wasn't certain she could get to her front door, much less negotiate the stairs to her bed.

"You're a good friend, Nola," she said, pleased that her words weren't as slurred as before. She must be sobering up. "I think I can make it on my own now." She pushed away from Nola. But she must have pushed harder than she'd intended for the younger woman went sprawling. "Are you hurt?" Ginny asked, bending over her friend. The action made her head ache, so she straightened abruptly.

"Is everything all right?" Mary called from the taxi.

Ginny waved to them reassuringly. "It's okay. I just didn't know my own strength." She turned back to Nola, who still sat on the ground. "Come on, I'll give you a hand." Suddenly, Ginny started giggling. Nola glared up at her, then got to her feet. She looked angry. "I'm sorry, Nola. Honestly, you looked so funny sitting there."

"Give me your keys," Nola demanded, holding out her hand. Ginny stifled her giggles and dug out the round disc that held her keys. Without a word, Nola opened the door to the vestibule and guided Ginny up the stairs to her bedroom.

"Thanks for taking me out." Ginny hiccuped. "I had more fun than I thought I would."

"You're going to have a hell of a headache in the morning," Nola said, switching on lights.

"I already have one." Ginny was holding her head. "Whew, where are the aspirins?"

"I'll get them." Nola turned toward the bathroom.

"No, that's all right. I can get them," Ginny said, dropping gingerly onto an overstuffed loveseat. "Thanks for coming up with me."

"That's what friends are for." Nola was standing in front of Ginny, her expression warm and caring.

Through a painful haze, Ginny studied Nola's face. Nola's expression was as frank and open as it had always been. "I'll see you tomorrow, friend."

"Are you coming in?" Nola paused at the door and glanced back at her.

"I'll be there. I have too much work to miss a day."

Nola looked doubtful. "Nothing you can't put off. Why don't you come in late? I'll cover for you."

Ginny flinched and placed icy fingertips against her temples, moving them in small circular motions. "I'll consider it. Thanks."

The door closed behind Nola, and Ginny sat clutching her head, trying to sort out instincts that seemed to have gone haywire. Thoughtfully, she rose and crossed to the window that looked down on the street. The taxi was still waiting. Nola came out of the shadows of the building. Her shoulders were hunched, and one hand clutched her cheek. Alarm swept through Ginny. Had Nola fallen and hurt herself? She gripped the window sill and peered through the mist of falling snowflakes. Nola had reached the cab now. Mary had gotten out to greet her. They stood talking for a moment, then both women looked up at Ginny's bedroom window. Ginny waved to let them know she was all right. Neither of them waved back. They got into the cab, and it drove away. Ginny stood staring down at the empty street. Something wasn't right, but she couldn't quite put her finger on what it was. Sighing, she turned away from the window and went in search of a bottle of aspirin.

She went to bed without creaming her face or brushing her teeth. She was lucky to get into her nightgown before flopping under the covers. Her thoughts went back to the blond dancer who looked so much like David. He'd awakened something within her, some sensuality that she'd thought dead. Now it was clamoring inside her, reclaiming its role in her life. She could feel it in the aching yearning of her breasts and the flood of heat in the pit of her stomach and between her thighs. Muscles and flesh remembered the feel of hot turgid flesh, the rhythm of loving, the sweet pain of release.

She thought of the first time she'd seen David striding across campus. She'd been struck first by his tall well-made body and broad sloping shoulders. As the autumn sun had glinted off his pale hair, he'd looked virile and incredibly handsome. It had taken her nearly three weeks to finagle an introduction. He'd seemed as taken with her as she'd been with him. He'd asked her out immediately, and they'd gone back to his room and made love after that first date. It was the beginning of the sixties, of a new attitude. They'd been lovers for all of her freshman year, and then, anguished at the thought of separation during the summer, he'd asked her to marry him. She hadn't hesitated, knowing her destiny was forever entwined with his.

Ginny fell asleep, remembering the feel of his skin beneath her hands, the taste and hardness of his body. Sometime during the dream the images changed. It was no longer David bending over her. Alex's dark eyes captured her gaze while his slender hands slid over her body. She felt the intensity of his desire and reached for him, encountering his engorged shaft. It was hard and hot and satiny smooth, and it invaded her with exotic intimacy, causing her to writhe against him. She awoke with a throbbing deep within her. Moaning she hid her face in her pillow and tried to tell herself it had been David in her dreams, but she knew differently. She'd dreamed of Alex before.

Ginny groaned and turned on her side. Her hands ran over her breasts and her stomach. "David, why did you leave me?" she whispered. She placed her hands between her thighs, feeling and smelling the flowery, heated scent of her own flesh through her gown. Finally, curling her legs up to her chest, she lay, wishing, wanting, needing.

She woke in the morning with a pounding headache and a fuzzy mouth. Standing in front of the bathroom mirror and staring at her reflection, she thought about staying home as Nola had suggested, but a long empty day with nothing to occupy her was not appealing. Besides, she was supposed to pick up the girls after work. Sighing, she reached for the cleansing cream and tried to repair the damage her night on the town had caused.

"Mr. Russell wants to see you right away," Mary said when she arrived at the office.

Ginny shrugged out of her coat and hung it up. "Tell him I'll be there as soon as I can get my hands on a cup of coffee. Where's Nola?"

"Umm, around somewhere," Mary said evasively. She seemed strangely subdued this morning.

"Did you survive the night?" Ginny asked, putting away her bag and gloves. She'd long since decided the best way to handle last night was to make light of it.

"Well enough." Mary's expression was unresponsive.

Ginny had no time to dwell on that now. She had overslept, and her six-year-old Lincoln hadn't started. There were a hundred things she had to do, and this meeting with Alex would take more of her time. "Tell Nola to stop by my office when she has a minute." Ginny poured a mug of black coffee and carried it to Alex's office.

"Hi! You wanted to see me?"

"Come in, Ginny." Alex got to his feet. His air of formality seemed foreign to him. "How was your night out?"

"Don't ask." Ginny sat down and crossed her long legs with a silken swish of nylons. In spite of her pale face and the dark circles beneath her eyes, she looked fashionable in a smart Anne Klein blazer and skirt. Alex had a bemused look in his eyes as he watched her settle herself. How could a woman spend the night as she had and then arrived starched and polished the next morning? He wasn't really surprised. That was Ginny's style, just like the matching silk blouse beneath the jacket. Large gold earrings were the only jewelry she wore, and yet she looked chic and sleek. He liked the way she sank into the chair and looked at him expectantly, not fussing with her clothes.

"To top it off, my car wouldn't start."

"You should trade it in for a newer model."

Ginny sipped. "I know. I just can't seem to find anything I like better. What did you want to see me about?" she asked quickly to forestall any lectures. "Problems with our new account already?"

"Nothing we can't handle. Have you seen Nola this morning?" Again that air of formality, even withdrawal.

"She was busy when I came in."

"Have you seen the morning papers?"

Ginny looked puzzled, the smooth wings of her brows flickering delicately above her expressive hazel eyes. "I didn't take time to glance at them. Did I miss anything important?"

"I suppose that depends on how you view such things." He passed a paper over to her. "Read it for yourself. Page three."

Glasses perched on her nose, Ginny picked up the paper and scanned the page. "Oh, my god," she lamented quietly when she'd finished reading one of the columns. Her eyes were large as they peered at him above the rims of her glasses.

"There's even a picture," she yelped disbelievingly, and glanced back at the large display covering three columns widths. "Grandmother gets her man!" she read aloud. She glanced from the bold headline to Alex, then continued. "Mike Shay's All-Male Revue has the ladies battling to get on stage as evidenced last night. Ginny Logan, a fifty-year-old grandmother who works for the Russell and Taylor Advertising Agency by day frequents the new Chez Rue Club where the revue is being staged. During the dance numbers, Ms. Logan, who was celebrating her half-century birthday, danced in the aisles along with other sex-crazed gyrating women before slipping a bill into the young dancer's G-string. This scene is not uncommon when lonely, desperate middle-aged women attend the lively show. Twenty-one near-nude male dancers . . ." She crumpled the paper in her hands. "Half-century birthday! How could they have gotten that picture and all that information about me?"

"Nola said you gave the reporter the information."

"I couldn't have!" She couldn't stay seated. Furiously she paced from one end of the office to the other. "I wouldn't have been so indiscreet as to give the name of the agency."

"Nola says you were pretty well out of it. You'd had a lot to drink."

"Well, obviously. It doesn't take much for me, Alex. I seldom drink."

He didn't contradict her.

"She said they tried to stop you last night, but you were depressed about . . . things."

"But I haven't been." Ginny crossed to his desk and leaned across it. Her expression was tight and angry, and tiny lines stood out at the

43

corners of her eyes and mouth. She's a damned attractive woman, Alex thought, and an angry one.

"My life is going great," she declared. "I feel as if I have things under control for the first time since David died."

His brown eyes studied her. "Have you, Ginny?"

She glanced back at the wrinkled newspaper. "I thought I did. Last night . . . I don't know. I felt out of place with those younger women, and I thought why not just let my hair down a little. The next thing I knew this dancer was gyrating in front of me. What was I supposed to do?" Her voice had slowed and deepened. "He looked like David when I'd first met him." She stopped talking and took a deep breath. Her face showed how upset she was as she turned to Alex. "If I've hurt the agency in any way —"

"Don't worry about that," he said quickly. "But you have to let go of David."

"I have, Alex. It's just . . . this young man reminded me of him."

"You haven't, Ginny. You still talk about him. You still live your life exactly as you did when David was alive, except now you're alone."

"You needn't say these things to me. I've accepted the fact that David is no longer here."

"I hope so. I hate to see you hurting yourself and the people who care about you."

"I didn't think I was." She was defensive, pulling her aloofness around her like one of the fashionable capes she wore.

"You need to talk to Nola," Alex said, and disappointment was evident in his eyes. It hurt. She was surprised to feel how much. She'd always had Alex's approval and admiration. To think she might have lost that because of one night out on the town . . . it seemed unfair. He'd been her friend for a long time.

"What about? Is there a problem there as well? Never mind, I'll find out myself," she said tightly and headed for the door.

"Ginny," Alex's voice halted her halfway there.

"What is it?" She faced him.

"Go easy." His brown eyes held some message she couldn't fathom.

"I don't understand." She felt she'd walked in on the middle of a play and everyone knew the plot but her.

"Just that. Go easy." The words were a warning. A warning! From Alex? About what? Thoughtfully she closed the door behind her and walked to the center office.

Three

Nola was bent over Mary's desk, her back to Ginny, her voice low and subdued. Ginny watched her for a moment, feeling her anger grow. If Nola hadn't insisted on going to that night club, she wouldn't be in this embarrassing position. Her chin tightened in resolve as she crossed the corridor.

"Nola, I want to talk to you," she began crisply. Nola swung around, and Ginny gasped. Nola's cheek and one eye were bruised, the skin around them an ugly purple and blue. She'd tried to hide the damage with makeup, which only made it stand out more. "My god! What happened to you?" Ginny demanded, her anger forgotten. She put out a hand to touch Nola's shoulder, but the younger woman shrank away. For a moment she stared at Ginny as if possessed, then, whirling, ran toward the ladies' room. Her muffled sobs were loud and unmistakable in the too-quiet room.

Everyone had stopped working to watch the scenario. Ginny glanced around at all the accusing faces turned toward her.

"What's wrong with Nola?" she asked Mary.

"Can you blame her?" Fran demanded. "After what you did to her, I'd run too."

"I'll go see about her," Mary said, pushing her chair back and disappearing down the hall after Nola. Ginny looked at Fran's angry face.

"I didn't do that to her."

Fran made no answer. The rest of the office staff remained silent. Ginny had an insane urge to cry out her innocence, but common sense prevailed.

"Get back to work," she said instead and, head high, fled to her office. Seated behind her desk, she tried to get going on the pile of paperwork, but her thoughts kept straying to Nola. Had she had a fight with a boyfriend? She tried to remember whether Nola had mentioned a man recently and realized for all her bright humor and seeming openness, Nola actually revealed very little about herself.

Most of the stories she told about friends and family were a little too farfetched to be entirely true so Ginny had dismissed most of them, taking Nola at face value, overlooking her tendency to exaggerate. Now she wondered how, being someone who valued honesty, she'd come to accept Nola's fabrications. Except that Nola had told each story with great charm, making her listeners laugh, entertaining them. Advertising depended on a flair for fracturing obvious truths into fresher viewpoints. What was the real Nola all about? What off-center notions about Ginny had she begun to instill in the office help—and in Alex?

Time and again Ginny went over the evening, ending with Nola helping her from the taxi and up the stairs. There had been no angry words between them, nothing that would have presaged a blow. Besides, Ginny prided herself on her even disposition. She'd never struck anyone in her life. But that didn't matter, for Alex and the office staff thought she had struck Nola.

Ginny rustled the papers on her desk and reached for a tissue to dab at her forehead. That damned sweating again. Impatiently, she threw the tissue away. She was annoyed, determined to ignore the beads of moisture on her scalp and brow. Suddenly she felt old and useless, yet she'd never felt that way before, not even when Scott had moved out of the house and into his own apartment. She'd made it through so much, she'd survive a little sweating. Defiantly, she reached for another tissue and swiped at her brow and upper lip.

"You're still needed," she said out loud.

"The girls depend on you now that Diane is gone. They're looking forward to spending the night with you." But she felt she was borrowing legitimacy from a woman who'd too easily given up her role as a mother.

Ginny buried herself in her work, not pausing for lunch. She was surprised when Mary brought her a cup of coffee in the middle of the afternoon.

"How's Nola?" she asked, putting aside the last of her paperwork and stretching.

"She went home this morning," Mary answered quietly. "Alex told her it was okay."

"Of course it was," Ginny said. "Has Nola said anything about trouble with a boyfriend?"

Mary looked at her strangely. "I don't think that was the problem."

"Look, Mary, I didn't give Nola that black eye. I've never struck anyone in my life. There has to be some other explanation. I just don't understand why Nola's allowing everyone to believe I did it."

Reluctantly, Mary opened her mouth and sighed. "When she came back to the cab last night, she was holding her cheek. She said you swung at her when she tried to stop you from having another drink."

"Mary, that's not true."

Mary didn't quite believe her. Ginny could see it in the secretary's troubled expression. Loyalties waged a battle within the young

49

woman, and finally she shrugged. "If you did do it, I don't believe you meant to hurt Nola. It was just the alcohol."

Ginny stared back at her employee for a full minute, weighing the desire to restate her innocence against Mary's effort to be fair to both parties.

"I do appreciate that, Mary," she said quietly. "But I did not strike Nola, and I'm sure when she returns we'll get this all straightened out. You may go back to your desk now."

"Yes, ma'am," Mary said and silently left the office.

Ginny tried not to think about Nola and the misunderstanding for the rest of the afternoon, concentrating on her work and on the commitment she'd made to her granddaughters. When she left the office, she drove out to Canton to pick up the girls. Scott had kept the two-story colonial he'd bought when he and Diane married. How happy and proud he'd been the first day his parents came to visit. He'd grinned from ear to ear. Ginny stood in the driveway, remembering that day when all they'd ever dreamed or wished for had seemed to be theirs, as if some higher being had marked them for only the good things in life. How right it had seemed. How easy to take for granted their happiness.

But there had been a shadow in Diane's eyes, the desperate look of a trapped creature.

Then she'd smiled and the look had gone. Ginny had thought they'd quarreled and tactfully had not probed too deeply. She hadn't wanted to think there were shadows in her perfect world, hadn't wanted to admit it might not seem so perfect to everyone — or that the price was too high.

After Diane left, Scott had talked of selling the house and moving into an apartment closer to his office, but he'd liked the schools in Canton.

Ginny walked up the crushed stone path and rang the bell. Immediately the door was thrown open.

"Hi, Grandma," twelve-year-old Tracy cried, throwing her arms around Ginny. Ginny hugged her back, feeling the difference in her young body. She was changing, her delicate frame fleshing out, as if she were gaining back some of the baby fat she'd once carried. She was starting to become a woman, and Ginny felt saddened at the thought. The years moved too quickly.

"Gwandma's here!" Steffi squealed in her tiny Cindy-Lou-Who voice. Her blue eyes danced with excitement.

"Hello, Steffi-eff," Ginny called catching the blond three-year-old up in her arms.

"Grandma, look what I made for you in kindergarten today."

"That's beautiful, Candi." Ginny praised the

green and yellow abstract that was supposed to be a flower. Candi grinned with pleasure and danced away, her slim six-year-old body imbued with energy.

"Hello, Marnie," Ginny called to the angular gray-haired lady dressed in a hot pink sweat suit and tennis shoes.

"Hello, Mrs. Logan. They haven't had supper yet," the housekeeper said as she helped the girls get their bags zipped.

"Good, we'll go out for supper."

"Showtime Pizza," the girls cried in chorus. Ginny made a face. Marnie laughed.

"I put in jeans and tops for school tomorrow. Steffi-eff has to be at her nursery school by nine at the latest. They've planned a field trip. I'll pick her up afterward," said Marnie.

"Do you have my phone number in case there's been a change in plans?"

"Scott gave it to me. Kiss me goodbye, girls." The girls crowded around Marnie. Watching, Ginny wondered how Scott could have managed without the elderly woman. She'd answered his ad and he'd almost not hired her, thinking her too old for housework and child care, but she'd been stubborn, calling and returning to see if the job was still available. Finally he'd given in, and then Marnie had pitched in as if she were part of the family. At first Ginny had been bothered by the attachment between Marnie and the girls,

52

feeling her own role was being usurped, until she'd realized how badly they needed someone they could depend on every day.

Kisses done, coats zipped, they all trooped out to the car, waving farewell to Marnie.

"Would you consider some other place for supper?" Ginny asked.

"Showtime Pizza," Steffi chanted from the back seat.

"Grandma, you might as well give in to the inevitable," said Tracy. "These two have been planning this all afternoon."

As often happened, Ginny was startled by Tracy's vocabulary. Gifted though the child was, an inaptitude at math had kept her from testing in the genius range. But David had predicted that long before she reached school age. Now, driving back toward town and listening to the bright chatter of the girl seated beside her, Ginny longed for David to be with them. A stab of guilt quickly followed. Perhaps Alex was right. She was still dwelling on David way too much. But was it so wrong to remember the good times in life and to long for them to return?

The girls, filled with excitement, vied for equal time to tell about the day at school, their friends, and teachers. It often seemed to Ginny that they all talked at once. Laughing, she quieted them down before arguments erupted. Then they sang songs and shared funny knock-knock jokes that made their grandmother grit her teeth and laugh anyway. Amid much good humor they arrived at the combination pizza and game arcade.

Ginny sat on a hard bench eating rubbery pizza while the girls chattered excitedly. Blinking lights and whizzing noises marked the game area. Suddenly the darkened stage area lit up, and for one mad moment Ginny imagined she was back before the male dancers at the Chez Rue. Then the stage floor rose, revealing a mechanical overstuffed bear wearing a goofy hat and an even goofier expression. As piped music played, the bear's oversized eyes shifted from side to side, and his big hands moved up and down on a banjo.

The children cheered. The adults smiled indulgently and gulped their diet sodas. While the girls tried all the games, spending silver tokens at an alarming rate, Ginny wandered from one attraction to another, keeping one eye on her spritely granddaughters and the other on the proud parents and grandparents who tagged after their charges.

One family caught her attention. The husband and wife were young and good-looking, and they had a gray-haired mother in tow. The couple smiled a lot as if they were very happy. Their eyes met often, their sense of belonging to each other like an armor around them. Now and then the man dipped his head to talk to the aging woman who walked on the other side of him. She used a cane and appeared tired and clumsy among the animated children. Protectively the couple stood on either side of her.

Do I look like that? Ginny wondered. Though her gray streaks had been carefully covered by an expensive hairdresser, did she still give the impression of age? In contrast to the carefree youthfulness around her, did she seem old and tired? Was that what was happening to her at work? Amid the fresh-faced girls with their quick, light chatter, did she appear heavy-handed and outdated in her thinking? Did others see her in the same way she saw this woman?

"Grandma, we're ready to go," Tracy said.

"I'm not." Candi tried to scoot out from under her sister's herding arms, but Tracy was too quick for her. "School tomorrow," she reminded Candi, and the younger girl's shoulders slumped in acceptance of her sister's edict.

Ginny was glad they'd provided some distraction from her thoughts. Happily she gathered their coats, and within moments they were out in the cold night air, bundling themselves into the car, everyone shivering and complaining until the heater got going. It was only a few blocks to Ginny's condo. The girls carried up their bags and spent the next half-hour seeing to baths and the brushing of teeth. By the time they were ready to settle down, Ginny was exhausted.

"Do you ever ride your bicycle anymore, Grandma?" Candi asked, performing her own brand of gymnastics in an attempt to make the wheels of the stationary bike go.

"Usually," Ginny said, creaming her face. She'd shed her clothes and pulled on a gathered nightgown.

"Are you going to wide it tonight?" Steffi asked from the bed. She already had a stack of books beside her.

"Not tonight," Ginny answered. "I'm going to read to you tonight." Steffi's smile was instant and beatific. Ginny felt her heart swell with love for the blond imp who often exasperated her but always won her over. She finished creaming her face, reached for the bathroom light, and paused, watching the three girls pile onto the bed. Even though it was kingsized, they'd never sleep comfortably. Before the night was out she'd have to carry one or two of them to the guest room, but for now, she was content to have them here. The bed was too big and too empty. She'd often thought of getting a smaller one.

"Ready or not, here I come," she called and snapped out the bathroom light. Only the lamp on the nightstand illuminated the room, casting soft shadows. The girls squealed in anticipation and made room for her. With girls curled all around her, she read several stories. Steffi fell asleep, her face rosy in the lamplight. Tiredly, Candi yawned and snuggled closer.

"You know, Grandma," she said sleepily, "sometimes I miss Mommy."

Ginny's heart contracted. "Do you still remember Mommy?" she asked in surprise. Candi's head nodded affirmatively against her shoulder, and her soft breathing came even and steady. She'd fallen asleep clutching an old worn-out teddy bear Diane had given her long ago. Tenderly, Ginny smoothed aside the girl's shiny hair. It lay around her face in red-gold ringlets. Steffi never mentioned her mother. She'd been too young to remember her, but Candi hadn't, nor had Tracy. Ginny glanced at Tracy and was startled to see her profile sharp and angry, her eyes scrunched tightly closed.

"Do you miss her too?" she asked softly.

Tracy shook her head and swallowed hard. "No," she said fiercely.

Ginny felt her hurt and reached out to her, but Tracy rolled away and lay on her side. After a long while Ginny saw her shoulders move slowly and rhythmically. She was asleep. As cramped as they were, Ginny couldn't bear to disturb the girls. She rolled over and turned out the light. Long into the night, she lay thinking of the beautiful, dark-haired woman who'd run away from her family.

"You fool," she whispered bitterly.

At some point she fell asleep and woke in the cloying hot darkness of midnight, feeling unable to break free of the restraints that held her prisoner on the bed. An alarm bell sounded again and again, further adding to her panic. Her scalp tingled and her pillow and nightgown were drenched in sweat. With a start she realized she'd been having a nightmare. The alarm bell was the telephone, the restraints a tangle of legs and arms—the girls'. Trying not to disturb them and without switching on the light, Ginny reached for the phone.

"Hello?"

"Mrs. Logan? Oh, thank goodness I've reached you."

"Who is this?"

"Marnie! I—oh, Mrs. Logan, it's terrible. I didn't know what to do. Those poor babies."

"Wait a minute, Marnie. Slow down. What's wrong?"

"The plane crashed. It just crashed. It fell right out of the sky. They don't know why. It was trying to land." The elderly woman was crying and babbling, but her message was horrifyingly clear.

"How do you know?"

"The news. It was on the late-night news

bulletin. I heard sirens when the Canton police and fire department headed for the airport."

"Oh, God, no!" Ginny cried, and she switched on the lamp as if she were still caught in a nightmare and light might help her wake up. "Are you sure it was his flight?"

"Yes, ma'am. He always leaves his flight information with me. I double-checked. What should I do? Do you want me to come over there?"

"Yes—no! Go to the house. He may not be on this flight. He may try to call. Someone should be there in case he does. I'll go to the airport. I'll . . . do something."

"Call me if you hear anything."

"Yes, I will. Stay by the phone. I'll check in with you." Ginny hung up and sat numbly staring at the phone. She couldn't think, couldn't function.

"Is something wrong with Daddy?" Tracy asked.

Ginny's head jerked up, her eyes registering the fear she couldn't hide. "I don't know," she whispered through stiff lips. "Surely, he's all right. He might have taken a later flight."

"Or an earlier one. Maybe he's home now," Tracy suggested. Hopefully, they stared at each other. With icy fingers, Ginny dialed and listened to the phone ringing at the other end. She tried to imagine Scott asleep in his bed, his hair tousled, his face relaxed and easy in slumber. She let the phone ring, willing him to be there as she pictured him, willing him to come awake, to swing his long legs over the bed and reach for his ratty old bathrobe, to reach for the phone. She willed it so hard, for an instant she thought she heard a click at the other end.

"Hello, hello. Scott?" she cried, but the phone just kept ringing in her ear. Slowly she replaced it and stared at Tracy. One of the younger girls stirred in her sleep, and Ginny automatically reached for the light switch. Darkness closed around them.

"Grandma?" Tracy said, and her voice sounded scared the way it had when she was small and she'd crept into bed with David and Ginny.

"Don't disturb your sisters," Ginny said softly. "Try to go back to sleep. Your father will call soon. He'll know we'll be worried." She heard the rustle of bedclothes and guessed Tracy had obediently settled back against the pillows. She sensed the girl's tension.

Easing out of bed, Ginny made her way barefoot through the darkened rooms. The sweat had dried on her brow and arms, and she shivered with a chill but made no move to find her robe. Without putting on a light, she groped her way to the window and cracked the blinds so she could peer down into the deserted road. Street lamps cast pools of golden light across the shadowed snow. Everything was still and silent and dreamlike. She stood for a long time as if in a trance. The same numbness she'd experienced as she'd waited to hear David's fate had settled around her, like a curtain shutting out pain. She seemed to be drifting. As long as she made no move to find out the truth, nothing could hurt her.

"Grandma, are we going to the airport to find out about Daddy?" Tracy asked. She stood, disheveled and shivering, in the unlit room. Her voice was full and sharp edged as if she were about to cry.

Ginny turned to face her across the dark abyss of the room. In the face of Tracy's bravery, she felt all the more a coward. She sighed, feeling a heaviness settle on her chest.

"Yes, I'm going," she said, and her voice sounded vague and uncertain to her own ears. She had to pull herself together, for Tracy's sake if for no other reason. "I'll call someone—Nola—to come stay with you."

"You don't need to. I can watch the others." Like her father, Tracy was strong, sure.

"I don't want you to be alone right now," Ginny said. She ached to hold out her arms to the girl, but she couldn't. It was too premature, too much like giving in. To dissolve into tears would be too devastating to them both.

She crossed to a table and switched on a lamp, blinking against the sharp flare of light. Gathering her courage and forcing a ragged smile, she turned to Tracy. The girl stood just as Ginny had expected, with her arms crossed over her chest and one hip jutting out as if nothing in the world could hurt her. She could handle anything. It was a pose, demanding by its very nature that others assume a pose as well. Ginny didn't want to be strong. She wanted to scream her denial of what was happening, but with a calmness she didn't feel, she picked up the phone and dialed. The phone rang several times before it was answered.

"Mmm! 'Lo!"

"Nola?"

"Mmmmf!"

"This is Ginny. I need you to come over here right away to watch my grandchildren."

"Ginny?" The voice at the other end had grown more alert. "Are you all right?"

"There's been a plane crash." Ginny turned away so she couldn't see Tracy's stark expression. "I have to go to the airport. To see if Scott was . . . on that flight. I'm sorry to ask you to come out in the middle of the night, but you're close by and—"

"I'll be right over."

Ginny's hands were shaking as she put down

the receiver. She stood for a moment, biting her lower lip to keep from crying before facing Tracy. When she did turn around, Tracy was gone. Ginny made her way to her bedroom and paused in the darkened doorway. Tracy had gone back to bed. Her back was to the door, her young body rigid and somehow untouchable, as if it might fly into a hundred little pieces if anyone touched her. Ginny crossed to the closet and, without noticing what she pulled out, quickly dressed. She pulled on gym socks and a pair of boots, got her coat and keys and handbag, then stood by the window waiting for Nola's car to drive up. When it did she threw on her coat.

"My God," Nola said when Ginny opened the door for her. She hugged Ginny briefly. "It sounds bad. They had it on the car radio. Was Scott supposed to be on that flight?"

"Marnie said he was. Maybe . . ." Ginny paused and stared at Nola. "God, maybe he didn't take that flight. Maybe . . ." Her cry was a prayer.

"Go find out. Do you want someone to go with you?"

"No, stay with Tracy. She knows. She's awake. I'll call as soon as I hear anything."

Ginny hurried to her car. Her fingers were icy with fear so her movements were clumsy. Every step necessary to insert the key and start the motor seemed magnified, time maddeningly elongated until it lost shape and dimension. She drove automatically, without thinking, and arrived at the airport unsure of how she came to be there. Sirens wailed in the distance, and far off an orange halo of light could be seen against the dark wintry horizon. Police had cordoned off the streets leading to the airport. A burly, uniformed man came over to her car.

"Sorry, ma'am, you'll have to go back. These streets have been blocked off."

"I have to get to the main terminal. My son may have been on that plane."

Immediately, his expression changed from impatience to sympathy. Glancing over his shoulder, he called to someone, one brawny arm gesturing. Ginny waited in mute numbness while he stepped away from the car. The look on the policeman's face had made it all more real, more nightmarish.

"Follow that squad car up ahead, ma'am," the policeman instructed. "They'll escort you to the main terminal."

"Thank you," she said and eased her car into gear. Carefully, she followed the silent police car with its steady blinking light. Carefully, she parked the car where they indicated, and carefully, she followed their instructions as to where to go—as if the care would earn her some reprieve. It didn't work that way. She knew that, but she hoped—because it was part of her upbringing. If you were good and decent and did everything right, bad things didn't happen to you and to the people you loved.

As instructed she went up the stairs to the second floor and along the corridor. A uniformed clerk met her and led the way to a room where other people waited. Ginny walked in and looked around. After her throat-clogging fear, the waiting room was anticlimactic. They might have all been waiting for a plane themselves, waiting in bored indifference for schedules to be kept, delays overcome so they could fly off to their destinations and continue their lives. She sank onto an unpadded seat. Life was suspended. Minutes crept into an hour and more. People grew restless, moving about, lighting cigarettes; their faces pale and stark above the blue haze of smoke. Now and then someone began to weep quietly, then stopped. Occasionally someone stalked over to the airline representative guarding the door and demanded to be told something. Politely but firmly they were turned away. Coffee was brought and passed around. There were no windows, and Ginny guessed the airline people had chosen this room for that reason. Still, she could envision the orange halo on the horizon as she'd last seen it, and she knew the plane was burning, burning away to metal, the steel framework of its body.

One hour dragged into two and then three. More coffee was brought and Ginny caught a glimpse of gray dawn in one of the corridor windows before the door swung closed again. Close behind the coffee came three official-looking men wearing rumpled overcoats and weary expressions. Anxiously people flocked toward them, their voices raised in a demand to know something — anything — about the crash.

"Folks, if you'll just settle down, we'll try to get to each and every one of you," said the beefy-jowled, white-haired man who gripped a computer printout and seemed to be in charge.

"Now, flight 416 from Boston crashed last night on landing. We don't yet know the cause of the crash."

"Fuck the cause," a man shouted angrily. "What about the passengers?"

The official shifted his papers and cleared his throat. "I wish I — I had some good news about the passengers," he said and paused, glancing down at the floor as if trying to steel himself for what he was about to say. When he looked up, he seemed to be reciting the information, giving it swiftly, without dilution.

"There were a hundred and thirty-one passengers and eight crew members. So far we've found no survivors." He paused, pinching his lips together as a wail of grief rose from the listeners. After a few minutes he went on. "I have the passenger list here. If you want to find out whether your family member actually boarded, we can check that out."

Ginny had made no outcry. None of the horror around her seemed to touch her. Numbly she got in line. When her turn came, she gave Scott's name and watched the pencil skim down the line and come to a stop before making a tiny check mark.

"I'm sorry," the man said. "The airline will contact you about claiming the remains." She nodded and walked away.

Claiming the remains. Ridiculous phrases. As if there was anything of life left to claim. On a different level her mind noted the idiosyncrasies of people responding to catastrophic death, but she didn't feel the loss. She left behind the brightly lit corridors, the waiting rooms already filling with people, to walk out into the gray overcast day. The cold damp wind struck her face, yet she felt nothing at all.

"Ginny!"

In slow motion she turned to look at the gray-faced man waiting by her car. "God, Ginny, are you all right? I tried to get in last night to be with you, but they only let family go in."

"Alex, how long have you been waiting

67

here?" she asked vaguely.

"Ever since I heard last night. I waited by your car because I didn't want you to go through this alone. Have they found out anything?"

She couldn't say the words.

He read it in her expression. "God, no," he said, pulling her roughly against his shoulder. She could smell wet tweed and tobacco and aftershave, and guessed he'd come from a date. She smiled at the thought of Alex leaving the exotic warmth of some woman's bed to wait in her cold, empty car; yet she was untouched by it. He sensed her rigid stance and drew back to study her face. "Why did this have to happen to you?" he muttered raggedly and hugged her. His cheek was cold and rough against hers. He felt her shiver. "You're cold. Come on. I'll drive you home."

"I have to go to the funeral home and make arrangements for the . . . remains." Pain ripped at her now. She gasped and her hands curled into fists.

"I'll go, Ginny. I'll go." His breath came out in short, jerky vaporous gasps. "Get in the car. I'm driving you home." Like an invalid, she allowed herself to be led to the car. He even strapped the seatbelt over her trembling, numb body. The door closed, and she was encased, alone and tomblike, in the cold car.

Then Alex was beside her again, sliding into

the driver's seat, switching on the motor, the heater, the wipers. She watched the newly fallen snow whirl away from the windshield wipers and concentrated on not feeling. It was best if she could maintain that detachment. She was aware that Alex was casting anxious glances at her, but she didn't turn her head to look at him. It was easier not to. He was alive, Scott was dead. He was alive, David was not. Why couldn't it be David beside her?

At her building, he helped her from the car and to her front door. Nola was waiting.

"Where are the children?" Ginny asked.

"I sent them home with Marnie. They wanted to go. I hope that was all right."

"Yes." Ginny headed down the hall and into her room, where she closed the door securely behind her.

Alex and Nola watched her go, then looked at each other, silent and tense, waiting for something, not sure of what until they heard its absence.

"Didn't she cry at all?" Nola asked. Alex said nothing. Her answer was in the hurt-filled silence.

"Damn!" he said finally, and turned toward the door. "Stay with her," he ordered, his hand on the knob.

"I will," Nola said.

Ginny heard the door close as he went out. It echoed in her head over and over, the finality of its sharp sound undimmed by repetition. There was no life, no death in the place where she existed, only a vacuum and the final closing of a door.

People moved around her in a shadowy world, coming and going, telling her information that made no sense, requiring of her that she move, bathe, dress, drink black coffee, lie down, get up, answer questions. She did it because it was part of her upbringing to be good and decent and do everything right so nothing bad would happen to those you loved.

Through it all she was aware of three small pale faces, the eyes tragic. These small girls clung together in a world that had once again proven to be unstable. The very ones they must depend upon were taken away. Ginny stood with her arms around the girls' narrow shoulders, aware of photographers probing with their cameras, of pencils poised to record her granddaughters' grief and share it with a shocked city, aware of the curious who'd neither known or cared about her or her family until tragedy had overtaken them, aware of how she and the girls must look in their black clothes with grief-ravaged faces. She felt helpless to protect the children from curiosity, pity, and horror.

Alex and Nola were there, weaving in and out of her life, making funeral arrangements, talking to reporters, shielding her; and when it was done and the poor charred remains of her beautiful son were laid to rest beside his father's grave, Ginny sent the girls home with Marnie and went back to her apartment, to lie on her bed while the numbness left her and to understand that hell was only beginning for her because she must go on living in a world that had once again lost its meaning.

"You have to pull yourself together for your granddaughters," Alex said. He was seated on the small Victorian bedside chair she'd covered with her own petit point. "They need you now."

Slowly, she turned her head and looked at him. The lamplight fell across one side of his handsome face. His skin looked gray beneath his habitual tan.

"Alex!" she said as if seeing him for the first time. She studied his face and long elegant frame and slowly shook her head. "So handsome! What a waste when there are men like David and Scott who—" She broke off, catching sight of his shocked expression. She'd been unforgivably cruel. "I'm sorry," she whispered.

He seized her hand and held it tightly. "I understand," he said gruffly. His grasp was strangely comforting. She fell into a restless, tortured sleep then, and when she woke in the night, Alex was gone. She dragged herself from bed and crossed to the mirror to stare at the woman still dressed in black. David had hated black. She could understand why. She looked like some menacing bird of prey, her features all sharp as if whittled from stone and dark shadows beneath her eyes. Her fingers became talons, ripping at the black cloth, shredding it, tearing it from her body until it lay in strips around her; then she sat on the edge of the bed and wept, her cries hoarse and tearing, leaving her throat raw. She couldn't stop. The door opened and Nola came in.

"Get out," Ginny sobbed, motioning her away. Nola hesitated, then backed out of the room. Ginny rolled up into a ball on the bed, cradling a pillow against her middle, but the momentum of her grief had passed and she wept softly, hopelessly, until her exhausted body surrendered to sleep.

Four

"I'm ready to come back to work."

"Are you sure? It's a bit soon."

"It's best I don't sit here brooding. You said so yourself, Alex."

"How are the girls?"

"As well as can be expected under the circumstances. Marnie's been a godsend." Ginny paused. Alex waited patiently on the other end of the wire. Funny, how she'd come to depend on these calls from him every evening. Funny, how he'd found the time to make them. "I must be interfering with your love life," she said and forced a semblance of a laugh.

There was another long pause from Alex but different from the last, as if he were taking a deep breath and counting to ten. "To hell with my love life," he finally answered. She sensed she'd angered him.

"I've appreciated the time you've taken to call, the support you've given me, Alex, but it's time to get everyone back on track."

"It might be the best thing for you. Nola says it's been rough for you."

Ginny made no answer. A wave of irritation passed over her. She wished everyone would stop relying on Nola's assessment of her emotional state. She opened her mouth to say as much, then bit back the words. Everyone had been kind and giving, Nola more than anyone. If Ginny found solicitous hovering rather smothering, she couldn't hurt Nola by saying so. The sooner she got back to work and showed everyone she was strong and able to cope, the better.

"Tomorrow's Saturday. Could Marnie watch the girls for you while we go out to dinner?"

"I don't think that would be a good idea. They need me to spend as much time with them as I can."

"I want to talk to you."

"I promised to take the girls out to dinner," Ginny hedged.

"Splendid. I'll join you. That is, if you don't mind."

"Alex, I think you ought to know the girls have a special place picked out already."

"Anyplace will do fine. I'll pick you all up at seven. Good night, Ginny."

"Good night, Alex."

Thoughtfully, she replaced the receiver. She should have warned him about the girls' choice, but perhaps she was worrying too much. The girls had grown accustomed to Alex and he to them. He'd even encouraged them to call him Uncle Alex. What on earth could he want to talk to her about enough to willingly volunteer to go out with three troubled little girls and their morose grandmother? She should have warned him they wouldn't make good company. All that wonderful patience of his would soon dissolve, and he'd return to his carefree bachelor existence. It was dear of him to make time for her, though. She hadn't thought he had that kind of sensitivity in him. No. That wasn't true. She'd always been aware of a certain empathy with Alex, had sensed an underlying sensitivity in him. She'd even found it intriguing, until she'd recognized where such thoughts might lead and she'd quickly clamped a lid on her curiosity. She'd been happily married to David, and happily married women didn't find other men fascinating, no matter how attractive and sensitive they were. At least, not in her world.

Shaking her head as if to deny these thoughts, Ginny turned out the light and walked down the hall to the bedroom. She'd been bunking at Scott's house, unable to uproot the girls yet knowing the time would come when she must. She changed into a white nightgown with tiny wildflowers embroidered over the yoke and collar. Standing before the bathroom mirror, a toothbrush in one hand, she stared at her pale reflection. Everything about her seemed grayed down, as if grief had leached away the vibrancy of life. For two weeks, she and the girls had been drifting together, staring with dull eyes at the flickering screen of the television, hearing the canned laughter of people untouched by the sorrow, seeing the bright colors and sound yet unable to take sustenance from it.

She'd read children's books until she knew them by heart, but had continued to read, sensing that her droning voice was one of the constants the girls could hold on to in a shifting, empty world. She'd used puppets to interact with them, had talked to counselors, had read articles and books dealing with children and grief. Burying herself in her granddaughters' needs, she'd softened the cutting edge of her own pain. Finally, having found no magic formula for their particular malady, she was sending the girls back to school. They were objecting.

"The pain will pass," she told them, yet standing here barefooted on the cold tile floor, her toothbrush forgotten in her hand, her eyes dark and wounded looking in her too pale, too thin face, she didn't believe her own words. But she had to move on. To stay at this place in time was unbearable. For all their sakes, she had to strive to reach some place where her pain would be muted a little. She began to brush her teeth.

There were decisions to be made about all their lives, but she seemed incapable of making them just yet. Going back to work was her first big step. Getting back into a routine would help her meet the other decisions. One day at a time, she reminded herself as she rinsed her toothbrush. She was shivery with cold, so it felt good to climb into bed and snuggle against a small warm body.

"God! Nola was right. You look terrible. Aren't you sleeping?"

"Thank you, Alex. And Nola. You always know just what to say."

"I can't lie to you."

"You might try. Sometimes lying has merit."

When he didn't answer she glanced around. His expression was bemused.

"What's wrong?"

"Strange to hear that coming from you. It sounds like something I might say, slightly cynical, slightly off center."

"I feel off center," she answered truthfully. "Girls, let's go."

Once there would have been chatter and noise and clutter. Now the girls greeted Alex quietly and reached for their coats and boots. Ginny knelt to help Steffi with her zipper. Silently Tracy did the same with Candi. Alex watched, his face somber and thoughtful. Ginny felt uncomfortable under his darting bright gaze. He saw too much for her liking. Far better to talk to Alex by phone. On the other hand had she revealed more to him, to his warm friendly voice floating across miles of wire, than she might have under his unyielding gaze? Well, the damage was done, if any. Alex was her friend as well as her employer, and whatever he had to say today, she'd listen and not talk much herself.

"We're ready," she said at last. One by one they filed out the door, Ginny last so she could check the lock. Ahead of her, Alex settled a tweed-clad arm around Tracy's shoulders in a protective gesture. The girl shrugged it off and got into the car. There had been no words, not even a glance, but her rejection was patently clear. Sighing, Ginny ran down the sidewalk and got into Alex's BMW. It was cramped, so she sat with Steffi on her lap and directed Alex through the traffic.

"Turn left here and into the first driveway on the right. You can park anyplace."

He did as she bid and then stopped, staring at the bright neon lights of a popular fast-food hamburger chain. "Here?" he asked. "I kind of thought we could go someplace and have steak or fish. Wouldn't you like to do that, kids?" He looked appealingly at them. Somberly the two younger girls shook their heads.

"I did try to warn you. Besides, red meat isn't good for you anymore, Alex, haven't you heard? You're about to have a five-hundred-calories-plus hamburger."

"Oh, goody," he muttered under his breath, but he opened the car door and they all got out. Standing in line, Ginny imagined how different this must be from his usual Saturday night—dining at an upscale restaurant, followed by drinks at an English-style pub. When their food orders had been shoved at them, Ginny turned toward the tables.

"There's a quiet corner," Alex said, nodding to a table and chairs surrounded by imitation silk plants and fake leaded-glass windows.

"Sorry," she said. "The girls like to sit over here." Steffi and Candi had already taken up residence under a garish plastic tree dripping with hamburgers and french fries. Mushroom tables and stools scaled down to fit preschoolers encircled the tree. Ginny tried not to smile at the expression on Alex's face as he folded his long, lanky frame onto one of the low stools. His knees were nearly level with his chin, and he was evidently irritated.

His expression softened when he looked at Steffi's solemn face, though. Gravely, she passed around the hamburgers and, with exacting care, the french fries and finally the drinks.

"Do you eat here often?" Alex asked Candi. The normally active child had listlessly waited for her food. Slowly she nodded.

"Don't you like it here?" she asked, her gray eyes enormous in her small face.

"It's my first time. It looks interesting though, lots of atmosphere." He glanced up at Ginny then and winked. She saw the desperate attempt at humor, the caring, the sensitivity, and she was touched by it. She held his gaze, caught by the personal warmth of the man. He seemed so bright and alive next to their wanness.

"Oops," Steffi said, her small hand losing its grip on the chocolate shake. The paper cup fell on its side, and the lid came off. Spewing chocolate, the container rolled to the edge of the table and began its downward plunge.

"Watch out," Alex cried, trying to leap out of the way, but his long legs couldn't unfold fast enough. His knees bumped the little table, rocking the other shakes, and his head struck sloping plastic branches as he leaped up. The milkshake hit the floor, splashing some of its sticky contents on his wool trousers.

"I'm sorry, Uncle Alex," Steffi sobbed, her chubby hands pressed to her mouth.

Brows drawn together like thunderclouds, Alex used a napkin to wipe at the gooey chocolate on his trousers. Without a word, Tracy went to get someone to clean up the mess.

"It's all right, darling. You didn't mean to do it," Ginny said soothingly.

Alex ceased muttering under his breath and glanced at Steffi. "No harm done. It's barely noticeable," he said, although his suit, if not ruined, would clearly need an expert cleaning. "The problem is I need another shake. Are you going to buy me another one?"

Steffi buried her face in Ginny's neck and continued sobbing, her arms in a choke hold about her grandmother's neck.

Alex watched them a moment, then stepped forward. "Come on, Steffi. You owe me a shake. You have to pay your debt."

Steffi screamed.

"Leave her alone," Tracy commanded stiffly. "You shouldn't have come with us. We didn't invite you here."

"Tracy!" Ginny remonstrated. "Uncle Alex is my guest. I invited him, and I expect you to show him some courtesy." Chastised, Tracy's face became closed and she turned away, watching stoically as the waitress came with a mop to clean up.

"Come on, Steffi, let's go get Uncle Alex another shake," Ginny said, desperate to ease the tension. The pair made their way back to the counter and waited until the shake was made. With an encouraging smile, Ginny handed it to Steffi.

"Give it to Uncle Alex," she instructed.

Steffi hesitated. Alex waited, making no move to urge her into action before she was ready. Only his eyes shone with humor. Humor! Steffi seemed as reassured by his patience as Ginny had been and with a charming little smile, she passed the carton to him, then once again buried her face in Ginny's neck.

"Thank you," Alex said gravely. No gushing, no baby talk. That seemed the appropriate touch, for as they all settled once more around the mushroom table, Steffi contrived to sit next to Alex and she gazed at him unblinkingly as she nibbled at her food.

"I think you've made another conquest," Ginny observed. They'd finished their hamburgers, and Tracy had come to claim Steffi and Candi and take them to the carousel over in the corner. As they rode, she alternately bossed and cajoled them, watching over them like a mother hen.

"They're nice kids," Alex said. "How are

they handling the loss of their father?"

"You saw. Steffi clings, and Tracy rejects any attempts at comfort from anyone. Even Candi who's normally so active is like a little lost soul."

"It's a bit soon. They'll bounce back."

"I don't know, Alex. It occurred to me the other day that we're a fractured family, and I'm afraid I can't put the pieces back together again."

"Take it one day at a time, one piece at a time," he said.

"That's good advice, but I'm afraid there will always be scars. It's just so damned unfair, first Diane and now Sco—" She swallowed hard and hugged herself, blinking rapidly. Oh lord, don't let me cry here in a restaurant with Alex looking on, she prayed silently. He made no move to touch her or comfort her, giving her the time she needed to bring her emotions back under control, and when she had finally stilled the tremor, she looked up and met his gaze. "Sorry."

"Have you ever heard from Diane?" he asked, as if she hadn't uttered that last lament.

Ginny shook her head. "She's somewhere in California. Scott's lawyer has her address."

"Maybe you should call her, let her know what's happened."

"No!" The denial was explosive. Diners

seated at other tables turned to look at them. Tracy's eyes were enormous, suspicious as she stared at them.

"They don't need to deal with their mother's rejection right now."

"What are you going to do, then?"

"I'll raise the girls myself," Ginny said fiercely. She hadn't realized she'd started trembling. "I'll be their father and their mother."

"That's a pretty big undertaking, alone and at your age."

"What's age got to do with it?" Ginny demanded furiously. "Surely if you're able to bed half the young women in the Metro area, I'm capable of raising my grandchildren."

Alex's face flushed a dark red. "I didn't mean it that way, Ginny," he said slowly. "And I'll overlook your outburst concerning my private life. I meant only to point out that raising three children alone is a big undertaking, even when you're a young mother. To do it now when you've . . ." He paused, seemingly at a loss of words.

"When I what?" she demanded, cut by his words, because they echoed too clearly her own fears.

"There's no need to be so defensive. You haven't had a chance to recover yet from your own loss, and you're going through—" He broke off and flushed.

84

"Through what? Finish what you were about to say," Ginny challenged.

Alex sighed. "Nola told me about your problems," he began in a low voice. He looked embarrassed.

Ginny got to her feet, gathering up coats and mittens. "It seems Nola's told everyone what my problems are. Perhaps she should tell me. In the meantime, I have to get the girls home. It's their bedtime."

"Look, I'm sorry if I've spoken out of turn," Alex said contritely. Ginny almost felt sorry for him. Almost!

"You have," she said, unwilling to back down. She'd been beastly to him, but it was his fault. "You don't know the first thing about women like me, Alex. Stick to the age group you're used to, young women whose hormone problems are at the other end of the spectrum, running amok. You're very good at handling that kind."

His grasp on her arm was unexpected, unyielding; his eyes were dark with anger. She read the outrage on his face and knew he had a right to feel that way. She hadn't been able to stop goading him.

"You're the one who doesn't know the first thing about me. You still believe those wild tales David used to tell you about my young days," he spoke quietly, but his intensity caused others to look at them curiously. "I

85

offer you my friendship and my shoulder, if you need it, but I'm not about to be the butt of bitchy remarks every time someone says something you don't like."

"How dare you speak to me like this?" she gasped, twisting her arm. He released her.

"I dare, as you have, to presume on an old friendship. I think it can withstand a few misunderstandings—and truths."

Ginny looked away then, because his dark eyes had peered too deeply inside her, had made her see her own pettiness. "I'm sorry," she whispered.

"I know," he said in a low voice. "You didn't have to say it." He paused and glanced at the girls. "I'll bring the car around for you." He walked away, leaving her to gather up her grandchildren, but she couldn't resist looking after him, couldn't help noticing how gracefully he carried himself, causing other women in the restaurant to gaze at him. A tall, elegant man out of his element in this place, yet he was trying. She had to give him credit for that.

The drive home was tense. Tracy stared at the back of Alex's head with undisguised impatience. Even Steffi seemed to have lost her former fascination with him. She sagged against Ginny, her bottom lip drooping, her stare unblinking and reproachful.

"Thanks for everything," Ginny said when

the BMW drew into the driveway. She opened the car door and got out.

"I still need to talk to you, Ginny. Can I come in for a while?" he asked.

She leaned down to peer into the car. Dusk had gathered along the street, and a cold wind blew whirls of snow around the car. "It's late, and I'm cold and tired. Can it wait?"

He opened his mouth to protest, then glanced at the girls lined up on the sidewalk, watching them. Reluctantly, he nodded. "Sure, it can wait," he said putting the car in gear. "Good night, Ginny."

He waved to the girls. No one returned his farewell. Ginny felt sorry for him. "We'll talk Monday," she promised and closed the car door.

She watched the little sports car disappear down the street and turned toward the house.

"Let's go, girls. Brr! It's cold out here. If this snow keeps up, we'll skip church in the morning and have hot chocolate for breakfast."

"Yeah!" Candi shouted with some of her old exuberance. She darted up on the porch energetically, but by the time she'd reached the door, her shoulders were sagging.

"How about some popcorn in front of the fireplace?" Ginny forced excitement into her words. "We'll get into our pajamas and tell scary stories."

That generated some enthusiasm. The girls hung up their coats and scurried off to put on their pajamas. Ginny hurried to the kitchen to find popcorn and butter. I have to stop bribing them with food, she thought, hauling out a heavy saucepan, but right now she was desperate. She'd use anything that worked.

Monday dawned cold and clear, the near zero temperature turning the kitchen window panes into a crystallized collage. Candi sat pressing her tongue to the icy pane, her attention riveted on the wet dollops she left behind.

"I wouldn't keep doing that," Ginny said, pouring herself a cup of coffee and settling down at the table. Marnie was busy at the stove making scrambled eggs and toast.

"Your tongue'll stick to the window pane," Tracy said, coming into the kitchen.

"Unh-hunh," Candi said and pressed her tongue to the glass again.

"It will when the surface of your tongue gets cold enough," Tracy said. "Besides it's disgusting."

"Unh-hunh," Candi repeated without moving her tongue. When she tried to pull away, her tongue stuck and she put her hand over her mouth, her eyes wide with surprise and pain.

Tracy shook her head and rolled her eyes. "She acts like a retard."

"Tracy!" Ginny gently remonstrated.

"It's true, Grandma. I'll be glad when next year comes and I go to middle school so no one knows we're sisters." Candi stuck her tongue out at her older sister.

"Here you are now, eat up, so your brain cells can work at their peak," Marnie said, bringing plates of scrambled eggs to the table. She'd worn a black jogging suit ever since the plane crash. Ginny longed to tell her to go back to her original gaudy colors, but she remained silent, refused a plate of eggs, and finished sipping her coffee.

Steffi was still sleeping. She'd awakened during the night, sobbing for her father, and Ginny had spent a long time calming her. Let her sleep, she thought and longed to go back to bed herself. But she'd made a commitment to Alex, and she didn't want any speculation at the office about her ability to cope.

Candi was toying with her eggs, but Tracy proceeded with her meal, showing it the intense concentration she'd been prone to lately. Of the two older girls, Ginny wasn't sure which one she worried about more.

"Finish eating, girls. You don't want to be late on your first day back to school."

"I don't want to go," Candi said, throwing down her fork and jutting out her bottom lip.

"Of course you do." Ginny forced a bright note into her voice. "I'm looking forward to going back to work."

"That's different," Tracy said, putting down her fork and crossing her arms over her chest. Her lips were pressed together in a prim grimace, and her brows were pulled low in a frown. "You won't have kids staring at you like you've grown two heads and expecting you to break down and bawl at any moment."

"Oh, some people at the agency will do that," Ginny said. "It will be very hard for all of us this first day back, but we'll get through it and tomorrow will be better. When people see we're going about our business in a calm everyday manner, they'll do the same. Trust me."

"That's different, Grandma. There are grownups at work."

"That makes no difference. They'll act just like the kids at school."

Arms crossed, Tracy shook her head, certain she was the only one about to undergo some special torment devised only for twelve-year-olds who'd just lost their fathers.

"I'll tell you what," Ginny said touching her arm. "When someone stares at you today, just imagine it's Nola or Alex or someone at my office, and when it happens to me, I'll

90

imagine it's one of the kids from school. Tonight we'll compare notes."

"Grandma," she said in disgust, but at least she picked up her fork, cast a quick glance at the clock, and began eating again. One down, one to go.

"Candi, don't you do gymnastics today after school? What are you going to work on, somersaults? We'll have to remember to pack your gym bag."

"I want to wear my pink tights," Candi said.

Five

Ginny was late getting off to the office. The girls needed her attention. Pink tights couldn't erase the sorrow of a lost dad or still the fears of returning to school, but reminders of life without tragedy helped. Her grandchildren needed reassurance that the world hadn't changed so drastically after all. Then there were her own fears. . . .

She took extra pains with her appearance, knowing, as Tracy had known, that the girls in the office wouldn't stare outright as the kids at school might, but that they'd be watching her nonetheless. When she'd finished her makeup, she stood looking at herself, a woman who'd just turned fifty, but didn't show it, a small-boned woman with regular features except for a too big, slightly crooked mouth. She looked too pale, she decided and picked up her rouge pot and reapplied the coloring.

She chose a Claude Montana lightweight wool in her favorite shade of hunter green. She'd been saving it for a special occasion, but couldn't think of a time when she'd need its uplift more than she did now. The color did look good with her glossy dark hair. Her eyes seemed too large in her pale face; otherwise she looked calm and capable.

She turned away from the mirror, from the image of a woman alone and vulnerable and scared. This was the image she'd present to the people in the office whether she wanted to or not. She pulled brittleness around her like a cloak, forced a bright smile that didn't quite ring true, assumed an aloofness that wouldn't let anyone reach her. Her haunted eyes said, Don't try. It was a soft shell, easily penetrable, she knew, but these were the only defenses she could muster.

As she pulled on a black silk and wool coat she wondered briefly why she felt the need for defenses. She'd worked with Alex and some of the office staff for years. Over the past nine months, Nola had become a friend. She'd been the first one Ginny had turned to on that dreadful night Marnie called. Why then did she feel this need to hide her feelings? Because they were still too raw, too near the surface. She answered her own question as she got into the Lincoln and turned it toward the Southfield Freeway. And because she was scared, but wasn't sure what she was afraid of. She hated this stomach-gripping terror that claimed her.

She drove automatically, giving little thought to the traffic around her. She'd always been a good driver, so she relaxed, letting old routines and skills resurface. She felt as if she'd been on a long journey and was just now returning to find everything the same yet different.

Bright sunlight was reflected from glass walls and the metallic edgings of the roofs of high rises as she left the freeway and made her way along I-96 to the Farmington Hills suburb where Russell and Taylor had relocated their offices years before. The brick and glass building, the third floor of which was occupied by Alex's ad agency, rose to a mere six stories. Though overshadowed by neighboring buildings, its clean lines and unique design made it stand out. Ginny pulled her car into the basement parking area, left her keys with the attendant, then took an elevator to the third floor. In that heartbeat of a moment when the car had slid to a stop and the doors had not yet opened, she breathed deeply and steeled herself. When the doors did open, she was smiling brightly — idiotically since no one else was in the car with her.

"Good morning, Ms. Logan. Welcome back," Francine Whittaker called, her glance bright and curious.

"Thank you, Fran. It's good to be back," Ginny acknowledged without halting her stride. She forced one foot in front of the other, not allowing her gaze to dip or her thin smile to waver. Though she nodded in acknowledgment of greetings, she had little idea to whom. At last she reached her office door, the metal handle smooth and firm beneath her cold fingers as she turned it and stepped inside.

Nola Sherman sat in Ginny's chair, her work spread out on Ginny's desk, Ginny's phone pressed to her ear. She glanced around as Ginny closed the door firmly and faced her. Nola didn't look surprised or abashed at having been caught using Ginny's office. Instead she held up one finger to indicate she'd be with her in a moment and spoke into the phone.

"Of course, Burr, I quite agree. I'll see what we can come up with. We've had some problems in the office. One of our staff has been out on leave for several weeks for personal reasons. It left us shorthanded. I'll work on this and get back to you within an hour." She paused, listening, her dark gaze darting to Ginny and away again.

Ginny slid out of her coat and, crossing the room in long angry strides, hung it on the oak and brass coat tree. Deliberately, she took her time, striving for a calm even approach. Behind her, Nola's laughter came, low and rich, denoting a confidence born of easy contact with Burr Osgood. I shouldn't be surprised, Ginny thought. She knew Nola's way with people. Nola could get past the formalities, the pecking order, and forge an easy working relationship with anyone, even the formidable Burgess Osgood.

Nola hung up the phone, and Ginny swung around to face her, once again striving for an offhanded smile. Her face felt as if it might crack.

"Well, Ginny, you're back," Nola said brightly. She'd remained seated behind the desk, so Ginny was forced to stand on the other side like an awkward applicant about to be interviewed for a much-sought-after position. She couldn't help remembering when Nola had stood in her place, applying for a job as her assistant.

"Didn't Alex tell you I was returning today?" Ginny asked, unable to hide her annoyance.

Nola's gaze was too bright, as if she enjoyed her advantage. "Yes, he did. I just didn't believe you'd be ready to come back yet."

"Believe it," Ginny said, and to temper the situation, she leaned forward to pick up several pages. "What's all this? Looks like my work has piled up."

"No," Nola said. Getting to her feet quickly, she fairly snatched the papers from Ginny's hands and shuffled them into the others on the desk. "Actually, it was something I was working on. I just came in here because it was quieter and the lighting was better."

"I see," Ginny said smoothly. Now that Nola had vacated her chair, she moved around the desk and regained possession. Nola gave ground. Assuming a brisk air, Ginny opened drawers, taking out pens and pad. "Was that Burgess Osgood on the phone?" she asked, offhandedly studying her calendar. The pages were blank, but she wrote a couple of reminders to herself, meaningless reminders, but they set the stage. They said clearly she was back. Nola remained silent, but now she glanced up. "Is there a problem with the Osgood account?" Ginny persisted.

"He just had a suggestion to offer about his account. I'll take care of it."

"Now that I'm back, I'll take care of it,"

Ginny said, holding out her hand for the files. Nola hesitated. "Give me the Osgood files," Ginny said in a voice that brooked no argument.

Shrugging gracefully, Nola handed them over. "What problems have come up with the account?" Ginny asked, glancing through the files. Nola's chin came up. Her gaze darted away from Ginny's and back again. For a moment Ginny thought she meant not to answer; then she sighed as if surrendering against her better judgment.

"He wants the first television spot to take place in a more exotic location than the family dining room, perhaps at a fancy-dress ball with classical music in the background."

"Surely, you didn't go along with him on that? The strength of our appeal will be to the solid middle-class market. Besides, we're selling catsup, not imported wine."

"He wants the campaign to be a little classier."

"We agreed on a certain campaign at the beginning. What makes him think he can just change in the middle?"

"Maybe you'd better talk to him about it," Nola said and turned to the door. With it open, she paused and glanced back at Ginny. "Are you sure you're ready to come back to work?" she asked. "Perhaps you should have talked to your doctor first."

Anger spiraled through Ginny as she raised her head and glared at her assistant. "I am perfectly well, thank you," she snapped. "And while we're at it, Nola, I want you to stop discussing my private life with everyone in the office."

"I'm sorry," Nola said, her voice cracking. "I was only trying to make things easier for you. I know you've been under a strain." She closed the door behind her. Through the glass, Ginny saw her pause by a secretary's desk, her shoulders hunched, her head bowed as if she might be crying. Was I too harsh with her? Ginny wondered, feeling guilty. Nola had been a godsend those first few days after Scott's death, but her presence had come to seem overbearing, even bullying at times. Other women had come to gather around Nola; angry glances were cast at Ginny's office. Ginny tried to ignore what was going on in the outer office, but her feelings were too raw, too uncertain. She hadn't expected her return to be this hard. Pulling a tissue from a box in her desk drawer, she dabbed at her damp upper lip.

Settling in at her desk, she went over the Osgood files and placed a call to him.

"Hello, Mr. Osgood," she said, making her tone professional, yet friendly. "This is Ginny

Logan. I have your—"

"Who?"

"Ginny Logan from the Russell and Taylor Advertising Agency. I've been looking over your account."

"I thought Miss Sherman was in charge of my account."

"Only while I was away, Mr. Osgood. Now that I'm back, I'll be handling it."

"You were out on a personal leave?" he demanded.

"Yes, I . . . my . . ." she stammered, unable to discuss her son's death with so impersonal a man.

"I don't know what's going on there, Miss Logan," Osgood said brusquely, "but the last time I talked to Alex, he said Miss Sherman had been put in charge of my account and that's the way I like it. If there are to be any changes, I want to hear about them from Alex himself and not some member of his staff. Do your homework, Miss Logan, before you call me again." The line went dead. Ginny sat as if stunned, then slowly replaced the receiver. She went over the conversation with Osgood, assessing everything he'd said. Slowly she got to her feet. Her hands were cold, her knees trembling. Punching the button on her intercom, she waited until the secretary answered.

"Is Mr. Russell in his office?"

"He just came in, but I believe he's on his way to your office." There was a note of unrestrained glee in the voice that came across the intercom.

"Thank you," Ginny said and snapped off the intercom. Striding across her office, she threw open the door and waited for Alex. He looked every inch the head of a successful business in his pinstriped suit. His dark hair was carefully combed into place, and his thin, handsome face and dark eyes distracted her for a moment as they always did, but she was too angry to be put off for long.

"Hello, Alex," she said stiffly. "Francine said you were on your way down. You have something to tell me?"

"Several things." Alex ignored the chair she offered, but Ginny perched on the edge of her desk, striving for an air of calm inquisitiveness when in fact she felt like railing at him. How dare he have left her in this position with Osgood?

"Perhaps we'd better start with the Osgood account," she said with deceptive mildness. Alex's head jerked up. His dark eyes studied her face.

"So you've heard. I've given the account to Nola."

"Oh, yes, I've heard." She got to her feet and paced around the room. "Burgess Osgood himself informed me about it this morning when I called."

"Damn! I meant to get here ahead of you and explain. I tried to tell you the other night, but . . . we got so distracted."

"You should have told me, no matter what the circumstances," Ginny snapped. "Didn't you think it was important for me to know? I've made a fool out of myself in front of Osgood, and that can't be good for the agency."

"I'm sorry it happened this way," Alex said. "I didn't want to break it to you on the phone. Didn't Nola tell you anything when you asked for the files?"

"Nola is interested only in telling me I should see a doctor," Ginny snapped.

"Is that why you two had a row first thing this morning?"

Ginny swung around to face him. "What makes you think we did?"

"Nola came to my office all upset and crying. She said you were enraged because she was handling the Osgood account. She even offered to withdraw from the account since it bothered you so. She thinks you feel threatened by her having it."

"I don't feel threatened by your giving the account to her, only by your not telling me."

"Then tell her that and try to mend this rift between you."

"There's no rift. I only asked her not to discuss me with the rest of the office, Alex. Is demanding a little discretion so unreasonable?"

"Depends on the way you ask. Nola said you're feeling a little paranoid."

Ginny's temper flared. "Maybe you should stop listening to what Nola says about my feelings and remember what *you* know about me."

"I am remembering," he said quietly, and she knew he was referring to her outburst at the restaurant the night before.

"Look, we've been friends for a long time. I care about you. You've helped make this agency. I should have made you a partner years ago, but somehow the timing just never seemed right. I will see to it, though. You needn't ever feel anyone can come in here and push you out."

"For heaven's sake, I don't, Alex. You don't have to placate me by giving me part of your business. I don't even want it. I'm just asking you to keep me apprised of things. I don't want to find out about them through someone else."

"You're right about that and I'm sorry. As for the rest of it, Ginny, I believe I'm a good enough friend to say certain things to you, personal things. Nola's worried about you and

I think she's right. She said she's urged you to go to a doctor for hormones."

"My son was just killed in a plane crash, Alex. Hormones aren't going to help that."

"But they might help with the way you cope with it."

"I'm grieving over the death of someone I—" She broke off, her voice cracking.

Alex stepped forward to put a hand on her shoulder. She could smell his aftershave lotion. It was like Alex, expensive and exotic. It made her feel uncomfortable. "I know this is a tough period for you," he said, "but don't be afraid to ask for help. Take the time you need to recover. You don't have to come to work so soon."

"You sound as if you're pushing me out of here," Ginny said.

Alex sighed. "You sound paranoid."

Anger swept through Ginny. "Get out of here, Alex," she snapped. "I have work to do. That is, if you haven't given away all my other accounts."

She sensed his tense stance as he regarded her a moment longer. Silently he turned to the door.

The week was tough, tougher than she'd expected it to be, but the alternative—staying home and wandering through Scott's strangely quiet house or the empty condo she'd once shared with David—was less attractive. She had to make decisions, she knew that. To go on supporting two residences in Detroit was madness. She had to make a choice, give up the condo and all the memories it held of David or take the girls from the only home they'd ever known. Then there was the lake house. She'd nearly forgotten that.

Round and round she went, her thinking muddled by grief and indecision, her hours equally muddled by the inconvenience of having half her clothes at her own place and the other half in Canton. She felt trapped between two worlds, unable to function efficiently in either one.

As the week progressed, she grew more tense, uncertain as to whether she'd caused the tension in her co-workers or whether she'd been affected by their wary attitudes. For they were wary, there was no denying that. Several times she'd rounded a corner or opened a door to find a knot of women talking, only to have them fall silent when they sensed her presence. Nola seemed to avoid her as much as possible, and Alex hovered around her, whether out of concern for her well-being or her job performance she wasn't certain. Her nerves grew frayed, and she was relieved to see

Friday approach.

The girls had been subdued all week. Working back into the routine of normal life was as hard for them as it was for Ginny. Then, as if in atonement for their ordeal of grief, the winter allowed them a reprieve, a time of warmth and sunshine in the midst of barrenness. January temperatures soared to the fifties and eaves dripped with incandescent runnels of melted snow and ice.

The children in the neighborhood put on their boots and stomped through wet snowdrifts, sending plumes of slush flying from beneath their feet.

"Maybe soon we can go to the lake and swim," Candi said as she wistfully stared out the window.

"This is January, you geek," Tracy said scathingly. "We can't swim until June."

"We could if it stayed warm," Candi cried, her gray eyes sad in her small face.

"It's going to snow and freeze again, Candi," Tracy explained with exaggerated impatience. "You know that."

"I want to go swimming," Steffi said, pounding her spoon handle against the table.

"Now see what you've done," Tracy shrieked, but Candi gazed back at her, apparently unmoved by guilt. She seemed too withdrawn.

Ginny reached across the table, rescued the spoon from Steffi's chubby fist, sent a warning glance to Tracy, and smiled at Candi. "You know we couldn't go swimming this weekend, but we could drive up to the lake and stay overnight."

"Could we?" Candi's gaze seemed to travel a long way to get to them, and her plain little face lit with a smile.

"I don't see why not. The weatherman said the whole weekend's going to be like this."

"Will we stay overnight?" Tracy asked, and Ginny noticed even she'd dropped the impatient, put-upon air she'd adopted of late.

"We'll stay overnight and have a fire in the fireplace."

"And roast marshmallows."

"And make s'mores!"

"And go for long hikes."

"Maybe no hiking," Ginny cautioned.

"And see if there are any ducks left on the lake."

"It'll be frozen, you ge—" Tracy glanced at her grandmother. "The ducks won't be there anymore."

"Maybe they will," said Candi, ever the optimist.

"Maybe they will," echoed Ginny, suddenly wanting to see ducks floating in the cold clear water, to hear the rush of their wings as they lifted into the air. It was the last thing they'd seen together in the fall when they'd gone down to close up the house for the winter. Scott had been with them.

Although they had Dick Chalmers bring in the boat and store it for them, Scott liked to go down one last time and check everything over. Just before they'd gotten into the car for the trip home, a flock of migratory geese had settled on the smooth surface of the lake. The girls had been awed. Even Scott's eyes had lit with wonder, and he'd hidden his face against Steffi's chubby body until she'd protested and insisted on being put down. His eyes had been red with unshed tears, and Ginny had known he was thinking of his father. Her heart had welled with love for him. They'd stood on the patio watching dog and children cavort on the green sweep of lawn, clucking, cooing geese bobbing on the water, and she'd felt a bitter-sweet joy. David wasn't there, but he'd never leave their thoughts.

"Grandma-a-a." Candi shook her arm impatiently. "I want to take my swimsuit, just in case."

"No, Tracy's right," Ginny said. "The lake will be iced over, and even if it's not, the water will be icy cold. You can't swim now."

Tracy stuck out her tongue at her sister. After breakfast they stacked their dishes in the dishwasher and packed overnight bags. Ginny raided the pantry for food.

Traffic on I-94 was light, so they arrived at the lake house in a little over two hours. She hadn't thought to call ahead and have Dick Chalmers plow out the long narrow drive leading down to it.

"Sorry, kids, we have to hoof it," she said, parking the car well off the main road and getting out. Amidst some grumbling, the girls picked up sleeping bags and duffels, and set off toward the low-slung two-storied cottage. Ginny brought up the rear, carrying her own soft-sided overnight bag and a picnic basket containing the groceries. The excited voices of the two older girls floated back to her. They saw this as an adventure. Even Steffi trudged along stoically, trying her best to keep up with her sisters.

Ginny had given no thought to the snow covering the patio and blocking the door. They had to force the storm door open, sweeping an arc in the snow; then they tumbled into the wide entrance hall with its plate-laden pine shelves and wooden pegs. On these pegs they draped jackets and long woolen scarves. And just like that, everything felt good again.

Rubbing their arms against the chill, they wandered through the rooms. Everything was just as they'd left it, the parlor with its stone fireplace, the mantel laden with David's collection of German beer steins, the walls covered with more plates, these from Holland and England bearing memories of past travels. The cushions on the couch and loveseat sagged comfortably, and glass shaded lamps from a bygone era, stacks of magazines, shelves stuffed with books, a stereo with some classical records beneath, and a VCR with children's tapes nearby made the place look lived in. The cleaning woman had been in months before, clearing away every glass, every forgotten saucer, yet discreetly leaving books neatly closed on the huge oak- and glass-topped coffee table and not disturbing well-loved rag dolls tucked into sofa corners. A pair of small, scuffed tennis shoes sat on the bottom step of the oak staircase. The cottage invited them, soothed them, enclosed them in its welcoming embrace.

Ginny turned up the furnace and knelt to set a match to the logs and kindling already laid in the fireplace. Tracy flopped on the couch and picked up a book, turning to the middle and burrowing in for a thorough read as if she'd just left off the day before. The two younger girls settled on the floor in front of the fireplace, their faces smooth and content in the light from the flames. Ginny went back to the kitchen and stored her cache of groceries in the roomy oaken cupboards with the glass doors. It felt good to be back, homey and safe and comfortable. The girls felt it too.

After a lunch of peanut butter sandwiches and hot soup, the girls put on their boots and coats and went out to look at the lake.

"Stay off the ice. It isn't safe," Ginny warned. Then she made her way to the attic, where she puttered among discarded skates and water skis, half-done needle projects and a stuffed deer head she'd never allowed David to hang above the fireplace as he'd wished. She smiled, remembering the row they'd had over it. She couldn't stand to see anything killed, and to mount an animal's head to hang for ornamentation seemed barbaric to her. David and Scott had ganged up on her on that one, but they'd made allowances for her sensibilities.

At last she found what she'd been looking for, a half-forgotten box of pictures she'd meant to paste into an album and never had. She shuffled among the bright squares of color reflecting on the laughter and the heart in her life before everything had gone so wrong. There were pictures of David and Scott at Scott's graduation, and some of Diane when Scott had first brought her to visit them. Her long elegant body was youthfully slim, her hair straight and fine around her pale face. There was one of her pregnant with Tracy, her slim body distorted by the unborn child, her lovely hair skinned tightly back from her thin tired face, her cheekbones standing out painfully, her eyes sunken and dark rimmed.

She'd had a difficult pregnancy with each girl. Surely that had been the reason for the haunted shadows in her eyes. She couldn't have been that unhappy so early in her marriage. Ginny sat studying the pictures. Had she failed to notice her daughter-in-law's distress? Had it been so apparent back then or was it only hindsight?

Ginny shoved the pictures deep into the box and carried it downstairs. The girls were still outside. She could see them through the window. They stood talking to a tall, thin man who was a stranger to Ginny. Alarm sounded through her, and she reached for her coat. Strangers didn't show up at Big Cedar in the winter unless they were staying in one of the cottages without the owner's consent. Settling the coat around her shoulders, she stepped outside. The temperature was dropping again. The snow crunched beneath her shoe-boots. The girls were laughing and didn't hear her approach, but the bearded stranger glanced up. He was sandy-haired, closer to Scott's age than her own although his face seemed older, and his eyes held a sadness and a wisdom beyond his years. An Irish setter frolicked in the snow.

"Grandma, come meet Jason," Candi cried running to take Ginny's hand and pull her forward. "He tells funny stories."

She hadn't needed to hear that. Even Tracy's red-cheeked face was bright with laughter.

"Hello, ma'am," the stranger said, straightening momentarily. He was even taller than she'd at first supposed. All too quickly his lanky figure sagged back into its comfortable slouch.

"Who are you?" Ginny demanded abruptly. She was aware that Tracy's smile faded and Candi stared up at her, startled by her tone of voice, but she paid them no heed. She was all too aware they were here alone, surrounded only by empty cottages. She couldn't afford to be careless.

The man looked startled, then relaxed once more. "I don't blame you for asking," he said. "You probably didn't expect to find anyone out here. Neither did I. That's why Redder and I came over to investigate."

"Redder?"

"That's his dog, Grandma," Candi cried, running to throw her arms around the Irish setter who greeted such a display of affection with a moist lick across one cold red cheek.

"I'm Jason McCann. I'm staying at the De-Fauw cottage."

"In the dead of winter?" Ginny knew she was being rude, but she felt suspicious. She hated the thought of packing up and leaving, but she couldn't risk the girls' safety if there was the slightest thing out of the ordinary with this sad-eyed young man. Too many years of living in the city had made her wary.

His smile was bleak, his frank gaze wavered, and he glanced off over the frozen lake. "They're in Europe for a year and I needed a quiet place to stay. I'm a writer."

"I see. Have you been published?"

He grinned, and she had a hunch he was amused by her cautious air, yet he continued to answer her questions courteously. "A couple of textbooks. I'm a clinical psychologist, but I've taken some time off to write something different."

"What are you working on now?" Ginny asked. Nothing like playing twenty questions, but she waited for the answer.

"I'm not sure yet. A mystery, I suppose."

He didn't sound convincing. Ginny drew herself up. "Come, girls, it's time to go inside."

"It's still daylight!" Candi protested, but

114

Ginny hustled them all toward the door. When she saw they were headed in the right direction, she turned back to Jason McCann.

"If you'll excuse us now . . ."

"Certainly," he said and, whistling for the Irish setter, turned back toward the DeFauw cottage. His long legs ate up the distance quickly, but halfway there he stopped and turned back to face her. "If you want to check out my story, I made myself known to the local police chief when I came out here. You can use my phone if you don't have one."

"Our phone is connected," said Ginny.

"No, it's not, Grandma, remem—" Tracy's mittened hand cut off Candi's words. "Don't!" Candi yelled, pushing at her sister.

"Come on, blabbermouth," said Tracy, and with a final shrug, she went inside.

"I'm sorry I startled you," Jason McCann said, "but I promise you I'm harmless. The girls told me about their father. I'm sorry to hear it. It must be tough on them."

"Yes." She didn't elaborate.

"If there's anything I can do to help . . . I'm used to dealing with these kinds of family tragedies."

"Thank you again," Ginny said stiffly. "But you can't possibly understand."

"I think I can. I lost my wife and baby son three months ago in an auto accident." He didn't wait for a further response. His long legs moved in steady strides across the snow-covered lawn until he reached the DeFauw porch, then he turned and gave her a final wave before disappearing inside.

Ginny went indoors and began supper for the girls. We haven't a corner on the grief market, she thought, remembering the naked pain on the man's face when he'd spoken of his wife and baby son.

Six

The time went by much too quickly. They ate a casserole in the big kitchen, then carried crackers and chocolate bars to the living room where they roasted marshmallows over the fire and reminisced about summers past. The day in the cold clear air had them all nodding early, so they banked the fire and climbed the stairs to their beds. There was a sense of peace here, of a day well spent, and the assurance of another day on the horizon. The little ones went to sleep halfway through their bedtime story. Then Tracy sprawled across Ginny's bed, and they talked.

"He's nice," she said, staring at the ceiling dreamily.

"Who, ducky?" Ginny asked, glancing up from her book.

"Jason McCann. I like the way he laughs, kind of like he's missed doing it lately."

"I suppose he has," Ginny said, thinking of the sad-eyed man when he'd spoken of his wife. Somehow, she kept remembering those thin shoulders of his, slumped and defenseless. They made her feel sorry for him, and she didn't like that. If she began to feel sorry for someone else, if feeling came back to her, God help her. She'd begin to feel the pain again. She shut it away.

"I don't want you girls to speak to Mr. McCann the rest of the time we're here," she said, turning a page. She'd been absorbed in the light mystery, but now it held little appeal for her.

"Why can't we talk to him?" Tracy demanded. "He's really very nice, Grandma."

"We don't really know anything about him, do we?"

Silently, Tracy regarded the ceiling. "He spoke to us, and he doesn't know anything about us."

"It's not the same."

Tracy sighed. "I suppose you're right. Nothing is ever the way it seems, is it?"

"What do you mean, honey?" Ginny stopped pretending to be interested in the book and put it aside.

"I suppose to people who don't know us well, we look just like ordinary people."

"We are ordinary people, Tracy. Nothing has changed that. We're just going through an extraordinary time right now. When we get through it, everything will seem normal again."

"Do you think so?"

"I know so," Ginny replied softly. "Now you'd better get to bed. You're going to want to get up early tomorrow."

Obediently, Tracy rose and started toward the door. Then she paused. "I think Mr. Mc-Cann is going through an extraordinary time too," she said softly.

"Why do you think that, Tracy?"

"I don't know. His eyes, maybe. Somehow we all sort of look alike."

"Don't worry about him, darling. He can take care of himself, no matter what's happened to him. He impressed me as a strong person."

"Do you think I'm strong?" Solemn blue eyes studied her, waiting for an answer.

"I think you are."

She looked pleased. "Like you. Good night, Grandma."

"Good night, darling." Ginny watched her granddaughter leave the room, then began to think over their conversation. They were just ordinary people having to bear an inordinate amount of sorrow, but they were strong, Tracy was and so was she, and the two of them would help Candi and Steffi to be strong too. They would all survive this. The healing was already beginning. But as she drifted off to sleep, the old doubts came back and Ginny wondered if she really was as strong as she needed to be.

When she woke in the morning, the sun was pouring through the window and she was reassured. The sound of a motor drew her out of bed. Fastening a thick velour robe over her flannel nightgown, Ginny hurried downstairs. Dick Chalmers' battered pickup truck, a snow plow attached to the front, was barreling down the drive, spewing sheets of snow from both sides of the blade.

"We're plowed out, girls," she called gleefully and ran for her purse while Chalmers made another pass down the long drive. By the time he arrived at the front door, she had a pot of coffee brewed and a crisp twenty-dollar bill ready for him.

"How did you know?" she exclaimed when he came into the kitchen amid a rush of cold air and stamped snow from his boots.

"Mr. McCann called me last night."

"Oh?" Ginny hesitated, wanting to question him about her neighbor yet wishing to respect the man's privacy. Curiosity won out. She pushed a steaming mug of coffee across the counter and beamed at him.

"How nice of Mr. McCann to think of it," she began. "Have you known him long?"

"Nope," Dick said, gulping down a large draught of coffee.

Ginny tried again. "When exactly did he move in here?"

"Last fall."

"Did the DeFauws tell you anything about him?"

"Nope. Just said he'd be staying there for the year they were in Europe."

"How's Mrs. Chalmers?" Ginny asked, acknowledging defeat. She'd have to be content with the thought that if the DeFauws trusted Jason McCann with their home, he must be all right.

The morning was spun sugar, the air crisp and biting. Ginny dug an old sled out of the garage and the girls piled on and streaked down the boat ramp and out onto the frozen

121

lake. Their squeals filled the pristine stillness. Ginny stood watching them, her heart surging with the sharp remembrance of what happiness could be like.

"Good morning," a male voice called, and Ginny turned, her lips still curved in a smile, her eyes filled with hope, her face smooth with contentment. Jason McCann's wide smile wavered as he looked at her.

"I hope you didn't mind my calling Dick Chalmers for you," he said, coming to a stop before her.

"You were kind to think of it," she answered, glad to have this opportunity to appear friendlier. He was dressed in a suede bomber jacket and faded jeans, with leather boots laced high up his ankles. The cold air had colored his cheeks and brightened his blue eyes. His head was bare and his longish brown hair lay across his brow.

"Sure turned cold last night." He drove one gloved fist into the palm of his other hand. He seemed uncomfortable with the silence between them, as if her unfriendliness the day before had left him uncertain of his reception.

"The girls don't seem to mind it," she answered, nodding toward the muffled figures who were trudging up the hill. The children saw Jason McCann standing with Ginny and waved enthusiastically.

"They're nice kids," he said, waving back. "How are they handling things?"

"Is that a clinical question, Mr. McCann?" Ginny asked, not wanting to discuss their problems with a stranger, and he was still a stranger. He had the grace to look sheepish.

"Sorry. I guess old habits die hard."

"What about you?" Ginny asked. "How are you handling things?"

His face turned bleak; his eyes gazed out over the frozen landscape. "I'm taking it one day at a time," he answered.

Ginny glanced away, not wanting to see his pain. She had enough of her own. "Someone advised me to do the same thing," she said lightly.

"It's good advice. No charge for service." His smile was nice, slow in coming, but real and warm once it got there.

"Aren't you lonely out here all by yourself?" Ginny asked, changing the subject. "Most of these cottages are deserted in the winter."

"That's the way I like it," he said, taking off his gloves and hooking long fingers into the hip pockets of his jeans. There were things about him that disturbed Ginny because they were so obviously masculine. In the clear sharp light she could see that he was older than she'd at first supposed—late thirties probably.

"You aren't becoming a hermit, are you?" she asked, looking down on the girls. They'd paused halfway up the hill to have a snowball fight. She was aware of Jason's sharp turn of the head and his measuring glance. She turned to face him. "One good turn deserves another," she said, nodding toward the plowed driveway. "You shouldn't stay out here alone. Don't you have family you can turn to?"

He shook his head once. "A drunk in a pickup truck ran a stoplight and took my family," he said, and his voice cracked. His eyes had that liquid, wounded look she recognized too well.

"I'm truly sorry. Nothing can stop the pain."

"No." He rubbed one large bony hand across his face as if to erase all traces of his brief weakness. "Do you need some help hauling that sled up?" he called down to the girls.

"Yes," Tracy called back.

"Excuse me, will you?" Jason McCann said, pulling on his gloves. He plunged down the snowy embankment, his longs jean-clad legs pumping vigorously. Ginny watched them for a while, then returned to the kitchen. She felt comfortable leaving the girls with him now. She prepared a pot of spaghetti and salad for lunch. They'd have to return to Detroit in the afternoon. She felt a reluctance at the thought. The broad patches of untouched whiteness were so serene. In Detroit the curbs would be banked with mounds of dirty snow. Even in the suburbs cars and people left their marks on the landscape, but here she seemed a part of nature itself. The thought was comforting, as if everything that had happened was part of an overall plan and all would come right in the end.

"I'm getting fanciful," she thought, bemused. Yet for a moment there she had known comfort, a sense of acceptance of the unacceptable. When all was ready she put on her coat and went outside to call the girls.

"You're welcome to join us, Mr. McCann," she offered. He was out of breath and laughing after his turn sledding down the hill. His hair had blown over his brow in silky strands. It's nearly as fine as a girl's, she thought and his face looks better, less strained.

"I wouldn't want to intrude, ma'am," he said. His chest rose and fell evenly with his fast breathing, and his cheeks were ruddy.

The girls gathered around him, pulling on his jacket, their faces bright.

"Please, Jason."

"Eat with us."

"Please!"

"Yes, please do. I've made extra," Ginny said.

He shrugged in acceptance, his smile taking them all in. I wonder what he was like before his wife died, Ginny thought. He was a man given to ready laughter. She could see that. The girls guided him to the door, helped him inside. Chattering sixty miles a minute they urged him to take off his jacket and scarf, showed him where the bathroom was for washing up. While Ginny dished up the servings, Tracy hurried to set the round oak table. When they were all seated around it, silence fell over them. They gazed at each other with bright-eyed interest, then Candi put her hands over her mouth and started giggling. That set them all off and the ice was broken. While they wolfed down seconds of spaghetti and hot bread, they all took turns talking.

Jason told them tales of his childhood on a Wisconsin farm, and each one of the girls contributed a story about her experiences at school. Ginny was amazed. In that short span

126

of time, she found out more about how their week had gone than she had with all her carefully couched questions. She even found herself laughing, something she hadn't thought possible in the past few weeks.

"That was good, ma'am," Jason said. "I get tired of my own cooking."

"I'm glad you enjoyed it, Mr. McCann."

"Oh, please, call me Jason."

"Only if you'll stop calling me ma'am. I keep looking around expecting to see one of my old schoolteachers."

Jason laughed, a generous sound, throwing his head back so his teeth showed. They were strong and white and the slightest bit crooked in front. Ginny rose and gathered up the dishes.

"Can I help you with washing up?" Jason asked, rising.

"That's the girls' job. Besides, we have to pack to go back to Detroit." The words were a dismissal, and he recognized it. He pulled on his boots and reached for his coat.

"Look, next time you're planning on coming down, call me and I'll see the drive is plowed out for you."

"We probably won't come again before summer," Ginny said. "This was sort of a spur-of-the-moment thing."

"Still, I'll give you my number, just in case the impulse strikes again." He jotted it on a note pad and handed the top sheet to her.

"Thank you. You're very thoughtful."

"I guess I'm lonelier than I thought. It was good to have someone around for a while. Thanks again for the meal, ma—"

"Ginny."

"Ginny." He smiled, fastened his jacket, and pulled on his gloves.

"You should have a hat," she said. "You lose heat from the top of your head."

He flashed her a smile, and she flushed and drew back.

"Sorry. I was always nagging Scott about such things."

His face had gone somber again. He made no comment. Waving at the girls who were busy at the sink, he opened the door and was gone in a quick swirl of cold air. The sadness came back, strumming at her nerves, and for one wild moment, she wanted to call him back. "He's not Scott," she whispered fiercely.

Returning to Detroit after the weekend was harder than she'd expected. The girls were quiet on the ride back, and she knew they were remembering the lake and the fun they'd had there. By the time she pulled into the driveway in Canton, their faces bore the same tragic expressions they'd displayed since the crash. Ginny felt the same way.

Monday morning she went straight to the office and settled in with the files that had been neglected while she was gone. Nola was avoiding her, and Ginny was almost glad, though the tension at the agency was becoming unbearable. In the afternoon when she saw Nola standing at the coffee machine, she decided to face the problem head-on in front of the staff, so the others could see she held no animosity. Picking up her mug, she strolled to the coffee machine.

"How are you doing, Nola?" she asked, filling her mug.

Nola glanced up and flushed, uncomfortable with Ginny's friendly manner. She seemed unable to hold Ginny's gaze for long, although she smiled broadly. "I'm fine," she answered. "Busy, but I like it that way."

"Are things going well on the Ozzie account?"

"Yes, of course." Nola's voice rose sharply. A couple of the secretaries had been pretending to work while they eavesdropped. Now they raised their heads and listened outright. "You have no right to question me on that account. Alex gave it to me. I'm sorry if you're having a problem with that, but you should take it up with Alex, not with me."

"But I'm not having a problem with it," Ginny tried to explain. "I'm just trying to be friendly."

Nola ignored her words. Her voice had risen, and everyone in the room could hear her clearly. "I know you've been under a lot of strain. We're all worried about you here, and we're all trying our best to make things easier for you. But we can't neglect our own jobs. If you can't handle the pressure of coming back to work, maybe you should take a leave of absence, see a doctor or something, Ginny. You just can't go on behaving as you have."

"I beg your pardon," Ginny began angrily. Don't raise your voice. Don't create a scene, she warned herself. That's what she's trying to goad you into. She spoke calmly. "I'm not the one ranting at the top of my voice, Nola. You are. I've tried to make a friendly overture, and you've chosen to misread it. I don't know what you're trying to do to me."

"Ginny, can't you see how paranoid you've become?" Nola said, her voice suddenly gentle and solicitous. "We don't blame you, Ginny. You've never gotten over the loss of your husband, and now losing your son is even more difficult for you. God knows you have a right to behave as you do. Some women go out of their mind over far less than you've been through. When a woman's going through her change, she can go off the deep end. You have to get help. Please!"

Nonplused, Ginny stared at Nola. The woman's face displayed concern, but her eyes were hard and shining like a marble underwater, reflecting back light but showing no inner emotion. Dread washed over Ginny. She was being manipulated by a real pro.

"You're the one who's gone over the deep end," she said quietly and walked back to her office. She could hear the buzz of the secretaries before her door swung shut. Hurt and mystified that she hadn't seen this coming months before, Ginny paced the office, dredging up old half-forgotten memories of times when Nola had jumped in to lighten the work load and the office had become fully aware that she was doing more than her job required, of coffee being brought while teasing remarks about hangovers were made, of papers misplaced and documentation missing. Ginny had been puzzled by many things over the past few months, but had pushed them aside. She had blamed some of the events on faulty memory or getting older. How many times had Nola set her up, and how many times had she failed to see it?

The thoughts were ugly. She couldn't understand someone who'd deliberately set out to sabotage another person just for a job. But what would this behavior net Nola? She already had Ginny's top account. Hurt and confused by what had happened, Ginny tried to get back to work, but her thoughts were too scattered. Finally she gave up the attempt and sat staring with unseeing eyes at the wall.

A knock at the door interrupted her brooding. With mingled trepidation and hope, she swung around in her chair.

"Have you got a minute?" Alex asked. His face was somber, his eyes evasive. Hope died; trepidation reigned.

"Of course. I always have time for you, Alex. You know that."

He settled into a chair across from her. His long legs automatically crossed as he slouched into a comfortable position. He'd taken off his suit coat and rolled up the sleeves of his crisp white shirt. He looked handsome as always. Ginny met his bleak smile with a cautious one of her own.

"I don't know how to begin."

"That sounds ominous."

132

"Why?"

"Are we fencing?"

"Are we?"

"Come on, Alex. You came in here. You must have something on your mind." Why did she sound so defensive even to her own ears?

"Ginny . . ." He rose and paced around the room, one slim brown hand rubbing the back of his neck. "Maybe you came back to work too soon."

"I don't think so."

Alex glanced at her, his face pained, his eyes pleading with her to relent and help him out of his dilemma, but Ginny merely waited for his next move.

"This thing with Nola has to be resolved. It's upsetting the whole office."

"What thing are you talking about, Alex?"

"This . . . this feud between you. Look, Ginny, I'm no good at handling women's hostilities."

"Is Nola hostile?"

"She says you are."

"And you believe her." Ginny's voice cracked in spite of herself. She was hurt.

"It's not a matter of believing her or you. I can see for myself that things aren't right. Nola's sitting out there red-eyed and upset, the secretaries can't concentrate on their work, and you're sitting in here brooding."

"I'm not brooding," Ginny snapped, her enforced calm fast diminishing.

"Well, you have to admit you haven't been yourself lately."

"I'm very much myself," Ginny stormed. "Nola has lied and dropped innuendos until everyone believes what she wants them to believe whether it's true or not. But you, Alex, I thought you were a friend, someone I could trust and depend on. Instead, you're being duped by another pretty young face and a plausible story."

"Before you go any further, Ginny, let me remind you that I've overlooked a lot of your innuendos about my private life. You should stop and consider that friendship can only bear so much."

"Is that a threat?"

"It's a warning."

"Of what? Of my losing my job? I quit!"

"Ginny!" Alex's exasperation was evident, and that only added to Ginny's anger. Pulling open the drawers of her desk, she began flinging its contents into her large handbag.

"I won't let you quit," Alex said.

"You can't stop me. I'll have my resignation on your desk within an hour and be gone."

"Ginny, be reasonable."

"I can't be," she replied whirling to face him. "I'm a paranoid, aging woman badly in need of a hormone fix." She slammed the desk drawer closed and crossed the office.

"You can't mean you're willing to walk out on me," Alex said quietly. His eyes were dark and angry. She sensed she was cutting old ties, burning bridges, ending something she might not want to be over. A tremor of uncertainty touched her; then she drew back her shoulders.

"Goodbye, Alex," she said with quiet dignity and closed the office door behind her. Every pair of eyes in the outer office watched her exit. Ginny kept her head high until she was in the Lincoln and headed back down the Southfield freeway. Then the tears came, blinding her so she was forced to pull over. She'd just lost another anchor in her life, and her hands trembled as she dug into her leather bag to fish out a crumpled tissue. When she was calm again, she took a deep breath and eased out into the traffic. Fine example I've set for the girls, she thought. How could she encourage them to go to school when she'd just walked out on her job?

True to her word, Ginny sent Alex her resignation, then tied into a major spring cleaning of the house just to keep herself from moping. She had no idea what she would do with her time or about money. She had enough to meet their immediate needs, and she had some vague idea of getting another job. Her years in the advertising business provided contacts. They'd pay off when she was ready. But each day she spent sweeping away cobwebs and straightening closets, her confidence ebbed. She was fifty years old. How could she compete against younger women who were probably as ruthless and goal-oriented as Nola? She'd never draw the salary she'd been earning at Russell and Taylor. In the middle of a mattress-turning which left Marnie red-faced and breathless, Ginny stopped to go over their expenses. Maintaining both the house and the condo was eating away at her resources. Scott had left a substantial insurance policy, but she'd put that, along with his modest savings, into a trust for the girls' college education. No matter what occurred, she wouldn't touch those funds. The picture was grimmer than she'd thought. The ringing of a phone interrupted her bleak musings.

"It's Mr. Russell," Marnie called from the kitchen. Ginny's heart squeezed painfully;

then she forced herself to be calm.

"I'll take it in here," she called, reaching for the desk phone.

"Ginny, how are you?" His voice sounded rich and warm.

I've missed him, she thought with dismay. "I'm fine, Alex," she said, keeping her voice even. "How are you?"

"I miss you. We all do. When are you coming back?"

"Didn't you receive my resignation?"

There was a brief silence at the other end. "I tore it up."

"You shouldn't have. I meant it, Alex."

"Why? Because of Nola? I'll get rid of her."

"That won't make any difference." There was another long pause.

"What can I do that will make a difference?"

"Nothing. Everything's been said and done. It can't be undone."

"Ginny, why do I have the feeling that I've failed you somehow? I've tried in every way to be there when you needed me."

She felt a shimmer of guilt; then her resentment hardened. "You weren't there at the right moment, Alex," she said, and knew she was being oblique.

137

"I meant to be. God knows I've tried." His sigh was weary.

"You did your best. Maybe this was bound to happen. Maybe I just needed a change, and Nola brought it about."

"Give yourself some time before you make any hasty decisions. I'll keep your place for you here at the office."

"Don't do that, Alex." Ginny paused, clenching her teeth to strengthen her resolve. "I'm really not even mad anymore." It was true, she realized. "I do need a change. So do the girls."

"My God, what are you planning?"

"I'm not certain yet."

"Ginny, stay in touch with me. Let me know when you have made up your mind."

"All right, Alex," she said, and knew she wouldn't. The change had to be complete, real, no halfway measure. Replacing the phone in its cradle she sat staring out the study window. Snow limned the spindly branches of the bare trees and lay in dirty mounds along the sidewalks. She thought of the lake with its untouched vistas of white, of the gleam of sunlight on ice and of the wind sweeping unchecked across the frozen expanse to whine around the cottage while she and the girls snuggled before a fire, roasting marshmallows. There had been something basic and reassuring about the stay there, a returning to a simpler existence where living each day was a celebration not a betrayal and ambition was gathering walnuts from beneath the towering trees or replenishing the cookie jar. Idyllic! Unrealistic! If she was going to run from reality, she could think of no better place to go than the lake house.

When the girls came home from school they found her packing.

Seven

She was mad. She had to be to do such a harebrained thing. She sat in the car at the end of the driveway and gazed at the cottage sitting below. She'd called ahead to Jason McCann, and he'd seen to it that Dick Chalmers had plowed out the drive. At least they didn't have to lug their luggage and groceries down this time. But suddenly everything else seemed overwhelming. The sun had already fallen below the black silhouettes of bare trees, leaving only a vague stain of red behind. Dark shadows crept around the sheds and pine trees, and a cold wind had come up, rattling the thin frozen branches of the apple trees and swirling snow across the cleared path. Dark clouds held a threat of snowfall. Thank God she'd stopped at the grocer's before driving out. They might get snowed in.

"What are you waiting for, Grandma?"

Candi asked when Ginny continued to sit with the front wheels on the drive and the rear ones still on the road as if she'd not yet decided to proceed.

Did I act too hastily, Ginny wondered, glancing at the eager young faces. They'd been as excited as she about it, but moving to the lake house permanently was far different from coming down for the weekend.

"Don't be scared, Grandma. We're with you," Candi said, and suddenly Ginny's indecision was gone. She wasn't alone; they had made this choice together. If it was the wrong one, she—they—would undo it. She'd only rented out the house and subleased the condo. They could go back if they wanted to. They'd set a course; now they needed to move ahead before they began to question their choice. She put the car in gear and rolled down the drive.

"Everybody grab a bag," Tracy ordered, punching a button to open the trunk. She portioned out the luggage and the grocery sacks according to size and strength. Arms laden, they made their way to the door.

"Look, Mr. Chalmers even shoveled off the porch," Tracy commented.

"Bless him," Ginny groaned, setting her load down by the door while she drew out the key. As before they piled into the cottage, feeling its hominess like a healing balm.

"We're home," Steffi sighed, and everyone smiled as if relieved that their reasons for coming here had been validated.

"I wish Marnie could have come," Candi said wistfully.

"Darling, she didn't want to leave her sister in Detroit," Ginny reminded her cheerfully.

"So she left us instead," Candi said. Steffi laid her head against her sister's chest, and they hugged briefly, sharing yet another loss in their short lives. Tracy just stood watching them, her expression unreadable.

"All right, let's get organized." Ginny looked at the piles of luggage and groceries. She had to keep them busy so they wouldn't have a chance to think about Marnie and their father and their old home.

Within an hour, they'd unpacked their bags and filled drawers and closets with what they'd brought. A moving van would bring the rest of their belongings in a day or two. The furniture from the house had been put into storage. Unable to bear storing all the treasures she and David had collected over the years, and not wanting to entrust them to the dubious mercies of strangers, Ginny had packed them. They, too, would be delivered with the rest of their belongings. As she looked around, Ginny automatically assessed where she would place her collectibles.

Groceries were put away, omelettes and toast made. By the time they'd eaten they were feeling more comfortable with their move. The girls' eyes sparkled with anticipation; smiles came readily. Ginny's spirits soared. Moving here had been the right thing to do.

"What're we doing tomorrow?" Tracy asked as they cleared away the dishes.

"I've had your grades transferred to the school here, so tomorrow we go down and get you all registered."

"So soon?" Three pairs of eyes stared at her in consternation.

"We're not on vacation now, girls. We live here. We're making this our home, remember? That means we have to go right on with life just as we would have before — and that means school."

Not one word of protest came from them, but their eyes were accusing.

"Sorry!" Ginny said, and she returned to loading the dishwasher.

"What if we don't like this school?" Candi asked stubbornly.

"You'll like it. You just have to give it time," Ginny reassured her.

"At least no one knows about our father

here," Tracy said. "They won't be watching us to see if we're going to cry."

A knock at the door stopped Ginny from answering. "Don't open the door until we know who it is," she called to the girls.

"It's Jason," Candi cried, brushing aside the ruffled curtains. The door was flung open, and Jason was ushered in amid high-pitched girlish chatter. His beard was frosted with snow; his eyes were bright with pleasure.

"Hello," he said. "Welcome back."

"Thank you for contacting Dick Chalmers," Ginny said, wiping her hands on a towel. "He did an excellent job. He even shoveled off the porch." She paused at seeing the look on his face. "*You* shoveled off the porch."

His laughter rang out, brief and masculine. He was pleased that she'd credited him with his good deed.

"Thank you," Ginny said warmly. "That was thoughtful of you."

"I'm glad you're back. It was lonelier after you all left."

"We'll be your neighbors all the time now," Candi said, slipping her hand into Jason's and gazing up at him confidently.

"You're the best neighbors I've ever had," he said, squeezing her hand.

Ginny watched him with the girls, the way

144

he talked to them, the way they responded to him; friendly and confident as if they'd known each other for years. The sadness seemed to leave him when he looked at their bright young faces.

"I'm sorry, girls. It's bed time."

Moans of dismay greeted her announcement. "You have to get up early in the morning."

"We have to go to school," Candi explained.

"I don't have to," Steffi said tugging at Jason's coat.

"Oh yes, you do," Ginny laughed. "Up to bed with you."

"I'll talk to you tomorrow after school," Jason said, picking up his hat.

"Good night, Jason. See you tomorrow."

"Maybe we'll get snowed in tonight." The girls disappeared upstairs. Jason's grin faded.

"Guess I'd better get back over to my place and let you get settled in," he said, pulling on his hat. "If you need anything, just let me know."

"You've been very kind, but we don't want to impose on you. We're here to start over, and that means standing on our own feet."

"I can understand that," he answered. "But everyone needs a neighborly hand now and then. That's all I'm offering. And in return, well, just to know someone else is around is enough." He turned toward the door, pulling on his thick gloves. "By the way, I took the liberty of calling the phone company for you. They'll be out tomorrow to hook up your phones."

Ginny smiled and shrugged. "I guess you're right. A neighborly hand now and then is awfully nice."

" 'Night, Ginny."

" 'Night, Jason."

She watched him trudge across the back yard to the opening in the winter-bare holly bushes. He disappeared from view; then a light flared on the snow as he opened his door and disappeared inside. Crossing to the sink, Ginny gazed out the side window. Jason's lights were diffused by the falling snow, but comforting nonetheless. She folded the dishtowel and hung it on the wooden rack Scott had made for her in high-school in shop. Running her fingers over the smooth varnished oak, she thought about those years and was touched by sadness as she knew she always would be.

"Gwandma, are you coming up?" a small voice called from the top of the stairs. Flipping the light off, Ginny grinned. "I'm coming," she called, and she made her way through the hall and up the stairs to where Steffi stood waiting, her teddy bear clutched to her chest.

We made the right decision, Ginny thought.

Her face twisted in a scary expression, her arms reaching out, she ran forward. Steffi screamed, her bare feet flying as she made for the big bed in the master bedroom. Ginny followed, growling and tickling the little girl until she giggled, then snuggled close. "It's nice to be here, isn't it, Steffi?" she said. Sighing, Steffi nodded and cuddled closer. The house was quiet except for the moan of the wind around the corners and the occasional creak and pop of old timbers settling. A movement at the foot of the bed caused Ginny to smile.

"Come on, girls," she sighed. "You can sleep with me tonight, but tomorrow you'll be in your own beds."

The morning was pristine, and crisply cold. Even the sun seemed intimidated by the unrelenting chill. A thick layer of snow softened the contours of earth and buildings, but the sky was innocent, not one menacing cloud to mar its passive image.

Ginny rose early, slipping into the thick robe and slippers she'd brought. The girls were soon roused, shivering and grumbling.

"You wanted to live in the country," Ginny reminded them before she hurried downstairs

147

to make oatmeal. Stirring the lumpy gray mass, she hummed to herself, feeling domestic and capable. Despite the modern conveniences of dishwasher and electric stove, it seemed she was only a hair's-breadth away from the primitive days of her forbears. By the time the oatmeal was dished up into the china bowls on the table, the girls were washed and dressed and downstairs.

"Ugh, what's this?" they demanded.

"Oatmeal," Ginny said loudly. "Don't tell me you've never had it before. I know Marnie made it for you."

"It never looked like this," Candi said, holding a spoonful up and letting it plop back into her bowl.

"What are these lumps?" Tracy demanded.

"I haven't made it in a while," Ginny admitted. "I'm kind of out of practice."

"Kind of!" Tracy's tone was scoffing.

"Well, I've forgotten just how to do some of these things, but I'll get it right the next time."

"I want peanut buttah and toast," Steffi demanded, pushing out her bottom lip mutinously.

"Me, too," Candi chimed in.

"Now look, girls."

"Grandma, we're used to having corn flakes for breakfast," Tracy said hopefully.

"Not cold cereal on a morning like this!" Ginny exclaimed. "You need hot food to warm your stomachs and give you . . . give you brain power."

"You sound like Marnie," Tracy said, and her gaze went to the ceiling.

"Well, it's true. You'll have a happier day if your stomach starts out with warm food in it."

"We'll have a happier day if we can just have some food that we like," Tracy countered.

Looking around the table at their unhappy faces, Ginny sighed. "All right. You win. Go get the Cheerios."

The car was sluggish after sitting out in the open all night. Ginny pumped the gas pedal several times and turned the key. The grinding moan sounded weaker with every try.

"Uh, I smell gas," Tracy complained.

"I think I've flooded it," Ginny said.

Tracy and Candi exchanged glances. "Hooray, no school," they cried in unison.

"I'll get it started." Ginny turned the key again. Someone knocked on the window, and she pushed the button. Nothing moved. After several more attempts, Ginny opened the door. Jason McCann hunkered down to talk to her.

"Got a problem?" he asked. His eyes were lively, their color brilliant in the cold. Bundled in his canvas parka and heavy boots, he

149

seemed bigger, more capable, undeniably masculine.

"I think I've flooded it," Ginny said again, and hated sounding like a helpless female. "I'm sure I'll get it started in a minute." She pumped the pedal and turned the key again. "It's not used to sitting out in the cold."

"It is flooded," he said. His breath came out in a white vapor. "Don't pump anymore. Push the pedal to the floor then try to start it." Ginny followed his instructions. After a few tries, the motor caught. When she was sure it wouldn't die again, she smiled at Jason.

He smiled back. "I had the same problem once," he said. "Listen, there's a double garage over at the DeFauws'. I'm only using one side if you want to put your car in the other."

"I wouldn't want to impose."

"You won't be."

"Thank you for the offer. I'll think about it." He sensed the dismissal and stood back. She reached for the door to pull it closed.

"Well, goodbye now."

She was sorry she'd been so stiff with him. He stood watching them, a tight little smile curving his lips as if he'd been hurt and didn't want to admit it. He was like a puppy that's been chastised unjustly.

"Do you need to go downtown? You can ride along."

He shook his head, shoving his hands in the back pockets of his jeans. She guessed that was a habit with him. "Nah, Redder and I are going to stay around here."

"Can I get you anything? After I drop the girls at school, I'm going to the grocery store."

He smiled then, that all-out giving response that was as much a part of him as the long gangly legs and brilliant blue eyes. She couldn't help smiling back.

"If I can't do something for you, could you do me a favor?" Ginny asked impulsively. His smile widened, and he nodded eagerly. Snowflakes scattered from his bare head. "If I don't get back before the men from the phone company come, will you let them in? I'll pay you back with a home-cooked meal tonight." She surprised herself by inviting him.

"Don't do it, Jason," Tracy said. "Grandma made terrible oatmeal this morning. All gray and lumpy."

"We had to eat Cheewios," Steffi chimed from the back seat, which occasioned laughter all around and gave Ginny an excuse for her heightened color.

"I thought grandmas were supposed to know how to cook everything," Jason laughed.

151

"Not this grandma," Tracy asserted.

"No, not this grandma," Jason said, and something about his tone and glance was unsettling.

Ginny remained silent during the ribbing, but now she spoke up, trying to erase some indefinable tension that had arisen. "Listen, you ingrates, if you expect ever to see food again, you'd better change your attitudes."

"You make good omelettes, Grandma," Candi said, leaning over the seat to place her cheek against Ginny's.

"And great spaghetti," Jason chimed in, the laughter back in his eyes. The moment was past. "I'll see to your phone. Don't worry. I think your car's warmed up enough so you won't have any trouble with it. I'll leave the garage doors open in case you change your mind."

He closed the car door, tucking them into the heated interior of the car. A large gloved hand cleared a streak of snow from the windshield, cracked ice off one of the wipers, and then rose in a gesture of farewell.

"He's nice," said Tracy, waving back with enthusiasm. Her face was alive and open as she turned toward Ginny. She looked more like the old Tracy. Ginny suspected she was developing a crush on this new neighbor.

She guided the car between the high snow-banks along the sides of the winding lake road and increased her speed when she reached the highway. In the back seat Candi and Steffi oohed and aahed over the fairyland of crystal-lized trees and roadside bushes. The world was changed, made beautiful by the mysterious forces of nature. Even Ginny felt the enchant-ment, and remembering Jason's bantering com-ments, she grinned and began humming a tune from the latest Andrew Lloyd Webber musical. The sunlight was stronger. It lay in bright patches along the roadside.

The school was a sprawling affair laid out over several acres. Elementary classes were held in the original building, which harked back to a different day and era. Wings had been added to both sides of it, and finally a new building had been constructed behind the back parking lot. Still farther back, overlooking one of the numerous lakes that dotted the county, the new high school perched on a slight hill, gaining stature by its size, modern lines, and slight ele-vation.

"Wow," Tracy said in one of her rare under-statements.

"Grandma, will I have to go up there?" Candi asked worriedly. Her small hand crept forward to find Ginny's.

153

"I think you start down here and work your way up," Ginny reassured her. Cheerfully, she took the hands of the younger girls. "We'll get Tracy registered first."

"Grandma, you aren't coming in with me, are you?" Tracy asked, her eyes flashing a plea to some unnamed God that would surely understand the distress of a near teenager who feared being treated like a baby.

"I'm only going to the office," Ginny promised.

"Do you have to?"

"I have to!" Ginny said firmly. She was somewhat miffed at Tracy's attitude.

By ten o'clock she had the registrations completed and each girl was safely tucked into a class. Candi had felt at home in the cheerfully cluttered first-grade room, and Steffi had stood in a corner, clutching her teddy bear but dry eyed, at the nursery school. If I hurry, Ginny thought, I can shop and beat it back to the cottage before the man arrives from the phone company.

Dalton was a small town, consisting of a few stores huddled together on the main highway, a post office down a side street, a drugstore, library, bank, and the sprawling, shoddy brick building that was the real hub of the town, Brannock's Groceries. Here one could drop off cleaning, have pictures developed, rent videos, and even replenish supplies of woolen socks and jeans, stone-washed preferences aside. Ginny hurried up and down the aisles, disappointed in the selection and the quality of the fresh produce. This was one of the handicaps of country living, she reminded herself. She'd become too used to the large chain stores with their variety. She'd adjust!

A truck bearing the emblem of the local phone company was parked in the drive when she arrived home. No one was in sight, so she assumed Jason had let the man in. She grabbed a couple of bags and headed for the door. Jason McCann's long lanky figure leaned against a counter. His arms were folded across his chest, his face was somber as he regarded the man working on her phone line. When she entered, he straightened and glanced at her bright face and laden arms.

"Let me help you," he said, taking one of the bags. His rough hands brushed against her as the exchange was made, but he didn't seem to notice and set the bag on the table. His easy manner made her easy too. Placing the other bag on the counter she turned to the workman.

"Your husband told me you wanted a phone here in the kitchen and one upstairs in the bedroom," the workman said over his shoulder. Ginny glanced at Jason. He was the one to look away.

"We're not married," he said gruffly and tugged at his gloves. "Well, now that you're here, I'll go. What did you decide about the car? Do you want it in the garage?"

Ginny glanced at the window and saw thick flakes drifting languidly to earth. "I think it might be best."

Jason nodded. "I'll put it in for you. Have you got your keys?"

She wanted to say no, she would do it, but she was aware of the workman listening. Shrugging, she handed her keys to Jason and watched him through the window as he folded himself into the big Lincoln and started the motor.

"You want the other phone in the master bedroom?" the workman said behind her, and Ginny turned away from the window.

"Yes. I believe there's already an outlet near the night table." Grunting, the man turned toward the stairs. Ginny saw that he hadn't taken off his boots and puddles of melted snow remained where he'd worked. Sighing, she got the mop. By the time the phone man left, she had to go pick up Steffi. It seemed strange to walk next door and retrieve her car from the neighbor's garage, but Jason had thoughtfully cleared a path from her drive to his. He was nowhere in sight when she swung the garage door open and backed out.

Steffi greeted her at the door of the nursery school, her face beaming.

"We seem to have made some friends today," observed the slender young woman in charge. "I think she'll do well here."

"Steffi, how wonderful. You made a friend?" Ginny squatted down to talk to her granddaughter at eye level while she zipped up Steffi's parka. She couldn't help feeling some irritation with Joan Stevens because Steffi's dependency had been so quickly diverted. She shook away the thought. That's why they'd come here. To find themselves again and become strong. Though Steffi still clutched her bear, it dangled from her hand by one arm while she began to tell of her new friend. When she'd finished, Ginny straightened and smiled at Ms. Stevens.

"You're very good with children."

Joan shrugged. "I like kids. They're resilient and tough. Steffi will be just fine. It must be tough. You're doing a good job."

In the face of such generous praise, Ginny regretted her first assessment of the young woman. With a final farewell, she guided her granddaughter to the car.

"How about if we two girls go out to lunch and poke around in the shops?" Ginny asked.

Steffi, buckled into her seatbelt, her bear tucked beside her, nodded happily. Her manner was already less babyish than it had been over the past few weeks.

They found a pizza place with country pictures, wooden booths, and a train track that ran around a ledge set below the ceiling. Wide-eyed, Steffi watched the train's progress, giggling every time it tooted. Stuffed with pizza and hot chocolate, they later ambled along the sidewalks, reacquainting themselves with the small stores. Snow had begun to fall again. With its old buildings whitewashed with snow, the shabby little resort town took on a picturesque quality. Ginny poked around in the craft shop, finally settling on a cross-stitch book and some yarn. Seeing Steffi's uninhibited yawn, she then took her back to the car and they headed home. It had been a satisfying trip, further enhancing her good feelings about their coming to Dalton to live. With Steffi tucked into bed for a nap, Ginny found herself with little to do, so she dug out an old cookbook and set about making cookies. She'd never been a grandmother who baked, but she could start doing it. She was soon immersed in the proper measurement of butter and sugar. The old cast-iron clock she'd once found at an auction added to her sense of contentment with its rhythmic telling of the minutes.

The older girls were delivered to the end of the drive by a big yellow school bus. They raced down to the cottage, their voices silvery and lighthearted, finally bringing gusts of cold air, snow, and life into the cottage. Ginny listened to them tell about their first day at the new school. She found out what they thought of their teachers, the other kids, and the curriculum.

"They stared at us," Tracy said with some disgust. "Just because we were new kids."

"Were they friendly?"

"Some were," Tracy admitted.

"I have a new friend. Her name is Laura," Candi informed her.

"There's a boy in my class who thinks he's so smart." Tracy paused. "He is," she finally added. "But he doesn't have to act like he thinks he is."

"I have fresh-baked cookies and milk for you," Ginny said when there was a lull in their conversation.

The girls fell silent and stared at her in consternation. "You made cookies?" Tracy asked.

"Yes. I can do those things," Ginny answered, grinning proudly.

"Are they like the oatmeal?" Tracy demanded suspiciously.

"They turned out very nicely, and if you don't keep a civil tongue in your head, I won't let you have any." Ginny's tone was light and teasing. Impudently Tracy grinned and headed for the stairs. "Don't you want some cookies and milk?"

"Later," Tracy called back. Ginny glanced at the other two girls.

"Candi? Steffi?"

"I'll like your cookies, Grandma," said Candi, ever the tenderhearted diplomat.

"Good," Ginny said, reaching for the cookie jar.

"But not right now, okay?" Candi shifted her book bag and headed for the stairs. That left only Steffi with her big, serious eyes.

"Boo!" Ginny said, and with a squeal the little girl bounded after her sisters. Ginny glanced at the pile of cookies. They looked good. She took a bite of one. It tasted good. The girls would try them eventually, and when they did, they'd be surprised. "They'll learn not to underestimate the power of a grandmother," she muttered to herself. She reached for the phone, intending to let Jason know what time to come over. The sound of giggles came to her.

"Hello?" she said automatically.

"Grandma, I'm using the phone." It was Tracy's prim voice that came along the wire.

"Sorry," Ginny said, and she put down the receiver. Humming she started supper. They'd gotten through their first day here. And it had been a good one for them all. Despite Tracy's complaints, she'd already found a friend, a confidante with whom to share secrets and information. Life seemed possible again. The red-orange glow of the sunset outside the kitchen window was no longer a sad sight. The sun would rise again. Tears stung Ginny's eyes, and she recognized that they weren't tears of sorrow. They were healing—all of them. Healing!

Eight

Each day slipped into a pattern. The children off to school, shopping, preparing meals, washing school clothes, picking up children, reading bedtime stories, helping with homework, and then getting up each morning to repeat the whole routine all over again. There was comfort in the repetition.

The moving van had arrived, bringing the rest of their clothes and personal belongings. Ginny spent one whole day carefully unpacking the crystal and porcelain collections and arranging them in the old china cabinet with the curved glass doors. It took another day to hang her prized plate collection. Jason arrived just as she'd hit her thumb with a hammer, and wisely did not offer to help. She hung her Hibel and Perillo plates on a west wall so the morning light hit them just so, revealing the beauty of the artist's work. Each day the cottage seemed more like home . . . in ways it never had before. She settled into it, drew in the serene isolation the season offered her, wrapped it around her like a woolen blanket, reveled in the long hours of quiet when there was no sound but the plop of melting snow falling from the roof peaks. Tranquility! Serenity! Peace! A surcease of the pain of loss. One hour slid into another, one day into a week, a week into many until with a start Ginny realized that spring was fast approaching. Icicles dripped. Snow loosened its hold on tree branches and slid ignominiously to the ground, where it lay in soft wet blobs that quickly melted into cold, brown runnels heading toward the lake. But the lake held its ice, unwilling to release itself to the seductive offer of springtime.

Drawn by the warm wind and the groan of ice in its death throes, Ginny walked down and stood peering out over the vast flat surface.

"I wouldn't walk out there," someone called, and automatically Ginny turned toward the De-Fauw property. She'd grown used to having Jason McCann nearby. He never intruded on them, but she had made it a practice to invite him over for supper now and then. The girls enjoyed his teasing humor, and so did she. Now she saw that he was busy fixing something on a rowboat. She walked over and saw that he was mending an oarlock.

"The ice is getting black. I think it'll be gone soon," she said, gazing out over the lake again.

"Sure looks like it," he agreed. He wore a light tan jacket which made his body look less bulky, trimmer, leaner, harder. She stopped looking at him.

"Mmmm, just feel that breeze. It's positively tropical."

He laughed, slow and easy, the way he often did. "That might be stretching it some," he said. "Getting a little cabin fever, are you?"

She laughed too and felt young and carefree. "Some," she admitted. "It was kind of nice to grow fat and lazy and contented when the snow was falling, but it's nearly spring and I can see contentment turning to boredom very soon now."

"Let's head it off. Want to drive over to Middleville for a movie?"

"That sounds lovely, but it's a school night. The girls have to be in bed early."

"I was thinking of getting a babysitter."

Startled, Ginny glanced at him. His expression was bland, his concentration centered on mending the oarlock.

"I . . . I don't think so tonight. I have some things to do."

"Another time then." His acceptance was so casual she felt relieved. It had been just a friendly invitation, made because they were neighbors. She watched him bend over the old rowboat, his long legs encased in a pair of the endless array of jeans he seemed to own, his rich brown hair falling over his forehead as he worked.

"You never wear a hat," she commented.

"Not my style, Ginny," he said in a tone that clearly indicated they were equals. She felt rebuffed, then relaxed a bit. Each of them had certain prerequisites. She didn't want to be thought an incompetent woman, and he didn't want to be mothered.

"You just like to go without a hat because it makes you look sexier," she teased, and was surprised when he raised his head to gaze into her eyes. The shock of his glance laced through her, and her teasing smile faded. His eyes were very blue, very direct, very compelling. She stood staring back at him, unable to turn away, unable to think she should want to. The breeze whipping against her cheeks had turned cold, making her shiver.

"You were right," she said, looking every place but at him. "The wind is cold." She faked a shiver. "I think I'll head in. See you later."

"Sure. Later," he said. She felt the heat of his eyes on her back, but only when she reached the safety of the patio did she allow herself to turn and face him. By this time, he'd bent over the boat again. A shock of brown hair falling forward hid his face from her. Thoughtfully, she made her way inside. I should make some cookies for the girls, she told herself, or do some mending or throw in a load of wash.

Instead, she lit a fire in the old stone fireplace and curled up on the couch to gaze into the flames. The memory of Jason's glance came back to her, and she felt a tingle of response in her breasts. I have to stop this, she thought wildly. He was a neighbor, almost young enough to be her son. My God, what was she thinking of. Was this some aberration caused by her grief for Scott? It was sick! She wouldn't think about it anymore. She wouldn't allow herself to feel these tingles, this achy need. Passion was behind her; it had ended when David died. Think of David, she told herself. Think of Scott. You haven't thought of either of them all day. I've been trying not to, she reminded herself. But not like this. Not these lecherous thoughts that had sprung to life when she'd looked at Jason in his tight jeans. This was depraved.

166

Unable to bear her own thoughts, Ginny hurried upstairs and spent the rest of the afternoon cleaning her closets. Steffi slept later than usual. When the slam of the back door roused her, she woke sobbing.

"I want Daddy," she cried piteously. Ginny hurried to smooth back sweat-dampened strands from her cheek and to hold her close.

"Do you know what that little animal did?" Tracy shrieked, coming up the stairs. "She's so disgusting. And now everyone knows she's my sister."

"Tracy, do be quieter," Ginny called over Steffi's wails.

Tracy appeared in the doorway. "What's wrong with her?"

"You woke her up, and now she's frightened."

"I'm sorry, Steffi baby," Tracy said, instantly contrite. She knelt beside the bed and patted her younger sister. Enjoying the extra attention, Steffi hiccuped and managed a few more pathetic sobs before allowing herself to be cajoled into a smile.

"Don't call me Steffi. I'm not a baby anymore," she pouted.

"What should we call you?" Tracy asked, amused. She truly adored this youngest sister.

"My name is Stef," the blond cherub said,

her cheeks dimpling as she smiled. Tracy and Ginny both laughed, then quickly agreed she wasn't a baby and henceforth would be called Stef. Then Ginny turned to Tracy.

"Now tell me what's wrong with you."

"I can tell you in one word, Grandma. Candi. *C-A-N-D-I.*" She spelled the name out to emphasize her point.

Ginny sighed and fought back a smile. "What did she do now?"

"She told everyone on the bus that I like Steve Howard."

"Isn't he the boy who thinks he's so smart? I thought you didn't like him."

"Grandma! You have to do something. You *have* to *do something.*"

"What do you suggest? Should I hang her from her thumbs? Put her in the attic with no food? Cut out her tongue and feed it to the fish?"

"I like that last one."

Ginny laughed despite herself. "Take it easy on her, Tracy. She looks up to you, and she has the kindest little heart. She'd never deliberately embarrass you. Just remember, you were six years old once too."

"Grandma, that's not the same, and it's not funny."

"I'm sorry. I won't laugh again. I'll have a

168

talk with Candi and explain why such comments are embarrassing to you." Ginny glanced toward the door. "Where is she now?"

"Oh, she went down to the lake. I think she's going ice-skating."

"On the lake?" Ginny's face went white. "Tracy, run down and tell her not to go out on the ice. It's too thin." She leaped to her feet, spilling Stef back onto the bed. Stef's wail of surprise went unnoticed as they both raced toward the stairs.

"Candi!" Tracy's cry was a shriek of terror. Her legs churned desperately. Ginny was right behind her. Without bothering to reach for coats, they flung open the back door and ran toward the lake.

"Oh, God, no!" Ginny screamed when she saw the yawning hole in the ice, bobbing in it a red hat that was Candi's. Her legs felt wooden. She slogged through the wet, clinging snow, feeling it ooze over the tops of her house slippers. It didn't matter, nothing could; for she'd caught a glimpse of a red-mittened hand reaching up from the icy water, scrabbling for a hold on the ice.

Ginny didn't pause when she reached the edge of the lake. Skidding and sliding, she ran across the ice, sometimes breaking through it, but always struggling out of the trough to inch forward again. The little hand had disappeared from view. It no longer struggled for a hold on life.

"Please, God," Ginny prayed. The ice beneath her feet gave way. She was out deeper now, so she went down and under. The shock of the cold water numbed her for a moment, but her terror for Candi took over and she flailed to the surface, hitting at the sharp edges of the ice that kept her away from that gaping hole.

"Candi!" she screamed. Her throat ached from the cry, but she repeated it again and again, like an animal looking for its wounded baby. She was unaware someone was beside her until a gloved hand pushed at the thin ice. Jason pounded and punched his way through, cutting a path to the hole. Ginny was surprised she could touch the cold sand at the bottom of the lake, but the water was too deep for a six-year-old, even a quicksilver girl who was tall and slim for her age.

"She's under the water," Ginny cried desperately as Jason reached the spot ahead of her. "I saw her go under." Then she stopped talking, for Jason was already diving beneath the ice. He came up, empty-handed.

"No!" Ginny screamed, clutching her clenched fists to her chest. Jason ignored her cry. His face was white from the cold water, his eyes wild as he looked around to get his bearings, then dove again.

Ginny stood where she was, although numbness was creeping into her legs and feet. She wondered if she might succumb to hypothermia. But it didn't matter. Candi was down there at the bottom of that cold, merciless lake. Her beloved Candi who never wanted to hurt anyone's feelings. She stood in the shoulders-high water in the hope that Jason who was now below would see her and use her as a guide back to the hole in the ice. God only knew how far under the ice the current had carried Candi. Enraged at the thought, Ginny wanted to scream, but she forced herself to remain calm. Jason would find her. He would find her. Candi loved Jason. She trusted him. He would find her. He had to. Her litany was a prayer, and as if to prove that prayers are answered, Jason emerged from ice and water, a small, limp body clutched in his arms. He began wading to shore.

"My God, is she dead?" Ginny whispered tearfully, following close behind. Candi's golden lashes lay still against her pale cheeks.

"I don't know. We have to get help. Tracy, call the first-aid squad," he yelled before he'd even reached shore.

171

"Call nine-one-one," Ginny yelled.

"There's no nine-one-one out here. Call the first-aid squad. It's faster. The number's on the first page of the phone book."

Looking confused, Tracy ran into the house.

Water streaming from their clothes, they reached the shore and, without pausing, rushed toward the house.

"We have to get her out of these clothes, get her warm," Jason said. Blindly, Ginny followed him.

"There's a fire in the living room," she said, and hurried after him. They laid the limp body on the carpet before the fireplace and began stripping away dripping, ice-encrusted clothes. Candi made no sound. She did not seem to be breathing.

"CPR! We have to give her CPR," Ginny cried when they had her wrapped in a thick woolen afghan.

Jason's strong hands felt for a pulse, and finding none, he began to press gently on Candi's chest while Ginny breathed into her mouth. She had no idea how long they'd worked, but suddenly the cottage was filled with men in white uniforms and boots. The first-aid squad quickly and efficiently took over, using a machine to do what Jason and Ginny had attempted. Ginny stood to one side, out of the way. Tracy, her cheeks tear-stained, crept forward to stand beside her grandmother.

"I didn't mean all those bad things I said about her," she sobbed.

"I know you didn't, honey," Ginny whispered, putting an arm around Tracy's shoulders. "Candi knows too."

"If she dies, it'll be my fault," Tracy cried.

"She isn't going to die," Ginny said roughly. "She won't!" But her heart caught each time she looked at the tiny form lying on the floor. The men worked over Candi until she gave a tiny cough.

"She's breathing!" Ginny cried, stepping forward.

"Yes, ma'am. But she's in bad shape. She's suffering from hypothermia. We're going to transport her now."

"I'm coming with you."

The first-aid man looked at her and shook his head. "It'd be better if you stayed here and changed into something dry and warm yourself. You may be suffering from exposure."

"I'm all right. I'm coming with you."

"Ginny." Jason's hand on her arm was a reprimand, his tone slightly chiding. "Do as he suggested. Candi's going to need you strong and well. Go change and I'll do the same; then I'll drive us all to the hospital."

"All right, but hurry." Ginny turned, gripping his hands intensely. "Hurry, Jason."

"I'll be right back." He glanced at Tracy's tearful face. "Get Stef's coat on her," he said. Tracy nodded and hurried to do as he'd ordered. Stef made no outcry as Tracy zipped her into her parka, and by the time Jason was back, Ginny had changed into woolen slacks and a sweater and had shoved her feet into a pair of boots. She'd also taken the time to gather up Candi's pajamas and her favorite rag doll.

Darkness had fallen, and Ginny was grateful that Jason was driving. She watched the headlights picking out the thin snow banks lining the road and her thoughts went back to that night months before when she'd driven to the airport not knowing if her son were alive or dead. Alex had come to her then, with his warmth and strength. Funny she should think of him now when Jason sat at her side, strong and brave and capable. But think of Alex she did, and she wondered what he would say and do if he were here. Suddenly, she longed to see him.

She pictured Candi when the ambulance attendants had placed her on a stretcher and had covered her with thick blankets. Candi's slim little body had hardly made a mound beneath the covers. She was so tiny, so delicate, so vulnerable. She couldn't die. Ginny had to believe that the God who ruled all their lives had not planned one more sorrow for them. They would never bear it. She looked at Tracy, silent and stiff in the back seat. Already she was pulling a shell around herself, preparing again for unbearable pain.

"She'll be all right," Ginny said. "She was breathing. Now they're just going to see to it that she won't lose toes or fingers, that's all."

Tracy made no answer. Even Stef remained silent, huddled in her car seat. Jason dropped them at the emergency entrance and went to park the car.

"I'm the grandmother of the little girl they just brought in," Ginny said to the woman at the desk.

"Is the mother with you?"

"No, I—She isn't here."

"We need the mother or father to fill out the forms."

"The children live with me. I'm responsible for them." Ginny was shaking.

"Do you have something in writing to prove you're solely responsible for them?"

"No, I—"

"What's wrong?" Jason was beside her.

"Are you the father, sir?"

"No, I'm a friend. This is their grandmother."

"I'm afraid we need one of the parents to fill out forms to allow the hospital to perform necessary treatment."

"The father is dead and we don't know where the mother is," Jason said. "Their grandmother is responsible for the children."

The nurse directed a distrustful glance at Ginny, then passed over forms clipped to a board. "Fill these out and bring them back to me."

Ginny's hands were shaking so, she could scarcely write. Jason took the board and pen from her. "Give me the information, and I'll put it down," he said kindly. In a stuttering voice, Ginny told him. When he'd finished, he carried the forms back to the nurse.

"It will be a while. They're working on her now," he said, slumping down into one of the chairs. They sat in numbed silence, staring at the sofa and chairs that lined the walls. A television, mounted high on a stand, emitted sounds of canned laughter and some Hollywood screenwriter's idea of middle-class American entertainment.

Tracy sat a few seats away from them as if she weren't part of their pitifully dwindling group. Her face was stern and set, the way it had been the night her father died.

"Darling, don't worry. She'll be all right," Ginny said, and knew she'd uttered the words too many times already. They'd lost credibility. Candi was somewhere behind those closed doors, having things done to her that would frighten her if she knew. But she didn't. The thought made Ginny sob out loud. She pressed her hands against her mouth, trying to hold back the sounds. She had to be brave for the girls. She glanced at Tracy and found her fighting back tears too. Ginny opened her arms and Tracy rushed into them. They clung together, sobbing. The sight of her older sister and her grandmother weeping without restraint frightened Stef, so she set up a wail of her own. Jason hoisted the little girl onto his shoulder and walked down the hallway. Ginny was aware of his thoughtfulness, but right now her thoughts were with Tracy and with Candi.

"It's my fault. I killed her."

"Darling, no. You were inside with me. How could this be your fault?"

"I should have made her come in. I never do what I'm supposed to, and I say such mean things, I drive everyone away."

"You haven't driven me away."

"I did Mommy." The words were out, so was the dark secret that had rested in Tracy's heart for a long time. Only the awfulness of her sister's accident had allowed it to escape.

"You didn't drive your mother away."

"I did," Tracy insisted. "I was jealous of Candi. Mommy always paid so much attention to her, and I thought she didn't love me anymore. I hated Candi sometimes, and I was mean to her. When Mommy had Stef, she must have thought I would be mean to her too, so she felt sad and went away. She couldn't bear to be around me anymore. I tried to be a better sister to Stef. I thought if Mommy found out how good I was being, she might come back."

"Oh, my darling girl," Ginny whispered, understanding now the animosity Tracy had always directed at Candi and the fierce protectiveness she'd shown Stef. "You were the apple of your mother's eyes. Diane was so proud of you. She didn't leave because of you."

"Why, then? Why?" Tracy drew away so she could meet Ginny's gaze. Her face was red and hot. Tendrils of hair stuck to her cheeks.

"I don't know why, honey. It was something between your mother and father. You weren't to blame, just as you're not to blame now. If this accident was anyone's fault, it was mine. I knew about the ice. I should have been downstairs to warn you all about it, but I was thinking of something else and forgot about that." Ginny's voice cracked with emotion. Tracy's arms went around her.

"Don't blame yourself, Grandma. You're trying really hard."

Ginny hugged her and felt the sturdy twelve-year-old's arms respond. Their cry had made them feel better, but their fear for Candi remained. They huddled on a sofa, Tracy's head on Ginny's shoulder, and waited. Jason returned with Stef, who, now reassured, was content to sit on his lap. Each minute seemed like an hour as time dragged on.

"You know what, Grandma?" Tracy said, raising her head to look at Ginny. "When Candi gets better, I'll never say a mean thing to her again. She can tell all my secrets on the bus, and I won't care."

A nurse came into the waiting room, looked around, then approached them. "Are you the family of the little girl who fell through the ice?"

"Yes," Ginny said, getting to her feet.

"You can go in to see her for a little while. She's been asking for you, but the doctor wants her to stay overnight."

"You say she's been asking for us. She's conscious then."

"Yes. But she's had quite an ordeal, so I wouldn't tire her too much. She needs to remain quiet."

"Thank you." Ginny couldn't keep the tears from her eyes.

Jason, with Stef in his arms, was right behind Tracy and Ginny as they made their way through the doors and down the line of beds. When they came to the gurney on which Candi rested, Ginny gasped and bit her thumb to keep from crying. At first she was struck by how small and pale Candi seemed. Tubes ran from bags of fluids to thin arms resting atop stiff white sheets. Her hands were bandaged. A thin dark-haired man wearing a white coat stood at her bedside, listening to her heartbeat through a stethoscope. He smiled when he saw them and motioned them forward.

"This little girl has had a close call. Lucky for her, you found her so quickly and got her warm and applied CPR as you did."

"Will she be all right?" Ginny asked.

"She'll be fine. We want to keep an eye on her for a couple of days, and then she can come home. She'll probably have to miss school for a week or two until her feet and legs heal."

"She isn't going to lose any limbs, then?" Jason asked.

The doctor shook his head. "As I said, she's a lucky little girl. We'll have her transferred to her room soon. If you or your husband want to stay with her, you may."

Ginny glanced at Jason, a denial on her lips, but she was just too tired to utter it. He made no effort to correct the doctor either. "I'll take the girls home and stay with them. You can stay with Candi," he offered.

"Thank you, Jason, for all you've done today," Ginny said, for the first time acknowledging his effort. If it weren't for him, she knew Candi would have died beneath the ice. She hadn't had the strength to break through it as he had done.

"I'm glad she's all right," he said, and she saw his eyes redden with unshed tears. She was moved by his caring. Impulsively she rose up on her toes and kissed him on one lean cheek. He looked startled, but he didn't pull away.

"Thank you again for everything," she said warmly.

"Goodbye, Grandma," Tracy said sadly. She'd hoped Candi would wake so she could speak to her, but the gold-tipped eyelashes never stirred.

"I'll bring you back tomorrow to see her," Jason promised, putting an arm around Tracy's shoulders. Ginny noticed she didn't shrug him off as she had once done to Alex.

True to his word, Jason brought Tracy and Stef back the next morning.

"He said we could skip school today," Tracy explained, handing Ginny an overnight bag. She then turned to Candi whose wan face had lit up at the sight of her sisters. "I brought a gift to you," she said and held out a gaily wrapped package.

"For me?" Candi asked in astonishment. She tore away the tissue paper and ribbons. When she saw the carved wooden box inside, she stared at her sister disbelievingly. "This is your treasure box," she said.

"Now it's yours," Tracy replied.

"Forever?"

"Forever. But you have to promise to take good care of it."

Ginny smiled. Despite her resolve, Tracy couldn't help bossing her younger sister. Candi took it with equanimity.

As Tracy and Stef perched on the edge of their sister's bed, Jason turned to Ginny and nodded toward the overnight bag. "We weren't sure if you wanted to stay with Candi or not, so we brought you fresh clothes."

"That was really thoughtful," Ginny said,

digging through the bag. "You wouldn't have happened to remember my toothbrush?"

"It's in there."

"And toothpaste."

"It's in there."

Ginny glanced up at him and smiled. He was grinning from ear to ear at their silly parroting of a television commercial.

"Listen, I hope you don't mind that I kept the girls home from school today."

"It was probably the wisest thing to do. I don't think they would have accomplished much."

"My thinking exactly." He hitched his hands into his back pockets and regarded her. "When the going gets rough, we make a pretty good team, don't we?"

"I guess we do," Ginny agreed.

Two days later Jason came to take them home. Amid a good bit of joking and tomfoolery, Candi was escorted to the cottage and carried into it. Ginny was certain Jason was trying to help her forget her near drowning, but Candi seemed to have no qualms as Jason swept her inside. It was Ginny who stood on the porch, gazing out on the lake with hatred in her heart. A wind had come up, and dark clouds had brought dusk early. The lake bucked beneath its containing cap of ice. Part of the coating had already broken apart, and on the distant half, Ginny could see stretches of wind-roughened water.

"Are you coming in?" Jason asked from the door.

"I'm thinking about selling off the cottage," she said out loud, and knew the idea had been in the back of her mind ever since she'd learned Candi was going to live.

"That's a hasty decision." Jason came out on the porch to stare at the lake as she had done.

"I can't risk one of the girls getting hurt out there again."

"You can't run to keep them from danger," he said. "No matter where you go there will be some. You just have to teach them to respect the lake and to understand it."

Ginny slumped, one white hand gripping the railing as if she couldn't stand alone. "For the first time I'm not sure I can teach them all they need to know in order to survive."

"You taught their father, didn't you?"

"Yes, but I'm older now."

"And wiser. So you know many more things, and you can teach them."

She thought about his words and smiled gratefully. "You always know the right thing to say, don't you, Doc?"

"Not Doc, just Jason. I've been there — and

had to learn a thing or two myself." She knew he referred to his dead wife and son. She wished she could help him as he'd helped them. She placed a hand over his and squeezed it gently. His hand felt warm. Then it turned and grasped hers as if she were a lifeline he desperately needed.

"Let's go inside," she said, and he nodded. Together they left the cold porch and went where there was light and the laughter of children.

Nine

Candi's accident seemed to pull them all together. They laughed more over silly jokes, played pranks, and shared thoughts and ideas. Jason was over often now, his presence accepted without question. He had saved one of them and thus had saved them all. He was part of them, his life wrapped around theirs. The girls adored him. Stef made pictures for him at school. Tracy shopped for special foods she knew he liked and instructed Ginny as to how to make them, and Candi looked at him with adoring eyes each time he came to see her. Sometimes he brought her a small toy he'd made himself or bought in some out-of-the-way shop. Sometimes he brought a book and sat on the edge of Ginny's bed reading it to Candi.

186

Nor did he neglect the other girls, sometimes coming to take them into the village for hot chocolate or enlisting their aid in some project of his. He was boyish and charming, and he seemed as hungry for laughter and companionship as they were. Ginny knew he was drawing too close, but was unable to be the one to turn him away. He needed them, perhaps more than they needed him.

One afternoon as Candi and Stef lay on the bed watching a children's video, Ginny sat at the kitchen table going over her checkbook and considering their future. So far they'd been living on her savings, but those funds wouldn't last forever. What would she do when the money was gone? She determined to start thinking about getting a job, but she hated the thought of leaving Stef with a babysitter. A knock at the door caused her to look up. Jason was peering unabashedly through the sheer curtains. Grinning, Ginny motioned him in. Broadly he shook his head in denial and motioned her out. Ginny wrapped her arms around herself and pantomimed a shiver. Looking disgusted, Jason opened the door.

"Come here," he ordered.

"What is it?"

"I want to show you something."

"It's too cold. I don't want to go outside."

"The sun is shining; that tropical breeze is blowing."

Ginny's smile died as she thought of the awful day she'd uttered those words. "Then I'm definitely not coming out," she said, and slammed her ledger closed.

"I insist."

"You insist?" Ginny arched one eyebrow at his presumptuousness.

"I insist, and you must obey me this one time."

"Obey you?" Ginny repeated, but she allowed herself to be led to the closet to have a coat tossed over her shoulders.

"You haven't been down to the lake since the accident."

"I've been busy."

"You've been harboring a stupid notion."

"You're a psychologist and you talk to people like this?"

"I always had trouble with my bedside manner."

"Aha, the truth comes out."

As they walked around the side of the cottage, she paused, silenced by the jingle of a hundred tiny bells. She looked around, enchanted, and brought her gaze back to Jason. He was like an eager little boy wanting to share his best secret with someone.

"It's the ice hitting against the rocks," he said. "See how it's breaking up. It'll be gone by nightfall." He led her down to the shore. The sun was bright and warm on her head, the wind against her cheeks was soft; but it was the ice that claimed her attention, tossing and twinkling like a thousand diamonds. And from the rock-strewn shore came the tinkling sound of cubes in fine crystal. The day was like champagne. She drew in a breath of clear, sweet air and couldn't help expelling it on a long contented sigh.

"Me, too," Jason said, his voice quiet and filled with awe. "I never want to leave this place."

"Someday you will."

"Maybe not," he said softly. "Why should I leave God's country?"

Ginny laughed. "You're a young man. You'll want to go back to your work one day."

Jason's movement was abrupt, causing her to turn to him in surprise. He saw the flash of anxiety in her eyes and forced a smile. "You forget I am working."

"Surely you don't consider us—"

"My writing," he interrupted gently. Ginny colored and glanced away at the lake.

"Sorry. I keep forgetting about that. How's it going?"

"My detective has run into some difficulty reading the clues."

"That sounds more like real life than fiction," Ginny quipped.

"Perhaps. But we're not going to discuss Detective Hoyt. We're going to find out what's troubling Ginny Logan."

"Ah, so you are indulging in your old field of work. Sorry, Doctor, I'm not willing to be your guinea pig."

"I'm not willing to be your personal psychologist," he snapped. "But I am your friend, and what I see as a friend is a woman who's had her emotions tightly under control ever since her granddaughter walked out on this ice."

Ginny hugged herself beneath the draped coat. The air was chillier than she'd supposed. "I don't want to talk about it," she said firmly. "It's past us now. I'm never going to let anything like that happen again."

"Is that why you stick so close to the house and hound the girls every waking minute?"

"I don't *hound* them. I just watch over them better."

"How do you figure the accident was your

190

fault?" Jason's gaze was unrelenting. His normally gentle blue eyes watched her with clinical curiosity.

"What makes you think I feel that way?" she asked with irritation. "You don't know everything about everyone, Doctor. Some of us don't fit into your casebook studies."

"You're classic, lady," he answered with an impish grin that failed to disarm her. "You're feeling guilty as hell. You think you failed at something, and it almost cost your granddaughter her life. You're wrong. Your quick action helped save her."

Ginny turned away then, not wanting him to see the tears his words brought. They stung the back of her nose and made her blink rapidly. She swallowed hard, knowing he was expecting an answer.

"If I'd just been downstairs that afternoon, I would have known immediately that she was going down to the lake. But I stayed in my room, thinking about myself and . . . my problems."

"You have a right to think about yourself and your problems. If you don't work them out, you won't be much help to the girls."

"But this wasn't really a problem, except that I . . . Well, I shouldn't have been thinking of myself that day. Oh, Jason, sometimes

I'm so afraid I can't do everything I should for them."

He took hold of her shoulders and turned her to face him. "Why do you feel that way?"

"Maybe I'm too old."

"Nonsense!"

"I'm a woman alone."

"You're not alone. You have friends. You have me."

"It's not the same, Jason. You know what I mean. Children need two parents."

"Are you proposing to me?" Her outraged expression brought deep, ringing laughter from him. "What do the kids say now? Chill out, Ginny. Lighten up."

"I meant no such thing."

"I know. But you give yourself too little credit. You're terrific with the girls, but you're scared to death you'll make a mistake. Don't you realize you're less likely to make mistakes than a younger mother? You have experience behind you."

"I don't have the energy and stamina of a younger woman."

"You look pretty damn good to me. Besides, you're all the family they have left. That makes up for any shortcomings. Don't be so hard on yourself."

"Thanks, I do feel better," she admitted

grudgingly.

"I knew you would," he said smugly and, picking up a handful of acorns, concentrated on pitching them one by one at the ice. The wind soughed through the leafless trees creating a soothing melody of its own.

"This summer I'd like to teach the girls how to sail."

"Oh, Jason, I'm not sure—"

He cast her a glance, one eyebrow raised.

"They'd love it," she amended.

"Do you sail?"

"I used to." Suddenly she was looking forward to summer and all the pleasures the lake offered. "All right, Doc. I'm cured." When she laughed, he turned to look at her in frank admiration.

"The girls are lucky to have you," he said softly.

This time the affection and good will emanating from him didn't scare her. Impulsively, she took his hand and swung it between them. "Our real luck was in having a detective writer move in next door," she teased.

"Speaking of which, I'd better hightail it back to my typewriter," he said abruptly, and breaking her hold on his hand, he headed across the muddy lawn to the DeFauw cottage.

"So who's afraid now?" Ginny muttered in amazement. She'd never seen Jason at a loss. He was always so self-possessed, so aware of those around him. She thought of his dead wife, and wondered what kind of woman she had been. Much like Jason himself, she imagined. Intelligent and self-assured, with a clear idea about what she wanted from life. Thoughtfully, Ginny headed back to the cottage, left her muddy shoes just inside the door, and walked barefooted into the kitchen to make a fresh pot of coffee. She was pretty sure they wouldn't be seeing Jason this night, even if she had issued an invitation to supper. Humming a tune, she took out meat and vegetables for a roast, then on a whim hurried upstairs to check on Candi.

The children's movie was over. Stef was sound asleep, half under the covers. Candi lay back against the pillows, her eyes drooping. When she saw Ginny, she sat up.

"Were you going to sleep?" Ginny whispered, crossing to the bed. Candi held out her arms, and Ginny sat down beside her and enfolded her slim body. Candi felt even more fragile since the accident. It was painfully evident as she cuddled against Ginny.

"Was the movie good?"

Candi nodded. "Grandma, do you think

God is mad at me?"

Ginny hesitated, wondering what had prompted such a question. "I'm sure he's not. Why do you ask such a question?" If Tracy had said something, Ginny swore silently, she would take away her telephone privileges for a week.

" 'Member how you told me when I'm scared I can make a cross and that's a prayer for God?"

"Yes."

"I forgot to make a cross before I went out on the ice." Candi's face was solemn, her brows drawn together in a worried frown.

Ginny felt like laughing and crying at the same time. "God isn't angry with you, Candi. He knows what a good, kind little girl you are."

"Maybe that's why he sent you and Jason to help me," she said softly. Her hug was convulsive.

"I think so," Ginny replied, smoothing back the silken tangle of red-gold hair. "He knew how much I love you, darling."

"I love you too, Grandma."

The words had the most precious ring to them. Ginny held Candi until she fell asleep. Outside the window, the sun shone golden light, casting diamonds on a lake that had

195

turned benevolent and playful. The capricious wind blew around the corners of the cottage, whistling irreverently. The whole world was filled with the sounds and motions of life. Life! They were reaching toward it with tentative hearts, but reaching nonetheless.

"Oh, David and Scott, I wish you were here," she whispered, and suddenly thought of Diane. Where was she now? How would she feel if she knew her daughter had come so close to dying? Not wanting to think of the tall, dark-haired woman who had given the three little girls life, Ginny gently settled Candi back against the pillows and went downstairs. It had been another day of examining her emotions and weighing herself as a parent. She didn't want to deal with Diane and old memories that were still hurtful. "Think of the positive," she said, and dug down in the onion bin for the biggest one she could find for the pot roast.

When had life at the lake stopped being enough? When had she grown bored and restless? Was it the steady slapping of the waves against the shore that stirred her into an unnamed longing?

The first day Candi returned to school,

Ginny put Stef down for her nap and took her oil paints out to the debris-cluttered patio. By the time she had her palette readied and a sketch made, she'd lost interest.

Instead, she swept dead leaves and pieces of bark off the patio; then, uncovering one of the patio chairs, she slouched down in it and spent the next hour thinking of little, letting her mind roam freely. She used to get her best ideas for promotional material this way. Inevitably, her thoughts turned back to the advertising agency. She thought of pompous Burgess Osgood and some of her other accounts. She thought of Fran and Mary and the rest of the office staff, and finally she thought of Nola. The sense of betrayal was still tangible. When she thought of the younger woman, some of her old insecurities flooded back. Abruptly she got to her feet and picked up the brush. She shouldn't just sit here mulling over old hurts, she told herself, and only then did she realize she was willing to do even that if she could avoid thinking of Alex.

What was he doing? Thinking of her? Wondering what she was doing? She'd heard nothing from him since she'd left his office that day. Had he tried to contact her? Hadn't he cared that she was gone? She shook her head and dipped the brush in a mixture of Prussian Blue and Alizarin Crimson, then worked steadily for the next two hours, taking advantage of the light. She stopped only to check on Stef, who was still sleeping. When she was finished she stood back and studied her work. A bit moody, but otherwise not bad. As she gathered up her wet canvas and paints and headed inside, she caught a glimpse of Jason working on a sailboat, and waved. But he made no response. Either he hadn't seen her or he was still sorting out his own feelings. She could respect that. Hadn't he allowed her the same kind of time?

The phone was ringing when she entered the kitchen. Hastily, she dropped her paint box on the counter and leaned the wet canvas against the sink. Concern for Candi gripped her as she grabbed for the receiver.

"Hello?" she said somewhat breathlessly. "Hello? Hello?" Only the dial tone greeted her. With shaky hands, she pressed the numbers of the school's phone. "This is Candi Logan's grandmother," she explained to the woman with the perky voice. "She's a first grader there. Did you just try to reach me?"

"No, Mrs. Logan. Candi is in her classroom. She's fine." Ginny picked up the receptionist's amusement.

"Look, this is Candi's first day back in school. She nearly drowned. I just missed a phone call, and I wanted to be sure she was all right."

"Oh, I remember her, Mrs. Logan. Candi's a nice little girl. We were so glad she's in school again, but I assure you, she's just fine. Someone else must have tried to reach you."

"Sorry to have bothered you." Ginny put down the receiver. Who could have called? Jason was outdoors. She could see him through the window. And Tracy's friends were still in school. Ginny shrugged. It could have been a wrong number or a salesman or any number of things. She hurried to put away her paints, then, finding Stef awake, she decided to drive down to the school and pick up the girls. That would save them an exhausting half-hour on the noisy school bus. Quickly dressing Stef, she led her downstairs.

"Hello-o, Jason," Stef called, waving to attract his attention.

"Hi, Steffi. Where are you off to?"

"I'm going to pick up the girls. Candi's first day back at school." Ginny ushered Stef into the car.

"How's she feeling?"

"Much better, but she'll probably be tired. I've made her favorite supper. Why don't you come over and join us?"

"All right, I will." His acceptance lacked the usual enthusiasm, and she looked at him sharply. Had she offended him? Had they leaned on him too heavily during the scare over Candi? She paused, wanting to reassure him but not wanting to offend. "See you at six," she called, and got into the car.

Jason arrived early that night, wearing a flannel shirt and jeans. The girls greeted him with their usual chatter, and after they'd led him to the living room and the closed-in porch overlooking the lake, which had become a workshop in which they carried out their many projects, Jason walked back to the kitchen.

"I see you managed to escape," Ginny said over her shoulder.

"For the moment. I wanted to talk to you."

"All right, but you'll have to help. Toss the salad."

Jason took up the wooden spoon and fork and held them over the bowl of greenery. "I wanted to explain why I've been so aloof the past few days."

"You don't have to." Ginny turned from the oven, her cheeks pink, her eyes shining.

She held a pan of hot homemade bread. Quickly, she set it upside down on a cooling rack. Jason watched her move about the kitchen. She wore a jogging suit, the uniform of most women these days, but on her it looked elegant. While she worked, taking the bread, brown and crisp, from the pan, he studied the sleek delicate lines of her back and shoulders, her slim legs. The bulky suit hid her body, but he could see the fineness of collarbone and chin. She was graceful, delicate, sensuous, yet not even aware of her effect on men. She treated herself as an asexual being, though she was one of the most alluring women he'd ever met. A perfect loaf of hot bread rested on the rack, and Ginny turned triumphantly, her face beaming with pride.

"Voilà. Nothing to it," she said, taking a bow. Then, seeing his somber face, she turned serious. "I know why you stayed away, Jason," she admitted, and on her face was naked truth. "For the same reason I hid in my room the day Candi had her accident." She walked toward him and put a hand on his arm. He could smell her perfume, light and flowery, mingling with the far more seductive scent of fresh-baked bread. She seemed a combination of all things a woman is sup-

posed to be.

"I understand that we're both vulnerable. We've both suffered terrible losses. We're drawn to each other because of this. Let's not confuse feelings of friendship with anything else."

"You're right."

"I need your friendship, Jason. Nothing more. And you needn't feel threatened by me."

"I'll remember that, Dr. Logan."

She grinned then, and her eyes flashed and her nose wrinkled slightly. When she patted him on his arm, much as a mother would a beloved child, he didn't fight it. His days and nights had been filled with longings for Susan, for the sound of his baby's cry. Now tears sprang to his eyes, and impulsively Ginny cupped his whiskered chin.

"You're not alone either, Jason. We're here when you need us."

"Thanks. That's helped me a lot."

They said no more. Their needs were too painful to talk about. What they wanted they couldn't have. They wanted their loved ones back. Wanted to hear a voice, feel a familiar touch—and no one else could give that to them. They were afraid to reach out, afraid they'd demand too much, afraid they'd give too little. They were crippled, and didn't know if they'd ever be completely healed. Yet they turned to each other, because only someone just as injured could understand. They'd hidden their own needs in concern for the children. Now they had time to feel again, and their pain was greater than they'd ever imagined. It might defeat them after all.

"Call the girls. Let's eat before this culinary achievement of mine cools off."

"Smells delicious." He paused before the wet canvas she'd hung in the back hall to dry. "This is new."

"I painted it this afternoon."

"You're very talented. Have you sold any of your paintings?"

"I've never tried to. It's just a hobby."

"You always have another surprise tucked up your sleeve," he said, shaking his head.

They gathered around the table, the adults drinking in the laughter and chatter of the children, the girls glowing in the undivided attention of Ginny and Jason. And when the night was over and the children had gone to bed, Jason stood at the door in his light jacket, smiling at Ginny.

"Thanks, friend," he said softly. "I needed this."

"We're here all the time, Jason. Come over

when you need us. Don't try to get through the bad times on your own."

"I'll remember that. Good night."

He bent to kiss her temple, and she sent him off with soft reassuring pats on the back. Then she watched him cross the lawn to his own house, thinking of how he must suffer beneath the lighthearted exterior he often showed the world. The devils had got him in the past few days, but she wouldn't let them keep him. She'd fight for Jason, and so would the girls.

Ten

The weeks slid into the warmth of spring. Each day started fresh and new. The grief was still there—it always would be—but now it was blunted by the smell of freshly mowed grass and budding trees. Ginny no longer parked her car in the DeFauw garage, but left it in her own driveway. Jason came and went. When she hadn't seen him for several days, she knew he was going through a bad time. She respected his need for privacy, but she worried about him. And when he returned to them, the smiling, warm man they knew, she searched his face for some sign he'd at last buried his devils.

The hot flashes continued to plague her, and finally she gave in and made an appointment with the local doctor. He seemed so young. Funny, all the men she met lately were young. When had she become an older woman? Dr.

Robinson greeted her with kind words and patted her hand, then gave her a prescription for hormone patches which she filled at the corner drugstore.

"Having hot flashes, are you?" the pharmacist said from behind his counter.

Ginny glanced around and reluctantly grunted an affirmative.

"My wife takes these. They help some." This man was not young, but he couldn't stop talking. Other customers were milling around, waiting for prescriptions to be filled. The pharmacist seemed unconcerned, greeting all of them by name and inquiring about each customer's health or the health of a spouse. By the time Ginny left the pharmacy, she knew all about Mrs. Hughes's arthritis and Mrs. Lerner's kidney infection, and she was equally certain everyone in town would soon know of her need for hormones. Distracted, she stopped at the grocery store and picked up some food for supper. Jason McCann was standing in the driveway when she drove in. The bus had just dropped the girls off.

"Hi," she called, getting out of the car and reaching for a grocery bag. Stef climbed out and ran to Jason.

"I just chased a raccoon over here," he

called. "He's been raiding my garbage cans at night."

"Where is he?" Ginny looked around. Jason pointed to a bushy-tailed creature with black rings around its eyes. "He looks like a bandit."

"Oooh, look at the puppy," Candi cried, running up.

"That's not a puppy, girls. Don't get too near him. He's wild, and he might have rabies."

"Look, he's shivering. He's scared," Tracy pointed out.

"Let me help you get your groceries in." Jason reached for a couple of brown bags.

"Wait, I have some things—" Ginny's words ended with a tearing sound. One of the bags had given out, and groceries rolled everywhere. The package from the pharmacy fell onto the ground. Ginny made a grab for it, but Jason had already knelt and scooped it up. She snatched the package from his hand, gathered up the groceries, and stormed into the kitchen, where she leaned on the kitchen sink fighting to calm herself. The girls stayed in the yard watching the raccoon.

Slowly, Ginny drank a glass of water, and when she felt reasonably calm again, she went outdoors. Her granddaughters were still studying the raccoon, and the rest of the groceries, neatly packed into one bag, sat on the back porch. But Jason was nowhere in sight. Ginny looked over at the DeFauw cottage, then went back inside and began putting the food away. Curiously, she looked at the box of hormone patches. God how she hated to give in to the idea that she needed them! She put the package away.

After supper, when the girls were in bed, she took out the box and read the instructions again, then opened one of the packets. Carefully, she peeled away the covering and then contemplated the best place to stick the patch. She finally decided on the fatty part of her buttocks. The patch was flesh colored and barely noticeable, but she glared at it before sighing in acceptance. "I guess I'll call this my patch-on-the-ass time of life," she told her reflection before she set about creaming her face.

In the days that followed she forgot about the patch, except when she showered or needed to change it. After a few days she began to feel less depressed, and the prickling heat that began at her scalpline and melted her makeup had abated somewhat.

May had arrived. Its warmer temperatures had the girls dipping a thermometer in the lake. "Not yet," she told them time and again when they tried to convince her the water was warm enough for swimming. She decided flowers would be nice along the walk and beside the porch. With the danger of frost well past, she drove to the nearest garden center and purchased a colorful assortment of plants. Then, eyeing the late afternoon sunlight, she put on a pair of shorts and the T-shirt the girls had given her for Mother's Day. Soon she was engrossed in getting the plants in the ground, placing them so their colorful blossoms would be shown off to advantage. Sweat beaded her forehead, but she wiped it away. This time it was different. It came from exertion and the rising temperature. She felt good.

After watering the plants, she realized she was tired and paused to rest, her bare legs stretched out before her, her head thrown back so her sweaty, dirt-streaked face was exposed to the warm sun. Tomorrow I'll have freckles, she thought, then shrugged the thought away. She was enjoying this too much to worry about such things. She shifted, and her glance automatically went to the DeFauw cottage. She hadn't seen Jason for days. Now she sat thinking about him, remembering the hurt look on his face. Impulsively, she got to her feet and, brushing off her fanny, walked through the hedge.

"Jason?" she called walking up on the back steps of the cottage. The door was open. She could see a puddle of water just inside on the floor. Ginny knocked and called out again. Is Jason gone? she wondered. Surely, he wouldn't leave without closing the back door. Puzzled, she walked out to the garage and looked in the window. Jason's jeep sat in its usual place. Troubled now, she headed back to the cottage and knocked again. The puddle of water gleamed up at her as if conveying a message. How had it got there? It looked as if rain had blown in, but there had been no rain, not since yesterday's brief shower.

Alarmed, Ginny tried the screen door. It was open. Stepping inside, she looked around. She'd never been in the DeFauw cottage before. She took in the neat countertop and the stack of plates drying in the rack on the sink. She wasn't surprised to find that Jason was an orderly man. She moved on into the large room that overlooked the lake and served as a combination living and dining room. Comfortable sofas sat across from each other at one end. Small tables and easy chairs filled the rest of the room. Tucked into one corner was a desk bearing a typewriter and stacks of paper. This is where he works, she thought, glancing about. From the desk he had an open view of the lake and of their cottage. No wonder he'd come over so often, drawn probably by the sound of children at play. She sensed the loneliness of his existence and grieved for him. Turning to the stairs, she took a tentative step.

"Jason?" she called out. The house was silent, too silent for a living presence. "Fool," she muttered to herself, and quickly mounted the stairs.

She found him in the east bedroom. That, too, faced their cottage. He lay sprawled on the single bed, still in rumpled jeans and shirt. His eyes were closed, his skin clammy and feverish. An empty whiskey bottle lay nearby. She wasn't sure if he was in a drunken stupor or very ill. In either state, he needed care.

"Wake up, Jason. Come on, wake up. It's Ginny." She shook him, trying to get him to respond, but he only grunted and rolled away from her. His breath was foul.

Suddenly she was pulling off his boots, unzipping those impossible jeans and slipping them down his long, hairy legs. She got him under the covers, gathered up the empty bottle, and made her way downstairs. In his cupboard she found instant coffee and a single can of soup. The man simply wasn't buying food for himself. How long had it been since he'd eaten decently? Since he'd last had supper with them, she decided. She made the coffee and warmed the soup. With a mug in each hand, she headed back upstairs. He lay as she'd left him.

Setting down the mugs, she went to the bathroom and held a washcloth under the tap. Returning to the bedroom, she wiped his face and neck, then settled the cloth on his forehead. When it became warm she returned to the bathroom and ran cold water on it. This time she got a response. Jason cursed and flung the cloth aside. His eyes were open now, bloodshot and glaring. When he finally focused on her, he gasped and lay back.

"Ginny, what are you doing here?"

"Administering first aid to a friend," she replied.

"Go 'way. Have hangover."

"Yep, I'd say that's true. But you also have a fever. You have to eat something." She picked up the mug of soup and held a spoonful out to him.

"No, no. Leave me 'lone." He pushed her hand away, spilling soup on the bedcover.

212

Ginny put the spoon into the mug and reached over to deliver a light tap on his cheek. Jason's head swung around, his reddened eyes glaring at her balefully.

"I am going to offer you another spoonful of soup," she said crisply, "and you are not going to splash it all over the bed, are you?" When she held the next spoonful to his lips, he dutifully opened his mouth. Soon the soup was all swallowed. "Now you may have some coffee," she said, and sat on the bed beside him so she could support his head and shoulders. His hands were shaky as he tried to hold the mug. When he'd taken a few sips, he gently pushed the mug away and turned his head into her shoulder.

"Leave me alone, Ginny. I'm not worth the trouble."

"I think you are," she said softly, and ran her hands through his hair. "I told you, you're not alone. We're right next door. We love you, the girls and I. You're a good man. You don't deserve what happened to you any more than we do. But bad things can happen to good people, and when they do, we just have to find a way to go on, to believe in ourselves again."

He cried then, turning in toward her. His head was heavy on her shoulder, but she wouldn't have shifted away from him for the world. His hoarse sobs were raw with pain, filled with loneliness and desperation. She rocked him as a mother would a child and uttered wordless, soothing sounds that she hoped eased his pain. At last the awful weeping ended and he pulled away, wiping at his eyes and sniffling. His face was ravaged.

"I can't take the lonely nights," he whispered. "The silence. Susan used to sing all the time, the way you do when you're busy. And Bobby!" He swallowed hard. "He was such a little guy, but when he wasn't crying, he was cooing and babbling already. I used to say he was going to be a talker like his mom." A sob cut off his words. He turned. His back to her now, he hugged a pillow to his chest while his frame shuddered with the effort not to cry.

"It's all right," she said. "You have a right to weep."

Tears were running unchecked down her cheeks as her hands soothed him, patting his shoulders, smoothing his hair. She talked to him, she hummed. She did whatever she sensed would make him feel that he wasn't alone, that another being was in the big empty house with him. At last he slept, whimpering now and then like a hurt child. When she was sure his

214

slumber was sound, she hurried down to nursery school to pick up Stef.

After a quick lunch, the two of them walked hand in hand over to Jason's cottage. Ginny settled Stef in for a nap in one of the spare bedrooms and then sat by Jason. He stirred several times in his sleep before a sound at the door made Ginny look around.

"I can't sleep in a strange bedroom all by myself," Stef pouted. "Can I lay down with Jason?"

"Bring your blanket," Ginny instructed. "You'll have to be very quiet so you don't wake him." She tucked the three-year-old on top of the covers, spreading her little blanket over her, and Stef soon fell asleep at Jason's side. Ginny looked down on the two of them, thinking of everyone's fundamental need to love and be loved. Finally she dozed in the chair until a sound roused her. Jason was awake. His arm was curved around Stef. While Ginny watched he placed a tender kiss on the little girl's cheek. His own cheeks were wet with tears. He looked around and saw Ginny watching him.

"Thanks," he said quietly, and she felt like weeping for him all over again. How little he needed. How much he gave. When Stef awoke and got up, Ginny left her telling Jason a story and hurried home to greet the girls.

"Where's Stef?" Tracy asked.

"Next door," Ginny told them. "Jason's been ill. Do you want to go visit him while I make supper?"

"Sure," Tracy said. "Come on, Candi."

Ginny worked quickly, whipping up a chicken casserole and setting it in the oven. She was just reaching for a head of lettuce when the phone rang. Thinking it was Tracy calling from Jason's, she picked up the receiver and spoke into it.

"Ginny. Thank God, I've found you!" Her thoughts were so centered on Jason and the girls, she didn't at first recognize the voice that had once been so familiar to her.

"Ginny?" Alex Russell said when she made no answer. "Are you there?"

"I'm here. You just caught me by surprise. How did you know where to find me?"

"I didn't. Nola and I have been searching for months. We didn't know where the cottage was. We hoped you had gone there. We even checked with Scott's housekeeper, but she said she didn't know where you were."

"Marnie told you that?"

"She told Nola," Alex answered. "We've been

216

so worried. Finally I took a map and started calling information for every little town in southern Michigan. I felt like a goddamn detective. But when I finally got your number, I couldn't get anyone to answer."

Hearing the frustration in his voice, conflicting emotions clawed at Ginny. "I'm sorry to have caused you so much trouble," she said. "I just wanted to get away from everything."

There was a pause at the other end of the wire, and she could picture him raking his hands through his hair. "How are you?"

Memories came. Of long lonely evenings when she'd groped for some explanation for Scott's death. And of Alex's voice, warm and strong, drifting over the wire. She was stronger now. She no longer needed his strength, but she still wanted his friendship. She hadn't realized how much she'd missed him.

"I'm fine. This was a good move. The girls are doing better in school—Stef's even saying her *r* properly. Candi fell through the ice, but we got her out. She spent a couple of nights in the hospital, but she's recovered now. And with the lake warming up, all the girls think about is going swimming."

He laughed, a rich, warm chuckle. "You sound happier, Ginny."

"I am. We're mending."

"When are you coming back?"

She hesitated, thinking of her dwindling checkbook. But the thought of Nola pretending to have talked to Marnie gave her pause. Why hadn't Alex called Marnie himself? She would have told any friend or business acquaintance where Ginny was. Nola had lied, and Alex had believed her. Not really, she reminded herself. He was on the phone with her now because he hadn't been willing to take Nola's word that she couldn't be found.

"I'm not coming back, Alex," she said quietly. "I made my decision, and I won't change it."

"You can't mean that." She heard the catch in his voice.

"I do."

"I won't accept that as your final decision."

"You'll have to."

"Not until I've had a chance to talk to you face-to-face."

"That won't make a difference."

"It might. When can I come there to see you?"

Ginny looked around the old-fashioned kitchen with its round table and oaken chairs, its open shelves and brick chimney. Alex just wouldn't fit in here, but she didn't know how to tell him so without hurting his feelings.

"Grandma, are you coming over? Jason needs you," Candi called through the screen door.

"I'm coming. Alex, I have to go. The girls need me."

"When can I see you?"

"It's not a good idea, Alex. I have to go. Goodbye."

"Ginny!"

She hung up on his outraged cry, trying to tell herself that part of her life was behind her. Alex was just an old friend who no longer fit into her new lifestyle.

Her thoughts turned to Jason who was next door and who certainly needed her. Was his fever worse? Were the girls wearing him out? She checked the casserole and then hurried after Candi. She could hear the girls' bright chatter from the bottom of the stairs. When she reached the bedroom door, she saw that they'd set up a monopoly board at the foot of Jason's bed. His face was set, and he only grunted monosyllabic answers to their questions. Ginny hurried forward.

"What's wrong? Candi said you need me?"

Jason looked at her with grateful eyes. "I

have a problem," he said. "I have to go to the bathroom, but I can't walk there by myself."

"He fell down when he stood up," Tracy said. "I made him lie down again."

"Tracy and I will help you," Ginny said, reaching for the covers.

Jason jerked them to him, tucking them around his waist while he glanced askance at the girls. "I don't have any pants on," he muttered to Ginny.

She stifled a grin. "Girls, why don't you run next door and get washed up for supper. I'll be right over."

When her granddaughters had left the room, she looked at Jason. "Well?"

He slung one foot off the bed and the other, then tried to rise. The coverlet slipped as he swayed and grabbed for a chair.

"For heaven's sake." Ginny yanked the cover away. "I'm the one who took off your pants. I've seen many a man without his trousers."

He grinned then, standing there in his flannel shirt and white cotton briefs, his long, hairy legs reminiscent of a gangling giraffe's. "Many a man?" he teased.

"Well, a couple of men, many a time," she amended and, placing his arm over her shoulders, helped him to the bathroom. "Do you need me to come in with you?"

"I think I can manage," he said, his cheeks turning ruddy.

"Hah!" she retorted, and let him go in alone. She fluffed the pillows and straightened his covers while she waited. When she heard him shuffling along the hall, she ran to help him.

"Why didn't you call me?"

"I thought I could make it. Don't know why I feel so weak."

"You've had a fever, and drinking all that whiskey when you were sick didn't help much. When was the last time you had a decent meal?"

"I'm not hungry. I feel like I could sleep for a week."

"Rest while I go feed the girls," she said, settling him on the bed and tucking the covers around him. "I'll bring you over a plate of hot food."

"You don't have to."

"I want to."

"Ginny." He caught her hand and gripped it for a moment. "Thanks."

"You've said that already," she reminded him brusquely. "Do you want me to turn on the television so you can watch the news?"

He nodded, and she switched on the small color set on the dresser. Adjusting the sound, she handed him the remote control and headed back downstairs. She was worried about Jason. His face was weary, as if he'd used up all his emotion and was just drifting now.

She hurried to finish supper. She was running late. The girls still had homework to do and baths to take, and there were bedtime stories to be read. When she got back to Jason, he was fast asleep and she hadn't the heart to wake him. She left the tray on his night table, in case he woke, then slowly made her way back to her own cottage.

The sky was star studded, the scented night air was warm and sensuous on her skin. Ginny walked down to the lake and gazed out over the water. The distant lights of other cottages were reflected in its dark mirrorlike surface. People were returning now for the summer.

She felt less alone and yet somehow lonelier. In those lighted houses people were laughing and loving—and belonging to one another. She had the girls, and God knew she loved them above all else, but was this all of life there was for her? She felt her mortality, standing there and gazing across the water, and she wondered if she'd already experienced what life had to offer her. The years since David's death had been lonely, difficult ones, and she'd given no thought to loving again. But now she thought of how it had felt to be held by a man, to be aware of passion surging between them.

She thought of Alex, so far away and no longer a part of her life. Thinking of him made her more lonely. She thought of Jason and smiled. She could still remember the feel of his body beneath the flannel shirt — warm and real and very masculine.

Ginny turned toward the cottage. She couldn't just stand in the yard, mooning like a sixteen-year-old over a much younger man. Maybe I'm taking too many hormones, she thought. Then she closed the back door and locked out the star-filled night and those secret longings.

Eleven

May was winding down amid days so hot they promised an impossible summer. The fluted tulips hung limply from their stalks, and the lilac blooms that filled the air with their sweet, cloying scent had begun to turn brown. The trees were fully leafed now, their shade welcome on the patio where Ginny and the girls had begun to take the evening meal. And the pansies and pinks Ginny had planted were already making a showy display of the flower-beds.

Under the onslaught of the sun, the water became warm enough for the girls to don their swimsuits. Dick Chalmers had long since come and put in the dock and boat. Despite the steadily diminishing amount in her checkbook, Ginny bought a paddle boat for the girls, and she often sat on the patio watching its gay canvas awning bob around the shoreline, powered by the churning brown legs of the girls.

If winter had given them long contented evenings before a blazing fire, summer gave them movement and energy and a new zest for life. Scott's death seemed less immediate. They were healing.

As Marnie had once been, Jason was now a part of their lives, someone who had come when they needed him most. Having already learned to substitute Marnie for the mother who had disappeared from their young lives, the girls now adopted Jason.

"They're great kids," Jason said. He sprawled on a patio chair as he watched the older girls cannon-ball off the raft.

"They are pretty terrific," Ginny answered. "I'm going to hate not being here with them all summer."

Jason looked at her in surprise. "What do you mean?"

"I have to go to work, Jason. I'm running out of money."

"Why didn't you say something? I have money."

"You have enough money to live on while you write your book," she said. "But that might take years."

"I have plenty. Besides, I could always take

on some patients, open an office or something."

Ginny shook her head. "You aren't responsible for us, remember? Besides, I'm not desperate yet. I still have some funds, but not enough to last till the girls are through school. I just thought if I went to work again, I could make sure they have everything they want."

"Like paddle boats?" he teased. "What will you do about the girls while you're working?"

She smiled. "That's the best part of all." She leaned forward in her eagerness. "I've been trying to convince Marnie to come live with us ever since we left Detroit, but she wouldn't. She was born there and declared she was a 'city gal.' When I called and told her I had to go back to work, though, she said right away she'd come and stay through the summer." Ginny laughed with delight. "I think she's missed the girls."

Jason watched her lively face a moment before he turned to stare out over the lake. "Do you have any idea what you'll do?"

"I already have a job interview."

"In advertising?"

A cloud dimmed the radiant smile. She shook her head once, matter-of-factly. "I didn't feel like working in advertising again. I'm interviewing for a receptionist job at a women's crisis center."

"Won't you be bored at such a low-level job?"

"I don't know. Besides I haven't got it yet."

"They'd be a fool not to take you."

Ellen McCallan looked at Ginny over her half-rimmed glasses and tossed her sandy blond hair over her shoulder. "What makes a woman in your position want to come to work here as a receptionist?"

"I honestly don't know," Ginny answered. She liked McCallan. Although this woman was about Nola's age, Ginny sensed a wariness in her and an impatience to reach out and help make the world better — tempered by determination.

"I've gone through so many major changes in the past few months, I just feel this is something I'd like to do. I can get references, very good references. I was with Russell and Taylor for more than ten years."

"I don't doubt your word on that, Mrs. Logan," Ellen McCallan said slowly. Her glance slid over Ginny's Anne Klein suit and Ferragamo shoes. "I need someone who's dedicated

227

to helping a woman who isn't sure where her family's next meal is coming from, a woman who isn't sure she can survive the next beating her husband dishes out. It's not pretty here at the clinic. Even a receptionist is called on to deal with people in crisis. And she's their first contact with us. If you're not sympathetic to some woman's plight, you may scare her away from a badly needed haven."

"It's true I don't have any personal experience with these kinds of problems, but I'm a woman—and I've had my own share of sorrow. I hope you'll give me a chance. Someone surely must have been willing to give you one."

Ellen's head came up. Behind the glasses, her gray eyes looked defenseless for a moment; then she shrugged and leaned back in her swivel chair. "I first came to the clinic as the victim of an abusive husband," she said. "I had nowhere else to turn. The clinic was my lifeline in those days."

Ginny stared at her in amazement. Surely this self-possessed, no-nonsense woman had never allowed herself to be abused. Yet something in Ellen McCallan's eyes, some tiny tremor of vulnerability, revealed that she spoke the truth.

"I'm sorry," Ginny said getting to her feet.

"Wait." Ellen's voice was warm. "I didn't mean to imply you have to be a victim yourself to work here."

"I can see that it would help in identifying with the problems some women have," Ginny answered, but she sat down again. She wanted this job, and it had nothing to do with her need for an income.

"I just don't want you to be shocked by the stories you're going to hear," Ellen was saying. "Do you think you can take it?"

"Yes, I do," Ginny replied. "If not, you can fire me."

"Come on, then, and I'll introduce you to the staff." Ellen got to her feet and led the way out of the office. "We're crowded for space as you'll see," she said over her shoulder. "We've had to improvise to have enough cubicles to allow minimal privacy." She swung around a half-wall. "This is Dr. Robert Schur. He's one of our licensed psychologists."

The burly man stood up and held out a fleshy hand. "Also known as For Sure Dr. Bob," he said. Humor brightened his pale eyes, and he pulled at his graying beard.

"Ginny's coming to work as our receptionist," Ellen explained.

"Welcome." Bob Schur took her hand in a

quick grip, then raised both his hands to the ceiling. "And thanks be to Allah!"

"As you can see, we're pretty desperate for someone to handle the front desk and phone," Ellen said, already leading the way down the tiny hall to the next cubicle. "Your job, besides the routine procedures, will involve talking briefly to the women who call or come into the clinic—and directing each one to the right person to help her. We have three psychologists, one psychiatrist, a nurse, and three counselors. They're not always here all the time. Some of them donate their time. Pam?" Ellen hailed an overweight, middle-aged woman with a load of mail in her hands. "Pam is our mail clerk. She's been with us for six months, and she's doing a super job."

The woman's round face broke into a cheerful grin, revealing a broken tooth. When she looked at Ellen, her expression revealed her gratitude. "I do my bes' for you, Ms. McCallan," she said. Ginny wondered if Pam had lost her teeth at the hands of an abusive husband.

"Is Norma in today, Pam?" Ellen asked, swinging off down the hall.

"She's in her office," Pam replied. Ginny hurried to catch up with Ellen. She'd begun to discern a restless energy in her and guessed the well-run center revolved around the energy this woman evoked.

"Norma, we have help."

"At last." A petite black woman turned to greet Ginny. "If I have to answer those phones one more day I'll go out of my mind."

"Don't scare her away before she starts," Ellen said, noticing the look on Ginny's face.

Ginny grinned. "I'm tougher than that."

Ellen studied her and then nodded as if she'd made up her mind about something. "I'll bet you are," she said quietly. Ginny felt like beaming with pride at this praise. She followed Ellen in and out of cluttered cubicles and was led at last to the even more cluttered front desk, on which a phone shrilled.

"This is your chance," Ellen said. "You want to take it?"

"Sure." Ginny picked up the phone.

"Is Dr. Bob there?" a soft female voice asked.

"I'll check and see. May I say who's calling?"

"Just tell him Jo."

"Jo who?" Ginny asked, picking up a pencil and pad.

"Just Jo. He'll know who I am."

Ellen was signaling to her. "Just a moment please." Ginny put her hand over the receiver. "She doesn't want to give her name."

"Often, they won't. Just connect her with Bob. He'll know who she is. She may be afraid to reveal her name—or ashamed. Many women think they're to blame for what's happening to them." Ginny put the call through, thinking of the hesitant voice on the phone.

"Can you handle this?" Ellen asked, sensing her mood.

"I want to try," Ginny answered. She'd come looking for a job, and already she felt involved in something far greater than a mere desire to make money.

"I think you'll do fine," Ellen said warmly. "Can you start tomorrow?"

"Monday. That's when Marnie arrives to help with my grandchildren."

"I'm looking forward to getting to know you better, Ginny," Ellen said, holding out her hand. Her gaze was frank and direct, her manner friendly and easy, yet Ginny had already seen the intensity of her response to the woman who had called.

"And I'd like to know you better," Ginny answered honestly. A phone shrilled again.

"That's my phone. I'll talk to you on Monday." With that burst of energy that seemed to mark most of her movements, Ellen turned toward her office.

Feeling rather dazed, Ginny made her way out to her car. On the way home she thought of the woman called Jo. What calamity had befallen her that she needed to talk to Dr. Bob? What had caused the tremor in her voice? And Ellen. What kind of man could have struck a woman so imbued with kindness and generosity of spirit?

Jason was in his back yard when she parked the car. "How'd it go?" he called, looking up from the sailboat he was recaulking.

"I got the job," Ginny said, and she wandered over to sit on a sawhorse and watch him work. She was quiet, reflecting on all that had occurred.

"Why so pensive? Wasn't the pay any good?" Jason's eyes were very blue against his new tan. He'd taken off his shirt and had tossed it aside as he worked. He'd filled out since she'd first met him, and she couldn't help thinking that she'd had something to do with it. She invited him over several times a week, and when he didn't eat with them, she nagged him to be sure he ate properly. Yes, he'd put on weight, and his chores had firmed the muscles in his arms and shoulders. He looked fit for the first time since she'd met him. In fact, she thought, glancing away from his bare chest, he looks a little too fit.

"Ginny?"

She stirred and shook her head. "The pay was adequate. The job's just not what I expected."

"Don't take it, then." He paused, studying her.

At these words, she looked up. "I couldn't bear not to," she said. "I would always wonder. I have a feeling I haven't taken on just a job, but a way of life. I'm not sure I can handle that much commitment. I'm already committed to the girls. Maybe I've made a mistake."

"Tell me about it," Jason said, putting down his brush. He listened, watching her sensitive face rapidly change expressions. He hadn't seen her so dressed up before. He studied the expensive suit and shoes, the long sexy legs encased in expensive stockings. This must be the way she looked back in that other life she lived in the city. She seemed alien to him somehow, and yet she was the same giving Ginny who'd first touched his life.

He listened to her clear voice and watched

the way her eyes crinkled when she was amused, the way her irises darkened when she was moved by something. She has a right to be concerned, he thought. She's not the sort of woman to hold back. At least not now. He guessed she'd held back from life in the past, but no longer. She was committed, fully committed, and she was scared. But not cowardly. When she had finished talking and sat staring out at the lake, he picked up his brush and went back to work on the wooden hull.

"What should I do?" she asked finally.

He looked up at her, surprised, a half-smile curving his lips. "I thought you'd already made up your mind," he said quietly.

Ginny laughed. "I guess I have. Why is it I always seem to bite off too much?"

"Because that's your nature, and now that you know about those women and that center you could no more walk away from them than you can from the girls."

"Thanks, pal," Ginny scolded, sliding off her perch. "I don't need this."

He sobered. "I think this is just what you do need."

"Time will tell. If you end up with a madwoman as your neighbor, remember, I came to you for advice."

"You're tough. You'll survive. You handled me, didn't you?"

"Oh, Jason," she reached out and ran a hand through his tousled hair. He caught her hand and carried it to his mouth, his blue eyes capturing her gaze. She colored as his lips touched her skin and jerked her hand away.

"I . . . I . . ." Her mouth opened and closed as she grappled for something to say, something disarming and innocent that would put their relationship back on a safe footing.

"Think you hear someone calling you, right?" he said, grinning. She flushed.

"Right!" she snapped and hurried back to her own yard.

He watched her go, waiting until she'd reached the porch, then he let out a long wolf whistle. She glanced back at him, her eyes too big and too serious; then her lips curved into a smile, and tossing her head, she sashayed across the porch, punctuating her exit with a well-executed bump and grind. He went back to caulking the boat, but he kept thinking of Ginny. He'd never met a woman like her. Just when he thought he knew her pretty well, she surprised him. She was a woman of many layers. He'd like to peel away some of them, especially the expensive suits and silky nylons. He liked her best when she was running around in shorts, freckles on her nose, her knees dirty from weeding.

"Ginny?"

"Alex!"

"I'm coming down this weekend."

"You can't."

"Why not?"

"I'm—I'm busy. I'm just starting a new job, and I'm not organized yet."

"I'm bringing Marnie."

"I can come in to get her."

"I want to bring her."

She was silent.

"Are you trying to avoid me?"

"I just don't think it's a good idea to see you just now. I'm awfully busy and—"

"Why did you get a job?"

"I need the money."

"I've made you a partner in the business. You can have your dividends quarterly or monthly, however you want them. I've set up an account for you."

"Alex, I wish you hadn't."

"I told you I was going to."

"I won't take the money."

"It's a done deed. I'll bring you the information on your account."

"I won't take your money."

"It's your money too. You've certainly earned it. The agency wouldn't be what it is without you."

"I got paid for my work."

"This is a bonus."

"Alex, please. I don't want it, and I do not wish to discuss it any further."

"Can I come down?"

"Not just now."

"I promised Marnie."

"I'll come and get her."

"Will you have dinner with me, then?"

"I don't think so, Alex."

"My God, Ginny, what have I done that's so horrible we can't even have dinner together?"

"Oh, Alex, you haven't done anything. Please don't make me feel guilty. I just need some time. I don't mean to offend you."

"Offend me?"

"Try to understand."

"I'll try, but I don't think I can. Who's your new job with?"

"I'm a receptionist at a woman's crisis center."

"You'll be good at it."

238

"Thanks for all you're trying to do."

"The Fourth of July."

"What?"

"If you haven't called to invite me down for the Fourth of July, I'm going to drop in on you. Be prepared. That's a whole month away."

"I know." She had hurt him by refusing to allow him to come down, yet he wouldn't give up. How many times had he swallowed his pride for her? "Alex, you are invited to the lake for the weekend of the Fourth of July," she said grandly.

"Thank you. I'll have to check my calendar."

She laughed then. He heard it over the miles of wire and wished she were closer. He wanted to see her, to know she was well and happy. She sounded happy—like the old Ginny.

"God, I miss you," he said, and the warmth in his voice made her shiver. He waited for her to say something back, but she didn't. She never had.

"I'll see you on the Fourth, Ginny. Take care and congratulations on your new job."

"Goodbye, Alex." Ginny replaced the receiver and sat staring out the window at Jason Mc-Cann, working on his boat. What was wrong with her? She was like one of those horrible, frustrated, sex-starved women the newspaper

239

article had likened her to. Here she sat, lusting after two men, certain she needed nothing more from either one than a satisfying roll in the hay.

"Maybe it's a good thing you're going to work at the crisis center," she muttered to herself. "At least you'll have help close by when you really go off your rocker."

MORE PASSION AND ADVENTURE AWAIT... YOUR TRIP TO A BIG ADVENTUROUS WORLD BEGINS WHEN YOU ACCEPT YOUR FIRST 4 NOVELS ABSOLUTELY *FREE*
(AN $18.00 VALUE)

Accept your Free gift and start to experience more of the passion and adventure you like in a historical romance novel. Each Zebra novel is filled with proud men, spirited women and tempestuous love that you'll remember long after you turn the last page.

Zebra Historical Romances are the finest novels of their kind. They are written by authors who really know how to weave tales of romance and adventure in the historical settings you love. You'll feel like you've actually gone back in time with the thrilling stories that each Zebra novel offers.

GET YOUR FREE GIFT WITH THE START OF YOUR HOME SUBSCRIPTION

Our readers tell us that these books sell out very fast in book stores and often they miss the newest titles. So Zebra has made arrangements for you to receive the four newest novels published each month.

You'll be guaranteed that you'll never miss a title, and home delivery is so convenient. And to show you just how easy it is to get Zebra Historical Romances, we'll send you your first 4 books absolutely FREE! Our gift to you just for trying our home subscription service.

BIG SAVINGS AND FREE HOME DELIVERY

Each month, you'll receive the four newest titles as soon as they are published. You'll probably receive them even before the bookstores do. What's more, you may preview these exciting novels free for 10 days. If you like them as much as we think you will, just pay the low preferred subscriber's price of just $3.75 each. *You'll save $3.00 each month off the publisher's price.* AND, your savings are even greater because there are never any shipping, handling or other hidden charges—FREE Home Delivery. Of course you can return any shipment within 10 days for full credit, no questions asked. There is no minimum number of books you must buy.

4 FREE BOOKS

TO GET YOUR 4 FREE BOOKS WORTH $18.00 — MAIL IN THE FREE BOOK CERTIFICATE T O D A Y

Fill in the Free Book Certificate below, and we'll send your FREE BOOKS to you as soon as we receive it.

If the certificate is missing below, write to: Zebra Home Subscription Service, Inc., P.O. Box 5214, 120 Brighton Road, Clifton, New Jersey 07015-5214.

FREE BOOK CERTIFICATE

4 FREE BOOKS

ZEBRA HOME SUBSCRIPTION SERVICE, INC.

YES! Please start my subscription to Zebra Historical Romances and send me my first 4 books absolutely FREE. I understand that each month I may preview four new Zebra Historical Romances free for 10 days. If I'm not satisfied with them, I may return the four books within 10 days and owe nothing. Otherwise, I will pay the low preferred subscriber's price of just $3.75 each; a total of $15.00, *a savings off the publisher's price of $3.00.* I may return any shipment and I may cancel this subscription at any time. There is no obligation to buy any shipment and there are no shipping, handling or other hidden charges. Regardless of what I decide, the four free books are mine to keep.

NAME

ADDRESS _____ APT _____

CITY _____ STATE _____ ZIP _____
(   )
TELEPHONE

SIGNATURE _____ (if under 18, parent or guardian must sign)

Terms, offer and prices subject to change without notice. Subscription subject to acceptance by Zebra Books. Zebra Books reserves the right to reject any order or cancel any subscription.

Twelve

"Marnie, here we are."

"Hello, loves," Marnie called from the train window. Ginny hadn't gone to get her after all; she'd insisted on arriving on Amtrak.

"I've done me some interesting things in my life, but I haven't ridden on a train yet," she'd said in her matter-of-fact way, and Ginny had known better than to argue with her. Now here she was in her Reeboks and sweat suits even though it was a hot summer day. The girls ran to hug her, and Marnie sniffed and fixed each one of them with watery eyes.

"Have you been good for Ginny?"

"We have. We have, Marnie," they replied.

"*I* have," Stef chimed up.

"Ooh, look at you. You've gotten bigger," Marnie crowed.

Stef nodded with satisfaction. "I'm wearing Candi's swimsuit," she revealed, obviously intent on holding Marnie's attention as long as she could. But the other girls clamored for equal time, and Marnie's bags had to be collected and then carried, by the children at their own insistence, to the car. Only after all that was done did the two women have a chance to greet each other.

"Marnie, it's so good to see you," Ginny cried, throwing her arms around the old woman.

"How are you, Mrs. Logan?" Marnie asked, taking hold of her and walking arm in arm to the car.

"Marnie, call me Ginny. We're old friends now. As for how I'm doing? I'm fine now that you're here. I'm going to make it. In fact, I think we all are."

"God love you, you surely will. The babies look good, happy and feisty like they were before their father died."

"They still have some hard times, but they're handling things," Ginny said. "They'll be even better now that you're here with them."

"I've been missing them," Marnie said, and Ginny saw her pale eyes water. She patted the old woman's hand.

"I'm sitting beside Marnie."

"No, I am. You always get to sit in front.

242

Now you can't come in back with Marnie and me."

"Girls, girls. I'll be around awhile. You'll all have a chance to sit by me. Pretty soon you'll be fighting because you have to."

"I won't, Marnie. I'll always sit by you," Candi said, laying her head against Marnie's shoulder.

With a little further discussion, they arranged the seating for the trip home. Tracy sat in front as she usually did, and Marnie sat in back with a girl on either side. Glancing at the three in the back in the rearview mirror, Ginny couldn't decide who was happiest to see whom. When they reached the cottage, the girls were fireballs of energy, hauling in Marnie's bags, escorting her to her room, showing her the lake, introducing her to Jason.

Ginny hurried to the kitchen and began preparing supper. Humming, she set about making the shish kebabs.

"I've planned a cookout for us," she said, when Marnie offered to help. "I'm doing everything today. You just rest from your trip and visit with the girls. They're so glad to have you here."

"What about that Mr. McCann next door? The girls said he's coming over to eat with us."

"Yes, he has supper with us three or four

243

times a week. You'll like him, Marnie. He's been a godsend to us."

"Humph. I don't think I'll like him as much as I do Mr. Russell."

Ginny halted in her preparation. "Have you talked to Mr. Russell then?"

"He came to see me several times since you left."

"That was nice of him." Ginny waited for Marnie to go on, but for a woman who was usually talkative, she'd become strangely reticent. "How is he?" Ginny asked.

"Who?" Marnie turned from peering out the window.

"Alex!"

"Fine, just fine. Healthy. He's a damn sight better looking than that young pup next door, but then I always was partial to men who look like Cary Grant."

"He does!" Ginny said remembering Alex's dark eyes and lean face. "Jason is a friend, Marnie. You'll see."

"What's Mr. Russell? He used to be your friend. Now you won't even let him come out here to see you."

Ginny sank down on a stool. She'd known this conversation with Marnie was inevitable, but she hadn't thought it would be so soon or so direct.

"I still need time, Marnie. Things happened at the agency. Things that hurt me. I felt so disappointed in Alex."

"Don't see much about him to disappoint you."

"What do you mean?" Ginny asked, hoping to draw Marnie out and divert her from further questions.

"I just think Mr. Russell is a fine man," she said, and turned away. "Guess I'll go watch the mermaids do their water tricks."

"They've been practicing for days." After Marnie left, Ginny felt unsettled. Why had Alex gone to visit her so often? Once was enough to find out where she was. Had he asked about her? Had he kept going back because Marnie told him about her weekly telephone conversations with Ginny? It was obvious he still cared about them all, but was that due to an old friendship or a sense of obligation. Why should it matter why he'd acted as he did? "Damn, Alex," she muttered after poking herself with one of the skewers. She didn't want to think about him. Not yet. She might have to make another decision, and she wasn't ready for that, not yet. She stood at the sink, running cold water over her hand.

"Anybody there?" Jason yelled from the porch.

"Come on in," Ginny called back as she wrapped her hand in a clean dish towel. Jason entered, looking scrubbed and boyish in a clean pair of jeans and a chambray shirt. He'd trimmed his beard so it was barely more than a Vandyke. Ginny couldn't help staring.

"What's wrong? My ears don't match?" he asked good-humoredly.

"Sorry. You just look nice with your beard trimmed."

"I do clean up good, don't I?" he said. "What have you done to yourself now?"

"I'm wounded, speared through the hand by a lawless shrimp."

"Do you need surgery?" He set down the bottle of wine he'd brought, and held out his hand.

Obediently, Ginny exposed her injury. Jason's fingers were cool and dry on her flesh.

"Ummm," he said, making a great show of examining the cut. "I zink ve must amputate." He waggled his eyebrows. Ginny drew her hand back, feigning alarm.

"Do you mind if I get a second opinion, Doctor?"

"Not at all. In ze meantime, I vill make ze shish kebab."

"Good idea. I'll watch."

"Good." Jason picked up a skewer and began pushing chunks of onion and pepper onto it.

"The girls seem mesmerized by Mrs. Lansky."

"They love her."

"Mrs. Lansky is not mesmerized by me."

"She needs time to warm up to you. Look how long it took the girls and me. As I recall you didn't sup with us until the second day. I know this must be hard on your masculine ego, but there are some women who are harder to win over."

"I'm all too well aware of that," he said, glancing up at her.

Ginny avoided his gaze. "How's your book going?"

"Ah, my book." Jason grinned at her abrupt change of topic. "Detective Peters—"

"I thought his name was Detective Hoyt."

"I changed it. Hoyt is now his subordinate."

"Is Detective Peters more clever?"

"No more so than his creator. And, my dear hostess, your shishes are kebabed."

"Lovely. Can you start the grill?"

"Whatever happened to the independent woman bit?"

"Now that I've prove my point, I can take advantage of superior male brawn."

"Yeah?" Jason's look was intentionally lascivious. "I'm willing."

"Thought I'd see if you needed any help in here!" Marnie's rough voice made them both jump like guilty children.

Jason recovered first. "How do you like the country, Mrs. Lansky?"

"Call me Marnie, and I don't know yet," she answered, staring down her nose at him. "I'm still making up my mind."

"Making up your mind," Jason muttered. "Well, I'll go light the fire."

"Seems to me you've already been trying to light some fire," Marnie snapped. "Maybe it'd help if you used matches on this one."

"Yes, ma'am." Jason went out, completely cowed by the old woman's sharp tongue.

"Take it easy on him, Marnie," Ginny said lightly, her eyes dancing with humor. "You'll have him flayed and grilled before sundown."

"He can take it," Marnie said. "Now, tell me about him." And Ginny did, while they both worked on the salad. Marnie clucked sympathetically and soon took over the rest of the preparations, ordering Ginny about as if she were an apprentice. Ginny grinned at the crusty old woman with tightly permed gray hair. It felt good to have her with them again. When everything was ready, Ginny called for help in carrying everything out to the patio table.

"Do we need salt and pepper?" Tracy asked.

"Not with Marnie here," Jason said, and he grinned.

"Touché!" the older woman snapped as she thrust a platter of shish kebabs at him. "Get busy and earn your supper," she ordered. "No more freeloading around here."

"Marnie, I'm deeply hurt that you'd think me a gold bricker." Jason was turning on his charm full circuit, Ginny decided. And Marnie was right; he could take it. The two of them were already settling into a bickering love-hate rapport that was comfortable for them both.

"I'm glad you two have hit it off so well," Ginny said, bringing up the rear.

They sat around the patio table, already set with gay stoneware plates on a hot pink cloth. Jason manned the grill, and Ginny passed around foil-wrapped baked potatoes, salad, and hot garlic bread. The girls chattered nonstop, vying for Marnie's attention, her opinion, her praise.

"Poor you," Ginny said to her as the girls cleared the table and served after-dinner coffee and pie.

"Ah, this'll wear off in a day or two, and then they'll ignore me like they used to."

"I'm almost jealous," said Jason. "They usually make a fuss over me."

"Don't go getting your nose out of joint," Marnie retorted. "I'm not real sure I'm going to stay the summer."

"Marnie, you promised," Ginny cried.

"I promised I'd try it," Marnie said. "I don't know if I can sleep without the sound of traffic."

"You'll get used to it," Ginny assured her. "We did. Now I'm not sure I could stand to go back to the city."

"Humph! I don't see much here to recommend the country," Marnie answered, but the next morning Ginny found her sitting at the edge of the pier, dangling her feet in the water and watching a loon skim the mirrored surface of the lake. She didn't disturb her, remembering her own fascination with the lake and its inhabitants when she'd first come here. There was something seductive about water and sky. She went back into the house, leaving Marnie to her meditation.

Monday morning she drove into Grand Rapids, to the battered neighborhood where the center was located. Parking her car, she silently prayed that tires and chrome would still be on it when she came out. Carrying her brown-bag lunch, she hurried into the building and stopped dead. Pandemonium reigned. Ellen was speaking loudly and rapidly into the phone, while Dr. Schur stood behind her, offering advice. Seated on the waiting room chairs were a woman and three children. They all looked frightened. The woman's face was bruised, her upper lip was split. Her thin fingers nervously smoothed a little boy's hair. A girl Candi's age sobbed and leaned against her mother's shoulder, but a boy of about thirteen sat a little apart from the others, his eyes dark and angry, his elbows on his knees, his pale hands twisting together in sheer frustration.

"I tell you the father is on his way down here now. He's called and made threats against the center if we help his wife."

Ellen paused to listen. "Yes, she's here now, along with the children. No, they seem unhurt. The mother has bruises and a cracked lip."

Ellen listened again, her lips tightening in anger. "It isn't what he's already done that we're worried about. It's his threats. He means them. I know you can't arrest anyone for making threats." Ellen stopped talking and peered at the door. "He's here," she said frantically. "Get them in back. Emily, go with Dr. Bob. Hurry." She spoke into the phone again. "Lieutenant, the husband is here at the center now. He looks angry and dangerous. We need you."

Ginny heard a door open behind her. The woman called Emily and her children were still in plain view down the long hall. Without thinking, she swung around and blocked the doorway. A tall, dark-haired man wearing a dirty T-shirt and worn jeans stepped inside.

"May I help you?" Ginny asked calmly, although her heart was beating so hard, she was sure she would pass out on the floor at any minute. The man halted, staring down at her as if undecided what to do. His face was brutish, the lips thinned in anger. His hard gaze said very plainly he had little use for women, especially those who wore linen suits and French perfume. Ginny smiled pleasantly.

"This is the women's center. Are you sure you want to be here?"

"Yeah! I want to be here," he said, doubling his fists and taking a step forward. Ginny didn't back up as she knew he'd expected, but her smile did waver a bit.

"Where's my wife?" he bellowed.

"I'm not sure your wife is here. If you give me her name, I'll check."

"Emily, Emily Fuller."

"Well, Mr. Fuller. If you'll just have a seat, I'll go inquire."

"You have a seat and I'll inquire," the man snarled.

"Good morning, Ginny." Ellen now stood at her side, and Ginny wanted to hug her. Her knees were trembling from fear, and her mouth was stiff from the effort to smile. "Good morning, sir. Have you been helped?" Ellen continued calmly.

"He's here inquiring about his wife. What was her name again?" Ginny asked, stalling for time. Surely Bob Schur had the woman and her children out of sight by now.

"I want to see my wife, *now!*" the man bellowed.

"What is her name?" Ellen asked. "We can't help you if we don't know her name."

"You know it," the man pointed a stubby finger in her face. "I know she's here, and I know what you're trying to do."

"What is that, sir?"

"You're trying to stall me until the police get here. Well, I'm leaving now, but I'll be back. You just watch for me." He turned and stalked out. Ellen expelled her breath. Ginny leaned against the wall, waiting for her legs to be steady again.

"You were great," Ellen said with a grin. "Sure you haven't had experience with this before?"

"One hundred percent certain." Ginny tried not to slide down the wall.

"You need a cup of coffee after all that." Ellen took Ginny by the arm and headed for her own office. Shoving Ginny into a chair, she filled two paper cups with strong black coffee and set them on the corner of the desk. Settling into her chair, she opened a bottom drawer and pulled out a bottle of Irish whiskey.

"I always keep a little for emergencies," she said, pouring a generous dollop in each cup. She handed one to Ginny.

"Go on, take it. Even if it *is* nine o'clock in the morning, you need it."

Obediently, Ginny sipped, coughed, and sipped again. Ellen was right. She needed the burning liquid that brought life back to her numbed limbs and choked lungs and heart. "I never want to be that scared again," she gasped when she'd emptied the cup.

"More?" Ellen asked, holding out the whiskey.

Ginny shook her head, so Ellen capped the bottle and put it back in the drawer.

"Now you know a little better what we're all about. Do you want to stay?"

Ginny sat studying Ellen's broad face, the untidy shock of blond hair, and the gray eyes. "You handle this sort of thing all the time, don't you?"

"Sometimes it's not as bad. Sometimes it's worse."

"How could it be worse?" Ginny asked. "If it had been any worse out there, someone would have gotten hurt."

Ellen said nothing. Ginny gasped and sat back, understanding at last what Ellen was trying to convey. People get killed when passions flare.

"Are you sure you want to stay now?"

"Are you trying to scare me off?"

"I'm trying to give you a dose of a different reality than you're used to," Ellen answered. She waited while Ginny sat staring at the floor.

Gone were all her plans for this job, her unrealistic dream that she would make things right just by being here.

"Have I been naive?" she asked finally.

"No, you've dreamed," Ellen answered. "Dreaming for a better way is never wrong." She leaned forward and tapped Ginny's hand, which lay on the desk. "We could use some dreamers here. Some of us have become way too cynical. We only look at the hard line."

Ginny stirred herself. "Then I'd better get to my post," she said. "Because if it's a dreamer you want sitting out there, then I'll be the best dreamer you ever had." She stood up, looping her purse strap over her shoulder. "I want to help. That's why I came. I want to do something to stop some of the pain."

"To stop your own pain?" Ellen peered up at her.

Ginny shook her head. "I didn't come here for

me."

"Yes, you did, Ginny. We all did. We're looking for answers to questions we don't even know."

Somberly, Ginny walked back to the receptionist's desk and sat down. She looked around—at the clutter of papers, the phone that was blessedly silent for the moment, the battered file cabinets, the vase with a bunch of zinnias. Bulletin boards covered with schedules and posters announcing workshops, day-care centers, and self-help programs covered the walls. The dreams to be found here were of ordinary things like learning a job skill or finding someone to care for a child during working hours. They could use some dreamers, Ellen had said, and looking around her, Ginny knew she was looking at the dreams of hundreds of women. She'd been so enfolded in her own safe world, she'd given little thought to the other worlds that existed right under her nose. She had been pampered. Her life had been orderly, pleasant, untouched by need. She felt guilty, then pushed that emotion aside. She was here now, and if she could make a difference, she would try.

Pulling a stack of papers over, Ginny began sorting through them. No one had filed any for some time. She spent the morning seeing to this mundane business. The phone seldom rang.

"It gets like this sometimes," Ellen said when they took a break to eat lunch. Neatly she'd handled the police when they'd showed up, placating them for the false alarm. The rest of the morning she'd been in her office, working.

"You go like a fiend to catch up on your paper work when it's like this because you know the lull won't last. Soon there'll be a flood of women needing your help. It's especially bad on a full moon."

Ginny laughed. "I've heard that before. I thought it was just an exaggeration."

"Not a bit. You just watch and see. A full moon seems to bring out the craziness in everybody. Men beat their wives, teenage girls get pregnant or run away, women finally get up the nerve to leave their husbands, or their husbands abandon them, leaving them with no money or food for the kids."

Bob Schur returned halfway through their lunch. "I left Emily and her children at a safe house," he reported, raking his fingers through his hair.

"Did you get a chance to talk to her?" Ellen asked. "Is she going to prosecute?"

Wearily Bob shook his head and drummed his fingers against a file cabinet. "She's worried about her husband eating right without her there to make the meals."

257

"Why should she care?" Ginny asked in dismay.

"She loves him," Ellen answered. "That's what makes it so tragic."

"She says he's been out of work for a while. The usual hardships and frustrations. She says he's a good man. He just beats her all the time."

"Do you think she'll go back to him?"

He nodded. "Yeah. She'll go back." He stalked off to his office, his shoulders drooping in defeat.

Ginny put her sandwich down and looked at Ellen. "Don't you ever burn out?"

Ellen shook her head. "I remember how I felt when my husband abused me. It wasn't the physical pain that was so bad, it was the feeling inside me that I wasn't worth much and was just getting what I deserved. And the despair. Whenever I think I've had enough, I look at another battered frightened face and I know I haven't. I'm out of all that. I go home at night and know no one will hit me or make me feel bad about myself, but there are women and children out there who haven't escaped."

"How do you keep from thinking of men as the enemy?"

Ellen turned her contemplative gaze on Ginny. "I've never met any who are not," she said softly. "I'm sure they're out there, but I haven't met them yet."

"So you're a man-hater?" Ginny asked, somehow disappointed to find this crippling scar in so savvy a woman.

"No," Ellen answered. "And I'm not a lesbian, though I've been called that by some irate husbands. I keep thinking someday I'd like to meet a man and get married again and have children." She shrugged and grinned, as if the dream wasn't that important to her. "I'm just more cautious than I might have been otherwise."

Driving home that night, Ginny thought of her first day of work and of all the things she'd experienced. She thought of Ellen and the way her plain face lit up and became really beautiful when she smiled. She thought of Emily Fuller who was sitting somewhere in a safe house, agonizing over the decision to leave her husband or return to his abuse.

She was depressed by the time she got home. Marnie and Jason were sitting out on the patio, a pitcher of lemonade on the table between them. The girls were swimming. The scene was so tranquil that for a moment Ginny ached with joy just at being home, being a part of the life they all shared. I'll call Ellen tomorrow, she thought, and tell her I can't continue at the cen-

259

ter.

But the next morning when the sun pushed through her bedroom curtains and the plaintive call of a nesting dove sounded, she rose and reached for a plain cotton skirt and blouse. It was far more suitable for the job she would be doing at the center.

Thirteen

"You're looking kind of down," Jason observed. "Is your job going okay?"

"Yes—no. I don't know. I think I'm just down because the girls are going away this weekend with Marnie." They were seated on the patio, sipping lemonade. Though it was only mid June, a haze lay over the lake and freshly mowed yard. The heat and humidity had become unbearable in the city, and Ginny was glad to be home.

"Where's she going?" Jason asked, crossing his bare legs. He was clad only in a swimsuit, his uniform for the summer. Sometimes Ginny was tempted to ask him to put on a shirt, but she didn't.

"She's going back to visit her sister," she answered, "and since the girls have never ridden a train, they're going with her."

"They were telling me about that." Jason

glanced at her. She looked tired, her dress wilted, her makeup shiny across her nose. She fiddled with her glasses as if restless. "Why don't you go with them? You've been working hard at your new job. You need a change."

Ginny shook her head. "I don't want to go back to Detroit. It's probably as hot as Grand Rapids."

"Is that the only reason?"

"What other reason would there be?" Her voice was shrill with impatience.

He shrugged. "Just asking?"

"Sorry." She felt silent again.

"How about a movie and dinner out tonight?" he asked.

"You don't have to do that," Ginny sighed. "I wouldn't be good company."

"You don't even have to talk to me if you don't want to."

She said nothing.

"We could go dancing. I understand women love to dance."

"I do." A tiny break in her reserves. He tried again.

"I'll take you to a fancy restaurant. You haven't been out to a nice place since you moved here."

"You're right," she said. "I haven't dressed up in weeks, months. That's what I need. A night out on the town, perfume and diamonds and good food and wine served by a man in a waist-coat." She turned to him. "We'll go dutch of course."

"I never make my ladies pay," Jason said.

"You can't afford the kind of evening I have in mind."

"I'll manage."

"How is Detective Peters coming along?"

"He's been fired and Lieutenant Lansky's mother has taken over the case."

"Jason! Does Marnie know?"

"Am I a stupid man?"

Ginny leaned back in her chair and laughed. "She'll be delighted."

"I'm not taking that chance until I've finished the book. By the way, it's going well. I just needed to get the right main character."

"Then we'll celebrate tonight." Ginny smiled. "I have to take Marnie and the girls to the train station in a half-hour and come back and wash my hair and get dressed. How about seven o'clock?"

Jason nodded in approval and got to his feet. "I'll leave you to it, then. Don't get too fancy. I won't recognize you."

"I'm going to dazzle you," Ginny promised.

He looked at her sparkling eyes. "You already do that, Ms. Logan," he said lightly, and tipping an imaginary hat, he strolled away.

Knowing she had an evening planned made saying goodbye at the train station a little easier. Ginny kissed them all and waved them off.

"If I happen to run into Mr. Russell, is there anything you want me to tell him?" Marnie asked just before boarding.

"Just give him my best," Ginny said and stepped back. "Have a good time. 'Bye."

On the way home, she wondered briefly why Marnie had brought up Alex, but shoved the thought away as she concentrated on what she would wear that night and how she would arrange her hair. When Jason's jeep pulled into her driveway and he got out, she could only stare. She'd never seen him in anything other than blue jeans. Now he wore a navy blue pinstripe suit and a pale blue dress shirt set off by a positively trendy flowered tie. His hair was neatly parted and combed into place, although she could see from her window that the silky brown strands were already falling over his brow.

Suddenly she was glad she'd taken so much pains with dressing. She'd thought she was doing it for herself; now she realized she wanted Jason to be as pleased with her appearance as she was with his. She grabbed up the floral silk shawl that matched her dress and hurried downstairs to answer the door. His eyes widened when he saw her.

"What, no whistle?" she asked, turning this way and that for him to get the full effect of her low-cut dress.

"I'm nearly speechless," he said. "Blue is my favorite color—forever."

Ginny laughed, pleased by his reaction. The high heels gave her enough height to meet his gaze almost at his eye level. "So where are we going?"

"Sam's Joint."

"Oh." Her ebullient mood sagged for a moment, then she shrugged her shoulders. "I'm in your hands tonight."

"Words to make a man's heart beat a little faster," he said. "I warn you, I'll hold you to that."

His tone was just teasing enough, his glance just admiring enough to make any woman feel beautiful. Ginny loved it. She thought about offering her Lincoln, but Jason had obviously washed and waxed the jeep.

"I don't think I've ever seen a jeep with a wax job before," she said swinging her long legs into it.

"Nothing's too good when I take a lady out." He grinned. "Fasten your seat belt so you don't fall out."

Sam's Joint was a low-slung, shedlike building

that might have given her alarm if not for the light blazing through the leaded windows. Jason helped her out of the jeep and escorted her to the door.

"How did you know about this place?"

"The DeFauws told me about it when I moved in."

"Looks interesting."

"Wait till you see the inside."

The interior did not disappoint. Every available inch of walls and ceiling was hung with a hodgepodge of antiques, art objects, and leaded lamps. They were shown to a booth, and drinks appeared almost at once. Ginny leaned back against the cushioned seat and began to relax.

"Thanks, Jason," she said. "I needed this."

"Don't thank me yet," he admonished. "We haven't been served yet."

"I don't care. It just feels good to get out and do something different."

"Is your job getting you down?" His gaze was sympathetic, inviting confidences. She gave in.

"I love feeling I might make a difference somehow, but it's much harder than I thought it would be. I think everyone expects me to possess an enormous amount of wisdom and expertise just because I'm older, but I'm out of my element. I'm a baby at this." She paused. He said nothing, waiting.

"When I look at Ellen and all she accomplishes—and what she wants to accomplish but can't—I just get . . . frustrated, angry. When those women come in and they're alone—their husbands have died or left them and they don't know how they're going to survive without them—I want to shake them, and yet I feel so sorry for them. I know how they feel, lost . . . knowing you're alone."

"If it's too tough, why don't you quit?"

Her head came up then, her eyes blazing with indignation. "I can't do that. They need people to help, to care."

Jason's hand covered hers. "Are you sure you're not biting off more than you should? If working there is making you relive the loss of your own husband, is it worth it?"

"I never realized how lucky I was until now," Ginny replied, shaking her head. "I can't turn my back on those women. Their plight is so pitiful, but they're so . . . brave. Like nothing you've ever imagined. Women don't get a chance to be brave very often, and when they are it isn't on a battlefield or someplace where they win medals, it's a different kind of bravery. Do you have any idea how difficult it is for some of them to take those first steps into the unknown? Yet they do it, driven by desperation and the hope they can better themselves."

She paused. Jason's eyebrows had drawn together in a frown. She sensed he didn't like hearing the things she was saying. "I'm sorry to go on and on about my job. I won't mention it again tonight."

His frown disappeared. "Let's talk about how beautiful you look tonight," he said teasingly.

Supper was delicious, well served and accompanied by plenty of wine. And Jason was charming company. Though Ginny was not unaware of the glances cast his way by some of the women, he seemed not to notice. His blue eyes were compelling as they regarded her across the table. Soon she was caught in the spell he was weaving. He made her feel feminine and desirable again. She reveled in it.

"Want to dance?" Jason said, holding out his hand. A small band had set up at one end of the dance floor.

"Love to." Ginny slid out of the booth.

He held her close, one broad hand spread across her back, the other cradling her hand as he guided her around the floor. "You're a good dancer," she said, peering up at him.

Jason's heated gaze captured hers. "Relax, Ginny," he whispered. His voice was husky. "I won't eat you, unless you want me to." His breath was warm against her temple. Her limbs felt liquid, giving. He drew her closer, and they danced cheek to cheek, hip to hip, thigh to thigh. She felt the heat of his body, the raw-boned strength of it; and desire flooded through her. She glanced around, afraid people could see her thoughts and desires, but the others were dancing slowly and dreamily too, clasped in warm embraces, eyes closed, lips seeking lips in tiny kisses, and exchanging slow sensuous smiles when the number was over.

Jason didn't release his hold on her as they waited on the dance floor for the music to begin again. Their gazes never wavered from each other. Ginny gave no thought to time and place. They were man and woman, their awareness of each other encompassing. A Latin tempo began and Ginny moved her hips to its rhythm, her gaze on Jason's face. He placed his hands on her hips, keeping her close to him, yet giving her space to move. She felt sensuous, passionate, free. Jason was leading her off the floor, and she wasn't sure whether the music had stopped or continued only in her head. He reclaimed her wrap, paid the bill, and led her out to his jeep. This time he didn't tell her to buckle up. His long arm reached for her, dragging her against his side, and he drove one-handed. He made no move to touch her breasts. His hand stayed at her side, polite yet possessive, restrained yet demanding.

The night seemed to be holding its breath as they wove through back-country roads to the lake. The moon was full, and briefly she thought of what Ellen had said. There would be a rash of women in need of help after a full moon. But that didn't touch her, not here. She was back in her own world now, where moonlight brought pleasure and passion and romance, where pretty women and handsome men danced together and reached through the dark shadows for each other. Jason had brought this back to her, had reminded her of pleasures past and yet to be found. She reached for him, her hand brushing across his lap, and she heard him groan. Her arms wound around his slim waist, and she cuddled close while the warm breeze whipped her hair.

She tried to push away the inner voices that said: Don't do this; don't reach for something that may be wrong for you, that may not last. He's younger than you. You've shared grief; it's drawn you together. But what will hold you together? What will tomorrow bring? One day you may be like those women, abandoned, bereft. You may be opening yourself to still more pain. She drew away from him.

"What's wrong?" he asked, but she couldn't answer. They were nearly home now. He pulled the jeep to a stop and turned to her. "Ginny,

270

what's the matter?"

"Oh, Jason, I'm so sorry," she said. "The moon is full."

"What? What's the moon got to do with us?"

"Everything and nothing. At least it should be nothing." She climbed out of the jeep. He followed. "You can't come in with me, Jason." She was backing away from him, edging away from the threat he represented. "We can't—I can't do this. You're younger than I am. We're lonely. We're confusing friendship with something else. Thanks for taking me out." She slammed the door behind her, locked it, then stood with pounding heart, wondering what she would do if he knocked. Go away, she willed him. I haven't enough will power to resist forever.

She heard the jeep start up and back down the driveway. Still, she stood listening until it reappeared in the next drive. She shouldn't have. She didn't need to know he was so near that all she had to do was fling open the door and call out to him.

"What are you thinking of, you fool?" she said, and went upstairs. Getting ready for bed, she couldn't help standing in front of the mirror to study her image. Her eyes were bright, shiny with some emotion she didn't recognize. David would have known. He would have sensed the aura of sexuality clinging to her like a second

271

skin. Had Jason sensed it too? Hastily, she creamed away the makeup and showered away the expensive perfume. When she was scrubbed and devoid of all artifice, she stood before the mirror again and saw the lines about her eyes and throat. They weren't ugly, but they were there, signposts of her years of living. They were part of who she was, just as the heavy full breasts and long sleek legs were. She couldn't wash away who she was—and what she was.

She stared at her reflection, feeling her body's demands, and finally accepted that part of herself she'd denied too long. Drawing on a cotton gown trimmed with lace, she went downstairs and let herself out the back door.

The grass was dewy beneath her bare feet. She stood at his door and hesitated to knock. Then, pushing open the screen, she stepped inside. He was seated on the floor in front of the fireplace, feeding small bits of wood shavings to the hungry flames. He looked up, and seeing her standing there, he stood. His eyes held a question, then seemed to know the answer, for he crossed the room in long strides and put his arms around her.

"Ginny," he whispered, his mouth hungry against hers. His beard brushed her cheeks, her throat, as he trailed kisses over her face. When they both were breathless, he took her hand and

272

pulled her down to the floor. He was impatient, as needful as she. In a jumble of limbs and heavy breathing, he stripped away his clothing. She wasn't surprised by him, she'd seen him so often in his brief swimsuit; but the sight of his hard shaft excited her. He tried to caress her, to ready her, but she reached for him, pushing aside his attempts, pressing him to her, glorying in the remembered weight of a man. Their mating was swift, lustful, satisfying in spite of its brevity. They reached a climax before the roaring fire, and when their breathing returned to normal, they reached for each other again, this time going more slowly, seeking to please each other in the intimate manner of lovers.

She rose in those cool gray hours before dawn and, drawing on her nightgown, made her way back through the dew-slicked grass to her own cottage. Her body felt sore and tired and alive. She showered, then, unable to sleep again, took a cup of coffee out to the end of the dock, where she watched the sun come up.

Funny, that the day was different because of what the night had brought. She wasn't the same Ginny she'd been yesterday. She never would be again. She'd succumbed to the moon's madness, but for her there was no regret. She had prepared herself mentally before she'd gone to Jason. She felt almost guilty, for she had used

273

him. There had been no love between them, only need, and that had been enough.

The sun rose, heating water and land. She slipped off her robe and dove into the lake. The water licked at her arms and legs as she moved through it with long lazy strokes. She reached the raft and clung to its edge, dipping her head backward so the water caught her hair and tamed it into a long sleek wet curtain.

Hands, cool and smooth, reached for her, sliding up from below the water's tranquil surface, bringing tingles, waking desire. Jason's head broke the surface gently. His hands pinned her waist.

"I want you," he whispered.

"There's no more full moon," she protested.

"The madness is still there." He was drawing her closer, sweeping her under the raft, seeking privacy among the barrels. She glanced around. Only a solitary fisherman could be seen in the distance, a silver reflection on the water. Jason's mouth hovered close to hers, and she could offer no resistance.

Her breasts were buoyant in the water. He weighed them in his palms, his thumb flicking across the nipples until she licked her lips and moaned. Then he gathered her close, lifting her so her long legs wrapped around his middle. He was ready for her, his shaft hot and hard, pinning her so that for one exquisite moment she couldn't move while waves of desire rippled over her. He was hot, the water cold. He was hard, unyielding, the water moved languidly around her. He moved against her, and she arched backward, seeing her nipples, gleaming and wet, jut out of the water. He moved against her again and she moaned, and then she came, all hot and moist and trembling. He held her, smoothing her back, while the tremors that claimed her carried him over the edge, his throbbing tip inside her. She cried out once and would have done so again, but his lips claimed hers, hushing her wild climactic song.

They made breakfast and ate at the breakfast counter. They had little to say. Their eyes and touches spoke more clearly than words. They found delight in each other. They swam again, drifting far out beyond the raft to the middle of the lake, then swam back side by side, stroke for stroke. In the evening, after supper, they took out Jason's sailboat and watched the sunset turn crimson and orange against the sky. When dusk fell, they made love in the bottom of the boat and laughed gleefully when a speedboat went by and teenagers hooted and catcalled. Nothing touched them. They lived in a magic place where reality couldn't intrude. Jason slept with her in the big double bed she'd shared with David and

275

with her granddaughters. During the night, he woke and, sensing she, too, was awake, made love to her, chasing away the shadows of memories. Gratefully, she clung to him and wept. In the morning he was gone, and she knew reality must begin again. She showered and dressed and drove to the train station to pick up Marnie and the girls.

"Mr. Russell asked about you," Marnie said when they were in the car. "He said to remind you that he's looking forward to the Fourth."

The Fourth. Two weeks away. Ginny had forgotten Alex had been invited. She'd forgotten many things in the blaze of the summer weekend. Suddenly, in the pit of her stomach, she felt certain she'd just made a horrible mistake.

Fourteen

Monday morning brought a return of sanity. She hadn't resolved any of her problems by having a weekend fling with Jason. If anything, she'd created new ones. What had she been thinking of, full-moon madness aside? This was a relationship neither she nor Jason could build on. She didn't want to be one of those women who denied their age by clinging to a younger man. Yet the memory of their hours together teased her, so when she lay in bed at night, she hugged her pillow to her stomach imagining she could catch a whiff of Jason's scent, imagining the fluffy softness of her pillow was Jason's hard young body. She couldn't stop the images that came to her in the darkness or deny the desire that, wakened after so many years, could no longer be held in abeyance.

By Thursday night she was unable to sleep,

blaming her wakefulness on the heat. Through her window she could see the glow of light from Jason's room. Tossing and turning on her lonely bed, she thought of his long, nude body sprawled in masculine disregard, his legs and chest glistening, his manhood rigid and smooth. Her fingers curled, remembering the feel of him.

The house was silent around her, the girls resting in innocent slumber after their hours of play. Marnie retired early and rose early, and neither heaven nor earth could move her when she slept. Ginny imagined herself rising from bed and creeping down the stairs and reaching the freedom of the dew-wet grass, the inviting warm darkness of Jason's cottage. She imagined and then moved as if in a dream.

He heard her coming and was waiting at the top of the stairs, his long arms reaching for her, his kisses urgent and hungry. She laughed deep in her throat at his impatience. Without releasing her, he tugged her gown from between their molded bodies and pulled it over her head, dropping it on the hall floor. He lifted her high, urging her legs around his waist and she clasped her ankles around him, clinging to him, feeling her weight sag against his groin. She was moist and ready for him.

He impaled her, forcing himself deep inside, his tongue thrusting in a rhythm that was repeated by his hips. They couldn't make it to the bed. They didn't try. He pinioned her against the wall, his hips hammering at her. Their bodies moved together, their moans mingled; their release was mutual and searing.

Ginny clung to him, gasping for air, feeling the moist sleekness of her body. Something inside her had died, and the sweet pain of its going still lingered somewhere deep in the core of her. Slowly she opened her eyes and looked at him. His head was flung back, his eyes closed, his mouth slightly open. He was breathing hard from his exertions. Ginny collected the sweat from his cheek and wiped it on her own sweat-soaked breasts. He opened his eyes and grinned at her.

"Are you okay?" he asked huskily.

She nodded and sighed, leaning her head against his shoulder. He shifted his hold on her buttocks and carried her to the bed. Their bodies were still connected, though muscles had begun to relax from their intense effort. He pulled away from her and reached for a towel; then he was back beside her, cradling her, pulling her warmth to him. She reached for the covers, tucking them around his shoulders, for she'd learned he quickly grew chilled after making love. They held each other, glad to be together again, and slept, their bodies nestled in on each other spoon-fashion. When she woke, the windows were still dark. The red eye of the clocks said midnight. She moved and Jason's large hands closed around her, pulling her close again. He gave her no chance to turn toward him. Gently he nudged her up on her knees and entered her, his strokes long and silky, causing her to gasp with pleasure. His tall body hovered over her, his hands cupped her breasts, kneading and caressing her nipples until she mewed with gratification. Their climax was no less staggering than the first had been and when they were finished she lay satiated, unable to move. They slept again, and near dawn she rose and, unable to find her gown, donned one of Jason's long shirts. Legs flashing bare in the moonlight, she ran back to her own cottage.

The house was silent as she made her way up the stairs and settled back into her own bed. She still had an hour or so of sleep before she had to get up. She ran a hand over her sore breasts and down to her stomach. Her body still tingled from Jason's lovemaking. She felt voluptuous, sensuous, hedonistic — and not the least bit sorry. She would save regrets for later.

After a short sleep she rose, feeling better than she would have thought possible. A hot shower washed away all trace of Jason from her body, but not from her senses. Dressed, she quickly made her bed, tossed Jason's shirt into the dirty-clothes hamper and hurried downstairs.

"Are the girls still sleeping?" she asked Marnie, who served up a cup of coffee and a plate of scrambled eggs, bacon, and toast.

"They won't come down till ten or thereabouts. They've become real slugabeds."

Ginny laughed and began eating. "That's what summer's all about," she said.

"I guess you're right about that." Marnie brought over a cup of coffee and perched on a chair across from Ginny. "You were right to bring the girls here. They needed this change."

"They do seem happy, don't they? I think it's worked well for all of us. How about you? Are you growing used to the country?"

Marnie took a swallow of coffee and peered at Ginny over the rim of her cup. "It's too quiet. No roar of traffic. You can get used to that sound; it's constant. You know what it is. When it's so quiet, I can hear every little

281

sound the house makes, every squeak of the stairs, every door that opens and closes."

Ginny flushed in spite of herself. "These old cottages are always making noises. The timbers are settling, and they creak and groan."

"That's what I mean," said Marnie, setting down her cup. "Say, I haven't seen you eat like that before."

Ginny glanced down at her plate. "I guess I was hungrier than usual. I'll have to skip lunch to make up for all these calories."

"I already got your sandwich made," Marnie said indicating the brown-paper sack. "You look kind of tired around the eyes this morning. Didn't you sleep well?"

"Like a log. I'd better get moving or I'll be late." Ginny grabbed up her lunch and made for the door. "See you tonight, Marnie."

All day she had trouble concentrating on her work. By lunch time, she was preoccupied and quiet. All her misgivings about an affair with Jason had come back to bedevil her.

"Is something bothering you?" Ellen asked as they settled in a back office and unwrapped their sandwiches.

"Good Lord, no," Ginny answered. "What

could be bothering me?"

"Maybe man trouble?"

"Man trou— No. Absolutely not." Ginny shook her head, then hesitated. "What would make you think I had man trouble?"

"The way you looked Monday morning and again this morning when you came in to work, kind of glowing and heavy lidded, and you've been distracted and almost secretive."

"Secretive?" Ginny shrugged and picked up half a sandwich. "I have nothing to hide."

"Not even a secret lover?" Ellen teased.

Ginny colored and looked away.

"Ouch. I've stepped on some toes," Ellen said. "Sorry."

"No, that's all right. It's just something . . . I'm not sure how to handle."

"You don't need to tell me about it if you don't want to."

"It might help to talk about it to someone."

"It might," Ellen agreed. "I'm not sure I can advise you, but I'll try."

"He's younger than me." Ginny waited for Ellen's reaction.

"That's it? That's your problem? He's younger than you?"

"You don't understand. He's more than ten years younger than me, twelve to be exact."

"I still don't see the problem. He's of age, a consenting adult."

"Ellen, I could almost be his mother."

"Highly unlikely. You would have been eleven at the time of his conception."

"My son, Scott, was thirty-two."

"Six years difference."

"Not very much. I feel as if I'm taking advantage of Ja— of him."

"Did you force him?"

Startled, Ginny looked at her friend and boss. "Of course not."

"Did you get him drunk and seduce him?"

"No. He'd made it clear for some time that he was interested, but I kept my distance. I tried to keep everything on a friendship basis."

"He wasn't happy with that?"

"Yes, but he wanted more."

"And you wanted more, and now you both have what you wanted. What on earth's the problem? Ginny, surely you aren't being prudish about this. Women date younger men and go to bed with them and even marry them."

Once again Ginny looked startled. Then she slowly shook her head. "I don't want to get married. I don't love him." She hung her head and stared at her hands twisted together in her lap.

"Ah, I see the reason for the guilt. You only want his body. What's wrong with that?"

Ginny sighed in exasperation. "Maybe I shouldn't have brought it up."

"You didn't. I did. Do you want someone to tell you this is wrong and you're a dirty old woman for bedding down with a nubile young male in his late thirties?" Ginny's face twisted with self-disgust. "I won't be the one to do that, Ginny, because I don't believe it's so. Is it the man next door, the one who lost his wife and child?"

Ginny nodded without looking up. Ellen reached forward and took one of her hands. "You're not doing anything wrong. You're a human being reaching out to another. What you two are doing is very human. For God's sake, don't muddle it up with all these guilt feelings."

"I can't help it, Ellen. What if I hurt him? I don't love him, at least not the way I loved David." -

"You could never deliberately hurt anyone," Ellen said. "Maybe you've given more to this man than you'll ever guess."

"I just feel so guilty. Maybe if it were so . . ." She flushed.

Ellen grinned. "Are you bragging or asking

advice?"

Ginny laughed. "Neither. And next time I need to talk to someone, I'll pick a lamppost. I'll get more sympathy."

"When you need sympathy, Logan, it'll be there. But, honey, you've got a lusty young male hankering after you. You don't need any advice from me."

As usual Ellen's no-nonsense attitude made Ginny feel better. Ellen seemed to know how to cut to the quick of a problem and discard anything that wasn't pertinent. She'd helped Ginny see that she and Jason were just two people who needed someone, so for now they should enjoy the pleasure they found in each other. Grateful Ginny gave Ellen a swift hug before returning to her desk.

Marnie was taking clothes off the line when Ginny got home. "It was a good day for drying," Ginny said, starting to help her. "I love the smell of laundry that's been hung outside."

"Country air is better for drying," Marnie conceded.

"Where are the girls?"

"Jason took them sailing."

"I hope they have on life jackets." Ginny

paused to stare out over the lake.

"You know Jason. He'll see they have."

"He's very good with them, isn't he?"

"Yep." Marnie folded a towel and dropped it into a basket. "He's awfully fond of the girls."

Ginny smiled. "They love him too."

"I sometimes worry about him, though."

Ginny looked at the old woman. "What are you trying to tell me, Marnie?"

"Well, he acts like those girls are his. It's going to be hard on him when he has to part from them." She held out a garment to Ginny. "Here's his shirt. It's been washed."

Ginny took the folded blue shirt from Marnie and clutched it to her chest. Her eyes went to the sailboat wafting across the gleaming water. She could hear Stef's squeal and Tracy's and Candi's high-pitched voices. Jason's deeper laughter mingled with theirs. They looked like a father and his children out for an afternoon sail. Ginny felt tears leap to her eyes.

"Ellen was wrong," she whispered, gripping the shirt tightly.

"Who's Ellen?" Marnie asked.

It was Friday night and they'd promised the girls a bonfire. Jason came over just before dusk to help set the ring of stones and lay the logs. Ginny stayed indoors under the pretense of having work to do. From the screened porch, she watched the girls and Jason.

"Grandma, come out," Candi called.

"You can't avoid the problem like this," Marnie said. She sat in a chintz-covered armchair, her sewing basket on the floor beside her, the lamp making a pool of warm light around her.

"I don't know what to do," Ginny confessed. "I fear I've made a dreadful mistake."

"Ain't no mistake you can't make right."

"It's not so simple," Ginny said.

"No, I never thought it was."

"Grandma, we're going to light the fire."

"You'd better go out there," Marnie urged. "Sometimes, things have a way of working out."

Ginny drew a light sweater around her shoulders and walked down to the lake. The moon was a quarter gone, but its light was intense as it rose over the dark line of trees, casting gold on the water.

"We've got marshmallows, Grandma," Candi said. "See!"

"Uh-oh, sounds like s'mores to me. There goes my diet."

"You don't have to diet, Grandma. You look beautiful enough," Tracy said.

"I concur with that," Jason said from across the fire. His grin was slow and sexy, his eyes filled with secret messages. Quickly, Ginny looked away and caught Tracy watching them intensely. She made a face, and Tracy's features relaxed into a smile.

The girls bubbled with talk, marshmallows were toasted and sometimes burnt, and chocolate melted on their fingers so they sat licking them. Jason told them a story that had the three of them screaming and huddling against Ginny, but Stef fell asleep long before the others were ready to call it a night.

"I'll carry her upstairs for you," Jason said, taking her from Ginny's arms.

"That's all right. I can manage," Ginny said lamely, but she relinquished her burden. Silently she followed him up the stairs and set about removing Stef's jeans and tennis shoes.

"Let her sleep in her T-shirt," Jason said. "It won't harm her one night." Ginny concurred and tucked the covers around Stef's grubby chin.

"They had fun tonight," she said, looking down at her granddaughter's smudged face.

"I had fun too," he said softly, placing his

hands on Ginny's shoulders. "Are you coming over later tonight?"

"Not tonight," she answered, unable to meet his gaze. "I have a headache."

Jason studied her face, then released her. "I hope you soon feel better." He placed a quick kiss on her cheek before turning to the door. It was so spontaneous, so much a part of the relationship they'd developed over the past months that she wanted to throw her arms around him and hug him. They were all so vulnerable, despite their new shows of strength.

"Jason!" He turned back toward her. The hall light shone behind him, casting his face in shadow, but she sensed his disappointment. "Thanks for all you do," she said.

He shrugged that away. "Take some aspirin, and get a good night's sleep," he said, and lumbered down the stairs. Ginny stayed where she was until she heard him bid the girls and Marnie good night, then she went to her own room. For a long time she sat in the dark, staring out over the moonlit water. This time last week, she and Jason were still just friends, having dinner at Sam's Joint. The dancing was what started it all, she reflected, the dancing and the moonlight. But she knew that wasn't true. This thing between Jason and her had started long before that. It had started when two lost people reached out to each other.

Despite Marnie's admonition, for the rest of the weekend, Ginny avoided being alone with Jason. She saw the puzzled look in his eyes, but could do nothing about it. She knew she had to break some of the ties they'd woven around each other. Or did she?

She didn't love him. What she felt was lust, and that couldn't be enough, could it? When she dwelled on their lovemaking, her resolve faltered. He'd awakened surprising things in her. She was grateful to him. Maybe that was enough, that and lust. Maybe she never would love anyone again. Maybe she should stop worrying and just enjoy whatever came as Ellen had advised. Maybe Marnie was a bigger worrier than she was!

"Let's go swimming," Jason called from his side of the fence. Ginny sat on the ground in front of her flowerbeds, ostensibly weeding, but she'd done very little. Now she glanced up at Jason and shook her head.

"Can't. Work to do."

"Can't you let it go for a few minutes? I've been trying to get you alone all weekend."

"I know." Ginny concentrated on her flowerbed. Jason looked too handsome, too sun-tanned and healthy, too nude in his swimsuit. "Why don't you wear a shirt once in a while," she said crossly. "I have granddaughters running around here."

"They never seem to notice. You're the only one objecting." His grin was impudent, saying he knew all too well why she objected. "Come on. You're hot and sweaty. I can see it from here. Take a swim and cool off."

Again Ginny shook her head. "I'm not going into the water with you, Jason."

"Coward!" His gaze was bold and lazy, the way his lovemaking was. She tried not to think about that.

"Dammit, Jason. I have a problem and you're not helping matters."

"Sorry. Can I help?"

"You are the problem."

"Me?" He pointed to his bare chest, and when she didn't respond he grew serious. Crossing the hedge fence, he came to sit on the ground across the flowerbed from her. "Maybe we'd better talk."

Now that he was here, now that the opportunity to tell him her fears had been given to her, she didn't know what to say—if anything.

"What's wrong?" His blue eyes regarded her across a row of yellow and orange marigolds.

"Marnie knows."

"I guessed as much when she hung my shirt on the fence. That doesn't have to be a problem. We're both single. We aren't doing anything wrong."

"That's what Ellen said."

"Ellen knows?"

Ginny nodded.

"How'd she find out?"

"I told her."

"Why?"

Ginny raised her head to look at him. "Because I needed advice." Jason looked upset.

"If I were older or you were younger, would you have needed advice or would you just have accepted the fact that we are two people who find each other attractive and have acted on that attraction."

"But we are what we are. And we've both been through so much." She tugged at a stubborn weed. It came out, spewing clumps of dirt over her smooth brown legs. Absently she brushed at her knees. "I don't want to take advantage of you," she mumbled.

"What?" Jason said, cupping his ear. "I didn't hear you. Could you repeat that?"

"I don't want to take advantage of you," Ginny said louder. Then she looked around guiltily and lowered her voice. "You've had a tremendous loss. I don't want to . . ." She hesitated, seeking the right word. Jason just waited for her to go on, a grin waiting to happen in his eyes. "I don't want you to think I seduced you in your moment of weakness."

"You mean when the moon was full?"

"Yes, something like that. And not just me, but the girls as well."

"What have the girls got to do with you and me?"

Ginny swallowed. "Maybe that's why you were so . . . susceptible to me."

He didn't answer. He rested his arms on his upraised knees and lowered his head so she couldn't see his face. What is he thinking? she wondered. She saw his shoulders quiver and felt alarm. Had she upset him so badly? The sound came—of someone suppressing weeping or . . . laughter!

"You bastard!" she cried, leaping to her feet. "I'm trying to be so considerate of you and your feelings and you're laughing at me."

He showed his face then. It was red from suppressed laughter. "I'm sorry." He shook his head and sprawled back on the grass. "It's just that you looked so earnest, like a little girl who's sorry she's broken the cookie jar."

294

Ginny threw a clump of dirt at him. Then, leaping across the flower bed, she pelted him with her fists. He laughed and threw up his hands.

"I'll kill you, Jason McCann. You are the most obnoxious, obtuse, self-centered, insensitive—"

His hands caught her arms, taming her, pulling down on the grass beside him. "I can be better, much better, given an incentive," he said. "The girls are off riding their bikes, Marnie's napping in her chair on the front porch. Come over to my cottage for a while."

She caught the intensity of his body, and a tenseness in her own responded to his words. She shook her hands free of his grasp and sat up, brushing the grass from her hair and clothes.

"I can't, Jason. That's what I've been trying to tell you. I just can't. I've started something that I don't know how to handle. I have to think."

"Don't be a thinker," he said next to her ear. His breath against her cheek sent shivers down her spine. "Be a doer." She couldn't fight him. She could feel herself weakening.

"All right. I'll be a doer," she said, getting to her feet. Jason sprang up effortlessly. His face was smug with victory. Ginny walked toward her cottage.

"Hey, where are you going?" Jason asked.

"A woman's got to do what a woman's got to do," she said, deadpanning à la Clint Eastwood. She'd gained the porch now, and she didn't look back. "Goodbye, Jason," she called and firmly closed the door behind her before taking a deep sigh of relief. Jason was as hard to resist as chocolate, and this was a battle she'd have to wage every day.

Fifteen

The moment she saw Alex again, she knew just how much of a mistake she'd made.

"Mr. Russell's here," Marnie fairly sang out as she hurried out to greet him, but Ginny stood at the kitchen window, watching him get out of his BMW. He looked hot and tired after his drive from the city, but he was just as handsome, just as endearingly familiar as always. Wings of silver swept up from his dark hair at the temples. Glancing about, he stretched his kinked muscles. She was almost grateful to see his suit pants and white shirt were rumpled and limp. It made him more human.

The girls had run up from the lake to see who had come, their tanned bodies in bright neon-colored swimsuits looked sleek and cool next to Alex's.

"Uncle Alex is here," Tracy called, and

Ginny had no more excuse for stalling. Fixing a smile on her face, she went out to meet her guest.

His dark eyes brightened when she appeared. In spite of the chatter around him, his gaze went to her face time and again.

"Alex, it's so good to see you," she said, going to hug him. His shoulders were thinner than Jason's. She couldn't help the comparison and flushed with guilt. He looked his age, as if he'd been under stress.

"God, Ginny, you look so good."

When he held her close, she drew back and peered into his face. Deep lines marked his eyes and thin cheeks. A wave of fondness washed over her. He'd always been her friend, and he'd always stood by her. He was part of her life, and he'd come here because he was concerned for her.

"You look tired," she said, affectionately looping an arm through his. "You need a swim and a drink."

"Could we reverse that order?" he asked, matching his long stride to hers.

"You're the boss," she answered lightly. "Let's get you settled on the patio, and I'll get you something. Scotch and water, isn't it?"

Gratefully he nodded.

298

"You two go ahead. I'll bring it out to you," Marnie ordered.

"I can swim now, Uncle Alex," Candi said. "Want to see me?"

"Give him a chance to rest, girls, then he'll change into his swimsuit and join you."

Satisfied, they raced back to the lake.

"They look like Indians, they're so brown and healthy." Alex turned his gaze from the lake to Ginny. "You all are. No wonder you don't want to come back to the city."

"We do like it here. You will too by the time you leave. How long are you staying?" Ginny sank into a cedar armchair and Alex settled into the one across from her so he still had a view of the lake.

"I don't know," he answered, looking around. "It's really beautiful here. I may stay awhile."

"You're welcome."

His gaze locked with hers. "Am I?" he asked. "Then why did it take so long for you to let me come out?"

Ginny looked away. "I needed time, Alex. I'm sorry if I've offended you."

"I wasn't offended." His hand landed on her knee in a brief, reassuring pat, then was removed. "Just worried."

His touch had been almost impersonal, but the warmth of it stayed with her. Marnie arrived with the drinks and passed them around.

"Aren't you going to join us?" Alex asked when she turned back to the cottage.

"You didn't come all this way to talk to me," Marnie said. "Besides, I've got supper to make and a pie in the oven."

"Homemade pie. What kind?"

Alex was surprisingly boyish. Ginny had forgotten how charming he could be.

Marnie was not immune. She tittered and shot a coquettish glance from under her lashes. One wrinkled brown hand went to her tightly permed hair, tucking in a frizzled curl. "Key lime pie. I remember you once said you liked it."

"Ummm, Marnie, you're a doll." The lines and tense muscles of his face had relaxed so, he was already looking younger. His teeth flashed in a smile as Marnie simpered under his dark gaze, and Ginny would have sworn the older woman's flat hips wriggled a bit as she walked back to the kitchen door.

Ginny laughed.

"What's so funny?" Alex asked with a half-grin.

"You are," Ginny gasped. "You aren't here

an hour and you have my granddaughters and my help eating out of your hand. Young or old you're a danger with women."

She'd expected him to laugh with her, but his face grew somber. "I'm not a womanizer, Ginny," he said seriously.

"How could you be anything else?" she said. "Oh, it isn't your fault, Alex." It was her turn to touch his knee in a conciliatory gesture. "You're so good-looking, you just naturally turn their heads. Tell me honestly. Have you ever had a failure with a woman?"

His eyes were fathomless. "One," he said, and got to his feet. "I'm ready for the next part of your agenda."

Ginny set aside her glass. "Come on, I'll show you to your room." She led him up the path to the back porch, where they'd left his overnight bag. Alex picked it up and followed her inside. His whistle of approval was low and heartfelt as he looked around the cottage.

"I pictured you making do with minimal comforts. I see I was wrong."

"Thank you. David and I did a lot of work on this place when we first bought it. After he died I just couldn't come out here—until Scott and the girls got interested in it. So we added a lot of things to make it comfortable and homey."

"You did a good job." He followed her up the stairs, his gaze taking in slim, rounded hips and long slender legs.

"I hope you don't mind fuzzy, stuffed animals and posters of the latest teenage idols." She paused. "No, that's not quite right, teenage hunks, I think they're called."

"Am I putting the girls out?"

"Only Tracy. She's bunking in with me for the weekend."

"I could have done that." His face was solemn, his eyes twinkling. He looked half-serious. Ginny chose to treat his comment as a joke.

"We run a moral house here, Mr. Russell," she said primly and suppressed an urge to do a bump and grind. What on earth was happening to her? Where was the serious, responsible adult she once had been? She'd have to remember this was Alex, older and therefore more proper, not Jason with his mischievous grins that dared her to be different.

"That door leads to the bathroom, which you'll have to share with Tracy and me." She looked around to see if he needed anything else. "I'll change into my suit and meet you downstairs."

302

Her perfume lingered after she was gone. Alex chided himself for his remark. He'd been trying to introduce a little levity between them. He'd sensed Ginny's stiffness. But the comment hadn't come out right. Yet, he'd seen the quiver of a smile lurking in her eyes, he'd noticed the slight jutting of a hip, and he now pondered what was so different about her. She glowed. He slipped into his swim trunks and grabbed a towel from the bathroom. True to her word, Ginny was already on the patio waiting for him. She wore a tropical-print swimsuit, soft fuchsias and purple. Her legs were tanned, sleek, and about a mile long. He had trouble keeping his gaze from them.

Ginny felt his hot gaze flick across her figure, and nervously turned and led the way down to the lake.

"Hey, Uncle Alex, look at me," Candi called and cannonballed off the raft. Stef was busy making mud pies along the sandy shore. Tracy was sunning herself, although the late afternoon light was already waning. When she saw Ginny and Alex approaching she leapt up, her eyes shining. Ginny couldn't help but remember how Tracy had shrugged off Alex's hand that disastrous winter night when they'd all had dinner together. But now Tracy seemed eager to see him and talk with him. He'd always been a part of the girls' lives too, she realized with a start. Why had she always thought he wasn't a man who cared for children? He'd brought them gifts at Christmas, taking time to have a drink and watch them open their presents. And his gifts had reflected thoughtfulness as to their interests and age level. Remembering this, Ginny felt guilty that she'd taken him so much for granted, and she took his hand as they waded out to deeper water.

"It's good to have you here, Alex," she said.

"Is that an admission that you've missed me too?"

"I believe it is." She let go of his hand and pushed forward into deeper water, where she floated for a moment and then swam in long easy strokes toward the raft. Alex was right beside her. They arrived at the raft at the same time and laughed as if they'd run an unofficial race and were glad neither had won.

"Look at me now, Uncle Alex," Candi cried, and somersaulted off the raft.

"Wonderful," Alex called, his laugh deep and rich.

Tracy joined her sisters and added her gymnastics to the show, and when the girls had tired themselves out, Ginny and Alex floated on their backs, staring at the flat blue sky and relaxing in the warm water. Now and then they dog paddled and talked. Ginny didn't ask him about the agency. She didn't want to know if Nola was there or not.

"Looks like we have company," Alex said, nodding to a third swimmer.

"I've told Tracy she can't come out this far," Ginny said, but the dark head that broke the surface spewing a plume of water was not Tracy's.

"Hello," Jason said, his gaze going from Alex to Ginny. Something in his tight expression made her feel uncomfortable.

"Hello. Alex, this is Jason McCann, our next-door neighbor."

Jason glanced at her accusingly, and she was aware she hadn't mentioned that he was also a friend.

"How do you do," Alex said, treading water. "I've heard a lot about you."

"Ohh?" Jason glanced at Ginny questioningly.

"Yes, Mrs. Lansky and the girls seem quite taken with you."

"Well, I'm taken by them." Again that half-lazy glance in Ginny's direction.

"Have you lived here long?"

"Since last fall. Is this your first time here?"

"My first, not my last." Ginny sensed the challenge between the two men.

"Alex is an old family friend," she said. Then, remembering she'd been rather sketchy about Jason's status, she rushed on. "Jason is . . . a friend also."

"A new family friend," said Jason. His voice was heavy with meaning, and he paddled closer to Ginny in a movement that was clearly possessive.

"Well, isn't this cozy?" Alex looked from one of them to the other.

"Grandma! Marnie says supper is ready," Tracy called.

"Oh, we'd better go in then," Ginny said in relief. "Marnie hates to have her food get cold."

"Are you joining us, Mr. McCann?" Alex asked.

"Yes, of course," Ginny said quickly although she'd deliberately not invited him for that night, wanting a chance to get comfortable with Alex first. "Jason has a standing invitation to eat with us."

Jason cast a triumphant look at Alex.

"How nice," Alex remarked. "Well, we'd better swim in and change. I know Marnie can be a bear."

"Not if you know how to handle her," Jason remarked, and anger shimmered through Ginny. She had little doubt the two men were not talking about Marnie now. She shot Jason a warning glance and swam away from them both.

Alex had caught up with her by the time she reached shallow water. "He seems a nice enough fellow," he said, wading out of the lake and picking up his towel.

"He's been a good friend to all of us." For some reason she wasn't able to meet his eyes.

"I'm sure he has." Alex draped the towel around his neck. "After you." He followed her up the brick path to the patio.

"Is he married?"

"Widowed."

"Oh? Children?"

"No. I think that's why he enjoys the girls so much."

Alex grunted again. "What does he do besides swim and eat with you often?"

"He was a psychologist, but he's taken a hiatus to write a detective book."

"He's a writer?" Alex's voice registered alarm. His expression was dour as he glanced over at the DeFauw cottage.

307

"There's nothing wrong with being a writer," Ginny said. "Besides, he was a psychologist first."

"The worst kind," Alex grumbled. "First they analyze you; then they put you in a book."

Ginny laughed. "Actually, Marnie's the one he put in a book, and she loves it."

"Traitor!" Alex grunted under his breath. They were at the cottage now, and with a last grin, Ginny ran lightly up the stairs and disappeared into her room.

Alex wandered back to the kitchen, where Marnie was putting the finishing touches on her meal. "Ach, you've had your swim. You look better."

"I feel better." Alex hesitated, then, taking the bull by the horns, spread his towel, and sat down on an oak chair. "Tell me something about your neighbor," he said, fixing Marnie with a stern eye.

She shot him a dubious glance and went back to mixing a bean salad. "He's a good neighbor. He helps out around here. He's good with the girls. He makes them laugh."

"Does he make Ginny laugh?"

"I wouldn't be knowing about what's between the two of them," she said, then dropped the mixing spoon into the sink with a clatter. "You'd best be getting yourself dressed. No one comes to my table in a swimsuit, not even a guest."

Unsatisfied, Alex went to his room to change. Glancing out the window, he could see Jason McCann emerging from the house next door, so he hurried to pull on fresh slacks and a collared knit shirt. He was determined to beat out Jason McCann in spending time with Ginny. After all, the guy was here all the time. Alex only had the weekend with her.

By the time he had shaved, combed his hair, and slapped on aftershave lotion, he'd taken far longer than he'd wanted. Jason and Ginny were on the patio, where a table had been set. Strings of lights hung from the trees and citronella candles flamed at each corner of the patio. The girls were already seated around the table, their hair freshly brushed, their suits changed for T-shirts and shorts. Ginny was beautiful in a sprigged cotton sundress that showed off her tan. Her bare brown feet were shoved into sandals.

"Here's our guest," Jason said. "We were just wondering what had happened to you."

"You may sit here in the place of honor," Ginny said to Alex, pulling out the chair at the head of the table, "and you Jason may sit at the other end."

"How practical," Alex said. Jason walked past Alex's chair and paused, holding his nose to the wind. "Lovely perfume someone is wearing." Alex's hands tightened, but he ignored the gibe.

"Marnie, can I help you carry out anything else?" Ginny asked, but Marnie shook her head.

"It's all out. Sit down."

Obediently, Ginny sat and looked around the table, smiling. "Well, isn't this nice?" she said. "Here we are with good friends at our table." No one answered. The girls seemed to have picked up on the tension between the adults. Marnie harumphed and snorted in indignation as people picked at her food, and Alex and Jason spent the meal glaring at each other across the table.

"How much mileage do you get out of that little number in the driveway?"

"When you drive a BMW, you don't worry about the mileage," Alex said. "What do you drive, Mr. McCann?"

"Call me Jason. Ginny and the kids do." His tone was possessive. "I'm a practical man, Mr. Russell."

"Please, do call me Alex or even Uncle Alex.

310

Ginny and the children do."

Jason frowned. Ginny frowned. Tracy giggled and hid it in her napkin. Stef's eyes got bigger, and Marnie glowered.

"As I was saying Mr. —" Jason smiled. "Alex, I'm a practical man. I drive a jeep."

"I would have guessed that, Mr. Mc — Jason."

"Yes, here in the country we like dependability, serviceability."

Ginny choked and reached for her water glass.

"But no subtlety, Jason?" Alex asked softly. "There's no romance in a jeep."

"I kind of figure romance doesn't belong in a jeep. It works better for me in a—"

"Is everyone ready for dessert?" Ginny cried, leaping to her feet.

"My land, they ain't hardly eaten anything," Marnie said.

"I'm finished." Alex handed over his half-full plate.

"I guess I am too," Jason said. Ginny had never seen him leave anything less than an empty plate until now. Marnie had once remarked she feared he meant to eat the pattern right off the china, but his plate was nearly full as he passed it over. Fussing under her breath, Marnie toted the plates back to the kitchen.

"I've never seen either of those men act like such a fool before," she fumed, handing Ginny the dessert plates.

Ginny remained silent. She wasn't sure how to handle the verbal combat that was going on. Part of her was ready to scream in frustration, but a tiny part of her, that part deep beneath practicality and sensibility was touched by her two Lotharios.

"Maybe your Key lime pie will cool them down," she said, grabbing forks and spatula from the drawer. Everyone was silent when they reached the patio again. The two men were studiously ignoring each other, while the girls stared from one to the other, their heads swiveling to and fro as if they were watching a tennis match.

"Oh, lord," Ginny said as she tripped over the leg of a lawn chair. Instantly two chairs scraped backward, two sets of hands reached for her, steadying her. Two handsome faces peered at her in concern.

"Are you all right?" Jason asked.

"Yes, I was just clumsy."

"Are you sure you're okay?" Alex said. "Let me take those things from you." As Alex took her small burden, Jason led her to her chair and held it until she was seated. The girls stared at her in consternation. They'd never seen anyone treat their grandmother in such a fashion. They weren't sure what to make of it.

Marnie dished out the Key lime pie, and they all picked up their dessert forks.

"This is delicious, Marnie. Thank you for making it for me," Alex said.

"How did you know it was my favorite?" Jason asked. "Ginny must have told you."

"I didn't make it for either one of you," Marnie grumbled. "I made it for myself."

"It's delicious, no matter who you made it for," Ginny said with false brightness.

"Grandma, why are you talking like that?" Stef asked. Her blue eyes were large and solemn as they regarded Ginny.

Ginny cast a desperate glance at Marnie, who relented and came to the rescue. "Girls, it's past your bedtime. Help me take these dishes back to the kitchen and then get to your showers. Stef, I'll read to you tonight, since Ginny has company."

Ginny wasn't sure whether Marnie's action had been a rescue or not, for she was left seated at the table with a glowering man on either side of her. "Coffee anyone?"

313

"I'll have a cup," Jason said.

"Certainly," Alex replied.

"Cognac?" Both men nodded and waited silently while she poured a dollop in each cup. When that was done and the cups were passed, an uneasy silence fell over them.

"When are you returning to Detroit, Alex?" Jason asked and his tone made it clear any time soon wouldn't be soon enough.

"As I told Ginny, I'm not certain. I may stay for a while. I need a vacation."

"You'll likely find us boring around here," Jason said.

"Not if I'm selective about my company," Alex answered.

Ginny faked a yawn and stood up. "I'm really exhausted," she said. "I think I'll head up to bed myself."

Alex got to his feet. "I'm tired too," he said genially. "I'll go up with you." He smiled at Jason. "Sorry to rush you off."

"You couldn't," Jason said, unfolding his long length from the chair. He took Ginny's hand. "Good night, Gin. I'll see you in the morning." Playfully, he touched the tip of her nose with one long finger. His smile was lazy and sexy and self-assured. Before she could respond, he dropped a light kiss on her lips and

314

stalked away into the dark.

"Well"—Ginny looked around the patio at a loss as to what to say—"looks like the mosquitoes are coming out." She crossed to a flare and set the metal cup over the flame, smothering it. Silently, Alex did the same at the outer corner. The patio was flooded with darkness broken only by the multicolored lights hanging in the trees. They faced each other across the darkened space. She could sense the questions he wanted to ask, but he remained silent. Holding out a hand to her, he nodded his head.

"Come on, let's go for a walk," he said.

Hand in hand, they meandered down the drive. The moonlight was shadowed by a cloud.

"I should have gotten a flashlight," Ginny said. "We can't see anything."

"We don't need one," Alex responded. "It's more adventurous this way. Besides you don't have to be scared with me. I can take care of you, even if I do drive a BMW."

He'd meant for her to laugh, and she did, a sort of breathless sound of relief.

"I'm sorry, Gin," he said. "I acted pretty abominably tonight."

"You both did."

"We both did," he echoed. She felt the unasked question, but he turned it aside. "Tell me how things are going with you and your new job," he said instead, and she told him about Ellen and Dr. Bob and Emily Fuller and her husband and all the other people who filled the center with drama and laughter. He heard something new in her voice and took heart. He let her talk, learning new things about her, things she'd only explored herself these past few months. He listened to the sound of her voice, felt her slim hand resting in his and wished they could go on like this forever, but all too soon they were back at the cottage. The windows were dark except for a soft glow from the light Marnie had left for them in the kitchen.

They climbed the steps to the porch, their voices soft, at home with each other again. At the door, Alex told hold of her arm.

"Wait, Ginny," he said, and slipping his arm around her waist, he drew her to him. His kiss was gentle, undemanding, a statement making itself heard, a pledge not to give up too easily. She hesitated; then, caught in the wonder of Alex, she returned his kiss, her lips soft and sweet beneath his. When he released her, she stood back and stared at him, her eyes wide in the dark shadows, trying to see beyond the old familiar concepts that might blind her.

"Good night, Ginny," he said softly. He placed his palm against her cheek as if needing to touch her in some way, then he slipped inside the cottage. She heard him climb the stairs to his room and the closing of his door. Standing alone on the porch, Alex's kiss still warm on her lips, Ginny knew just how much of a mistake she'd made.

Sixteen

A summer Saturday morning at the lake held all sorts of possibilities. First, there was lolling in bed, listening to the skitter of tiny feet as squirrels played tag across the porch roof and to birdsong as brilliant and poignant as the dabbled sunlight pouring into the room. On Saturday there was no reason to spring out of bed, unless you just didn't want to miss one moment of the golden day, no reason to worry about anything. Concerns could be put on hold for another day. Ginny usually slid into her swimsuit, knotting an oversized T-shirt at her hips. In spite of Marnie's fussing about a proper meal, she usually took an oversized cinnamon roll and a cup of coffee down to the dock, where she dangled her feet in the water and watched the first sailboat race of the day. Sometimes Jason came to join her. The day was filled with working on the flowerbeds, swimming with the girls, boat-

318

ing, or curling up in the big swing down by the lake and reading the latest mystery. Saturday was for no makeup and wind-blown hair and lazing away long hours swinging back and forth and staring at the sky.

But this was not a normal Saturday. Alex was here, and suddenly Ginny felt terrifyingly shy and confused about who she was and what she was about. It had all seemed so simple before. Before what? she wondered. Before her affair with Jason? Before Alex came and saw too much and guessed what existed between them? He'd said not one word, made no accusations. How could he? Hadn't he engaged in affairs with younger women? Why should it be so different for her just because she was a woman? She marshaled her defenses, fine-tuned her arguments, and practiced them to herself alone in her room, the sunshine and birdsong temporarily forgotten. But, in the end, she knew she'd never have a chance to utter them, for Alex would never question her behavior. He was too fine. He would simply accept the fact she'd chosen to have an affair with Jason and leave it at that. She felt deflated. It is for the best, she thought. I can't possibly handle two suitors. Jason is quite enough, perhaps too much.

Ginny reluctantly got up and spent an inordinate amount of time in making the bed, showering, and dressing. No swimsuit and baggy T-shirt this Saturday. She drew on a pair of shorts and a matching halter top, then buttoned the matching skirt partway, so there was a flash of brown knees when she walked. When her hair and makeup suited her, she went downstairs. No one was around except Marnie, who was puttering in the kitchen.

"Good morning. Where is everyone?"

"The kids took Mr. Russell out in the canoe," Marnie grunted. "I ain't seen Jason yet."

"He's probably sleeping late." Ginny poured herself a cup of coffee.

Marnie glanced around and noticed her dress. "Where you going all dolled up like that?" she asked.

"I'm not dolled up, Marnie," Ginny said pleasantly. "I just thought, since I have company, I should wear something else besides a faded old swimsuit. I'll be out on the patio, if anyone should want me."

The sky was cloudless, the sun on the water decadently seductive. In the distance sailboats gathered near a starting buoy. A majestic blue heron flew past the end of the dock, and sea gulls settled on rafts, their raucous cries mocking the owners who'd mounted fake owls in the hope of scaring away these messy visitors. Despite her unease over Alex and Jason, Ginny allowed the peace of the lake to ease into her limbs. She walked down to the swing and sat on it, slipping off her sandals and pulling her feet up on the wooden seat. The canoe was returning, and the bright voices of the girls carried over the water.

"Look out, sit still," Alex admonished them.

"It's all right, Uncle Alex. She won't fall out," Candi reassured him.

"I'm not worried about her falling out. I'm afraid she'll tip us over," Alex said, and he made a grab for the little girl.

"She's too little to tip us," Tracy said. "If you or I stood up in the boat—" Her warning came too late. In his effort to secure Stef, Alex had gotten to his feet. The canoe wobbled dangerously, rolling from side to side.

"Lookout," he cried and tried to shift his weight. He overcompensated and the canoe listed deeply to the other side.

"Watch out, Stef," he called, still worried about the little girl.

"Sit down, Uncle Alex," Tracy called, hanging onto the sides of the canoe with both hands. Ginny sprang to her feet.

Even as she watched, the canoe rolled one last time, took on water, and flipped over. Alex and the girls spilled into the water. Barefooted, Ginny rushed to the end of the dock, preparing to dash in and rescue her granddaughters if need be, in spite of the shallow water. Alex's head surfaced and he stood up, clutching a sputtering Stef to his chest.

"I've got you," he cried triumphantly. "You're safe with me."

"Uncle Alex," she cried reprovingly, one chubby hand rubbing the water from her eyes. "You tipped the canoe."

Candi and Tracy had emerged from the water now, and they all stood glaring at Alex. He took in their accusing faces.

"Look, I was trying to save Stef," he said lamely.

"She didn't need rescuing, Uncle Alex. She always crawls around in the canoe."

"But the canoe was tipping."

"Because you stood up," Candi said.

Alex looked from the girls to the bottom-up canoe to Ginny, standing barefoot on the dock, trying to hide her laughter. "Well, I warned you I wasn't good at this sort of thing." He waded over to set Stef on the dock.

"We didn't think you'd flip the canoe," Tracy said, hands on her hips.

Alex glanced up at Ginny. The sunshine brought out red glints in brown hair, and her face was bright with humor. How could she look so crisp and perfect standing there barefoot and windblown? he wondered, and was suddenly aware of how bedraggled he must appear. He pulled his wet shirt away from his chest and turned back to the boat.

"So how do we get this thing back to shore?" he asked in disgust.

"We'll have to turn it over and dump out the water," Tracy explained.

"Need some help, old man?"

Alex didn't need to turn around to know who had offered. Jason McCann stood beside Ginny on the dock. His eyes were mocking.

"I suppose I could use someone at the other end," Alex acknowledged with the best grace he could muster.

Jason grinned and swung down into the water. He wore only a swimsuit, and his upper body was very brown and fit looking. Alex was aware of every one of his years as he waded back to the boat. He figured he must look ridiculous to Ginny in his wet shirt and dripping shorts and tennis shoes. She certainly seemed amused. Next to nature boy, he felt citified and incompetent.

To make matters worse, two of the girls stood in the water and supervised his efforts, while neither of them seemed to think Jason needed help. Together the men turned the canoe, the air in its flotation chambers helping it rise. They then got it to shore, where Jason helped Alex

323

empty out the rest of the water. Tracy and Candi waded out, dragging the paddles. Ginny had brought Stef up to the swing and wrapped her in a towel.

"Maybe next time, we'll use the paddle boat, Uncle Alex," Tracy said earnestly. "It doesn't tip quite so easily."

"That's not necessary," he protested. "This was just an accident."

"Still, I wouldn't go out in the canoe alone, old man," Jason said.

"So good of you to be concerned about me."

"Not at all." Jason grinned. "You'd better get out of those wet things. You wouldn't want to catch a cold."

"Quite right." Alex's gaze went to Ginny. "If you'll excuse me . . ."

"Girls, you'd better get into dry clothes too," Ginny said, and she concentrated on drying Stef, so briskly the child protested. When the girls had disappeared into the cottage, Jason stood regarding Ginny. She folded the towel and hung it neatly on the back of the swing.

"Well, that's one adventure that ended safely," she said without meeting his gaze.

"Ginny . . ." Jason's voice was soft. He stepped forward and took hold of her hand. She had to meet his gaze then. Honesty demanded she do so.

324

"Is he the reason?"

"The reason?"

"You need time to think?"

"I— No, he wasn't."

"Wasn't? Is he now?"

"Oh, Jason, please." She pulled her hand from his. "I . . . I just need time to sort everything out. I didn't mean to start an affair with you. It was better when we were just friends."

"I don't agree."

"It was less complicated then."

"That's true. But you can't just take the easy way all the time. You needed me. Don't you need me now?"

"Jason, I don't know what to tell you. I don't want to hurt you."

"Did you have an affair with him?"

She flared. "You have no right to ask me such questions."

"Are you having one now?"

"No, on both counts. Now I think you'd better leave."

He turned to go, then hesitated, one slim hip jutting in that slouch he affected when he was hurt and trying not to show it.

"I'm sorry," he said. "I know I have no right to make demands of you. But you can't blame me for feeling jealous of this guy."

"Jason, you have no reason to be jealous.

Alex and I have been friends for many years. That's all. He's . . . well, he likes younger women. I'm just not his type."

Jason looked at her solemnly; then his mouth widened in a grin. "You sure don't know how to read guys," he said, "but I won't argue with you. If he's willing to pass up someone like you, he's really not as smart as he looks." He strode away to his side of the hedge, whistling a tuneless melody.

Ginny watched his lanky, brown body, remembering how it felt against her own, and a flush crept over her cheeks.

"Your friend has gone home, I see," Alex said from close behind her. "I meant to thank him." He'd changed into cotton shorts and a fresh shirt.

"That isn't necessary," she said, trying to hide her reddened cheeks from Alex's knowing gaze. "Everyone pitches in and helps when there's a problem. After all, you aren't the first person to tip a canoe, and you won't be the last."

"I expect not." He walked to the swing and sat down. Her sandals still lay on the ground where she'd left them. Hesitantly, she joined him. Jason's questions still hung in the air, and she remembered Alex's kiss the night before. Had she been mistaken when she'd told him Alex wasn't interested in her?

326

"How are you, Ginny? I mean aside from your job and the lake. How are you feeling about things now?"

"I'm coping. When I left Detroit I didn't think I could bear all that had happened. It just seemed to be too much, but now I can put it in perspective."

"Have you heard from Diane?"

"No, why would I?"

"I was just remembering what you told me about Candi's near drowning and the problem you had at the hospital. Perhaps you should contact Diane and get her power of attorney in caring for the girls."

"I suppose that makes sense," Ginny said reluctantly. "I'll think about it."

Alex said nothing more about it. Somehow they'd begun to swing, their legs pushing against the grassy sod in unison, their bodies swaying slightly with the gentle rhythm of the swing's movement. It felt good. Alex glanced at Ginny and smiled.

"I haven't done this in years," he said. "I'd forgotten how great it is."

Ginny laughed softly. "I know. I felt the same way, as if all the years were lifting away. If you lean your head back and stare at the sky you can nearly hypnotize yourself."

They swayed in companionable silence until

Marnie called out that lunch was ready. Together they walked to the cottage and joined the chattering girls who still had much to say about Alex standing up in the boat. He took their ribbing with good humor, even laughing at himself. After lunch everyone settled onto lounge chairs and sofas to read and relax. Ginny tried to finish her latest mystery, but she was distracted.

"Want to take me for a sail?" Alex asked, bending over her chair. "I'm determined not to take a nap until I've reached my ninetieth birthday, but that requires drastic measures."

"A sail sounds good to me too." Ginny put aside her book. "Sail boats tip though," she warned impishly.

"If this one does, I vow I won't rescue you as I did Stef."

"Just promise you won't stand up."

He colored slightly and crossed his heart.

"Good enough." She laughed. "I'll meet you at the boat in five minutes. I have to put on my swimsuit," she paused, eyes sparkling, "just in case." Alex couldn't help laughing at himself.

She dashed upstairs and dug out the new swimsuit she'd been saving. It was black and sexy. She didn't ask herself why she chose to wear it now.

Alex was waiting for her when she got downstairs. He'd changed into a swimsuit as well. Although his lean body wasn't as fit as Jason's, Alex was no slouch, she noticed. They pushed off in the boat, and Ginny set the sail. There was just enough of a breeze to send them skimming across the water.

"Ah, this is great," Alex said. "I remember when my buddy and I used to sail on Lake Charlevoix."

"Was your parents' boat large?"

"The boat wasn't my parents'," he said. "They couldn't afford a boat."

"I thought you grew up in Grosse Pointe."

"I did, but my parents weren't wealthy. They worked for people in Grosse Pointe. My mother was a housekeeper, my father was a gardener, chauffeur, a man of all trades."

"I always thought you came from a wealthy family."

"Part of the myth I used to maintain when I thought it was important."

"I see." Ginny took a while to digest this new information. "How did you get the money for the university and to start your business?"

"I won a scholarship." Alex shrugged. "And I worked my way through. While the other guys were off with their sports and fraternities, I was back in Grosse Pointe working weekends for Hoyt Taylor. When I got out I married his daughter." He took a deep breath. "The mar-

329

riage didn't last long. I worked too many hours, and she wanted a husband with money. She'd grown up with it, and she wasn't willing to wait."

"Oh, Alex, I never knew. I'm so sorry. I always thought your marriage failed because—"

"Because?"

"*You* wanted it to."

"Be honest, Ginny. You and David thought it failed because I couldn't be faithful to my wife."

"Yes, that's what we thought," she said quietly, and studied the water curling away from the transom.

"Don't feel bad. I let everyone think that about me. It made me feel tough at the time, as if Carly's leaving me really didn't hurt after all."

"But it did."

"Yeah, it did. Say, this isn't meant to be confession time."

"I'm glad you told me, Alex," she said, putting a hand over his. Quickly she drew it away and pretended to adjust the tiller. "Did Mr. Taylor blame you for the failure of the marriage?"

"Hoyt knew his daughter pretty well. He came and apologized to me as if it were somehow his fault. Carly went to Europe and stayed. Hoyt and I went into business together."

"The agency?"

"The agency. He had a lot of confidence in

me, a lot more than I had in myself. When he died, I was prepared to buy out his part in the business. I didn't want to have Carly as a partner, but she said she wouldn't sell. Then Hoyt's will was read. He'd bequeathed me his part of the agency, and Carly was given everything else. She was furious."

"Why?"

"I've never understood why she needed it. I think she just wanted to control me. Without a share of the business, she couldn't do that."

"No wonder you chose women who were—"

"What?"

"Young and without any real power."

"Is that what I've been doing?"

"I'm sorry. I didn't mean to sound like a psychoanalyst."

"Some of Jason rubbing off on you?"

"I guess so."

"Ginny, why did you leave? I never understood."

She smiled, thinking how endearing he was even when he couldn't see her side of things.

"I just couldn't stay, Alex. I felt as if everything I was as a woman was put on the line and found wanting. It scared me."

"But why would you of all people feel so vulnerable?"

"When you've spent your whole life relying on

your intuition, and then suddenly you reach a certain age and people begin to tell you that you can't trust your instincts, that they're wrong, you get confused," she said earnestly. He liked the way her eyebrows pulled down when she was thinking something through. "Oh, people don't tell you that in so many words, just in their responses to you. Once your opinion, which was largely based on intuition, was held in some esteem and suddenly, when the big *M* word occurs, you lose every ounce of esteem you once enjoyed."

"What big *M* word?"

She cast him an exasperated look. "Menopause."

"Oh!"

She remained silent for a time. "You know it's so unfair because it isn't caused by anything you've done except have the unmitigated gall to grow older, to reach that age when your body changes, when you can no longer make babies, although God knows that's not so important to women these days anyway."

Alex listened in silence, but she was too fired up now to need input from him. She'd bottled all this up, and he sensed she just needed someone to listen. He could feel a thigh muscle tightening with the advance warning twinge of a cramp, but he didn't move, lest he stem the flow of words.

"Do you know, Alex, that in nearly every society, our own included, puberty is celebrated, but menopause is treated as a shameful thing? No wonder women become depressed! Their whole lives they struggle for equality and recognition for their contributions, and when they enter menopause, they seem to lose what ground they've gained."

She was mad now, just plain mad. She was the old Ginny again, passionate, articulate. The passivity she'd adopted ever since David's death was gone. She'd been down, she'd lost her husband and son, her belief in herself had been shaken, but she was fighting back. The wind blew her hair out from her head in funny little spikes that would have made her laugh had she been able to see them. But she couldn't. He stared at her wind-tossed hair, at her shiny face glowing with renewed purpose, and at soft hazel eyes that had gone dark with intent. Emotion shook him right to his fingertips, and he wanted to sweep her forward off the side of the boat and into his arms. The thought was unsettling as hell.

"Damn!" he yelped, leaping to one knee, his other leg stretched before him.

"What's wrong?" asked Ginny.

"Cramp! Get me to shore—fast," he grunted.

Without another word, she hauled over the jib sail and turned the little boat about. When they were skimming straight toward her dock, she cast him a quick glance.

"Try kneading it," she called. His long brown hands worked at his thigh muscle. He could feel the knots, shifting and clenching. His teeth were gritted, his face tight and red.

She raised the rudder and ran the little boat right up into the shallows. Stepping out, she hauled the bow up on the sand and ran back to help him ashore. She put her shoulder beneath his arm and braced one hip, but his weight carried them both to the earth in a tangle of limbs. He lay still, grimacing and cradling his thigh. Ginny extricated herself and knelt beside him.

"Roll over," she ordered, pushing him onto his side. Her fingers were strong and soothing on his thigh. She worked from the outside edges of the cramp, kneading and massaging toward the core of the pain, while Alex lay with his cheek pressed into the earth, watching her buttocks clench and weave just inches away. She had pretty good legs for a fifty-year-old woman. Hell, they were great legs for anybody, long and slim, the skin smooth and tanned from her summer in the sun. His glance moved back to her fanny and the rhythmic motion it made as she concentrated on tending his cramped muscles.

Hell, he was getting another cramp just watching her.

"How does that feel?" she asked, sitting back on her heels and regarding him with concern. Alex rolled forward onto his stomach to hide the condition he'd been brought to by his lascivious thoughts.

"Much better," he answered, and realized the cramp was gone. A bigger problem assailed him now. How was he going to face her with his swim suit sticking out in front as if he were a randy young bull. "Hand me my towel," he said, his voice muffled against his forearm.

"Your towel?" Ginny repeated, straightening in one sweeping move. How in the hell had she done that? Hadn't she heard of arthritis? She brought the towel back and stood over him. "Do you need some help getting to your feet?"

"No! I can manage." Alex snatched the towel and balled it in front of him high against his thigh. Awkwardly he got to his feet and stood crouched over.

"Oh, Alex. The towel isn't going to help you," she scoffed gently. Humor was beginning to seep back into her voice. If she knew, he was sure she'd laugh.

"It helps," he ground out. Sweat was standing out on his forehead.

"You look positively awful," she said. "Lean

on me and I'll help you in." She took hold of his towel arm. In a panic, he shook her off. Ginny's smile faded instantly. Her eyes looked hurt and uncertain again. He hated himself for hurting her even the least little bit, but he had to get away from her, at least until his libido had settled down.

"I'll talk to you later," he said and staggered across the lawn to the house. His thigh muscle was still sore, and knowing she was watching him, he exaggerated his limp shamelessly. But when he'd reached the screened porch, he couldn't resist a look back. Ginny was standing at the hedge, chatting with Jason. They both looked in his direction, so he knew she was telling him about his cramp. His dislike for the young man grew.

A hot shower helped his cramped muscle, one of them anyway. He turned the nozzle to cold to help the other problem. Jesus, he hadn't had to do this since he was a teenager. He came out, goose pimply and shriveled. He stood nude before the mirror, studying himself, assessing what he was, what he'd become. What he saw was a tall slender man with gray temples, a permanent squint from smoking too much, and a soft middle from sitting behind a desk too long. He wasn't much competition for Jason McCann, he decided.

Ginny wasn't the only one to face changes in life. Men had them too, and they were just as traumatic, but he'd be damned if he'd tell her what they were. No doubt Jason would do that. Besides sleeping together, they seemed to have an uncommon rapport.

"Face it, old man," he told his reflection. "You're jealous as hell because she's sleeping with a younger man."

He threw himself across the bed and lay staring at the ceiling, thinking of the things Ginny had told him in the boat and of his response to her on the beach. He'd always cared about her. He'd gotten used to seeing her smiling face at the office every day, of hearing her bright greeting, of walking by her office and seeing her bent over her drawing table or hearing her charm some potential client over the phone. She was good at her job. She had a way with people, kind of friendly and sincere. People didn't laugh at her jokes as they did at Nola's, but they often felt more comfortable with Ginny. There was a credibility in all she did. She'd been a dynamic force in the agency, and he missed her more than he'd ever guessed he would.

But here on the lake, he was seeing Ginny in a different way. He saw the earthy, loving woman she was underneath the professional image and the grandmotherly facade. My god, the roles she juggled. No wonder David had admired her so, had been proud of her, had thought of her first before even going out for a drink. Alex had thought of him tied down, had pitied him even, thinking his freedom forever gone. Now at the ripe old age of forty-nine—well all right, fifty-three—Alex was having an awakening. David was the one who'd had it all, a son and a wife like Ginny, while he with all his highly prized freedom had gained what? A thousand nights with a thousand different women, each one more meaningless than the one before. The faces ran together into a blurred collage, the tragic trophy of a man who'd been afraid to take a chance again.

He thought of Ginny with her face scrubbed free of makeup, laugh lines at the corners of her eyes and mouth, freckles dotting her nose, her hair blowing free in the wind. There was real freedom, he realized with a jolt. He'd sensed something about her, but hadn't been able to put his finger on it. Ginny didn't care what others thought about her, whether she fit the popular concept of a woman her age. She was so involved in living her life, she probably never gave it much thought. Suddenly he remembered the agency and the things he'd been told about Ginny. Things he should have been able to sort out. There had been a power play. Ginny had called it right that last day she'd been at work.

But Nola had seemed so concerned, so genuinely dedicated to Ginny's best interest that he'd believed her. Of course in his own defense he'd been preconditioned by old notions about women who have reached a certain age. Ginny had certainly turned that around. She'd been right about a lot of things. The question was, how did he go about making amends and getting her back to the agency. It wasn't just the agency he was concerned about. He wanted her back where he could see her every day and smell her perfume and hear the sound of her voice. He wanted her away from Jason McCann.

Yet he remembered that old Ginny. Beneath the smiles and warm greetings was always an air of sadness, of loneliness. Did he want her to go back to that? Could he be that selfish? He sat up and put his feet on the floor and hung his head while he pondered.

From the open window he could hear her laughter. Jason's deeper tones mingled with hers. There was a high-pitched squeal of delight, signifying the girls were back, and no doubt Jason had swung Stef up on his shoulders. What a pretty picture they no doubt made. He certainly couldn't fit into it. Could he?

Seventeen

Monday morning was a relief. Alex had left early on Sunday, preoccupied and strangely quiet. Jason had stayed at his own cottage, sulking. When everyone was gone, Ginny had taken out the sailboat and stayed on the lake until the sun was dipping perilously close to the tree line. She was more troubled than she'd ever thought possible by Alex's visit and his quick exit. She wasn't certain what she'd expected after his tender kiss on Friday night and their frank conversation during their sail, but it hadn't been his cool and polite withdrawal. By the time she waved him goodbye, they'd seemed more like strangers than old friends.

"Not a good weekend?" Ellen asked when they met at the coffee pot.

"I've had better." Ginny sipped the hot brew absently.

"Need to talk?"

"I'm not sure what I'd say," Ginny admitted. "Maybe I'd better just let things stew for a while. How was your weekend?"

"Simple, quiet. I did my laundry, my nails, my hair, and my legs, and when I was all done, I realized there was not one person out there in the world who cared if my legs were shaved or not."

"Ouch!" Ginny said. "One of those weekends."

Ellen tilted her head thoughtfully, her dark blond hair swirling over her shoulders. "I think I'm ready for a change," she said, "but I'm not certain what change I need to make."

"I know that feeling." She glanced at the woman who was her boss and friend. "How about coming to the lake next weekend?"

Ellen shook her head. "I'm not the hardy outdoors type. I get seasick in the bathtub, and I don't get a kick out of nature. I'd be a drag."

"You could never be that. If you don't want to go outside, you can stay in the kitchen with Marnie or put puzzles together on the porch. We have running water, electricity, a VCR!"

"Mmmm, that sounds a little better. I'll give it some thought."

Ginny settled at her desk, and before the morning was half over, the phone rang. She sensed before she picked it up that someone on the other end was in trouble and needed help.

"Is this the place that helps women?" The woman was scared.

"Yes, this is the Women's Crisis Center. Who is this please?" Ginny automatically reached for her pad and pencil.

"What is your name, please?" she repeated. There was a long pause at the other end.

"Imena!" the sound was so small Ginny had to strain to hear it.

"Is that your name?"

Another long pause. When Ginny thought the woman had hung up, finally the affirmative came, low and whispered.

"Are you in danger at this moment, Imena?"

"No. My husband, he went out. He say he not coming back." She was crying now. "I got no family here, no friends. I see this number on TV. They say they help people."

"We do, Imena. Can you come here? Do you know where we're located?"

"No, no. My child, she sleeps. I don't know if my husband come back. If not, how do I pay the rent or buy food? I don't know."

"Imena, I'll let you talk to one of our counselors here. We can help you. Don't hang up. Wait!" Ginny buzzed Ellen's office, knowing she handled much of the financial portion of the clinic and would be the one to offer money for food and housing. After the call was transferred, she sat thinking. Somehow all her problems seemed unimportant compared to the ones these women faced.

"Were you able to help her?" Ginny asked Ellen later in the day when they had a break.

"I reassured her we were here for her. She didn't want to come in, and she didn't want me to go to her apartment. She's going to wait and see if her husband comes back. Apparently, he's disappointed with her because she had a daughter instead of a son."

Ginny thought of Imena's husband that night when she pulled into the driveway and sat watching the girls run up from the lake to greet her. Their hair flew around them in wild disarray, their bright faces bore eager smiles, and their brown, sleek young bodies glowed with health. How could a man not want daughters such as these? How could a mother walk away from them? Ginny got out of the car and held out her arms. The girls flew to hug her, their voice shrill with eagerness to share the day's events. Ginny determined she would dwell on the joy her life held and forget about the restless yearnings that had bedeviled her of late. She'd given in once to those feelings and started an affair with Jason. It had been a disastrous thing to do. She wouldn't make a similar mistake.

343

But in a week that had started out so disquietingly, the unexpected was bound to happen. On Wednesday evening as Ginny settled down to watch a video with the girls, the phone rang.

"I'll get it," Marnie said, passing out bowls of hot buttered popcorn. She was back immediately. "It's for you, Ginny."

"Who is it?" Ginny asked reluctantly.

"She wouldn't give her name, but she said it's very important."

Immediately, Ginny thought of Ellen, of some crisis at the center. "I'll take it in the kitchen. Start without me." She hurried to the phone.

"Ginny?"

The voice wasn't Ellen's. It was familiar but Ginny couldn't place it. Private numbers were never given out at the center, so she eliminated those possibilities.

"Yes, this is Ginny. Who is this?"

"Ginny, this is Nola!"

Startled, Ginny said nothing, unable to believe this was really Nola Sherman, yet she knew no other Nola.

"I guess you're kind of surprised to hear from me," Nola was saying. "I didn't give Marnie my name because I was afraid you wouldn't speak to me."

"Why should you think that?" Ginny asked stonily.

344

"I don't know. You seemed so angry with me before you left. I wasn't sure if you'd gotten over those feelings or not. When Alex said he'd been to the lake last weekend and you were your old self, I decided to take a chance."

Nothing has changed, Ginny thought bleakly. Nola was still insinuating that everything was Ginny's fault.

"What do you want?" she asked impatiently.

"Just to see how you are. I still consider myself a friend even if you don't think of me as one."

"Friends don't wait six months to check on friends."

"I didn't know where you were. No one did."

"Marnie told you we were here at the lake. She gave you the address and the number, information you chose not to pass along to Alex."

"I thought it was best for everyone. I was trying to give you time to recover. I thought if you wanted us to contact you, you would have given us the information."

As usual Nola's arguments made sense, and they simulated a thoughtful, caring attitude on her part — but this time Ginny wasn't buying. "It was nice of you to call," she said preparing to end the conversation.

"Don't hang up," Nola said quickly, and in

her voice was an emotion new to Ginny's ears, panic perhaps.

"All right," Ginny said calmly. "Let's cut through the little games and get right down to the bottom line. Why did you call, Nola?"

There was a long pause, reminding Ginny of the calls she received at the clinic from women who were in over their heads and had no place else to turn.

"Nola?" she prompted.

"Ginny, I'm . . ." A heavy sigh Ginny was sure she wasn't meant to hear. "I'm having problems with the Osgood account."

"Why tell me? Why not go to Alex?"

"Alex told me he's made you a partner in his business. I thought— You and I used to work well together. I thought you might help me out."

"Alex wouldn't fire you just because you're having problems with the Osgood account," Ginny said. "He knows how difficult Osgood can be."

"I . . . I know he told me to come to him if I have any trouble, but I told him I . . . had everything under control."

"Tell him the truth."

"Ginny, Osgood is threatening to pull the account and sue the agency."

"My God, why would he think he could do that?"

"I . . . I haven't been able to deliver what I promised."

"What did you promise him, the moon?"

"Spots on the 'Today' show."

"Nola, those shows won't go along with a commercial enterprise. That's why they sell advertising space."

"I know. But Ozzie just kept demanding more and more, and I had to promise him little extras to keep the account."

"This is highly unethical, Nola. It reflects badly on the agency."

"I know. What am I going to do?"

"What about your advertising spots?"

"They're awful. Even I can see they won't work, but that's what he wants. Help me out, Ginny."

Ginny hesitated, loath to be pulled back into the backbiting, stressful world Nola Sherman inhabited. But what of Alex? He was her friend. He'd done many things for her. Could she stand by and see him lose one of his biggest accounts?

"Fed Ex me what you have on the account," she instructed. "I'll go over it and see what I can come up with. I'll also talk to Osgood. He's pushing you around because you're new at this business. He knows you can't deliver. You're going to have to push back."

"I can't, Ginny."

347

"Why not?"

"I . . . Ozzie and I—"

"Never mind," Ginny snapped. She thought of Burgess Osgood and his corpulent hairy body. If Nola chose to sleep with him, that was her business. "Whatever you do in your personal life, it can't affect your business ethics. I'll talk to Osgood tomorrow after I get your material."

"Thank you, Ginny." The relief in Nola's voice was evident.

"You're not out of the hot water yet," Ginny said ruthlessly. "You'd better plan to come down here on the weekend, and we'll see what we can work out."

"All right." Nola's voice was almost meek.

"You do know how to get here?"

"I'll find it. I'm good at directions." The old arrogance was creeping back into her voice.

"We'll see about that," Ginny muttered.

"Ginny, one more thing," Nola said quickly. "You won't tell Alex, will you?"

"I won't lie to him about anything, Nola," she said, then relented, "but I won't volunteer information about this unless we can't fix it."

"That's fair enough," Nola said.

More than fair, Ginny thought.

She was hardly able to concentrate on the movie with the girls. She smiled when they laughed, and cheered with them for the ending, but later she couldn't have told anyone what the movie was about. Her thoughts were on the agency. She was almost tempted not to help Nola. The woman had acted in a most unprofessional manner, and certainly her ethics could be questioned. Burgess Osgood could hurt the agency, though, and Alex had put his life into it. She couldn't allow Nola to bring about its destruction without doing something to stop that.

"Looks like you didn't sleep very well," Marnie said next morning as she passed Ginny a cup of hot coffee. "Was that phone call bad news?"

"Just a person I used to know who's in trouble," Ginny answered, slowly stirring her coffee. "By the way, we'll be having a house guest again this weekend."

"Is Mr. Russell coming back?"

"No, this is a lady." Ginny sipped her coffee. She doubted Alex would ever return to the lake as a guest. His leavetaking had been too cold.

But she was wrong. Later that day, the phone rang. "Ginny? I'm sorry to call you at work."

"That's all right, Alex." She held the receiver tighter. She was inordinately happy to hear from him.

"Are you busy this weekend? I thought I might drive down again."

Damn Nola! Ginny thought. "This is a bad weekend, Alex," she said.

"Look, I know I left rather abruptly and you're probably not ready to go through another awkward weekend. I . . . well, I was trying to sort some things out. Now I have, and I want to talk to you."

"Is it something you can tell me over the phone?"

"I don't think so."

"I'm sorry, Alex. This weekend just won't work."

"I see!" She heard the flatness in his tone.

"Why don't you come the following weekend?"

"That's nearly two weeks away."

"I know, but it's the best I can do."

"All right." He sounded less confident than he had at first.

"I hope all is well with you, Alex."

"I'm fine. Don't worry. I'll see you in a couple of weeks."

"Goodbye." She felt hollow as she hung up the phone. He wanted to talk to her about something, and in typical Alex fashion, he wanted to do it now. She understood his impatience. Likely he simply wants to apologize, she told herself, and then she tried to concentrate on the outlines and proposals Nola had sent her. Now that there was a lull at the center, she'd taken them out and was trying to make some sense of them.

Nola's work had always been rather slapdash, depending on the unexpected, the daring, to make it stand out rather than skill and thoughtful application. Some of her ideas were good, actually inspired, but impractical. The cost of executing such plans would have been far too high. Ginny picked out the best of the lot, made notes, and finally put a call through to Burgess Osgood. He was belligerent, unwilling to talk to her, and sulky when she couldn't be bullied. By the time the call ended, Ginny had abated much of his anger toward the agency and had promised a new format for his advertising campaign. She then put in a quick call to Nola to tell her how things had gone and to advise her how to proceed with Osgood.

"Well, thanks, love," Nola said. "You did me a big favor."

Ginny could hear voices in the background and knew Nola was trying to cover the identity of her caller. Anger at the younger woman's continuing duplicity tightened Ginny's grip on the phone.

"I'm doing you more than a favor," she snapped. "I'm saving your ass. Be at the lake this weekend." She hung up.

Nola arrived late Friday night. She'd brought a briefcase full of papers, and as they settled into the deep, cushioned chairs, she plopped the stack onto Ginny's lap. "Maybe you can read these while we're sitting here," she said, settling back on the loveseat and tucking her feet under her. She sipped hot coffee while she stared into the fire Marnie had built for them.

"What are they?" Ginny asked.

"Some other accounts that have given me problems," Nola answered with an eloquent shrug. Irritation crossed Ginny's face, but she said nothing, simply laying aside the additional work. Nola glanced at the discarded pile, but said nothing.

"This is wonderful," Nola said, stretching. "No wonder you don't want to come back to the agency, the hustle and bustle. You can hibernate out here and bake cookies and knit afghans just like a proper grandmother."

"Actually, I don't do any of those things," Ginny said. "I work at a women's crisis center. We stay amazingly busy."

Nola laughed. "You know I would have guessed you'd do something like that when you retired. You're so generous."

"Well, I haven't exactly retired," Ginny said, and watched for emotions to play across Nola's face.

"Are you coming back to the agency?" Nola asked, bending her head so her hair hid her expression.

"We can never tell what the future holds for us," Ginny responded obliquely. Then she stretched and got to her feet. "We'd better get to bed. We're getting up early in the morning to work on the material for the Osgood account."

"Ummm, I'm not an early riser on Saturday," Nola said. "If you get down first, just start without me."

"I don't think we'll work that way," Ginny answered. "We'll both be down here by eight o'clock."

Nola met her firm gaze, then smiled, although her eyes remained serious. "You're the boss, Ginny," she said and got to her feet and followed Ginny upstairs. "This really is incredibly kind of you," she said when they'd reached the landing. "I don't know how to thank you."

"I'm not doing this for you, Nola. I'm doing it for Alex."

"Well, good night, then."

"Good night. I'll see you at eight."

Puffy-eyed and sullen, Nola was up and dressed at eight o'clock. Ginny set up their work on the porch, on the glass-topped patio table the children used for playing board games. By the time Marnie had served them black coffee, Nola's brain cells were kicking to life and she bent over the work as eagerly as Ginny.

"It's like old times, isn't it?" she said when

they paused to replenish their cups.

Ginny grunted a noncommittal answer. She didn't want to pretend with Nola. By evening they had a new presentation hammered out.

"Don't let Osgood budge you on any of this," Ginny warned as they gathered up the papers. "He's manipulated you successfully up to now, and he'll think he can get away with it again. You'll really have to stick to your guns."

"Thanks for the tip," Nola said lightly. "By the way, who is that hunk who's been out there with the girls all afternoon?"

Ginny glanced up. "That's Jason McCann, a next-door neighbor."

"Ummm, nice. He reminds me of one of those dancers we saw last winter." Nola cast a bright measuring glance at Ginny.

"He's anything but," Ginny answered casually. "Jason is a psychologist and a writer."

"Is he married?"

"He lost his wife and child in an automobile accident more than a year ago."

"So he's unattached."

"You might say that," Ginny answered.

Something in her tone finally registered with Nola. She swung her bright probing gaze around. "I hope you don't mind that I'm interested in him."

"Not at all. Just take it easy on him. He's vulnerable and easier hurt than you might imagine."

"I'll keep that in mind," Nola said, shaking back her hair. "I think I'll stroll down and meet him."

Ginny watched as Nola sashayed down to the dock and struck up a conversation with Jason and the girls. She tried not to watch. Jason was a grown man, but Ginny knew how Nola could work her magic. She heard Jason's laughter ring out and glanced up. He stood in the water, facing Nola, head thrown back, his face bright and interested. Well, it's no business of mine, she thought, and she gathered up Nola's papers and stuffed them into her briefcase. Then she hurried upstairs for a hot shower and a change of clothing.

"Ginny?" Nola knocked at her bedroom door and stuck her head in. "I hope you don't mind, I've done the most inconsiderate thing. I've invited your neighbor for supper."

"I expect we can manage," Ginny said without revealing Jason often ate with them.

"He's so charming, and I just thought it might be fun to get to know him better. I'd better hurry and freshen up." As she withdrew, Ginny took malicious pleasure in the thought that Nola had overstepped herself. Humming she put on one of her prettiest dresses and a pair of huaraches, and hurried downstairs. When Jason arrived she greeted him with more warmth than she'd shown him since their weekend together. He looked surprised, and then his face settled into one of his endearingly boyish grins. When Nola came down, Jason and Ginny were seated on the patio, drinks in hand, and were engaged in a heated debate over the lake association's fight with the DNR to cut a channel through the swamp end of the lake.

"DNR?" Nola asked.

"Department of Natural Resources," Ginny answered and continued her discussion with Jason.

"If a channel's cut through that swamp, it will destroy a natural sieve that keeps pollution from run-off water out of the lake," Jason said. Nola remained silent while they debated the issue, her bright eyes studying first one and then the other. Throughout the meal, Ginny felt Nola's assessing gaze, but it wasn't until the evening was over and Jason had bid them good night that she learned where Nola's thoughts had turned.

"My God, you're having an affair with him," Nola said, clapping her hands lightly.

"Why would you think that?" Ginny hedged, trying to look indignant.

"The way he looks at you. Why didn't you tell

me? I wouldn't have tried to horn in."

"You weren't. Jason and I are just friends."

"Sure you are!" Nola grinned.

Ginny felt her anger rise. "How many times have you jumped to conclusions about me, Nola, and built on those conclusions, whether or not they were the truth?"

Nola's grin faded. "I don't know what you're talking about," she said.

"Don't you? I know." Ginny faced her. "Time and again, you set me up at the office, made me look like a half-crazed, incompetent woman. You misplaced work I'd completed and claimed I didn't give it to you, told lies to Alex and the office staff. You even gave a reporter information about me for that article about the male dancers." Nola didn't deny the accusations, but her eyes glittered victoriously.

"Why, Ginny, I thought you were better," she said softly, "but you're just as paranoid as ever."

"Don't play your games with me, Nola. Don't make that mistake a second time. You've left me with a lot of ammunition."

"Are you threatening me?"

"Am I? That's something you'll have to figure out all by yourself."

"I see." Nola was silent for a moment. "I came here thinking I'd gotten my old friend back."

"No. Whyever you came here, it wasn't to find an old friend," Ginny answered quietly.

"I'm sorry you feel that way," Nola replied. "Perhaps I'd better leave tonight."

"It's a two-hour drive back to Detroit. I hardly think leaving now is necessary. Your room is prepared for you. It's late and you're tired."

"I can't stay here knowing you feel about me as you do," Nola replied stiffly.

"Whatever you do, is your decision," Ginny said, and she turned away to gaze over the lake. She knew she appeared calm and untouched by their conversation, but inside she was shaking from anger and disgust at ever having been taken in by Nola. The woman's true character was patently clear to her now. When she glanced around, Nola had left the patio. Ginny sank into a chair and stared out at the lights twinkling on the water. After some time had passed, she heard the back door slam and a car start up. Nola had chosen to leave after all. Ginny slumped in her chair. She hadn't realized how tense she'd been during Nola's visit. She was glad to be rid of the woman.

She thought of Alex and was glad she'd done all she could. Although he was unable to see through Nola's machinations, he didn't deserve to have his agency damaged. She wondered where he was tonight. He'd sounded disappointed that she hadn't let him come this weekend. She wished he were with her. Sighing she watched the moon rise over the trees and settle low in the sky. Soon it would be full again. Sighing, she got to her feet and went inside.

Eighteen

She'd given no thought to the long-term effect the weekend with Nola would have on her life. She'd tried only to secure the Osgood account and quietly help the agency. But Nola's visit had exonerated her somehow, for her suspicions had been proven right. Nola had never really been a friend. She'd been waiting to jump on the main chance when she saw it, even if it meant sabotaging her boss.

The unfairness displayed by the agency staff had been generated by Nola. Ginny was sure of it, just as she was sure all that was behind her. She'd never be a victim of such machinations again. She'd learned that much from Nola's visit, or maybe it was from Ellen's heaven-sent belief in women's power regardless of age and color. Funny, that at a place where women seemed so helpless, Ginny was learning to believe in herself. She went to work each morning imbued with confidence, anticipating what the day would bring. She'd never felt so complete, so capable. She, Virginia Alma Gordon Logan, could handle anything. She was invincible.

Late in the week Alex called, and her shield of invincibility fell away, splintered. It wasn't that she needed a man to be a whole woman, and certainly she didn't need Alex, but she couldn't help feeling deflated as she listened to him.

"I'm disappointed you aren't coming this weekend," she said smoothly, happy that her words and tone conveyed polite regret without revealing how desperately she'd looked forward to his visit. "Perhaps another time?"

"I'm not sure, Ginny. The agency is pretty busy right now, and I have some social engagements pending."

"I see. I thought you had something you wanted to say to me."

"What? Oh." His tone was flat. "It wasn't that important. I'll stay in touch. And you call me if you need anything. In the meantime I'll have my lawyer mail you the papers on the new partnership."

"Alex, I don't want to be a part—" A click cut her off. The rest of the day passed in a blur. Imena called to say her husband had returned and forgiven her for the birth of their daughter. He would give her another chance to produce an

361

heir for him. Emily Fuller returned to the center with her children. Her son sat with sullen lips and dark suspicious eyes. Dr. Bob left on vacation and Ellen was tied up with finding new funding resources due to the cost-cutting rampage on the state budget. By closing time, Ginny felt drained and depressed. Even the drive back to the lake through winding tree-shaded country roads did nothing to lift her spirits.

Jason was waiting to speak to her when she arrived. She begged off.

"Not tonight, I'm just too tired. We had a busy day at the center. Can it wait?"

"Sure," he said, hooking his hands in his back pockets. His shoulders sagged a bit, but his blue-eyed gaze was sympathetic. "How about a sailboat ride tomorrow night after the girls are in bed. We'll talk then."

Ginny nodded absently, relieved he hadn't been insistent. She barely spoke to Marnie and the girls before making her way up the stairs to her room to change clothes. She hadn't given Jason an excuse. She really was exhausted. Her big bed with its pretty floral cover and plump pillows beckoned, and she succumbed to temptation, sprawling across it in her slip and bra. Her lids were heavy, her mind fuzzy. She closed her eyes for just a minute, and when she opened them again, the room was dark, the house quiet.

Leaping up, she drew a silk robe on over her slip and left her room. Marnie's door was open. She lay in bed, reading one of the mysteries that had captured her imagination ever since she'd learned Jason was putting her in his book.

"Are the girls in bed already?" Ginny whispered.

Marnie nodded.

"You should have awakened me."

"You looked like you needed the rest," Marnie said. "It didn't hurt the girls not to spend one evening with you. Are you hungry? There's leftovers in the fridge."

Ginny shook her head and yawned. "If everything's under control, I'll just go back to bed. Thanks for all you do, Marnie. You're a godsend."

"You get some rest," Marnie said, ignoring her thanks. "You try to handle everyone's problems. You can't do that all the time. It's taking a toll on you."

Ginny shrugged. "You know, I remember how Tracy loved David so. She used to call him perfect, Mr. Perfect. I guess, now that he's gone, I feel like I have to take over the role."

"Can't nobody be that perfect, Ginny," Marnie said. "You got to think about yourself a little bit."

Ginny regarded the old woman whose beliefs

were as set as her iron-gray curls, and she couldn't repress an affectionate grin. "You will stay with us when the summer's over, won't you, Marnie?"

Marnie put down the book and glanced at her. "Other than my sister Sophie and her son back in Detroit, I haven't got a family," she said with surprising quietness. "I guess maybe God just sent me to you 'cause we both have a need."

Ginny crossed the room to give the garrulous woman a hug. "Bless you," she said. "The girls love you so much. They'd be devastated if you didn't stay."

Marnie returned her hug, then sniffed and flipped the covers fussily. "Oh, now, let's not get all maudlin. I'm not staying just for the girls. I figure you need me about as much as they do. You may think you're Mrs. Perfect, but I know better."

Ginny laughed. "You don't let much get past you, do you?"

"Not as much as you do," Marnie said, fixing her gaze on Ginny. Ginny sensed she was talking about Nola's visit.

"I'm learning," she said. "I may be a little slow, but I am learning."

"You know that woman asked me all kinds of things about you and Mr. McCann just before she left. She also wanted to know what Mr. Russell and you talked about when he was down here."

"What did you tell her?"

"That it wasn't none of her business," Marnie snapped, folding her arms across her chest in satisfaction. Her gray curls bobbed. "She tore out of here like a scalded cat. Already had her bags packed."

"I'm afraid she found us a pretty ungracious lot." Ginny grinned. "Thanks again, Marnie."

"No need to thank me. I don't spread gossip about my family members. Now go to bed and get some of that rest you need."

"Yes, ma'am." Ginny scooted back to her room. In spite of the fact she was now fifty years old, Marnie managed to make her feel like a little girl. She couldn't repress a grin as she thought of their conversation. Right to the bitter end, Nola had sought to find some way to strike out. Why? Ginny wondered, getting under the fresh sheets. She had left the agency, giving Nola a clear field to her job. How could the woman still feel threatened . . . unless Nola feared Ginny might return. Alex had made it very clear she'd be welcomed back as a partner. But Nola didn't know about the proposed partnership. Alex had said he was keeping it between the two of them. Why else then? Perhaps she had set her cap for Alex. Was that why she'd been so insistent that Ginny not tell him about her affair with Osgood? She'd put little past her former assistant, and her conclusions about Nola's designs on Alex bothered her so, she spent the rest of the night tossing and turning.

By noontime on Friday, Ginny was so exhausted and distracted that Ellen came to her desk and studied her with some concern.

"Go home now," she said. "You look terrible."

"I'm all right," Ginny insisted. "I don't want to leave you short of help."

"Things are quiet around here. Bob is sitting back twiddling his thumbs. I'll have him man the phones."

"Are you sure you can get by without me?"

"Only for the afternoon," Ellen said. "Otherwise, I don't know what we'd do without you."

Ginny's smile was brief. Not like her, Ellen noted. Quickly Ginny gathered up her purse and umbrella and headed for her car. She felt guilty to leave so early, but the getaway was welcome. She'd let things get her down lately. No one ran to greet her when she arrived at the lake, so she walked down to the patio, where Marnie sat knitting and watching the two older girls swim. Jason was nowhere in sight, so she assumed he

366

was at his cottage, working on his book.

"Where's Stef? Napping?" Ginny asked as she settled into a chair."

"She wore herself out this morning," Marnie answered. "You got off early."

"Things were slow." Ginny stretched and looked at the idyllic scene before her. If she ever needed anything to restore her, this was it. "I think I'll change clothes and get out my oil paints," she said.

She spent the rest of the afternoon trying to capture the serenity of the sun-dappled lake and shoreline, then decided her morose frame of mind was creeping into the picture for she'd used too many darks and shadows.

"Looks like a scene from a V. C. Andrews book," Tracy said, standing back to look at the picture.

"And since when do you read V. C. Andrews?" Ginny asked.

Tracy shrugged. "You told me I could read anything I wanted from the school library."

"School is closed."

"I know, Grandma," Tracy said impatiently, "but the school library has some of V. C. Andrews' books, and I got one this summer from the local library."

"I'd rather you didn't read those just yet."

"Uhhh, you treat me like I'm a baby."

"I don't mean to, Tracy, but you're not as grown-up as you think you are."

"You're just so square, Grandma."

"Be patient with me. I'm trying hard not to be. In the meantime, leave the V. C. Andrews books in the library for a few more years."

Tracy rolled her eyes and stalked away. Ginny watched her go, tempted to call her back and tease her into a hug and kiss. She'd always felt particularly close to her, but now Tracy was growing up. She'd just turned thirteen this summer, and it seemed to make a difference in her outlook about things. Well, why not? We're all entitled to identity crises, based on the turning calendar.

Ginny had nearly forgotten her promise to go for a sail with Jason after supper. He'd not shown up for his usual Friday night-supper visit.

"He's got an agent interested in his book," Marnie explained. "He's trying to get it ready to send off." Mindful of the deadlines she'd once had to meet at the ad agency, Ginny curled up on the old couch on the porch and proceeded to read a book. But she was restless, and the novel did little to claim her attention.

"Ready?" a voice called from the other side of the screen door.

"Jason? We didn't think we'd see you anymore until your manuscript was finished." Ginny willingly put aside the book.

"I need a break," he answered. "Besides, I want to talk to you." He sounded serious.

Ginny rose. "I'll just get a sweater and be right with you," she said. She watched as he turned away and headed down to the boat landing. What does he want to talk to me about? she wondered, and her spirits sank even further. She had little doubt it was about the two of them and the way she'd been avoiding him lately.

Under Jason's expert touch, the sailboat skimmed across the moon-silvered water. Ginny raised her cheeks to the soft summer breeze, kicked off her sneakers, and leaned back, stretching her long, slim legs across the boat. She seemed unaware of the sensuous, feline quality of her movements or of their effect on Jason. His mouth tightened, and he yanked the tiller, bringing the boom around. Deftly, Ginny ducked below it and glanced at him.

"Sorry," he said.

"It's okay."

"Ginny, I . . . I just don't understand why you've been avoiding me these past few weeks."

"I know I've been unfair to you not to have discussed this with you," she answered, suddenly terribly ashamed of the way she'd treated him. "You've been such a dear friend, I haven't wanted to hurt you in any way, but I'm afraid I have."

"Look, this doesn't have to be complicated for either one of us," he said, then cursed as the wind changed and his jib went limp. "I'm heading in," he added irritably. "Looks like a storm brewing."

Ginny glanced at the horizon. Lightning flared in the distance, then died away, leaving a quiet stillness. Dark clouds had scudded up from nowhere and nearly covered the moonlight. "I think you're right," she called.

When they reached the dock, she helped him haul the boat up on the lift and tie down the sails. The dark clouds were closer now, and the air was hot and sticky and heavy as if the coming storm had sucked all the oxygen out of it. Sweat rolled down Ginny's back and dampened her underarms. Why had she thought she needed a sweater? She stood on the shoreline and watched the storm approach. Thunder rumbled off in the distance, menacing and surreal.

A wind had come up by the time Jason joined her. It whipped at his hair, feathering it over his brow. He looked at her with deep serious eyes. "I want you, Ginny," he said, and she felt an answering excitement.

He stepped forward and caught her arms. "Come home with me. Spend the night with me."

"I can't. Marnie and the girls are here."

"That's an excuse, Ginny." He kissed her then, thoroughly and desperately so that her knees weakened. He saw the effect his touch had on her, and grinned and tried to pull her closer.

"No, Jason. I can't," she cried, pushing against him. "I don't love you. All I feel for you is desire, passion—not love."

"You care about me, Ginny. I know you do, just as I care about you. If it isn't love, then at least let's take advantage of what feeling there is. It's good to feel again, to know we're not dead." He said the words she felt, so she couldn't resist when he drew her close. His lips were hot and demanding on hers, and she kissed him back, greedily, her hunger matching his. He held her tightly, awakening a stream of fire along her nerves. Why not go along with him? she wondered dimly. Why not gather what joy they could, why not prove to themselves they were alive and still capable of feeling and responding? Then the thought of Alex came to her, and desire for Jason died. He was young and virile and caring, but she didn't love him. She drew away from him and opened her mouth to tell him all she felt, but a sound drew her attention and she turned to find Tracy staring at them.

Tracy stood in her white cotton nightgown. Ginny read innocence and shock and betrayal in her accusing gaze.

"I hate you," Tracy cried. "Both of you." Her eyes glistened with tears, and she looked terribly hurt. Whirling, she ran across the patio.

"Tracy, wait!" Ginny called. "Let me explain."

Jason, too, called to her, but she kept running. Ginny heard the bang of the screen door.

"She's going to Marnie," she said to him. "She'll be all right. I'll talk to her."

"God, I'm sorry, Ginny." His voice was full of anguish. "I love Tracy. I wouldn't hurt her for anything."

"I know. She knows that too. She was just shocked by what she saw. Marnie'll calm her down and talk to her. You'd better go now."

He shook his head and, his shoulders slumping, made his way back to the DeFauw cottage. Raindrops splattered against the end of the dock and on the dusty leaves of the maple. Wrapping her arms around herself, Ginny hurried into the house and climbed the stairs.

"Marnie?" she whispered. Tapping lightly on the old woman's door, she pushed it open and saw Tracy sprawled across the bed, her face buried in Marnie's lap. Marnie's worn hand patted her soothingly.

"Your grandma's here, and she can explain everything now—so's you'll have no reason to be upset."

"I don't want to talk to her." Tracy's voice was muffled.

"I think it's only fair you let me tell you what happened," Ginny began. "After all, don't I have to listen to every side when you do something wrong?"

Tracy raised a tear-streaked face to her. "You did everything wrong," she sobbed. "Jason was my friend."

"He was my friend too, Tracy," Ginny said.

"But not that kind of friend. You have Uncle Alex. We only have Jason, and now you're taking him away from us."

"Oh, God. No, Tracy. I'd never do that to you, honey. Listen to me."

Tracy's anger flared. "No, I never want to speak to you again." She began crying in a choked-up way.

"Maybe you'd better let her calm down a little bit," Marnie said. "You go on to bed and talk to her in the morning."

Reluctantly, Ginny followed Marnie's advice, knowing she couldn't sleep. She lay stiff and anxious on her bed, hearing the rise and fall of voices from Marnie's room and, finally, quietness. What had she reaped that one weekend when she'd abandoned common sense and given in to passion. She rolled over and buried her head in her pillow. She certainly didn't feel perfect now, unless she was the perfect fool.

After a restless, nearly sleepless night, Ginny rose and tried again to talk to Tracy, but to no avail.

"Tracy, you know how much I love you, don't you?" Ginny asked, refusing to let this misunderstanding come between them.

"You just say that because you're our grandmother and you have to take care of us."

"That's not true."

"It is. If you had your way you'd go back to Detroit and go back to work. You had to leave because of us."

"Oh, Tracy, you're so wrong." Ginny was appalled at all the hurt her granddaughter had bottled up inside her.

"I left for all of us, and I've been happy here."

"Then why did you kiss Jason? He's our friend. You can't do that." She leaped to her feet. "I don't want to talk about it anymore."

"You have to let me explain."

"I did," Tracy cried, turning on her, "and all you said was the same lie—that you love me. That's not an excuse for what you did with Jason."

"It was only a kiss," Ginny protested, deciding to take a different tack. "Aren't you overreacting about this?"

"It wasn't just a kiss," Tracy said. "I heard what you said to each other. Grandma, you're too old!"

Ginny didn't know what to answer. Nonplused she stared at her granddaughter. She'd always known Tracy was bright beyond her years. She should have expected something like this. She shouldn't have given in to the moonlight and a whim.

She tried to reach Tracy again that weekend, but her granddaughter simply walked away. In the following week, Tracy contrived to be busy in her room when Ginny was present. If Ginny tried to start a conversation, Tracy made an excuse and quickly left. She spent a lot of time out on the water in the paddle boat. Ginny was troubled by her inability to communicate with Tracy. She could see that her granddaughter was suffering as much as she was over their alienation, but the week slid into another weekend. At Ginny's request, Jason tried talking to Tracy, but got nowhere.

Hot, somnolent July melted into August. The lake was beginning to lose its charm. What had once been a wondrous joy, now became an unappreciated part of daily life. The girls still swam and boated, but with less enthusiasm. Friends came to visit them and sat around talking about the new school year. Ginny hoped the change would do Tracy some good, for she had grown belligerent, became angry over the littlest things. And in her anger, she became destructive. Ginny found a row of flowers trampled. None of her granddaughters claimed to know anything about it, but Ginny saw a flicker of something in Tracy's eyes and guessed she knew more than she was telling.

"How can I reach her?" Ginny asked Ellen one day as they sat having lunch together. "She is so angry at me."

"I expect she's been bottling it up for some time."

"She has," Ginny agreed, "and I don't know how to break through that shell she's formed. You know I went along all spring and summer, thinking there'd been a miraculous change in them. Now Tracy acts like this, and I wonder if I've failed with the other two girls as well."

"Don't take on a problem before you have to," Ellen advised. "You said Tracy always kept her feelings to herself. I suspect it's just getting to be too much for her. She's really a little girl, and she's had to deal with the loss of her mother and her father. Sounds like Tracy substituted Jason for her father, but you're her grandmother and you've acted out of character. It makes her feel threatened. This new life she's adjusted to feels very fragile to her."

"What can I do?"

"Give her time. When she sees nothing has changed, she'll begin to relax a little. Give her extra love and attention."

Easier said than done, Ginny discovered in the days that followed. She did her best, but Tracy shouldered aside her attempts, showing by a curl of her lips that she held Ginny in great disdain.

Steffi and Candi had begun to notice Tracy's hostility toward Ginny and were troubled by it. Ginny felt like weeping at times. Where was all that brave talk of being invincible? Where was that brave new strength she'd discovered within herself? Fool again, she berated herself. She missed Alex. She wanted desperately to talk to him, to see his face, to hear his calm voice providing answers where there seemed to be none. She wanted to feel his hand holding hers, strong and sure, and she wanted his kiss. With a flash of clarity, she saw that her desire for Jason was misplaced. She'd desired Alex for a long time, but she'd run from it. Well, she'd run head-on into a mess. This one she had to resolve herself.

Then one day, just when she thought things couldn't get any worse, a car pulled into the driveway, and a slim, dark-haired woman got out and walked toward the cottage. Having just colored her hair and rinsed it beneath the kitchen tap, Ginny was drying it. She squinted to make out who had come calling. A knock sounded at the back door. Knowing Marnie was down in front with the girls, Ginny wrapped a towel around her head and flung the door open, her mind going numb as it registered the identity of her caller.

"Hello, Ginny. How are you?" Diane Logan asked.

Nineteen

Ginny was speechless at first, the towel sliding from her hair, her mouth gaping as she stared transfixed at the woman who was at one time familiar to her. Diane looks older, she thought inanely, then realized it had been nearly four years since she'd seen her. There were fine lines around her daughter-in-law's eyes and lips as if the years had not been kind, yet she was dressed in an expensive Liz Claiborne silk suit and Bally pumps. Gold earrings glittered at her lobes, and the diamond on her finger testified she wasn't destitute. Her dark hair was arranged in a sleek coil at the back of her head. The look was dramatic, accenting her cheekbones and those eloquent eyes.

"Let me come in and talk to you," she said. Ginny wanted to deny her, to say no, but words crowded into her head, wanting to be spoken. Silently, she opened the screen door and let Diane into the back hall. Diane hesitated, waiting to be invited into the living room, to be asked to sit down; but Ginny remained in the entrance hall, staring at her with dark, accusing eyes.

"I'm sorry I've startled you so," Diane said, her voice low and well modulated. "I just felt coming here directly was the best thing to do."

"How did you know we'd be here?"

"At first, I wasn't sure. When I heard about Scott . . ." She paused, and a spasm of pain passed over her features. She controlled it, bringing the serene exterior back as a shield. "When I heard about Scott, I didn't know what to do. I tried calling the house in Canton, but they said the number was disconnected. So was the one at your apartment. I panicked and then I thought of the lake. Then I was afraid to come."

Her gaze was direct, unflinching. She'd always been self-possessed, Ginny remembered. Now she stood waiting for a response. When it didn't come, she took a deep breath and looked away, her eyes blinking rapidly. "I'm sorry about Scott," she said in a low voice.

"Why?" The one explosive word Ginny spoke

brought Diane's head around, made her eyes widen in wounded disbelief.

"I loved him, Ginny, though you may not believe that."

"A woman doesn't abandon a husband and children she truly loves."

Diane looked away again as if unable to meet the accusation. "In your world, I suppose that's true," she said finally.

"In my world?" Ginny scoffed. "You make the idea of loyalty and fidelity sound archaic. There's no excuse for leaving a husband, a baby, and two little girls who needed you desperately."

"I know that." It was an anguished cry. Those expressive eyes held pain, liquid and fresh. "You could never understand, Ginny, how it felt to be a woman drowning. Scott didn't either, although I tried to tell him." She laughed, a short painful sound. "He used to tell me to talk to you, to try to follow in your footsteps. You were content and happy. I would learn to be too. I couldn't seem to get out of your shadow."

"Don't tell me this," Ginny cried, gripping the towel as if it were a lifeline. "Don't try to turn this around and make me the scapegoat. You were the one who walked out and Scott—

Scott . . . Every day, he hoped you'd come back."

Diane was crying then, standing in the back hall of the lake house, the place where she and the children and Scott had come in the summer to laugh and play. She cried without making a sound. Only her shoulders trembled slightly. Ginny guessed she'd cried like this many times before. There was a dull defeat to it. She felt trapped in this small space with this woman's guilt and grief.

Too much! She, Ginny Logan, had borne too much grief herself to bear anyone else's. This was grief Diane had invited when she'd made the decision to leave; let her deal with it. Ginny tried to close her heart and mind to the weeping, but she couldn't. For some reason she thought of the women who came to the center, despairing, frightened. But Diane wasn't one of those. Here she stood in her Bally pumps and silk suit and gold earrings and designer perfume. There could be no sympathy merited here. She was undeserving. Ginny turned away. When Diane spoke again, her voice was calm, with barely a trace of the emotions she must be feeling.

"I didn't come here to excuse myself or my decision to leave my family. Whether you believe it or not, I truly loved Scott, but I couldn't continue as his wife. I didn't know who I was, what my worth was as a human being. I was sequestered and smothered behind suburban walls." She paused, but Ginny made no rebuttal. She felt too weary. She only wanted Diane gone.

"I've come for my children," Diane said softly.

Ginny whirled on her. "You must be mad," she half whispered, half shouted. "You can't just waltz back in here four years after you've abandoned the girls and expect to have them back."

"I'm their mother. They need me now."

"They don't need *you*. They have me."

Diane stared at her; then her expression hardened. "I ran away once, Ginny, because I didn't know how to exist in your world or how to stand up to your expectations of me. But I'm stronger now and I've come for my children. You can't stop me from taking them."

"I'll stop you with everything I have," Ginny said. The two women glared at each other with near hatred, the only emotion they'd shared in a long time.

"I'm prepared to take whatever steps I must to reclaim my children," Diane stated quietly.

"Why? There's no money involved."

"What?"

"There's no money for you to collect, Diane. I've tied it all up in trust funds for the girls' education." It was a cheap shot, Ginny knew, but she was angry and scared by Diane's threat. She wanted to strike out, to give pain to the woman who had caused so much pain to Scott and the girls.

Diane's face had gone pale. Her eyes darkened, and she brought her hand back, prepared to strike Ginny.

"Mama?"

Both women whirled to look at the girl standing on the other side of the screen door.

"Tracy," Diane whispered. Her smile was tremulous, a mother's love shining through a mother's pain. That touched Ginny as nothing else had—and it enraged her. She wanted to tear at Diane, to deny her the very right to exist. So great was her hatred, she shook with its intensity.

Diane took a step toward the door, her face shining with wonderment as she looked at her daughter. "You're so grown-up. Tracy, you're so beautiful. Your hair . . ." She put out a hand as if to touch the long blond tresses, but the screen was between them.

Tracy's face was touched with tragedy, with anger and love and distrust — and the need to believe again. Her hand rested on the screen of the door, and when Diane placed a hand on the other side of it, Tracy jerked hers away and stared at the woman she called Mama.

"Tracy, I've come back for you," Diane said.

"Diane!" Ginny's voice crackled in the air, drawing the younger woman's head around. "You have no right," Ginny hissed. There was a scraping sound on the porch, and when both women looked again, Tracy was gone, bolting away like a young colt.

"Tracy, wait!" Diane cried, pushing open the screen.

"You have your answer," Ginny almost shouted, following her. "If she'd wanted to see you again, she would have stayed."

Diane whirled on her. "You've turned my children against me. How could you be so cruel?"

"No, Diane." Ginny slowly shook her head for emphasis. "You turned your children against you. You were the cruel one."

Diane brought her hands up to her face to cover her trembling mouth, but her eyes were the mirror that revealed the extent of her agony.

"It's too late. You weren't here when Scott died. You weren't here when they needed you. They don't need you now. Go away and leave them in peace."

Without saying another word, Diane stumbled along the path back to the drive and her rented car. Once inside, she sat with head bowed against the steering wheel. Ginny stood on the porch, watching her. I should go inside, she thought dimly. This was something Diane should go through privately. A woman's need to adjust to defeat, to the loss of children she'd not valued highly enough, but Ginny was afraid the other girls would come up from the lake.

At last Diane composed herself and started the car. Ginny watched it turn out of the driveway and head down the road back to town; then she went in search of Tracy. She found her on the top floor of the old granary that had been painted and turned into a clubhouse for the children. It was hot, and dust motes danced in the sunlight.

"Tracy?" Ginny peered through the shadowy light. Tracy huddled in an old chair that had once sat on the porch. "Darling, are you all right?"

"Leave me alone," Tracy muttered. "I don't

want to see anyone."

"You won't have to see your mother. She's left."

Tracy raised her head and looked at Ginny. Tears streaked her cheeks. "She went away again?"

"Yes."

"Is she coming back?"

"I don't think so." Ginny waited, watching Tracy's expression in the dim shadows. "Do you want her to come back?"

"No. I hate her. I hate everybody," Tracy shouted.

"Darling, surely not me. I'm here for you, Tracy, anytime you need me."

"I don't need anyone. Go away and leave me alone." She buried her face in her arms, and Ginny withdrew and went to talk to Marnie.

"Poor lambs," the old woman said, rocking Stef who'd fallen asleep in her lap. "Poor little lambs."

"The others are adjusting, Marnie, but I'm worried about Tracy. I don't know what to do. I had a feeling upstairs that she blamed me for Diane's leaving in the first place."

"Don't start taking that onto your shoulders as well," Marnie scolded.

"Diane said the same thing, that she'd been

made to compete with me and she'd felt over-whelmed by it, so she left."

"Did you compete with her?"

"Never. Not that I knew of. I was in such a muddle after David died. I don't know, Marnie, maybe I called on Scott too much without realizing what it was doing to Diane. Maybe I am to blame."

"I don't think so." Marnie shook her head. "Whatever drove Diane away was between her and Scott—and in her own head. You can't take the blame of it."

"In the meantime, what do I do with Tracy? Ellen says she's just acting out a lot of the anger and fear she's kept hidden through all the things that have happened to her. She says we just have to give her time and assure her that we love her and will always be there for her."

"You've done a good job of that, Ginny," Marnie said approvingly. "It's going to work out. Tracy's got a good head on her shoulders and she worships you. She tries so hard to mimic you."

"Me?" Ginny looked at Marnie in consternation.

Marnie nodded. "She'll come around. Just give her time."

Ginny wanted to believe that was so, but as

the days passed and Tracy remained aloof, she began to doubt Marnie's judgment. One morning Tracy came down to breakfast and her long hair had been chopped off.

"Why'd you do such a fool thing as that?" Marnie demanded, her hands on her hips.

"Because I wanted it short," Tracy said. Her bright, hard gaze flashed to Ginny's face.

"I'll take you to a beauty shop and get it trimmed up for you," Ginny said, unperturbed.

"I like it this way," Tracy said, angered that she hadn't gotten a rise out of Ginny as well. Despite Ginny's attempts in the following days, Tracy simply wouldn't consent to having her hair cut professionally. The beautiful blond spears hung in jagged, uneven lines around her face. Ginny crept into Tracy's room when she was out and collected the long strands that had once trailed down Tracy's back nearly to her hips.

Two days after her visit, Diane called Ginny.

"I've had time to think," she said calmly. "Whatever mistakes I've made, I'm still the mother of those little girls, and I intend to have them back."

"I won't give them up without a struggle,

Diane." Ginny was gripping the phone so hard her knuckles were white.

"I know that, and I'm prepared to fight you if I have to. I'm engaged to be married to a man with considerable resources. He's reassured me he'll back me in whatever I must do to recover my family."

Her words, though quietly spoken, were thunderous in Ginny's ears. She could feel her knees begin to tremble. Without answering, she hung up the phone and just stood by it, trying to think what she must do. Whatever Diane's resources were, were they enough to win the girls away from her? Her fear was tangible now, surrounding her, cutting off her breathing, her ability to think. She didn't hear the knock at the door until it was repeated. On seemingly wooden legs she walked to the screen door, almost expecting to see Diane. When she saw it was Jason, she gasped and bent over, clasping her middle. Then her knees gave way entirely, and she sank to the floor and began weeping.

"Ginny!" Instantly Jason was beside her, picking her up, soothing her. He cradled her against his chest, rocking her back and forth. "What is it? What's wrong?"

Between sobs, she gasped out the story.

"Shhh, it's all right. She won't get them away from you," he crooned. "She abandoned them once. No court will give them to her again."

Ginny stopped crying and leaned back to peer into his face. "Are you sure?"

"The courts always go hard on parents who abandon their children. That's what it was with Diane, abandonment."

"But she says she has money. She's going to remarry. The courts will be impressed by that. The girls would have a father again."

"You and I will get married. The girls will have a father."

Ginny clasped her aching head, shaking it at Jason's offer. "I don't know what to do anymore."

"We'll figure out something. Trust me," Jason said. "You're not alone in this. I'll help fight for the kids."

"Would you?" she asked dully.

"I love them too, Ginny," he replied.

But love isn't enough, Ginny realized later, when Jason had left. She'd need attorneys and witnesses. Money to pay for everything. But she had very little money left, not enough for the kinds of lawyers she would need to fight Diane. Desperately, she pondered what to do, and then she remembered Alex and the account he'd set up for her. With trembling fingers, she called his office, but a woman's voice answered.

"Is this Alex Russell's office?" she asked, puzzled.

"Yes, it is. Ginny? Is that you?"

"Yes. Who is this?"

"Nola."

"Is Alex there?"

There was a slight pause, and Ginny could picture Nola's measuring expression. "He's busy at the moment. Can I help you with something?"

"I must speak directly to Alex," Ginny said. "Is he due in soon?"

"I believe he's here somewhere, he's just busy on another phone or something. Shall I give him a message to call you back when he has a minute?"

"No. Go find him," Ginny ordered. "Tell him this is an emergency. I'll hold on, and, Nola, don't play any of your stupid games with me or you'll regret it."

"Why, Ginny, is that a threat?" Someone had come into the office; Ginny could tell by the change in Nola's voice.

"Yes, it is," she said very distinctly. "Put Alex on, now!"

She waited while the phone was muffled and words were exchanged at the other end, and then Alex was there, his voice warm and sure and caring. She wanted to bawl. Instead, she bit her lip, cleared her throat, and told him quickly and concisely that she needed all the money her new position as a partner had allotted her, without telling him the reason why.

"Of course, I'll have it transferred right away," Alex said with no hesitation. "Will it be enough?"

"I don't know."

"If you need more, you know you have only to call me. Is there anything I can do to help?"

She told him then about Diane's visit, about Tracy's anger and withdrawal, about the threat of lawyers. She told him everything, and then she waited for his sympathy and support.

"Are you sure you're doing the wise thing?" he asked.

"What?"

"Diane *is* their mother."

"She abandoned them."

"Have you asked them what they want to

do?"

"I asked Tracy. She said she didn't want Diane to come back."

"Are you sure she wasn't just saying that because she's afraid of hurting you?"

"She wants to hurt me, Alex. She saw Jason kissing me, and she's been angry ever since. I don't know what to do."

"How about if I come down this weekend?"

"Not now, Alex. Not now. I simply can't handle anything more. Besides we'd only quarrel because you don't agree with what I'm about to do."

"I'll come down. Maybe I can help."

Ginny hung up the phone, wanting him there, yet wishing he wouldn't come.

At work the following day, she unloaded everything on Ellen.

"Wow!" Ellen said. "You've got your hands full."

"I'm going to fight for my kids," Ginny said. "I can't let Diane have them." She ran her hands through her hair. Ellen looked at her sympathetically. Ginny's normally impeccable attire was showing the strain of her preoccupation. For the first time her skirt and blouse

394

didn't match exactly, and her hair was messy because she kept running her hands through it and twisting the ends nervously.

"Would it help if I talked to Tracy for you?" Ellen offered. "I could come to the lake for the weekend. God knows you've invited me often enough."

"That might be a good idea," Ginny said. "Alex is coming down and Jason . . . Jason has asked me to marry him and he gets upset when Alex is there, and Tracy isn't speaking to me and . . . and— How did I mess everything up so badly?"

By Saturday, Ginny was nervously pacing the porch, waiting for all her weekend guests to show up. She wasn't certain it was wise to have guests when she was so preoccupied, but everyone knew of her problems and her guests had invited themselves. They would simply have to cope, come what may.

Alex was the first to arrive, followed close behind by Ellen, who got out of her car with a breezy smile and stood admiring the BMW. Jason sauntered over from his yard, and he stood staring at Ginny with accusing eyes.

"Why'd you invite him this weekend?"

"I didn't. He volunteered to come," Ginny said with some annoyance. Jason had become amazingly possessive in the past few days, since his proposal. Although Ginny hadn't given him an answer, he'd taken her silence as an affirmative.

"Hello," Alex said, escorting Ellen to the porch where Ginny waited. He even smiled at Jason who scowled in return.

Ginny made the introductions, then busied herself with showing Alex and Ellen to their rooms and slipping into her own to check her hair and makeup and take a deep steadying breath. When she went downstairs again, Alex's BMW was pulling out of the drive once more.

"Where's he going?" she asked.

"He and Tracy are going for a ride," Ellen said. "I like your Mr. Russell."

"Well, he's not exactly *my* Mr. Russell." Ginny noted the scowl on Jason's face. "Are you and Jason getting to know one another?"

"Actually, Mr. McCann has been regaling me with his opinion of what's wrong with present-day psychology and with how inefficient a center like ours is in giving help."

"Oh!" Ginny looked from one to the other. For a moment seeing the amusement on both their faces, she forgot her own problems. A solution to one of her problems might be presenting itself.

"Jason, would you do me a favor?" she asked. "I promised Ellen I'd take her sailing this morning, and what with this thing with Diane, I'm just too preoccupied. Would you take her out?" She could see Ellen's alarmed expression.

"Sure!" Jason answered. "So you like to sail?" he asked, leading Ellen down to the boat ramp.

"There's nothing like it on a clear day, with a soft breeze and popcorn clouds and molasses sunshine," Ellen said, making a face at Ginny behind Jason's back.

He laughed at her syrupy description. "I suspect you're putting me on."

"A bit," Ellen answered, cautiously eyeing the boat. "How many miles per gallon do you get with this thing?"

The sound of a car turning down the drive made Ginny leap to her feet and hurry to the back of the house. Alex whipped the BMW in with a flourish and got out. Biting the inside of her lower lip, Ginny waited for Tracy to emerge from the low-slung sports car. She'd had a haircut. The jagged ends had been trimmed into a becoming style that made Tracy seem taller and older. She ran to Ginny, her blue eyes shining, and threw her arms around her waist.

"I love you, Grandma," she said, drawing back and looking into Ginny's eyes. "I didn't know you felt lonely and frightened too."

"Oh, darling, I'm not afraid if I have you and the other girls nearby. I love you all so much."

"I know, Grandma. I'll never go away and leave you, no matter what Mama wants." Her gaze didn't quite meet Ginny's. Ginny cupped Tracy's face in her hands and studied guileless blue eyes.

"Where's Marnie? I want to show her my new haircut. Think she'll like it?"

"I think so. It's beautiful."

Tracy danced away and headed for the lake. Ginny turned to Alex, a stunned look on her face. "What did you do?"

"I just told her how hard things had been for you, Ginny. She really does love you."

"I know." Ginny smiled and hugged herself; then her smile faded. "I know she isn't all right, just like that. There were many things bothering her."

"Yes, there are."

Ginny couldn't meet his steady gaze. She looked at the flowerbed, the grassy drive,

398

and finally had to raise her head to look into his eyes. "She wants to see her mother, doesn't she?"

"She says she doesn't," Alex responded, "but I don't believe her."

"She was six when Diane left, and for a long time, she thought Diane left because she'd done something wrong." She paced along the drive, grateful that Ellen and Jason were out in the sailboat. She and Alex must find the solution to this problem. "What can I do?" she asked, and he sensed she expected no answer from him. She was thinking out loud.

"If I don't let the girls see their mother, they may hate me someday. I suppose I should at least do that much, but Alex"—she paused—"I won't give the girls up to her. I'm going to fight."

"If that's your decision, you can depend on me for support and for any money you need."

"You don't agree with my decision, do you?"

Slowly, he shook his head. "She made a mistake. No one's perfect. Now she wants to rectify that mistake. I think she should be given the chance."

"Even if it might cause pain and unhappiness to three little girls."

"It might bring them something else," Alex said. "They might feel better knowing their mother does indeed love them."

"I love them too." Ginny turned away so he couldn't see the welling of tears in her eyes. "I've been there for them through all the months since Scott's death. I've rocked them and soothed their fears and loved them."

"Yes, you have, Ginny, but maybe now your job is done. Diane is going to remarry. She can provide a father and mother, and you can go back to being their grandmother."

"No!" She rounded on him, her eyes flashing green-gold with anger. "I may be getting married too. Jason has asked me."

She saw shock ripple across his face. She hadn't meant to tell him that way, but she was angry at the stand he was taking. She wanted him behind her, wanted him to believe she was right, that she was entitled to have the children. Now she stood staring at him, thinking there were so many other things she wanted from life and was no longer likely to get. Alex gaped at her as if thunderstruck.

"Congratulations, Ginny. I wish you well," he said finally, and walked back to his car.

Twenty

"Is that all you have to say?" Ginny challenged.

"Why shouldn't it be?" Alex asked, staring at her over the roof of the sport sedan. "Nola told everyone at the office about you and Jason. She said it was pretty serious. I shouldn't have been surprised by your announcement."

"How did you find out Nola was spreading rumors?" Ginny asked curiously.

He glared at her in amazement. "God, Ginny, do you think after all this time I don't recognize your work? I was hurt you didn't see me that weekend until I put everything together. Nola said she'd come down as a friendly gesture, but that you were hostile to her. I might have believed her, but there she was with a damn fine promo layout that carried your stamp as much as if you'd signed it. I knew she'd been in trouble with that account for some time. I figured you did it for me and the agency. So despite the rumors I came back to see for myself."

"You came because I called you about Tracy and Diane."

His expression grew dark and impatient. "I came because of you," Alex shouted. He stalked around the car and grabbed her hand to jerk her into the passenger's side of the BMW. "I'm tired of being the proper gentleman, the understanding shoulder to be cried upon, the good sport who exits the field of honor when he sees he's beaten."

"What on earth are you talking about?"

"You and your marriage to Jason McCann," he snapped, and pushed her down onto the seat. "I've never heard of anything so idiotic and stupid in my whole life," he fussed while he tucked in her feet and skirt and slammed the door.

"Why should my marriage to Jason be idiotic, because of my age?" she asked when he got into his side of the car.

"That hasn't anything to do with it. He's just the wrong man for you. Fasten your seat belt," he ordered, starting the motor. They roared out of the driveway.

"Where are you taking me?" Ginny demanded. "I can't leave. I have guests."

"They can fend for themselves. Just once in my life, Ginny, I'm going to have you to myself.

I'm going to complete a conversation about you and about me and the way I feel about you."

Ginny felt her chest tighten. "How do you feel about me?" she asked.

"I love you," he said, taking his eyes off the winding road to glance at her.

"Look out," Ginny called as the car roared toward another curve. Alex jerked his head around and righted the wheel. At the edge of the curve, a dirt road led back into green-shrouded woods. Alex braked and turned down the narrow dirt path.

"You'll ruin your car."

"The hell with it." He brought the car to a stop in a deeply shaded clearing. Cutting the motor, he turned to her.

"Do you really love Jason McCann?" he demanded.

"Yes, I love him," Ginny answered, searching Alex's face for his reaction. "I love him as a friend." She saw what she wanted in Alex's eyes.

"Is that all?" he asked softly. His hand went to her neck, his thumb brushing across her cheek. Wordlessly, Ginny nodded, her gaze locked with his. Alex pulled her forward and kissed her. His lips were warm and gentle, but the mood quickly changed. He broke away, his glance sweeping over her face, his chest rising and falling unevenly. His breath was ragged and

403

fast. Silently, he unfolded his long frame from the sports car, and taking a blanket from the trunk, he spread it on the ground by Ginny's door.

"What are you doing?" she asked when he flung open her door.

Alex knelt on the ground beside the car. "I've waited too long to ask you this question," he said. "I waited, and some other man almost won you—but I won't give up without a fight."

She felt a thrill of happiness. It showed in her eyes as she looked at him.

"I love you, Ginny. I want you to marry me. I know I'm not young anymore. I'm not always as sensitive or thoughtful or patient, but I'll always be trying. I wa—" Her slender fingers on his lips stilled his words.

"Sometimes, you talk too much," she said. He took hold of her elbows, pulling her down on her knees on the pallet as his mouth settled over hers. Ginny leaned against him, taking in the dear, familiar scent that was Alex, elegant masculinity, a tinge of aftershave, a hint of tobacco. She lost herself in the taste and feel of him. Then, he tugged at her and they went sprawling onto the blanket, their mouths still clinging.

"Ginny?" Alex whispered against her cheek. She could feel the hard urgency of his body. Her own moved against his in an age-old invitation.

404

Her eyes were bright as she met his gaze.

"I thought you weren't going to be such a proper gentleman," she teased.

"Come here, woman," he growled, and she laughed, wrapping her arms around his neck and pulling his face to hers.

"You just can't go against the grain," she said, shaking her head. Her eyes were filled with laughter.

"Do you mind?" he asked, suddenly serious.

Ginny studied his handsome features, the dark liquid eyes, the dark hair peppered with gray. "No," she said. "I like you just the way you are."

He kissed her then, without even asking first, and his hands, long-fingered, sensitive, touched her in all the right places, skimming over her flesh, brushing aside her cotton dress. Nervously she looked around as they sat up, and he freed her elbow from her sleeve.

"Is this a good idea?" she asked.

"Haven't you ever made love in a field at high noon?" he asked. He sat back, looking at her. Her dress was around her waist, her skirt draped gracefully around her legs. Suddenly shy, she brought her arms up, crossing them over her bare breasts. She thought of all the young women he'd courted over the years, young women with hard, perfect bodies. They had no such inhibitions.

"Don't do that," he said gently. "You're beautiful."

"I'm a fifty-year-old woman," she said.

"Who's wowing a fifty-three-year-old man," he said. "You are beautiful in my eyes, Ginny. You always have been." She read the truth in his expression and slowly lowered her arms. Alex's dark eyes shone with love. He gathered her close, his lips sliding from her mouth to her cheek and down to the soft hollows of her throat. Ginny drew a breath and felt a shiver run through her. His lips slid down to her breasts, and she wound her fingers through his dark hair. The feel of his hot mouth against her breasts awakened her.

She'd hesitated, feeling hampered by the memory of her brief affair with Jason, but now, suddenly, she felt no more regrets. Whatever had happened to her until this moment had made her able to respond to Alex with a full, open heart and unabashed sensuality. She wasn't afraid to show him how his touch aroused her or to reach for him, touching him, caressing him until she felt his gasp of pleasure. And then they united, his body arching over hers, plunging against hers. The sunlight around them was golden, the grass sweet. She'd never felt such joy, such swift racing toward that arcing pleasure that claimed them both.

They collapsed against each other, cradling one another in a final expression of pleasure. Slowly muscles relaxed, bodies grew limp and heavy. They lay side by side, arms entwined, contented, then awareness of the world around them returned and they grunted, grinned at each other apologetically, and shifted away from the twigs and rocks on the ground beneath the blanket. Sitting up, Ginny reached for her bra and panties, then quickly pulled on her cotton dress. When she glanced up, Alex had already rearranged his clothes and once again looked elegant and unruffled.

"How do you do that?" she asked, brushing at her wrinkled skirt. "You always look so well dressed."

"Do you know the sexiest look a woman can have is that of just having made love."

"Well, you would know. You're the expert," she said crisply, then stopped and looked at him. "I'm sorry. I shouldn't have said that." She could see the disappointment in his eyes, but he shrugged.

"Forget it," he said, and he shook out the blanket and folded it neatly and placed it back in the trunk. She wondered why he carried a blanket, but decided not to ask. As they settled themselves in the car, Alex turned to her.

"We're older people, Ginny," he said. "We aren't youngsters just starting out with no history. We can't expect virginity and such things. I admit I haven't led a celibate life, but I haven't been as much of a skirt chaser as my reputation might suggest." He paused. "And I've finally allowed myself to fall in love with you."

"Oh, Alex!"

"I think I've wanted to love you ever since David first introduced you to me back in college, but you were so obviously — so shiningly — in love with him. I didn't want to admit, even to myself, that I was capable of feeling so much for a woman. Maybe that's what Carly felt, that I wasn't giving her all my love. Maybe that was part of the reason our marriage failed. Whatever it was, you won't have that problem. I feel like I've been waiting for you most of my life."

Ginny was crying now, tears of happiness that filled her eyes and rolled down her face. She figured she must look a wreck, but she didn't care. Alex held her hand, and she returned his grip with all the love she'd denied herself.

"I forgot all about Ellen and Jason," she said when they pulled into the driveway and saw the group gathered on the patio. A strange car sat in the driveway. "I wonder who's here."

They got out of the car and walked down the rest of the drive. Jason looked at her sharply, and she wondered if he could see all that had transpired. She'd have to tell him as soon as possible. Her gaze swept the others seated on the patio, and she drew in her breath, her features going rigid. Diane had gotten to her feet and stood awaiting Ginny's reaction.

"What are you doing here?" Ginny demanded. "How dare you just drop in as if you were a part of our family."

"Like it or not, Ginny, I am part of this family. I'm the mother of three little girls, and I came to see them."

Ginny's gaze flew to Marnie.

"Tracy and Candi are out in the paddle boat, and Stef's taking a nap," Marnie said.

Ginny felt as if her blood began to flow again, and she sank into a nearby chair. Diane perched tentatively on the arm of her chair, her gaze never left Ginny's face. She felt the hostility of the others, but she never acknowledged it. Jason's lip curled with something akin to rage as he looked at her.

"I think I'm ready for a swim," Ellen said, standing up. "Will you join me, Jason?" He made no answer, his attention was focused on the slender young woman who nervously twisted her hands in her lap.

"Jason, come on. You have to be my buddy. I can't swim, so if I start to drown, you'll have to rescue me." Reluctantly, he got to his feet and followed Ellen down to the dock and into the water. They struck out for the raft. Marnie went inside.

"Do you want me to leave as well?" Alex asked.

"No, Alex. Stay!" Diane said quickly. Ginny looked from one to the other, trying to deny some gut-wrenching revelation about to make itself known.

Diane began to speak in a low voice. "I know you're not a cruel person, Ginny. You've never deliberately hurt anyone. But the words between us so far have been harsh and threatening. They hurt and can continue to hurt." She raised her head, and her eyes were brimming with tears. "I don't want my daughters hurt anymore."

"Then go away," Ginny said. "They're happy without you."

"Do you know that for sure? Have you asked them?"

"I don't need to," Ginny said tightly. "I know how they feel."

"They've talked about me, then?" Diane asked hopefully. Ginny didn't answer. She was remembering Candi snuggled against her that horrible night before they received word of the plane crash. She'd expressed a wish to see her mother. Beneath their smiles, was there an empty place only a mother could fill?

"They never mention you," Ginny said, and saw a shudder of pain cross Diane's face.

"Stef wouldn't remember me. Candi may have forgotten, and Tracy—"

"Tracy feels angry and hurt. She thought your leaving was somehow her fault."

"Oh, no!" A slim hand flew up to Diane's mouth as if to cut off her strangled cry. She rocked herself back and forth while tears rolled down her cheek. "Tracy was the hardest to leave. I stood beside her bed for such a long time, watching her sleep, and I almost changed my mind then. How could I bear to be without her?"

"Yet you managed to walk away from her and the others, and never mind what you did to Scott. But you've managed to live quite well for the past four years without worrying about their welfare."

"I made a horrible mistake, Ginny. Can't you forgive me for that? Not everyone can be as perfect as you, as sure of who they are and what they want. I want to see my daughters. I want to ask them to come back to California with me."

Ginny couldn't meet the anguish on her face. She looked out over the lake and saw the paddle boat returning, its bright green-and-white striped awning bobbing gaily. Inside the house,

411

Stef had wakened from her nap, and Marnie was talking to her.

"Suppose you ask them and they say they don't want to go with you. Will you go away and leave us all alone?"

Diane was quiet for a long moment, and Ginny could see the effort it cost her to make a single nod of acquiescence. "I'd already decided not to drag this into court if the girls don't want to go with me," she said in a ragged voice. "You see, Ginny, in spite of what you think, I can be a good mother too."

Ginny wanted to deny that she'd thought her a bad one, but the girls had beached the boat and were racing up the sloping lawn to the patio. Tracy halted when she saw Diane. Candi paused beside her, looking with bright curious eyes from Tracy to Diane. She didn't recognize her mother.

"Candi," Ginny said stiffly, "this is your mother."

Candi's expressive face grew still; her wide gray eyes stared at the elegantly dressed woman. Shyly, she edged around behind Tracy, peering from behind her sister's shoulder.

"Candi, won't you come here and hug me?" Diane held out her arms. But Candi withdrew, so she was completely hidden behind her sister. Diane's arms dropped to her sides. Her gaze fixed on her oldest daughter.

"Tracy," she whispered, "please don't be angry with me. Try to understand. I was wrong to leave you, but I had no money, no way to care for you. I always planned to come back for you."

Tracy remained silent, her eyes huge in her pale face.

"I've come back for you now," Diane said. "I want you to come to California with me." Tracy made no response, except to look at Ginny's face.

"I'm getting married, and the man I'm marrying has a big house. There's lots of room for you. You can have your own room if you like. And . . . and the school—there's an excellent school right nearby. I've already checked into it. Mike, that's the name of my fiancé, he loves kids. You'll like him. He makes people laugh, and yet he's very warm and caring." Diane paused. Ginny could read a growing defeat in her expression.

"Tracy, darling, please say you'll come live with me again."

"I'm staying with Grandma," Tracy said. "And so are the little kids."

"I'm not a little kid," Candi said from behind Tracy. She peered out to see if her mother had heard.

"No, you're not a little kid anymore," Diane

413

said, smiling through her tears. "I could barely recognize you—except for your beautiful eyes." Candi drew back and closed her eyes. Diane laughed. "Will you come live with me, Candi?" Diane begged.

"Will you have lots of toys?"

Tracy pinched her and whispered something in her ear. Candi's gaze shifted to Ginny and then back to her mother. Solemnly she shook her head.

"I want to stay with Grandma," she said.

Diane sat down as if her knees could no longer support her. Her head was bowed, and Ginny wasn't sure if she was weeping. Tracy and Candi stayed where they were, as if frozen in place. Finally Diane raised her head and looked at Ginny.

"You win," she said softly. "If the girls want to stay with you, I won't fight you." She rose and walked toward the drive. Suddenly the back door swung open and Stef skyrocketed out in her usual fashion. She stopped dead when she saw Diane.

"Stephanie?" Diane said in disbelief. "Are you little Stephanie, all grown up into a big girl?"

Solemnly, the four-year-old shook her head in denial. "I'm Stef!" she said and grinned.

"Can you give me a hug, Stef?" Diane asked softly, holding out her hands. Shyly, Stef glanced around; then seeing her grandmother and sisters at hand, she pranced over to Diane and gave her a big hug. Diane's arms closed around the little girl as if she'd always been hungry to hold her baby daughter. Her face was transfixed for a moment, shining with love. She closed her eyes and buried her face against Stef's hair, taking in the sweet scent of the little girl. Stef wriggled to be free of her embrace, and Diane released her, sitting back on her heels. Wonderingly she touched Stef's blond hair and chubby cheek, then as if she could bear no more, she rose and walked swiftly to her car. Ginny stood watching her until the car disappeared. She felt someone grip her hand and turned. Tracy had crept forward and stood hanging on to Ginny as if she were a lifeline. Her face was crumpled, and sobs escaped her throat.

"Tracy," Ginny said, hugging her close. "Did you want to go with your mother?"

Vehemently, the girl shook her head. "I want to stay with you, Grandma," she said, wiping at her cheeks.

"I wanted to go with Mama," Candi said, and she began to cry.

"Shut up." Tracy turned on her fiercely. "Grandma needs us. She's the one who's taken care of us and loved us. She'll be lonely if we go away. We can't do that to her." She stalked to her younger sister and, grabbing her hand, led the way back down to the lake, where they huddled on the dock and talked. Ginny could see Tracy's arm snake around her sister's shoulders, and she guessed Candi was crying.

"My god," Alex said, and his face was gray. His dark eyes reflected all the pain he'd seen in the past hour.

"What is it?" Ginny asked.

"Those were my words to Tracy this morning, to make her understand why you needed Jason."

"That doesn't mean anything. They want to stay with me."

"Are you so sure, Ginny? Diane is their mother."

"You sound like you're on Diane's side. Why did Diane ask you to stay? What have you got to do with all this?"

"Diane called me in Detroit. I suggested she come this weekend and talk to you again."

"Is that the reason for that wild ride over the countryside?" Ginny asked, feeling a coldness settle over her. "Is that why you made love to me? Was it your job to detain me until Diane arrived and tried to convince the children to go with her? Only they weren't here. Your timing was a little off."

Alex gripped her arms. "If you believe that of me, then you can't love me as you claim," he said, shaking her lightly. Then he released her and stepped back. "You aren't thinking clearly now. When you do, you'll see you're wrong about me — and about Diane." He stalked back to his car, put the BMW in reverse, and roared down the drive. Ginny turned away, unable to see him leave when they'd finally been able to reach out to each other. Her life seemed very bleak indeed. Did the girls feel the same way, having watched their mother go out of their lives a second time? Ginny slumped onto a patio chair and tried to sort out her thoughts. The only sound of merriment came from the raft, where Jason and Ellen sat talking.

Twenty-one

Monday morning, Ellen was strangely subdued. Preoccupied with her own problems, Ginny gave her friend little notice until they paused for lunch.

"Are all your weekends like that one?" Ellen asked. The sun had streaked her hair, and she was sunburned. She'd also acquired a new peppering of freckles across her nose. Take away her glasses and that overly serious air, Ginny thought, and Ellen is really quite beautiful.

"I'm sorry it was so dismal for you."

"Don't worry about me. It was just so damn hard on the rest of you. I even found myself sympathizing with Diane."

Ginny rolled her eyes and half turned from Ellen in an unconscious gesture of rejection. "Did you get along okay with Jason?"

"We were talking about Diane," Ellen said. "She does have her own side on this."

"Yes, so Alex—and everyone else—has pointed out to me, everyone except the girls and Jason."

"They're all so loyal to you. I think they'd cut off their arms for you, Ginny. It's awfully nice for you to have that kind of devotion, but it may not be right."

Ginny flared. "Do you have something to say to me, Ellen? Just spit it out."

"Hey, I don't want to step on your toes. I'm *your* friend, but there are a lot of factors to consider here."

"I know, the kids need a mother and a father. Well, that doesn't have to be a problem. Jason has asked me to marry him."

"He did?" Ginny didn't catch the husky quality of Ellen's voice or see the darkening of her irises.

"Yes, as a matter of fact, so did Alex."

Ellen stared at her, then burst out laughing. "You amaze me. You sit there, cool as you please, and tell me two very handsome and intelligent men have proposed to you just as if it happened every day."

"Well, it really isn't anything all that amazing."

"Maybe not to you, but, honey, there are a lot of women out there looking for husbands and

419

having a tough time finding one."

"This isn't about finding a husband," Ginny said impatiently.

"I know." Ellen's voice had become somber. "It's about three little girls and who they end up with, but it's also about you, Ginny, about who you've become and where you're going in the next years of your life. And it's about Diane and what she's become, a very strong woman who wants her kids, but is willing to give them up if it makes them happier."

"All right, let's talk about the kids and what makes them happier. You weren't there when they chose me over Diane."

"Is that what it's about, Ginny? That they chose you over a woman who abandoned your son and grandchildren. Are you punishing Diane because she did the unthinkable?"

"How dare you say these things to me?"

"I'm your friend. That's how I dare." Ellen bit her bottom lip, then continued. "You're able to understand these women here at the center. You empathize with them, you help them. I've never once seen you judgmental because they're running away from their husbands."

"You could never compare Scott with the kinds of men who drive their wives here."

"No, I suppose it would be unfair to him. But

something in that marriage was wrong, and it drove Diane to take the drastic step of leaving him. She said she loved him, but she felt smothered, not a real person. Can you imagine the pain she must be feeling, the guilt she's carried all these years."

"She made her choices," Ginny said, getting to her feet and brushing at her skirt distractedly.

"So did the women who come to us here. We provide them with a second chance."

"The girls don't want to go with their mother, and I don't want to debate this anymore. Besides, Jason says I have a right to keep the children."

"Jason is wrong," Ellen said quietly.

"Does it ever cross your mind, Ellen, that *you* may be wrong? I've changed my life so I can be a good mother to those girls. I'd no sooner learned how to take care of myself when three more human beings suddenly needed me. Well, I've coped. I've gone back to PTA meetings. I've learned to get up in the middle of the night, to soothe hurt feelings, to sell candy for the classroom fund raiser. I've been a room mother, a den leader. I do anything I must to make the girls feel happy and safe. I've been as good a mother as Diane could ever be."

"But with all that," Ellen said, *"you* are

not their mother."

"I'm the one they want to be with."

Ginny's eyes were hostile. Ellen looked away first. Ginny had become a dear friend. She didn't want to hurt her, but she feared Ginny was on a course that was all wrong for her. She has lost too much in her life, Ellen thought. Now, if Ginny lost the children against her will, Ellen wondered what would happen to her.

"Maybe you're right," she said finally, and prayed it was so. "Whatever your decision, I want you to know I wish you the best."

Ginny was touched by Ellen's warmth. She gripped her hand momentarily in unspoken affection and then went back to her desk. I should be sure of my decision regarding the girls, she thought, but with each day, my certainty dwindles. She pictured Diane holding Stef to her, Tracy's face as her mother drove away. Her hands began to shake. God help her, she didn't know what was the right thing to do. What if Diane had the children and left them again? But somehow she sensed that wouldn't happen. The woman who had pleaded for the return of her children had gone through a fire of her own.

Brakes squealed in the street outside, loud voices sounded. Ginny glanced up, then went back to work. The banging of the glass door at the front brought her head up again. Dimly, she thought there'd been an accident, and someone wanted to call the ambulance.

It took her a moment to place the man who stood in the waiting room. She'd seen him before, seen his brutish face and fists. He'd threatened her the first day she came to the center. Emily Fuller's husband!

His shirt was dirty and torn, sagging at one side from something heavy he'd shoved inside. His boots and work pants were greasy, his hair hung in untidy strands across his forehead. But it was his eyes that held her attention. They were bloodshot and filled with a lifetime of rage.

"Can I help you?" Ginny said loudly, hoping Ellen — anyone — would hear her and come to the front of the building.

"Where's my wife?" His voice was guttural.

Ginny shook her head. "She's not here, Mr. Fuller." She tried to keep her voice calm. Don't show them fear, she'd been told when she'd started on the job, but no one had said how you were to hide it when your knees were shaking so, you were afraid to stand up.

"Liar!" he snarled, and he advanced on her. One dirt-encrusted hand swept the items from her desk in a single swipe. Ginny saw the picture of her granddaughters land on the floor, the

423

protective glass splintered. She bit her lips to keep from crying out. Her frightened gaze went back to Emily Fuller's husband.

"Let's try that again," he said, reaching inside his shirt and taking out a gun. His lips curled in a gleeful sneer as he held the barrel to Ginny's temple.

"No!" she cried, trying to draw away, but his other hand snarled in her hair and held her steady. She could feel the cold metal against the side of her face.

"Where is she?" he grated out. Spittle formed on his lips, and his eyes looked even wilder close up.

"She hasn't been in all day, Mr. Fuller."

"You got one more chance," he said, pressing the barrel against her temple so she flinched with pain.

Ginny remained silent. She was going to die, she realized, and she thought briefly of Marnie and the girls waiting for her at the lake. Jason would probably expect to come over for supper. They'd be sitting around, waiting. What would they say and do when she didn't arrive? She drew in a deep breath and held it, waiting for the sound of a shot.

"Oh, my God," Ellen cried from behind her. Someone screamed—a woman. Bob Schur entered the room.

"Look, fella, don't do something you'll be sorry for," he said placatingly.

"Don't come a step closer or I'll pull this trigger," Fuller warned.

"All right, take it easy. We'll do anything you say," Ellen said. "See, we're backing up. Just tell us what you want and we'll do it. Don't hurt our receptionist, though. She hasn't done anything to you."

Fuller looked at Ginny and tightened his hold on her hair, nearly yanking her out of the chair. She cried out despite herself. "She's just like the rest of you," he said. "She lied to me once before. She's lying now."

"Maybe she's not. Maybe she just doesn't know what you've asked her. What is it you want?"

"You know! Don't pretend you don't," Fuller cried, waving the gun toward them. "I want my wife, Emily."

"She hasn't been in today, Mr. Fuller. I promise you, we haven't seen her."

"That's what you said before when you snuck her out the back door. I know how you work things down here. You give women ideas about leaving their husbands, but you don't really help them."

425

"Mr. Fuller, you have a restraining order that states you must stay away from your wife and children. You've caused them enough harm already."

"They're mine, my blood. You can't take them away from me. You get her back to me or I'll shoot this bitch here and then I'll start on the rest of you."

Ellen cast a frantic gaze at Ginny, who sat helpless in the gunman's grip. "Emily hasn't called in yet today. I don't know where she is."

"I know where her apartment is," Fuller said. "You thought I was too dumb to find where you put her, but I did. I went over there to see her, but she and the kids ran out the back. They got no place to come but here."

"You're right," Ellen said quickly. "She'll probably call any minute. Why don't you release Ginny, and we'll all wait for her call?"

Fuller looked around the circle of frightened faces. "That's a good idea," he said. He waved toward the row of chairs along the wall of the waiting room. "Sit! All of you. Don't make any unexpected moves." He watched them warily as they filed past. When Bob Schur walked by, Fuller raised his gun and brought it down on the doctor's balding head. Someone gasped. Ginny wasn't sure if it was her or the volunteer or El-

426

len. Bob Schur slumped to the floor and lay still. The pink flesh of his balding head was split open and blood trickled down his shirt collar. Ellen made a move to help him, but Fuller waved her back.

"He's hurt. He needs help."

"He should have thought of that when he tried to take my wife away from me," Fuller said with some satisfaction. Now that Fuller's attention was focused elsewhere and he no longer held her by her hair, Ginny tried to sidle past him and join the others, but his arms lashed out knocking her back into the chair. It skidded backward and banged into a filing cabinet. Ginny's head bounced against the metal edge before she was thrown to the floor. She lay stunned, feeling blood trickle down her brow. Ellen tried to come to her, but Fuller brandished his gun.

"She's hurt," Ellen cried. "She needs a doctor."

"You'll need an undertaker if you don't sit down and be quiet," Fuller cried.

"I'm all right," Ginny called, pressing a handkerchief to the cut. Eyes wide, Ellen did as Fuller ordered. He pointed a finger at Ginny.

"Get up!" he bellowed. Slowly Ginny got to her feet and sat on the edge of her chair, gazing at him with wide, frightened eyes. Now that the others were seated, Fuller looked at Ginny, pointing his gun at her chest.

"Pick up the phone and put it back on the desk," he ordered and watched Ginny closely as she complied. "Now sit down, and we'll wait to see if Emily calls." Ginny pushed her hair out of her eyes. Her scalp ached where he'd pulled her hair. Sandy Parker, one of the volunteers, wept softly into her handkerchief. The minutes dragged by. Outside the center, cars went up and down the street, and people called to one another, unaware of the drama being played out inside. The phone was shrill in the tense silence. Ginny looked at Fuller. He brought the gun close to her temple.

"Answer it," he ordered, "just the way you always do. I'll be listening."

Ginny picked up the receiver. Fuller placed his ear close to it. She could smell his foul breath. "Women's Crisis Center," she said, and her voice sounded artificially bright. "Ellen McCallan?" Her wide gaze went to her boss.

Fuller grabbed the phone from her, cradling it against his chest. "She ain't here," he whispered to Ginny, then slowly gave her back the phone.

"I'm sorry. Ellen's left for the day. Yes, all right. I'll give her the message. Goodbye."

Fuller snatched the phone and placed it back

in its cradle. His eyes narrowed as he studied Ginny's ashen face. "You done good. That was real smart of you." He nodded approvingly.

He sat back on his haunches, his back against the wall, his gun trained on them all. The traffic in the street thinned. Ginny glanced at her watch. It was almost seven o'clock. Well past time for her to be home. Marnie would be starting to worry about now. Ginny's gaze went back to the photograph of her granddaughters, resting on the floor near the desk. Their smiling faces gave her courage. She had to survive. They wouldn't be able to cope with another loss. She didn't realize how long she'd been staring at the photo until Fuller spoke.

"What are you looking at?" he demanded. Ginny jerked her head up and met his enraged gaze. "What—what are you looking at?" he yelled.

"M-my grandchildren," Ginny stuttered. "That's a picture of my grandchildren."

Fuller stooped to pick it up and hold it out away from him while he studied the faces. He shook his head as if in approval. "Nice-looking kids," he said and thrust the framed photo beneath her nose. "You want to see them again?" he rasped.

Wordlessly, Ginny nodded. The movement

made her hair fall over her eyes. She brushed it away.

"If you do, you help me get my kids back, you understand?" Again Ginny nodded, her hair swirling around her face in disarray. "You understand?" he shouted.

"Yes, I understand. I'll help you all I can," she whispered.

The minutes dragged into hours. Fuller made Ellen lock the door and turn off the lights, and they sat in the dark waiting for the phone to ring, waiting for Emily Fuller to walk into the trap her husband had set for her. Bob Schur moaned once and then was silent. At least he's alive, Ginny thought dully.

"Emily won't call now. It's too late," Ellen said.

"She'll call you," Fuller insisted. "She has to. She has nobody else to go to."

"But she knows we're closed at night," Ellen persisted. "You might as well let us go. It's pointless to keep us here."

"I'll decide what's pointless," Fuller shouted at her. "You're not in charge now. I am. I tell you what to do. You don't tell me. Ain't anybody ever going to tell me what to do again. Sit down and shut up." He took a malicious pleasure in crossing the room to shove Ellen back into her

430

chair. When she tried to resist, he raised his gun and brought it down across her face. Blood gushed from a cut on her cheek. Ginny ran across the room and threw herself at Fuller, hammering his shoulders and head with her open hands. He slapped her, knocking her to the floor. She tried to get to her feet, but he was there with the gun, the barrel pointed right between her eyes. She stared at the black hole at the end of the barrel, thinking she was staring at death itself, but Fuller backed up.

"Get back over to the phone," he ordered.

"Do it, Ginny. I'm okay," Ellen said. She had a blood-soaked handkerchief pressed to her cheek. Slowly, Ginny got up and limped back to her desk.

They sat through the night in the dark, listening to the diminishing sounds of a city that finally rested. Once they heard voices outside the center, and someone tried the door and shone a light in. As the flashing red beam of a police car was reflected in the glass door, Fuller scuttled out of the open, pushing Ginny to the floor behind her desk.

"Make a sound and I kill her," he said in a low voice to those seated along the wall. Tensely, they waited. Ginny's throat ached with the desire to cry out for help. It was so close, just on the

431

other side of the door, but she remained silent.

"Everything seems all right here," a man called, and car doors slammed and everything grew quiet again. The phone began to ring.

"Don't answer it," Fuller said.

"Maybe it's Emily," Ginny suggested.

"She wouldn't call at night. You said so yourself, didn't you, bitch?" He stood over Ellen. Slowly she shook her head.

"No, she wouldn't call at night. She'd know we were closed."

Nervously Fuller wiped at his mouth and then took his place against the opposite wall, where he could watch his hostages and the front door. Incredibly, they dozed and woke, started momentarily and dozed again. Sandy Parker prayed out loud until Fuller ordered her to shut up; then she prayed silently. Ginny tried to do that too, but her thoughts were too scattered. She could think of nothing but the girls—if a policeman had to tell them she was dead. What would happen to them then? Diane would have to be notified, but how? No one knew how to reach her. Terror laced through Ginny at the thought that her granddaughters would be left to the tender mercies of the courts and foster homes. They might even be split up and lose track of each other, all because of her, because she was too bitter to forgive Diane. A small sob escaped her, and she choked it back. Fuller looked at her suspiciously, but made no comment, simply burying his head against his up-drawn knees.

Dawn came at last and Ginny prayed it would end their siege, but Fuller simply ordered Ellen to make a pot of coffee and he finally relented enough to let Sandy Parker apply cold cloths to Bob Schur's head. When Ginny tried to leave her post to help pass around coffee, Fuller ordered her to return to the straight-back chair she'd sat in all night.

"If that phone rings, I want you right there," he said. Ginny perched on the chair again. At eight o'clock, the phone rang. Fuller ran to stand beside her, motioning her to pick up.

"Women's Crisis Center?"

"Ginny? Is that you? Thank heaven, I've been half out of my mind with worry." Marnie's voice was sharp with concern. Ginny wanted to weep at hearing her on the line. She visualized Marnie standing in the kitchen in one of her jogging suits, her iron gray curls bobbing with impatience.

"I'm sorry there's no one here by that name," Ginny said, praying Marnie would understand.

"Ginny, that's you. I recognize your voice."

"Perhaps if you try later, she'll be here."

433

"What on earth's going on?" There was a slight scuffle at the other end and then another voice that made relief flood through her.

"Ginny . . . Ginny, this is Alex. Are you all right?"

"I'm sorry, you have the wrong number."

"Ginny, don't hang up."

"Hang up!" Fuller said, and she did as he ordered. His eyes were mean and dark. "What did they want?"

She tried to appear nonchalant. "It was a wrong number."

"They asked to speak to Ginny." He turned and studied Ellen, cocking his head to one side as if remembering something. "She called you Ginny last night."

"No, my name's . . ." Her mouth went dry. He was tearing at her handbag, digging out her wallet and flipping through the credit cards.

"Virginia — Ginny Logan," he said, pawing through them and throwing them onto the floor. He raised his head and stared at her with murderous intent. "Why did you do that?"

"I didn't want to worry them," she whispered, backing away from him. Mesmerized she watched as he brought the pistol up and pointed it at her. She was crying out deep in her throat, but the sound couldn't seem to come forth. She

434

rolled her head from side to side in wordless denial of what was about to occur.

"For God's sake, don't," Ellen cried. "You haven't done anything so bad yet, but if you kill her, you won't have a chance."

He paused, his eyes mad and staring, but some bit of sanity still remained for he slowly lowered the pistol. Ginny sagged, and mewing sounds came from her throat. Ellen came forward to put her arms around her friend. And then the phone rang. Fuller's gun was pointed at Ginny once again.

"No funny business this time," he said.

"No." Ginny wiped at her eyes with the heels of her hands. Taking a deep breath to steady her shaking, she picked up the phone.

"Women's Crisis Center," she said.

"This is Emily Fuller. I need to talk to Ellen."

"Yes, just a minute," Ginny lowered the phone and stared at Emily Fuller's husband. "She wants to talk to Ellen."

He motioned Ellen forward. "Tell her to come here to the center," he ordered.

Ellen shook her head. "I won't lure her to her death."

"Then I'm going to kill you," he said, pulling back the hammer on the pistol.

"No," Ginny cried, then whirled away from

435

him, taking the phone with her. "Emily, don't come down here. Your husband's here, and he has a gun."

"Emily!" he bellowed and fired. A bullet whined past Ginny's head and lodged in the wall. She turned, just as Fuller reached her and tore the phone from her hands. "Emily!" he yelled into the telephone. "Tell me where you are. Tell me, Emily. If I find you, I'll make you sorry you ever left me."

Fuller was so focused on this link with his wife, he didn't seem to hear the breaking of glass or the rush of feet.

"Emily!" he shouted into the phone, then slowly looked around at the circle of pistols trained on him.

"Put down the phone and set the gun on the desk, Fuller," a uniformed policeman said. "Carefully."

Almost sheepishly, the big man set the gun down and replaced the receiver. "I just wanted to talk to my wife, my Emily," he mumbled.

"Put your hands behind your head," the policeman ordered, and Fuller did so. His broad face broke into a grimace as he began to weep.

"She left me. My Emily left me. I just wanted to get her back."

"You don't do that with a gun," one of the

other policemen commented, clipping handcuffs around his wrists.

"Ginny!" a voice called, and Alex appeared in the shattered doorway. Without hesitation, she ran to him and was enfolded in his arms. She buried her face against his neck and remembered the morning at the airport when she'd just learned that Scott was on the plane that crashed. Alex had waited for her all night, ready to offer his strength. Now he was here again.

"You're bleeding!"

"It's nothing, just a scratch," she reassured him.

"Thank God, you're alive. When I heard shots, I thought . . ." He clutched her convulsively. "I love you, Ginny."

"I love you too, Alex," she whispered.

Twenty-two

"She's late!" Ginny looked at her wristwatch for the hundredth time and paced the floor.

"She'll be here," Ellen said. She rose from the chintz-covered armchair and crossed to the window to stare out at the lake. Rain sleeted against the window panes and turned the world beyond a pale gray.

It had been two weeks since Ben Fuller had held them captive in the Crisis Center. Bob Schur, who had been taken to the hospital with a concussion, had just returned to work, and Sandy Parker and the rest of the hostages were finally recovering from the trauma. Emily Fuller had never come back to the center, although she'd sent a letter saying she and the children were moving out of state to live with her sister. Her husband was in jail awaiting trial. And Alex had returned to Detroit, only because Ginny had insisted. Too much had happened. She'd needed to sort things out, and now she thought she had.

"Look, would you do me a favor?" she asked, glancing at Ellen. "Would you stop in and see Jason once in a while? He's going to miss us."

"Sure." Ellen turned from the window and smiled fondly. "*I'm* going to miss you." The two women embraced. Then, patting each other's shoulders, they laughed and wiped their wet cheeks. "Are you sure you want to do this?"

"I've thought of little else these past few weeks. Thanks for sticking by me through everything."

"Hey, what are friends for?" She glimpsed Ginny's whimsical smile. "What?"

"I was just thinking about friendships," Ginny answered, and didn't go into details about Nola. "I've just learned there are 'friends' . . . and there are friends. I feel awfully lucky to have gone to the center that day."

"Listen, the center where you'll be working in Detroit is really understaffed. Jane English is in charge there. I think you'll like her."

"She won't be you," Ginny said, "but I expect you and I will make good use of I-96. It can't take more than two hours between Detroit and Grand Rapids."

"Less. We won't lose touch." Ellen paused, her head held high as if she were a deer caught

439

in a clearing. "I thought I heard a car door close. Do you want me to check?"

"Marnie will answer the door if anyone's there. Stay here with me." Ginny's hands were shaking. Ellen reached out to clasp them. Ginny felt support flow through her square-tipped fingers.

"Thanks," she said. "I'm all right."

In the back of the house a door opened and closed. Voices mingled, the words unclear.

"Where are the children?" Ellen asked.

"They're upstairs."

"How are they taking this?"

"It's hard to know. I just have to trust my instincts on this." There was no time for more. Their visitor stood in the French doors opening onto the summer porch.

"Hello, Diane," Ginny said.

"Ginny." Neither woman made a move toward each other. Warily their gazes met.

"Won't you sit down?"

"Yes, thank you." Diane sank into an overstuffed chair and crossed her legs. She looked tired, Ginny noted. Lines radiated from her eyes and her makeup was faded.

"Did you come directly from the airport?"

Diane nodded. "My flight was late getting in."

"I'm sorry to hear that. Would you like some

tea or coffee?"

Diane nodded impatiently. "You asked me to come here. You sounded as if you meant to . . . to—"

"To let you have the children," Ginny finished for her and then had to sit down abruptly. The words had sounded so final. There was no going back.

"Why did you change your mind?"

"It doesn't matter why. I just have. You're their mother. It's best they're with you." Absently, Ginny twisted her fingers in her lap. She didn't want to see Diane's face, the joy reflected there was mirrored by an equal amount of sorrow in her own heart.

"When may I take them?" Diane asked, and Ginny could tell she was striving to keep her voice even.

"Now, today!" Ginny turned away to hide the tears welling up.

Diane watched her for a long moment. "You aren't losing them completely, Ginny," she said. "You're still their grandmother."

"I know," Ginny said, turning to her. Her eyes were red from crying, her beautiful face was pale. For the first time in her life she looked her full fifty years. Diane felt sympathy for the older woman, but before she could express it,

Ginny was gathering her resources.

"So help me, Diane, if you ever leave those children again—"

"I deserve that, I know, and it will take some time for you to trust me again, Ginny, but I promise by all that's holy, I never will." Her eyes were huge and moist and sincere.

"I'll be coming to California to visit them."

"You'll be welcomed by us all."

"And I'll want them to come back and stay with me some."

"Summers maybe, here at the lake," Diane said earnestly. "I don't want to take any more from them than they've already lost. They need us both, Ginny."

Ginny met her gaze then, and Diane rose in one swift movement and knelt before her. "Please forgive me for all the pain I've caused you. Let's take what we have left and try to make a real family out of it." Ginny knew Diane wanted to be hugged, to be assured that there was no anger left in her, but she could go no further. This woman with the dark needing eyes was taking away the people she loved most. Although she'd voluntarily given up her claim on her granddaughters, Ginny couldn't feel at peace about it.

"It will take time," she said, and took hold of

Diane's hand.

"I know. But it's a beginning for us all." Diane rose. "Where are the girls?"

"I'll tell Marnie to get them."

"I'll go, Ginny," Ellen said. She'd stood quietly by during their conversation.

"What have you told them?" Diane asked, and Ginny could sense a new tenseness in her.

"That you were coming back to take them home and they may go if they wish. It won't be easy for you, Diane."

"I know. But I'm prepared to try to win them back, however long that may take." Her eyes were bright with hope and purpose. Only the young can feel that hopeful, that sure that everything will turn out all right.

Silently, the three girls filed onto the porch. Diane caught her breath and waited. When no one spoke she took a deep breath and held out her arms. Candi was the first to move. Restless, energetic, the one most in need of love, she ran into Diane's arms, burying her face against her mother's breast. Tears rained down Diane's cheeks. Stef was next. Never wishing to be left out, she charged across the room and threw herself against Diane's legs. Smiling through her tears, Diane hugged and kissed the girls, touching their faces as if she'd been hungry for them a long, long time. Finally, her arms holding them close to her, she looked at the one girl who stood aloof.

"Tracy?" Diane asked tremulously. "Can you forgive me for leaving you? Can you give me another chance?"

With a wild cry, Tracy flew into her mother's arms. Ginny could bear no more. She crossed to the door and made her way back to the kitchen. Ellen was making a fresh pot of coffee.

"Are you all right?" she asked. Wordlessly Ginny shook her head. Ellen's arms went around her, and she rocked her. They stood for a long time, without making a sound. At last Ginny had recovered enough to sit down at the table. Ellen brought her a cup of coffee.

"Is everything going okay out there?" she asked.

Ginny nodded. "I . . . I thought I'd give them time to get to know each other again, without . . . without feeling disloyal to me."

Ellen's hand patted hers on the polished oak surface. "It hurts now, but in the long run, you'll see it was the best thing you could do for them."

"I don't want to hear that right now," Ginny said.

Nearly a half-hour had passed before Marnie joined them in the kitchen. The old woman's face was troubled. Ginny felt sorry for her. She'd been loyal and as generous as a mother with her love.

"You're going to miss them too, aren't you, Marnie?" Ginny said. "You've stuck with us through so much."

"I figure I'm not done yet," Marnie said without meeting Ginny's gaze. "The girls told their mother they wanted me to go with them. Miss Diane, she asked me if I'd come and kind of be a nanny or whatever."

"And you're going?" Ginny asked.

Marnie met her gaze then. "If you don't need me anymore, Ginny, and if you don't mind."

"Mind, why would I mind?" Ginny said. "It will be like being there myself."

"Miss Diane said I could travel back and forth with them when they fly back here for summers," Marnie said eagerly, "so it ain't like we'll never see each other again."

"No, and I'll have such peace of mind, knowing you're with them," Ginny said. She felt an easing of the lump in her stomach: Diane had meant it when she'd said the girls could come back for the summer.

"Well, I guess I'd better get started packing. Miss Diane's on the phone, making plane reservations for us." Marnie got up. "You'll be all right, won't you?"

Ginny smiled and raised her head so Marnie could see her face. "I'll be just fine," she said and meant it. One part of her life was over, another would start. She got to her feet. "I'll help with the packing," she offered.

In a matter of hours, the girls were gone. Phone calls had been made to the airlines and then to California. Ginny had listened shamelessly as Diane had told someone at the other end that she was bringing the children home with her. Whoever it was seemed as happy as she was, and promised to meet the flight. Diane was crying when she got off the phone.

They hadn't packed everything, just clothes enough for the girls to get by until Ginny could ship the rest of their things. Ginny stayed busy, searching for favorite stuffed animals and matching up shoes, but all the time inside herself she cried out that this was happening too fast while another part of her was glad the leave-taking wouldn't be prolonged.

She kissed their sweet faces, inhaling the clean, innocent scent of them, felt the baby softness of their cheeks and smiled and smiled until she thought her face might surely crack from the effort. Of the three girls only Tracy seemed to know how hard the parting was for Ginny. She

446

an back to hug her yet again and clung to her
eck, sobbing. Ginny almost broke then, despite
er resolve.

"I'll see you at Christmastime," she said. "I'll
y out there and you can show me California."

"I love you, Grandma."

"And I love you, my sweet girl. Get in the car
ow before the others start to cry. You're their
ole model, you know. They look up to you."

With a final hug, Tracy ran to the rental car and
ot in. Marnie was already in the front seat,
olding an overnight case on her lap. Diane
tood with her door open. Her face was radiant,
et filled with concern.

"We'll see you at Christmas, Ginny," she said.
Plan to stay with us. We have plenty of room,
nd the girls would like that."

"I'll plan on it." Ginny raised her hand in a fi-
al gesture of farewell. The girls waved and blew
isses until the car turned out of the driveway.
Ginny stood for a long time, watching the empty
oad. At last she turned back to the cottage. El-
en was waiting for her.

"I've decided to spend the night," she in-
ormed Ginny. "Jason is going to build a bonfire
lown by the lake and we're going to roast
narshmallows and hot dogs."

"Not tonight, Ellen. I just can't." Ginny

turned away to hide her face, but Ellen could see
her shoulders shaking with the force of her sobs.
She waited for a while then crossed to her friend
and put an arm around her.

"That's enough crying for now. You have dinner guests, and we won't let you be maudlin."

"I'm sorry, Ellen. Thank you for coming, but
I really want to be alone now."

"It won't work, Ginny. Come on. Help me
thaw out some steaks. You haven't eaten a bite
all day." She led the way to the kitchen. "I presume that since Marnie did the cooking, you're
not much of a hand at it."

Ginny blew her nose and threw away the tissue. Obviously, Ellen just wouldn't take no for
answer. Somehow she would have to make an effort to be sociable. "I'm really quite a good
cook," she said. "I make great macaroni and
cheese. Just ask the ki—" For one stark minute
she thought she might fly apart, but Ellen was
there, turning aside the panic.

"Okay, hot shot! Prove it!" Ellen held out a
saucepan.

Somehow, Ginny got through the evening.
They ate steaks on the summer porch, watching
the moonlight come up on the lake, and then Jason built a fire and they went down and sat on
the wet bank and roasted marshmallows and

448

told scary stories that turned silly. Ginny even laughed, and felt better for it. The empty place inside her heart couldn't be filled so easily, but Ellen's distractions were working. She was starting to think ahead to Christmas in California. She could, she told herself, even move out there if she wanted to, but she knew that wasn't a possibility she wanted to explore just yet. Ellen got her through that first night, Ellen and Jason with their easy banter. Sometimes Ginny saw a bleak look in Jason's eyes and knew he was going through a bad time himself over the girls' departure. That was when she looked at Ellen with renewed admiration. Her friend wasn't just healing one of them, but both.

When Ellen left to drive back to the center late the next morning, Ginny missed her almost more than she did the girls, but she knew she had to stand alone. She'd adjusted before, she could again. In the days that followed she kept herself busy, packing up the girls' clothing and toys for shipment, arranging with Dick Chalmers to take out the dock and store the boat, readying the cottage to be closed down for the winter. And she had another task to accomplish before she left. Jason McCann had been avoiding her ever since the girls had left. She knew he was still angry with her about her decision. She crossed through the opening in the hedge and knocked on his back door. He was wearing his swimsuit and had a can of unopened beans in his hand.

"Having supper?" she asked.

He shrugged and shoved the can into a cupboard. "Want some coffee?"

"Ummm!"

They settled at his kitchen table on which manuscript pages were scattered.

"How's your book?"

"I've got a nibble. My agent's negotiating right now."

"That's wonderful."

"They're interested in doing a series of books with this Mrs. Lansky character." He shrugged, but it was obvious he was pleased with himself.

"I'm very happy for you, Jason. No one deserves this more than you."

"What are your plans now?" he asked, obviously uncomfortable talking about himself.

"I'm going back to Detroit. The sublease on my condo is up and my renter's moving out, so I expect I'll move back there."

"Alone?"

"I'm not certain." She couldn't lie to him. They'd been too close for that. "I'm sorry for everything that happened this summer."

450

"What's to be sorry about?"

"I feel as if I used you."

"We used each other," Jason said, concentrating on stirring cream into his coffee. Then he raised his head and looked at her. "You know, I wasn't there just for the kids. You thought . . . well, you thought I was substituting you all for the family I lost—and maybe I was at first. But later, with you, it wasn't that. I find you very attractive, Ginny. My proposal still holds."

"That's very flattering to a woman of fif—"

His fingers pressed gently against her lips, stopping her words. His eyes were almost sad as he looked at her. She knew then she had to say it all, everything that was in her heart.

"You made me stop being afraid to be a woman," she said softly. "You took away the feelings of guilt, so I could open myself to the love of another man—after David. I'll always love you for that."

He leaned across the table and his lips brushed hers. Their touch was sensuous, because Jason was a sensuous man, and Ginny realized with a swift surge of joy that she was a sensuous woman. She smiled at him and got to her feet.

"Now I'm going to do what I should have done that first time last summer. I'm going to leave before I get myself into trouble again." She turned toward the door.

"It's Alex you're going to, isn't it?"

Ginny nodded. "Yes, it's always been Alex." She looked at him, fearful she'd brought him pain, but he grinned.

"Be happy then. You deserve it," he said, and she recalled that he'd always been a generous man. She remembered the first day she'd seen him, with his sloping shoulders and wounded eyes. Now he stood tall again, and if his eyes always carried a hint of sadness, that couldn't be helped.

"I did help you, didn't I?" she asked softly.

"Immeasurably," he said.

She carried the memory of his smile with her as she crossed back over to her cottage. Standing in the kitchen, she looked around for a final time. She couldn't think of anything else that needed her attention. Tomorrow she would return to Detroit. Tomorrow, she was going home to Alex.

Monday morning the freeway filled with vacationers returning from the Labor Day weekend. Matching her speed to theirs, Ginny thought she'd have to get used to the faster pace of the big city.

Closing the cottage that morning and walking

away from it, from memories of the months there, hadn't been as difficult as she'd anticipated. Now she actually looked forward to getting her furniture out of storage and moving back into her condo. Ginny's spirits rose as she drew closer to Detroit. Though some might give it a black eye, she'd come to have an affection for its ragtag, tough-town demeanor. Was that what Alex had meant when he'd questioned her decision to live in the country, that she was a city girl? Well, she was glad to be back. She took 275 north around the city, then, on an impulse, turned toward the office. Alex would be there and suddenly she didn't want to delay seeing him.

Going up in the elevator brought a rush of memories. She felt ridiculously glad she'd come, as if a part of her were coming alive again. She'd always enjoyed the challenges of her work at the agency, and by the time the elevator doors slid open, she was grinning with anticipation.

"Ginny, you're back," Mary said. Fran got up from her desk and came forward to hug her.

"God, you look great. What did you do to yourself?"

"We heard about your being held hostage. Glad you're okay."

The welcome was spontaneous and sincere.

When everyone in the outer office had greeted her, Ginny glanced around.

"Is Alex in?"

Fran grinned. "He sure is, and he's gonna be glad to see you. He's been the worst boss since you left. These past few weeks have been the pits."

Ginny headed toward Alex's office, her wide mouth curved in a smile of anticipation. The door to one of the other offices opened, and Nola Sherman stepped out. Startled, she stopped and stared at Ginny, taking in her suit and hair.

"Hello. Are you back?" she asked lightly.

"I am," Ginny said gaily without pausing in her stride.

"Don't you think you're rushing it a bit, after that incident with the gunman and all?" Nola called. "I mean, it takes time to get over something like that."

Ginny turned around and looked at her. "Perhaps for a younger, less experienced woman," she said kindly. She was still smiling when she walked into Alex's office.

"Ginny!" Alex stood up and looked at her in amazement. "I was just trying to call the lake."

"Yes!" she cried, her grin broad, her eyes glowing.

"What?"

"That's my answer to a question you asked me once in a field at high noon. Yes!"

He stared at her a moment, his gaze lingering on her face as if he were afraid she'd changed somehow. Then he grinned and walked around the desk. "Come here," he growled, and pulled her into his arms. His kiss was definitely ungentlemanly. She'd have to remind him of that later. And there was so much to tell him, about Diane and the girls and Marnie and Ellen and Jason.

"Let's go," he said when they were both breathless and considerably warmer.

"Where are we going?" she asked, following him out into the main office. He didn't answer, just pulled her along toward the elevator. The secretaries looked up and tittered affectionately. They've known for a long time, Ginny thought dimly.

"Where are we going?" she insisted.

"To find a field at high noon," he said. Then, suddenly he grew somber. "I love you, Ginny Logan. I'm going to marry you as soon as we can get a license. I don't intend to waste any more time."

"Nor do I," Ginny said. "I figure I only have fifty years left, and I'm not sure if that's enough time to show you how much I love you."

He pulled her into the open elevator and into his arms. His kiss was possessive and urgent. Ginny returned it with her whole heart. Just before the doors slid together, she heard the office staff cheering.

Twenty-three

Their wedding date was set, a mere two weeks away. The time between was a frantic time of discovery and adjustment as Ginny became better acquainted with the man who was to become her husband.

"Alex, do you think we might be rushing into this too quickly?" she asked as they wove in and out of freeway traffic in his BMW. "Maybe we need to take more time and work out all the little details. We may not even be compatible, you know."

"I know," he said softly. "Won't it be fun to knock off the edges until we are?"

She laughed again. It was so easy to do, to laugh and hold Alex's hand. She concentrated on the here and now and tried not to think about the girls and how much she missed them. She was determined not to be maudlin or worried. But having thought of her granddaughters, she was reminded of something.

"Alex, you do know that if things don't work out for the girls with Diane, they will come back and live with me."

"I know," he agreed, "and that's not a problem, Ginny. We're going to be a family. I haven't had one in a long time. I may do things wrong some of the time, but one thing I do remember about families is that they stick together."

Ginny gazed at his dark, fine profile and thought of the loneliness of his life. He'd never let anyone glimpse the truth, but now he'd opened himself to her. His trust was a gift she accepted with love. Leaning forward, she kissed him lightly on the ear.

"What was that for?" he asked.

"To remind you that I'm your family now," she said, "and you are mine." His dark eyes became suspiciously bright. Ginny saw the shine of emotion in them and was surprised and deeply touched by this sensitive, tender-hearted man. She thought of David and Jason. Each of them had given her something important, something she'd needed at the various stages of her life — young bride, mother, woman groping for a new understanding of herself. But it was Alex who'd touched her the

458

most deeply, awakening new dreams, breathing life into a heart of ashes. She was soaring again, rising like a phoenix from the ruins, reaching for the sunshine. Now her eyes were misty, and she couldn't seem to stop her mouth from curving into a wide grin.

Alex persuaded her to move in with him rather than reopen her condo. With their wedding only two weeks away, Ginny decided she had enough to do without the added burdens of having her place repainted and arranging for her furniture to be taken out of storage.

"I feel slightly wicked," she said as they stepped into the elevator in his building.

"Wait until I finish with you, my lovely little innocent," he whispered and drew her into his arms. His kiss was possessive, demanding, erotic, and it made her pulse race.

"I'll have to remember to stay out of elevators with you," she said when he finally released her. Her face was filled with laughter. She looked young and vibrant and alive. Alex squeezed her hand. She was his lady, and he'd never loved her more. The world was bright with promise.

"You overwhelm me," Ginny whispered when he busied himself planting tiny kisses on her throat and the lobe of her ear.

"I warn you, my beautiful, soon-to-be bride. I am insatiable where you're concerned." He blew in her ear, and Ginny moaned just as the elevator doors slid open. An older couple stood in the hall waiting for them to exit, their expressions knowing.

Blushing but head high, Ginny stepped into the corridor. Alex followed with her bags. She had to resist the urge to giggle, and she definitely wasn't the giggly type. When the elevator was gone, bearing the couple downward, she glanced at Alex and was surprised to see his masculine swagger.

"I'm not making a good first impression," she said lightly.

"I'm impressed as hell." He unlocked his door and ushered her in. "Welcome to your new home, Ginny."

With an expectant smile, she followed him through the spacious four-room apartment. It was far more modest than she'd expected the home of a man in his position to be, and although furnished with functional masculine taste, it showed no signs of being a playboy playpen. She was impressed by the shelves of books, the modest collection of really good paintings, and the surprising display of fragile jade carvings. She was less impressed by the worn leather chairs and sofas, the rack of pipes and the pungent odor of tobacco. These things would take some getting used to, as would the empty refrigerator, the never-used dishwasher and the array of cold cereals in the cupboards.

"Is this all you have to eat here?" she asked, holding a half-empty box of Count Chocula.

"I'm sorry. I always eat out," he said. "We'll get you settled in and go have a bite."

"That might be a good idea," Ginny said, staring at a jar of pickle juice, three eggs, and half a container of moldy yogurt. "I could whip up an omelette if you have some fresh yogurt."

"I hate yogurt," he called from the living room where he was sliding a CD into the player.

"Uh-huh!" Ginny said, and she dropped the yogurt container into the trash.

Strains of Debussy drifted through the apartment, dreamy and romantic. Alex appeared in the doorway, his gaze compelling. Ginny forgot about the yogurt left behind by some unnamed visitor and crossed the room. His hands went out to her, drew her into his embrace. His lips nuzzled her ear lobes, sought the sensitive hollows of her throat.

"I can't believe you're here," he whispered, caressing her in a languid, sensuous motion. "I've dreamed of this so often."

"Have you?" she asked, still surprised by his love for her.

"Didn't you ever dream of me?" he insisted, nibbling at her neck so she shivered deliciously.

"Yes," she confessed, remembering the disturbing dreams of Alex making love to her.

"Well, what did you dream? Tell me!" He was guiding her toward his bedroom, moving her backward in tiny steps, his knees bumping her thighs so she had no choice but to move as he dictated.

"I can't tell you my dreams," she murmured. "They're private."

"You'll have to tell me, eventually," he pressed. "I'll worm it out of you." His kiss was deep, hot, demanding. It left her whole body pulsing with need.

"Tell me," he whispered, slowly removing her clothing. He nudged her back onto the bed and bent over her, a half-smile curving his lips. "Tell me you love me," he said huskily.

"I love you," she gasped. His hands were working their magic on her. She watched as he stripped away his clothing. There was an air of purpose in his movements. They weren't in a field at high noon. They were in the privacy of their bedroom, and they could take the time to know each other in this mating, to seek and discover and find and delight. He bent her legs and pressed them apart.

"Relax," he said. "I want to see how beautiful you are." His head lowered and she felt his mouth against her. She flinched, startled by such contact; then waves of pleasure claimed her. "My beautiful, beautiful Ginny," he crooned, cradling her in his arms while she shuddered with ecstasy. Then slowly, sensuously, he began to caress her again. The long afternoon passed in a blaze of emotions and new responses. Alex teased her and cajoled her and wooed her, and always he was sensitive to her needs and desires. When she lay satiated and exhausted, he held her against him until she relaxed and slept. When she woke the afternoon was gone and Alex was watching her, a bemused expression on his thin handsome face.

"I must look a sight," she said, trying to rise, but he held her beside him.

"You look like a little girl when you sleep," he said, tracing her lips with one long finger. "My prudish, shy Ginny."

She chuckled and wrapped her arms around

him, hiding her face against his shoulder. "I'm hungry," she whispered.

"So am I," he answered, but his tone showed they weren't thinking of the same thing.

"I'm sore," she said quickly. "Take me to a restaurant and buy me some food and tomorrow I'll go shopping for groceries."

"You don't have to do that," he said, rising. "I'm used to eating out. You don't have to turn into a cook and drudge for me, Ginny. That's not why I'm marrying you."

"I know why you're marrying me," she said, grimacing. "But I don't want to live a transient sort of existence. I want to be a wife. I want a home, Alex, a home for you and me."

He paused in fastening his shirt and turned to her, his dark eyes serious as he regarded her. "I'm not sure I understand what you have in mind," he said finally. "I've lived a bachelor life—restaurants and apartments—for so long, I'm not certain I know how to live any other way. But if you're telling me you don't want to live here, we'll change that. It's just"—he paused and raked a hand through his dark hair—"I don't want to live at the condo where you and David were together."

Ginny stared at him in surprise. He was threatened by her memories of David, she realized and couldn't refrain from smiling. "I could sell my condo," she said, "and we could look for another place."

"You'd do that?"

Ginny nodded. "My life with David is over. My life with you is just beginning. I want to put all my love and energy into the future, Alex."

He squeezed her hand and resumed dressing.

"You know, we could look for a house," she said later, coming out of the shower, a fluffy towel wrapped around her.

"A house?" He paused in knotting his tie and gazed at his reflection in the mirror. "I haven't lived in a house in so long I'm not sure I'd know how to go about it."

"I'll teach you," Ginny answered. "You've taught me some pretty terrific things this afternoon. Now it's my turn to educate you." Her eyes glittered teasingly.

"I'm ready!" He began unknotting his tie.

"No!" she exclaimed in mock horror, but he whipped the towel away from her, his eyebrows wriggling lasciviously. She laughed and dodged away, but he caught her against him.

"Do you know what happens when you flaunt yourself before a starving man," he said ominously.

"How can you be in such need after the past few hours?" she protested laughingly.

"I'll show you," he whispered.

The evening had flown by before they finally dressed and went out to find a place to eat. He took her to Maria's, a little Italian restaurant around the corner from his apartment. From the way he was greeted, Ginny guessed Alex was a frequent customer. They consumed hearty dishes of spaghetti served with crusty bread, then lingered over cups of thick black coffee, discussing their plans.

The next day they got a marriage license and Ginny met with a realtor to put her condo on the market and begin the search for a home for Alex and her. Everything was happening so fast she had no time to think, not even at night when she lay beside Alex in bed for then he talked to her of his childhood and his dreams and the lonely years without her and she told him of her dreams of his making love to her and of the guilt she'd felt at somehow betraying David and of her agonizing decision to return the girls to Diane. He soothed her sadness with tender words, reassured her with vows of love and awakened her passions with his lovemaking. She'd never asked herself why she hadn't moved to California to be closer to her granddaughters, but now she understood, she could never have left Alex. She told him that and saw his eyes mist.

"You'll never be sorry you made that choice," he whispered huskily.

"I know," she said, and felt at home in his arms.

Although she had no intention of becoming a mere housewife and cook, Ginny took a few days off from the agency to shop for groceries and supervise the cleaning woman, who, after a few sullen glances, shrugged philosophically and accepted the fact that working for another woman was far different from cleaning house for a bachelor who was seldom there. After a few days the apartment looked much better. Contrary to his belief that he must sacrifice many of his comforts, Alex found his pipe rack still on the table beside his favorite armchair, now slipcovered into respectability. The dining-room table usually bore a vase of fresh flowers, and was the site of a carefully prepared meal. He began to settle into a routine that didn't include dashing out to an indifferent supper in a restaurant. There were other changes in his masculine abode. The scent of

Ginny's perfume lingered in his bathroom long after she'd left it, her nightgown hung beside his pajamas on the peg behind the door, his ample closet was bursting at the seams with his wife's clothes.

But there was one adjustment neither of them had given any thought to. Ginny was a neatnik, not obnoxiously so but still, seeing her belongings neatly arranged made Alex try harder. And there were other differences. He habitually dropped his clothes wherever they were taken off, thus his cleaning bill was astronomical. Ginny neatly hung her things in the closet. He liked to sleep late; she rose early — with boundless quantities of energy. She loved to read in bed; he was a television person. She liked popular music, even, Alex shuddered, some light rock; he preferred classical. She read mysteries, he preferred sci-fi. Yet he was delighted by all things about her, even the fact that she liked to loll in a long hot bath while he liked quick showers. The place they were the most compatible was in bed, and he tried his hardest to persuade her to stay there more often with him. Once he overcame her barriers of modesty, he found Ginny to be a delightfully sexual woman, a willing partner to any request. Her mouth was hot and sweet on his

468

engorged member, her teeth sharp and impudent on his nipples, her laughter bawdy and challenging. She was vixen, prim lady, and sensuous woman all wrapped up in one.

His friends adored her, her friends found him charming. For Ginny and Alex, it mattered little. They were in love and had little need of anyone else.

The day of their wedding, Ginny sent him off to the home of his best man. Ellen had arrived, and the two women took over Alex's apartment with their feminine fripperies. Ginny was radiant in a pale ivory satin suit and matching hat and veil. At the curved neckline, she wore a rope of pearls Alex had given her.

"You are so gorgeous," Ellen said, kissing her cheek lightly and then rubbing away any trace of lipstick that might have been left behind. She looked resplendent herself in a bridesmaid's dress of pale peach. Her thick blond hair was piled on top of her head.

"Too bad Jason couldn't be here," Ginny said, wishing he could see Ellen as she looked at this moment.

"He's getting over you, Ginny, but asking him to watch you marry Alex would be a little too much. I'm meeting him back at the lake tonight for a fall cookout."

Ginny hugged her, then finished dressing. All the while, she thought about Alex. What would he think when he first saw her? Would he think her beautiful? Was he frightened of this step? After all those years as a bachelor, was he getting cold feet? She had no doubts about her own feelings. She'd waited too long to love again, and she'd almost let Alex slip through her fingers because she lacked the courage to face her feelings. She was as certain now of marriage to Alex as she was about anything in life. The phone rang and Ellen picked up the receiver. She listened for a moment, and then her face lit up in a smile.

"Just a minute. She's right here."

"Who is it?" Ginny asked, for some reason thinking Alex was calling to tell her he'd changed his mind. Ellen just smiled and handed her the receiver.

"Hello?"

"Grandma!"

"Tracy." Ginny sat down abruptly. "How did you know where I'd be?"

"Uncle Alex called us last week and told us you were getting married." Tears slid down Ginny's face as she silently blessed Alex. He'd known she longed to hear from the girls, but had refrained from calling to give them time to adjust to their new life. "Congratulations, Grandma," Tracy was saying. "I'm glad you have someone so you won't be lonely."

"Are you happy there in California?" Ginny asked, trying not to be hurt by the happiness in Tracy's voice as she spoke of her new life with her mother.

There was a scuffle at the phone. "Candi, wait," Tracy said in some irritation.

"Grandma?" Candi's voice was small, but it was one of the sweetest sounds Ginny had heard in weeks. "Will you still love us, Grandma, even if you're married to Uncle Alex?"

"Oh, darling, of course I will. No one could ever take your place with me. Tell me about your school."

Ginny listened and laughed, tears of happiness sliding down her cheeks as each girl took a turn talking to her. Then Diane got on the phone.

"Congratulations on your wedding day, Ginny," she said. "The girls have missed you, but they're adjusting."

"I'm glad." Ginny couldn't help the reserve that crept into her voice when she spoke to her daughter-in-law.

"Mike, the girls, and I want you and Alex to come out here for Christmas this year. Will you think about it?"

Ginny felt the reserve melt away. She was crying again, weeping silently while tears slid down her face and over her smile. "Yes, Diane, yes. We'll come. Thank you for asking."

"No. Thank you, Ginny, for everything," Diane said softly. "I hope you're happy today. You deserve this."

"I am happy. And hearing from the girls was a wonderful gift. Goodbye, Diane."

"Goodbye, Grandma. We love you."

With the voices of her granddaughters ringing in her ears, Ginny hung up and looked at Ellen. She was smiling and weeping at the same time. Ellen thought she'd never looked more radiant, and then Jason came to her mind. Would she ever be able to erase his memories of this strong, beautiful woman? Taking up a powder puff, Ellen applied it to Ginny's tear-streaked cheeks.

"Time to go meet your man," she said gaily.

Alex was thunderstruck when he looked at Ginny. She'd never appeared more beautiful to him. Her eyes were glowing with love, her expression was serene, certain. He'd entertained no doubts about this marriage, but he'd been in hell, fearful she'd change her mind. Now, to see her walking down the aisle of the little chapel, carrying a bouquet of ivory roses and trailing orange blossoms, he felt like a kid who was about to get his deepest wish. He watched her approach and thought of all the ways he knew this woman, first as the wife of his best friend, when he had to hide his growing awareness of her; then as a widow, when he must practice restraint and respect her period of mourning; and finally as a woman ready to love and be loved. He knew the scent of her, the sound of her laughter, the satiny feel of her skin, the cutting edge of her wit, the tenderness and passion of her, yet there was so much more he would discover in the coming years, years when they'd grow comfortable with each other, years when waking beside her wouldn't seem such a miracle anymore. He'd never take her for granted, he swore to himself. He'd count his blessings each day.

She stood beside him now, her eyes all misty and glowing with love. He reached out and took her hand. Together, they turned toward the priest who would unite them in marriage. Her fingers clung to his, and when he placed the wedding band on her hand, she trembled slightly.

Only a handful of their closest friends had been invited to the chapel, but there were more than a hundred people at the reception — office staff, business associates, friends, and family. Ginny greeted each person with a smile, inquiring about this one's health or that one's tennis serve, seeing that all had been served food and champagne.

Alex had always known she was able to put people at ease and to provide a personal touch; still, it amazed him when he saw her in action. She seemed tireless. He watched her from across the room, listened to the lilt of her laughter, saw her smile, the lamplight gleaming in her hair and highlighting her cheeks and when he could bear it no longer, he crossed the room to claim her, tucking her elbow against his side.

There were shouts then, and crystal was lightly tapped with silverware so it rang out. The din ceased only when Alex kissed his bride, which he did thoroughly and without hesitation before escorting her to the bridal suite at the Hyatt Regency. The next day they would fly to Cancún for a brief honeymoon.

"Mrs. Alex Russell," Ginny mused, standing on the balcony and gazing down at the city's lights reflected in the river. "What a long journey this has been." She wore a pale ivory peignoir and held a long-stemmed champagne glass from which she occasionally sipped. Her hair had been loosened from its elaborate coiffure and brushed against her shoulders.

"It isn't over yet," Alex said, coming to stand beside her and wrap his arms around her. "We've just begun." He took away her glass and drew her into his arms. She went willingly to him, compliant and supple, her mouth eager beneath his. When they were both breathless with longing, Alex took her hand and led her to their marriage bed.

Twenty-four

"Do you think they'll ever get to be real friends?" Ellen asked. She was looking slim and pretty in a black sequined sweater and palazzo pants.

"I hope so," Ginny answered. "They had a pretty rocky start. I think once they overcome that, they'll do some male bonding."

"Ummm!" Ellen put the finishing touches on a tray of hors d'oeuvres and popped a stray olive in her mouth. They were preparing for a New Year's Eve cocktail party for the office staff. Ellen had volunteered her services, and Ginny had jumped at the chance to have her visit.

"I suspect when our guys see they have little choice, that we plan to get together often, they'll relent a bit."

"Have you and Jason finally set the wedding day?"

Ellen nodded happily. "June—at the lake. We thought you and Alex might stand up for us, since you two got us together."

"Oh, Ellen!" Ginny set down the tray of champagne glasses and put an arm around her friend. "I'd be so honored." The two women hugged each other, thinking for a moment of all they'd been through together and apart. "Seems like we're all due for a little happiness," Ginny said, pulling away. "I'm so happy for you."

"It was quite a year for everybody, wasn't it?" Ellen wiped at her teary eyes. "Have you heard from Marnie and the brats recently?"

"We went out there for Christmas, and of course the girls are coming here this summer. They'll be at the cottage for your wedding!"

"I know. I kind of planned it that way. I thought they could be my flower girls."

"They'll be so excited. They always ask about Jason. You were a dear to think of them."

"Well, you know Jason. He's such a sentimental fool."

"I'm certainly glad you were never that way." Ginny glanced at her friend from under her lashes.

Ellen laughed. "If you tell anyone differently, I'll slit your throat."

"A bit drastic."

"That comes from working at the center. No halfway measures. By the way how do you like working with Jane English?"

"She's wonderful, but not like you. She doesn't have your understanding of what the women who come for help are going through. I suppose none of us has. But she's competent and sincere."

"Do you go into the agency at all?"

"Three days a week," Ginny said. "I like working with Alex—I always have. He keeps threatening to retire, but he never will. He loves the challenge. I just hope I can get him down to the lake for a few weeks this summer. Otherwise he's going to commute."

"God, Ginny, you look so happy."

"I am." She glanced up at Ellen. "You and Jason will be too."

"Ummm! How are you and that woman—what was her name?—getting along?"

"Nola Sherman? She's left the agency. We gave her a good recommendation, and she moved on to Chicago."

"Bet you were glad to see her go."

"It didn't really matter to me one way or the other. Once I understood what Nola was all about—and understood myself better—I was able to handle things." Ginny grinned, then icked up some champagne glasses and a botle of chilled wine. "Shall we go find our guys ind see if we can hurry their male bonding ilong?"

"Good idea!" Ellen followed her through the iouse. The Christmas trèe was still up, and a ïre had been set in the marble fireplaces in the iving room and dining room. They found the nen in the study, going over a collèction of old maps that had claimed Alex's interest of ate. Ginny noticed how the lamp's glow high-ighted her husband's fine features and graying iideburns. She was still somewhat surprised :hat she was the wife of this handsome, distin-guished man.

He looked up and saw her and smiled in ap-proval. She'd chosen the pale green dress with pearl-encrusted bodice because she knew he liked it. Now she preened a little, feeling his admiring gaze on her. When she glanced at him from under her lashes, he grinned, pointed to his watch, and mouthed the words *High noon!* Ginny blushed and glanced around at their guests. Ellen's knowing gaze was pinned on the two of them. In silent approval she raised her glass.

Later that night, when the party was over, after bells and horns had filled the night with their raucous sounds and kisses had been exchanged and "Auld Lang Syne" sung and the guests had gone home, Alex and Ginny snuggled into bed and wrapped their arms around each other.

"Happy New Year, Mrs. Alex Russell," he whispered. His kiss was long and satisfying.

"Darling, do you like Jason?" Ginny asked sometime later.

"He's all right, I guess."

"Do you know that he's marrying Ellen in June? They want us to stand up with them."

"I like Jason better, knowing that."

"Why?"

"Because he's given up on you."

"He was never competition for you."

"That's not how I remember it." Alex nuzzled her ear. "You know what?"

"What?"

"I haven't made love to you yet this year." He disappeared beneath the covers, and she felt his hands doing strange and wonderful things.

"Alex!" she gasped.

"Did I shock you?"

"Ummm, a little bit. Do it again."

He laughed and did just that.